Praise for *Honor*

A Reese's Book Club Pick

"Complex and unfiltered, these are the type of characters that stick with you long after you turn the pages . . . [A] powerful story about family, devotion, and cultural truths all through the eyes of an incredible journalist." —Reese Witherspoon

"*Honor* is a novel of profound depths—cultural, personal, romantic, spiritual. It's also a story of tremendous grace, both in the understanding it shows its characters and in the ways they navigate a brutal but stunning life. The world may be on fire, but fortunately so is Thrity Umrigar." —Rebecca Makkai, Pulitzer finalist for *The Great Believers*

"A searing meditation on the meaning of dignity in a dehumanizing world . . . Umrigar writes not only as an elegant storyteller but as a sharp-eyed reporter . . . [and] takes us deep into the lives and minds of vividly realized characters . . . Crowd-pleasing . . . Umrigar convinces us that to read is to comprehend and to comprehend is to act." —NPR

"[An] intense story . . . that will infuriate and enlighten you, and melt your heart." —*People*

"An utterly engrossing novel . . . With insight and compassion, Thrity Umrigar writes masterfully about the complexities of hatred and love, estrangement and belonging, oppression and privilege, about holding on and letting go. *Honor* is a powerful, important, unforgettable book." —Cheryl Strayed, *New York Times* bestselling author of *Wild*

"In the way *A Thousand Splendid Suns* told of Afghanistan's women, Thrity Umrigar tells a story of India with the intimacy of one who knows the many facets of a land both modern and ancient, awash in contradictions, permeated by a smoldering mix of ageless traditions and new ideas, beauty and brutality, hope and despair, certainty and mystery. A place where love can sometimes involve the peril of defying convention . . . and ultimately risking everything for what matters most." —Lisa Wingate, #1 *New York Times* bestselling author of *Before We Were Yours*

"Powerful . . . A moving account of the multifaceted layers that are India—both the beauty and the ugliness." —Bookreporter.com

"This unfiltered novel is completely eye-opening . . . You won't be able to put down this thrilling tale of love and hope." —*She Reads*

"Umrigar aptly tackles honor killings in rural India and paints Meena with agency and depth . . . *Honor* boldly examines a system that continues to greenlight brutality and serves as a poignant reminder that despite all odds, 'in every country, in every crisis, there are a handful of people who will stand against the tide.'" —*Minneapolis Star Tribune*

"An intense and spellbinding novel, ricocheting between fear and hope, and betrayal and redemption. It is the story of the human heart in all its complexities, and love worth fighting for." —Connie Schultz, bestselling author of *The Daughters of Erietown*

"The kind of book that makes me want to sit for hours and read . . . Powerful and poignant." —*The Southern Bookseller Review*

"The many layers that comprise *Honor* unfurl like a peak-season peony." —*The Boston Globe*

"Propulsive . . . Umrigar offers readers a broad understanding of the complicated issues at play in contemporary India." —*Publishers Weekly*

"A book of horror and hope in India, inspired by extremists closer to home . . . Umrigar possesses a level of curiosity and compassion I rarely encounter in other human beings, even the many curious and compassionate authors I've interviewed." —*Los Angeles Times*

"Engrossing." —*The Christian Science Monitor*

"Thrity Umrigar's novel offers a well-rounded portrait of India . . . Whether she's writing about the bright lights of Mumbai or the poverty of village life, Umrigar excels at creating engaging situations and scenes. Readers will appreciate this novel's deep understanding of the many complexities of Indian society." —*BookPage*

"Thrity Umrigar brings a wise, compassionate lens to a brutal subject matter in *Honor* . . . Full-bodied and insightful, *Honor* is both a page-turning account of a horrific family drama and a meditation on the complexities of love—both personal and national." —*Shelf Awareness*

"[A] powerful story about injustices in rural India." —*The Cleveland Plain Dealer*

"Umrigar challenges traditions, perceptions and ideals of love in a modern India that still holds fast to ancient systems." —*Ms.* magazine

HONOR

HONOR

a novel

Thrity Umrigar

ALGONQUIN BOOKS
OF CHAPEL HILL
2022

Published by
ALGONQUIN BOOKS OF CHAPEL HILL
Post Office Box 2225
Chapel Hill, North Carolina 27515-2225

a division of
WORKMAN PUBLISHING
225 Varick Street
New York, New York 10014

First paperback edition, Algonquin Books of Chapel Hill, September 2022. Originally
published in hardcover by Algonquin Books of Chapel Hill in January 2022.
Printed in the United States of America.
Design by Steve Godwin.

This is a work of fiction. While, as in all fiction, the literary perceptions and
insights are based on experience, all names, characters, places, and incidents either
are products of the author's imagination or are used fictitiously.

LIBRARY OF CONGRESS CATALOGING-IN-PUBLICATION DATA

Names: Umrigar, Thrity N., author.
Title: Honor : a novel / Thrity Umrigar.
Description: First Edition. | Chapel Hill, North Carolina : Algonquin
Books of Chapel Hill, 2022. | Summary: "The story of two Indian women,
one a victim of a brutal crime and the other an Americanized journalist
returning to India to cover the story, and the courage they inspire in
each other"— Provided by publisher.
Identifiers: LCCN 2021026242 | ISBN 9781616209957 (hardcover) |
ISBN 9781643752174 (ebook)
Classification: LCC PS3621.M75 H66 2022 | DDC 813/.6—dc23
LC record available at https://lccn.loc.gov/2021026242

ISBN 978-1-64375-330-0 (PB)

10 9 8 7 6 5 4 3 2 1
First Paperback Edition

For Feroza Freeland,
whose light brightens our path

What we don't say
we carry in our suitcases, coat pockets, our nostrils.

—"Town Watches Them Take Alfonso," ILYA KAMINSKY

This place could be beautiful,
right? You could make this place beautiful.

—"Good Bones," MAGGIE SMITH

HONOR

HINDU WOMAN SUES BROTHERS WHO KILLED HER MUSLIM HUSBAND

BY SHANNON CARPENTER
South Asia Correspondent

BIRWAD, INDIA—Her face is a constellation of scars.

Her left eye is welded shut, while a network of stitches has reassembled the melted cheek and lips. The fire rendered her left hand useless, but after reconstructive surgery, Meena Mustafa is once again able to hold a spoon in her right hand to feed herself.

The fire that took the life of her husband, Abdul, has long since been extinguished. He was allegedly set on fire by Ms. Mustafa's two brothers, Hindus who were infuriated by her elopement with a Muslim man. Police allege that the brothers tried to kill the couple to avenge the dishonor caused by the interfaith marriage.

"My body did not die the night of the fire," Ms. Mustafa says. "But my life ended then."

Now, a new fire glows in her heart—a burning desire for justice.

This made her defy the wishes of her embittered mother-in-law and her Muslim neighbors, and demand that the police reopen the case. With pro bono help from a group called Lawyers for Change, Ms. Mustafa is taking her brothers to court. She says it is to seek justice for her dead husband.

In a country where dowry deaths, bride burnings and cases of sexual harassment are commonplace, such an act of defiance makes Ms. Mustafa a singular figure in her community. But the move has also made her a social pariah in this small, conservative Muslim village, where many fear retribution by the Hindu majority. Still, she is undeterred. "I'm fighting this case for the sake of my child. To tell my child that I fought for her father's sake," she says.

A petite, demure woman, Ms. Mustafa has a soft demeanor that masks an iron will. It is this same will that earlier allowed her to defy her older brother and get a job at the local sewing factory where she met her future husband.

Encouraged by her lawyer, she agreed to be interviewed in the hopes that her courage would inspire other Indian women to confront their perpetrators.

"Let the world know what they did to my Abdul," she says. "People need to know the truth."

BOOK ONE

CHAPTER ONE

———✦———

THE AIR SMELLED of burnt rubber.

That was the first thing that Smita Agarwal noticed as she stepped out of the cool, rarefied air of the airport and into the warm, still Mumbai night. The next instant, she recoiled as the sound hit her—the low rumble of a thousand human voices, punctured by occasional barks of laughter and shrill police whistles. She gaped at the sight of the wall of people, standing behind the metal barriers, waiting for their relatives to emerge. She wondered if the old Indian custom of entire families converging to drop off travelers still prevailed in 2018, but before she could complete the thought, she felt her throat burn from the smell of exhaust fumes and her eardrums thrum from the blare of the cars just beyond the waiting crowd.

Smita stood still for a moment, cowering just a bit. She traveled more days of the year than not, her foreign correspondent job taking her around the globe, and yet, barely a few seconds into India, and already the country was overwhelming her, making her feel as if she had been hit by a force of nature, a tornado, maybe, or a tsunami that swept away everything in its path.

Her eyes fluttered shut for a moment, and she again heard the lap of the waves in the Maldives, the paradise she'd left hours earlier. In that moment, she hated all the weird confluence of events that had brought her to the one place she had spent her entire adult life avoiding—the fact that she'd happened to be on vacation so close to India when Shannon had desperately needed her help, that Shannon's contact had procured her a six-month tourist visa in a matter of hours. Now, she wished his effort had failed.

Get a grip, Smita thought, echoing the stern talking-to she'd given herself during the flight. *Remember, Shannon is a dear friend.* A memory of Shannon making Papa smile during the dark days following Mummy's funeral flashed through her head. She forced herself to cast the image aside while peering through the mob, hoping to spot the driver that Shannon had sent. A man stared back at her brazenly and pursed his lips in a suggestive pout. She looked away, scanning the crowd for someone holding a sign with her name on it while reaching for her cell phone to call Shannon. But before she found her phone, she saw him—a tall man in a blue shirt holding up a cardboard sign emblazoned with her name. Relieved, she walked over to him. "Hi," she said, from across the metal barrier. "I'm Smita."

He looked at her, blinking, confusion on his face.

"You speak English?" she said sharply, realizing that she had asked him the question in that language. But her Hindi was rusty, and she felt self-conscious using it.

The man spoke at last, in perfect English. "You're Smita Agarwal?" he said, glancing at his sign. "But you were not supposed to get here until . . . The plane was early?"

"What? Yeah, I guess so. A little bit." She looked at him, wanting to ask where the car was, wanting to get out of the airport and into the Taj Mahal Palace hotel at Apollo Bunder, where, she hoped, a long hot shower and a comfortable bed awaited her. But he continued staring at her, and her annoyance rose. "So? Shall we go?" she asked.

He snapped to attention. "Yes, yes. Sorry. Sure. Please. Come around this way." He motioned for her to walk toward a gap in the barricades. She passed the boisterous, squealing reunions that were occurring around her, the profusion of kisses bestowed on the faces and heads of teenagers by middle-aged women, the extravagant bear hugs with which grown men greeted one another. She looked away, not wanting to lose track of her driver as he pushed his way through the crowd toward an opening.

On the other side, he reached for her carry-on suitcase, then looked around, puzzled. "Where's the rest of your luggage?"

She shrugged. "This is it."

"Only one bag?"

"Yup. And my backpack."

He shook his head.

"What is it?"

"Nothing," he said as they resumed walking. "It's just that . . . Shannon said you were Indian."

"I'm Indian American. But what does that . . . ?"

"I didn't think there was an Indian anywhere in the world who could travel with only one suitcase."

She nodded, remembering the tales her parents used to tell her of relatives traveling with suitcases the size of small boats. "True enough." She peered at him, puzzled. "And you are . . . Shannon's driver?"

Under the glow of a streetlamp, she caught the flash in his eyes. "You think I'm her chauffeur?"

She took in the blue jeans, the stylishly cut shirt, the expensive leather shoes—and knew she'd made a gaffe. "Shannon said she would send someone to pick me up," she mumbled. "She didn't say who. I just assumed . . ." She took in the bemused way he was looking at her. "I'm sorry."

He shook his head. "No, it's okay. Why sorry? Nothing wrong with being a driver. But in this case, I'm a friend of Shannon's. I just offered to pick you up since you were arriving so late." He flashed her a quick half smile. "I'm Mohan, by the way."

She pointed to herself. "I'm Smita."

He waved the cardboard sign. "I know. Same as the Smita on the placard."

They laughed awkwardly. "Thank you for doing this," she said.

"No problem. This way to the car."

"So, tell me," Smita said as they walked. "How is Shannon doing?"

"She's in a lot of pain. As you may be knowing, the hip's definitely broken. Because of the weekend, they couldn't do the operation. And now they've decided to wait a couple more days until Dr. Shahani gets back into town. He's the best surgeon in the city. And hers will be a complicated case."

She looked at him curiously. "And you're—you're close to Shannon?"

"We're not boyfriend-girlfriend if that's what you mean. But she's my dear friend."

"I see." She envied Shannon this—as the South Asia correspondent for the paper, Shannon could put down roots, form friendships with the local people. Smita, whose beat was gender issues, was hardly ever in the same place for more than a week or two. No chance to stay in any place long enough to plant the seeds of friendship. She glanced at the suitcase that Mohan was carrying for her. Would he be surprised to know that she kept two other identical bags packed in her New York apartment, ready to go?

Mohan was saying something about Shannon, and Smita forced herself to listen. He mentioned how frightened Shannon had sounded when she'd called him from the hospital, how he had rushed to be by her side. Smita nodded. She remembered the time she'd been laid up with the flu in a hospital in Rio, and how isolating it had felt to be ill in a foreign country. And that hospital was probably paradise compared with this one. Although Shannon had been covering India for—How long had it been? Three years, maybe?—Smita couldn't imagine her having to undergo surgery alone in a strange country.

"And the conditions in the hospital?" she asked Mohan. "They're good? She'll be okay?"

He stopped walking and turned to look at her, his eyebrows raised. "Yes, of course. She's at Breach Candy. One of the best hospitals. And India has some of the finest doctors in the world. It's now a medical destination, you know?"

She was amused by his wounded pride, his quickness to take insult, a quality she'd noticed in several of Papa's Indian friends, even the ones—*especially* the ones—who had lived in the States for a long time. "I didn't mean to be rude," she said.

"No, it's okay. Many people still believe India is a backward country."

She bit down on her lip, lest the thought that leapt into her mind escaped her lips—*It sure was, when I lived here.* "The new airport is gorgeous," she said as a peace offering. "Light-years better than most American airports."

"Yah. It's like a five-star hotel."

They walked up to a small red car, and Mohan unlocked it. He heaved her suitcase into the trunk and then asked, "Would you like to sit in the back or front?"

She glanced at him, startled. "I'll ride in the front if that's okay."

"Of course." Even though his face was deadpan, Smita heard the quiver of laughter in his voice. "I just thought . . . Since you thought I'm Shannon's driver, maybe you wish to ride in the back."

"I'm sorry," she said, vaguely.

He pulled out of the parking lot, eased the car into the lane, then swore quietly at the bumper-to-bumper traffic heading out of the airport.

"Lots of cars, even at this time," Smita said.

He made a clucking, exasperated sound. "Don't ask, *yaar*. The traffic in this city has gone from bad to worse." He glanced at her. "But don't worry. Once we get on the main road, it will get better. I'll have you at your hotel in no time."

"Do you live near the Taj?"

"Me? No. I live in Dadar. Closer to the airport than to your hotel."

"Oh," she cried. "That's ridiculous. I . . . I could've just taken a cab."

"No, no. It's not safe, for a woman to get in a cab at this hour. Besides, this is India. We would never allow a guest to take a taxi from the airport."

She remembered her parents driving to Columbus Airport through the sleet and storms of Ohio winters, to pick up visitors. Indian hospitality. It was real. "Thank you," she said.

"No mention." He fiddled with the dial for the air-conditioning. "Are you comfortable? Hot? Cold?"

"Maybe turn up the air a notch? I can't believe how hot it is here, even in January."

Mohan gave her a quick glance. "The joys of global warming. Imported to poor countries like India from rich countries like yours."

Was he one of those nationalist types, like Papa's friend Rakesh, a man who railed against the West and had plotted his imminent return to India for the past forty years? And yet, Mohan wasn't wrong, was he? She had often argued the same point herself. "Yup," she said, too tired to start a political conversation, her eyelids beginning to get heavy with sleep.

Mohan must have sensed her fatigue. "Take a nap if you like," he said. "We have at least another thirty minutes."

"I'm fine," she said, shaking her head, distracting herself by looking at the long line of shanties built on the sidewalk. Even at this late hour, a few men in shirtsleeves and lungis lounged near the open mouths of the huts, kerosene lamps burning inside some of them. Smita chewed on her lower lip. She was no stranger to third world poverty, but the tableau they were driving past was so unchanged from what she remembered from her childhood. It was if she had passed these very same slums and the same men the last time she and her family had driven to the airport twenty years before, in 1998. So much for the new, globalized India that she kept reading about.

"The government paid these people to vacate and go into government housing," Mohan was saying. "But they refused."

"Is that so?"

"So I've heard. But in a democratic country, how can you force people to relocate?"

There was a short silence, and Smita had the feeling that simply by staring so openly at the slums they were passing, she had made Mohan feel defensive about his city. She had seen this phenomenon often in her job, how middle-class people in poor countries bristled against the judgment of people in the West. Once, while she was in Haiti, a local official had almost spat in her face and cursed American imperialism when she'd tried questioning him about the corruption in his district. "I suppose you can't blame them," she said. "This is their home."

"Exactly. This is what I try to tell my friends and coworkers. But they don't understand what took you less than ten minutes to understand."

Smita felt unexpectedly warmed by Mohan's words, as if he'd presented her with a small trophy. "Thanks. But I used to live here, you know. So I get it."

"You lived here? When?"

"When I was young. We left India when I was fourteen."

"*Wah*. I had no idea. Even though Shannon told me you were Indian, I just assumed you were born abroad. You sound like a *pucca* American."

She shrugged. "Thanks. I guess."

"And you have family here?"

"Not really." And before he could ask another question, she said, "And you? What do you do? Are you a journalist, also?"

"Ha. That's a joke. I could never do what you and Shannon do. I'm not a good writer. No, I'm an IT guy. I work with computers. For Tata Consultancy. Have you heard of the Tatas?"

"Yes, of course. Didn't they buy Jaguar and Land Rover several years ago?"

"That's right. Tata makes everything, from cars to soap to power plants." He rolled down his window a bit. "So, we're going over the new Sea Link, which connects Bandra to Worli. It wasn't here when you were living here, obviously. But it will cut down on our driving time a great deal."

Smita took in the lights of the city as the car climbed up the cable bridge that spanned the dark waters of the Arabian Sea below them. "Wow. Mumbai looks like any other city in the world. We could be in New York or Singapore." Except, she thought, for the acidic smell of the warm air blowing into the car. She was about to ask Mohan about the smell but thought better of it. She was a guest in his city and the truth was, the knot in her stomach was growing as they got closer to their destination. The truth was, she didn't want to be in Mumbai. No matter how many beautiful bridges the city threw up, no matter how beguiling its new, bejeweled skyline, she didn't want to be there. She would spend a few days with Shannon in the hospital, and then, as soon as she could, she would clear out. It would be too late to rejoin the others in the Maldives, of course, but that was okay. It would be nice to return to her brownstone in Brooklyn for the rest of her leave. Maybe take in a movie or two. But there she was, in a car speeding toward her hotel room at the Taj. Speeding toward her old neighborhood.

Smita Agarwal looked out of the car window onto the streets of a city she had once loved, a city she'd spent the last twenty years trying to forget.

CHAPTER TWO

SMITA WOKE UP early the next morning and for a moment, as she lay in an unknown bed, she thought she was still at the Sun Aqua Resort in the Maldives. She heard the sound of the waves lapping against the shore and felt her body sinking into sand the color of sugar. But then she remembered where she was, and her body tensed.

She rolled out of bed and padded to the bathroom. When she returned, she made her way to the window and pulled open the heavy drapes to the brightness of the day, the sun alive on the dull, perennially brown waters of the sea. She remembered the first time she saw the Atlantic Ocean, how its pristine blue had astounded her, used as she was to the murky waters of the Arabian Sea. She remembered how Papa used to yell at the servants of the denizens in the buildings around the seaside when they flung bags of trash into the water and at the young men who urinated in the sea at Juhu or Chowpatty Beach. Poor

Papa. How much he'd loved this city that, ultimately, didn't love him back.

She looked toward the Gateway of India, the beautiful yellow basalt monument, with its four turrets and arch, that sat across the street from her hotel window. How solid and rooted it was, much like her childhood in India had once appeared to be. When she had played under its arch, had she ever imagined that she would someday be staying at this iconic grand hotel, one of the most opulent hotels in the world? Hell, everyone from George Harrison to President Obama had stayed there. She and her parents had celebrated birthdays and other happy occasions at the Taj's many restaurants, of course. But staying at the Taj was a different matter.

She glanced at her watch and saw that it was 8:00 a.m. Should she phone Shannon? Or would she still be sleeping? Just then, her stomach growled, and she realized she had not eaten since the afternoon the day before, her nervousness stronger than her appetite. She decided to get breakfast.

Half an hour later, she was at the Sea Lounge. The restaurant was fairly crowded even at this hour. The young hostess, radiant in a blue sari, approached her. "How many people in your party, ma'am?" she asked and, when Smita held up her index finger, led her to a small table by a window. Smita looked around the room, remembering its understated elegance from her childhood visits there with her parents, the hushed, impeccable service, the large windows overlooking the sea. She was pleased to see that the beauty of the restaurant remained unchanged. She caught the eye of the man at the next table, his face broiled red by the Mumbai sun. He gave her a crooked smile that she pretended not to notice. Instead, she looked out the window, blinking away the tears that filled her eyes. It was hard to be at the Sea Lounge and not think of her soft-spoken, genteel mother. Smita had been in Portugal covering a women's conference at the time of Mummy's death, and when Rohit, her older brother, had called to give her the news, she had yelled and sworn at him, made him a target for her wild grief. But sitting in her mother's favorite restaurant, Smita was warmed by memories of going to the Sea Lounge on Saturday afternoons, her mother ordering her favorite chicken club sandwich while her father sipped his Kingfisher beer.

She half wished she could order a club sandwich at this hour, in memory of Mummy. Instead, she ordered coffee and a spinach omelet. The waiter set the plate down in front of her with the care and precision of a mechanic setting down an engine part. "Can I get you anything else, ma'am?" he asked in a respectful voice. He was probably just a year or two older than her, but his obsequious manner, so typical of how working-class Indians addressed the rich, made her grit her teeth. But then, a quick look around this beautiful room told her that nobody else—not the many Germans and Brits in the room, nor the paunchy Indian businessmen out with their clients—seemed to mind the sycophantic manner of the members of the waitstaff; in fact, they seemed to expect and demand it. She had already noticed the snapping of fingers for service and the dismissive tone with which the other diners spoke to the servers.

"No, thank you," she said. "This looks delicious."

Her reward was a sincere, delighted smile. "Enjoy, ma'am," he said, and edged away, silent as a ghost.

She took a sip of the coffee and then licked the froth from her upper lip. She had tasted coffee all around the world, but God, how wonderful this cup of Nescafé tasted. She knew it would be an object of derision back home—"It's *instant* coffee, for Christ's sake, Smita," she could hear Jenna trill as they ate brunch at the Rose Water café in Park Slope—but what could she say? It was only in the last year of her time in India that her parents had allowed her to drink coffee, and that, too, just a few sips from her father's cup as he sat grading papers. One taste and she was transported to their large, sunlit apartment in Colaba, a short walk from the Taj, and to Sunday mornings as her parents bickered good-naturedly about whether to play his Bach and Beethoven CDs or her mother's *ghazals* on the living room stereo. Rohit would be in his room, still in bed as he listened to Green Day or U2 on his Walkman. Their cook, Reshma, would be making the South Indian *medhu vadas* and *upma* that was their Sunday morning breakfast treat.

Where was Reshma now? Surely, she was still living in this city of twenty million, working for another family? Smita would like to find her during this trip, but how, she hadn't a clue. Had Mummy stayed in touch with Reshma after they'd left? She didn't know. They had all worked so hard to forget what they'd left behind and to build a new life in America. Maybe it was just as well that she didn't know their old cook's whereabouts.

Reshma often used to accompany them to the Gateway, watching over Smita as she played under its arch. Every evening it seemed as if half the metropolis emptied out onto the promenade near the seaside, the smell of roasted corn on the cob wafting over them all. Smita remembered tugging on her father's tunic, asking him to buy her the mix of sand-roasted peanuts and *chana*. She'd watch as the street vendor filled a paper cone with the snack, twisting the bottom point of the cone into a tail before handing it to her with a flourish. As for those twilight evenings during the rainy season, when the spattering sun flung its embers across the sky and painted the city a luminescent orange? In all her travels, had any twilight ever compared with the twilights of her childhood?

The waiter cleared his throat, trying to get her attention. "May I clear this plate for you, ma'am?" he asked. "Was everything satisfactory?"

She turned around to face him. "Yes, thank you." She smiled. "Do you suppose I could order another coffee?"

"Of course, ma'am. You liked it?"

She heard the pride—no, it was more than that, the *ownership*, in his voice—and was touched by it. She longed to ask him about his life, how much he earned, what his living conditions were like, but noticed that the restaurant was getting even more crowded. "Yes, very much," she replied. "There's no coffee quite like this anywhere."

He nodded. "Where are you residing, ma'am?" he asked shyly.

"America."

"I thought so," he said. "Although most of our tourists are from Europe."

"Is that so?" she asked, having no interest in discussing her life. This was the great thing about being a reporter—you got to ask questions instead of answering them. She hoped he would get her that second cup of coffee soon. She glanced at her watch, but the waiter didn't pick up on the hint.

"It is my lifelong dream," he said, "to study hospitality management in America."

Smita heard some version of this wherever she traveled. The details varied, but the bones of the dream were the same—to get a tourist visa and gain a toehold into America. Then, to do whatever it took—drive a cab sixteen hours a day or work hard in a sweaty restaurant kitchen or have an employer sponsor you or marry an American. The goal was to someday get a much-coveted green card, the twenty-first century's version of the Holy Grail.

She looked at the thin, pigeon-chested waiter, and the eagerness in his face made her look away. "I need to get going soon," she said pointedly. "But I wish you well."

He flushed. "Yes, of course, ma'am. Sorry, ma'am." He hurried away and returned almost immediately with another cup of coffee.

She charged the expense to her room, leaving a 30 percent tip. She was getting up to leave when the waiter came rushing back. He was carrying a white rose. "For you, ma'am. Welcome to the Taj."

She took the single flower from him, unsure if this was their custom or not. "Thank you," she said. "Tell me your name again?"

He giggled. "I never told you the first time, ma'am. It's Joseph."

"It was nice meeting you, Joseph." She stepped away from him, then stopped. "Can you help me? Would you know how far it is to Breach Candy Hospital from here?"

"Sure, sure, ma'am," he said. "Not too far by cab. It all depends on the traffic, you know? The front reception can order a private cab with A/C for you. It will be costing you a little bit extra, ma'am, but what to do? It's worth it."

CHAPTER THREE

———————

THE FIRST THING Smita noticed when she entered the hospital were the *paan* streaks on the walls of the lobby. She was stunned. Breach Candy had been the city's finest hospital when she was a child, the place where movie stars went for surgery, and so she was surprised to see the streaks of betel juice. She swallowed her distaste and made her way to the information desk, where a tired-looking woman sat. "Can I help you?" the woman said.

"Hi. I need the room number for a patient. Shannon Carpenter?"

The woman spoke to a spot past Smita's shoulder. "Visiting hours start at eleven. No one is allowed up until then."

Smita swallowed. "I see. I just got into Mumbai late last night, and . . ."

"Eleven o'clock. No exceptions."

Smita's irritation showed on her face. "All right. But can I have the room number so that—"

"Eleven o'clock."

"Ma'am, I heard you. I'm just asking for the number so I don't have to disturb you again."

The woman glared at Smita. "Room number 209. Now, please take a seat."

And like a chastised schoolgirl, Smita had no choice except to wait in the lobby, under the woman's watchful gaze. She kept an eye on the clock, thankful that she didn't have a long wait. At the stroke of eleven, she got up and headed to the elevators, where a line had already formed. She looked for the stairway. Shannon's room was only two floors up—she'd take the stairs.

A kindly nurse pointed her toward Shannon's room when she got to the second floor. As she walked the hallway, she could see a small knot of people at the far end and heard a man's raised voice. She looked away, concentrating on reading the room numbers. She peered into an empty room, caught a glimpse of the sea outside the window, and was suddenly assailed by a memory of accompanying her father to Breach Candy when he was visiting a sick colleague. The sea appeared to be so close that she had thought the hospital was built on a ship. Papa had laughed at that, squeezing her shoulder as they'd walked.

She drew closer to the group in the hallway and was about to look away, not wanting to eavesdrop on what was obviously an impassioned argument, when she noticed that one of them was Mohan. But whereas he had been languid last evening, he now looked tense and angry as he glared at the nurse and a young man in a white coat. "I'm telling you, get Dr. Pal here immediately. The patient needs better pain control than this."

"But, sir, I told you . . ." the young resident said.

"*Arre, yaar*, how many times are we going to go round and round? I told you, we are not happy with her treatment. Now, go tell your supervisor to come talk to us."

"As you wish." The young man walked away briskly, the nurse following.

"Hi," Smita said, and Mohan looked up at her, startled.

"Oh, hi," he said. "Sorry. I didn't expect you to get here on your own. I was just getting ready to come pick you up."

"I'm glad to have saved you a trip." Smita glanced at the woman standing next to Mohan. "Hello. I'm Smita."

The woman, who appeared to be in her twenties, gave her a broad smile. "Oh, hello, madam. I spoke to you on the phone yesterday. I'm Nandini. Shannon's translator."

"Nice to meet you," Smita said. But a small part of her was resentful. Shannon obviously had all these people here to help. Had she really needed to interrupt her vacation? "Where's her room? Can I see her?"

"Yes, madam. Just a minute, madam." Nandini gave Mohan a flustered glance and walked away.

"They're giving her a bedpan," Mohan explained, following Smita's puzzled gaze.

"Oh." Smita shuddered. "How do they even . . ."

"Very, very carefully. Even though Shannon doesn't think so. I don't think these nurses have ever heard anyone curse like she does."

She saw that he was trying to keep a straight face. "I know what you mean. She's a legend in the newsroom, too." She cocked her head. "You're not working today?"

"No. I was supposed to be on vacation in Singapore this week," he said. "But the friend I was going with came down with dengue fever. So I canceled. Now, I'm off for two weeks."

"You didn't go by yourself?"

"Where's the fun in that?" He peered down at her and made a rueful face. "I'm not like you and Shannon. Independent. I *hate* traveling alone. In fact, I hate *being* alone, to be honest. I guess I'm a typical Mumbai boy in that respect."

Mohan's tone was ironic, as if he was mocking himself. Still, no self-respecting American male would have admitted to such a thing. If one of the Indian American men her mother had tried setting her up with when she was younger had made such a confession to her, she would have been contemptuous. But as she stood there in the hospital hallway, Mohan's admission felt normal. Human. She could see his point of view.

Smita sighed. "Well," she said, "looks like we both had our vacation plans upended."

A ward boy exited the room, and a moment later Nandini rushed up to them. "Come in, madam," she said. "Shannon is anxious to see you."

Shannon was lying down with the head of the bed slightly raised, her hair flowing on the pillow. Even though she mustered a smile, Smita could see the sweat on her forehead, her gray eyes hazy with pain. "Hi, sweetheart," Smita said, bending down to kiss her cheek.

"Hey. You came."

Nandini pulled up a chair. "Sit, madam," she said.

Smita held Shannon's hand as she sat. "I'm so sorry," she said. "Which side is it?"

"It's the right hip. And it's my own goddamned fault, for reading on my phone while walking. I tripped over a curb."

"Sorry." Smita looked up to see Mohan and Nandini talking at the other end of the room. "When are they saying they'll operate? Mohan said they're waiting on a particular surgeon. But surely there are other doctors who are equally skilled?"

Shannon grimaced. "It's a complicated surgery. I broke this same hip when I was in my twenties. Don't even ask. So they first have to remove the old prosthesis and then put in the new one. The bone has grown all around the old hardware. It's a mess. And this guy, Dr. Shahani, is apparently very experienced."

"Oh my God, Shannon. I had no idea."

"Yep." Shannon turned her head. "Mohan. Did you ask them to call for the fucking doctor or what?"

"I did. The resident said he would . . ." He looked up. "Actually, here he is."

Dr. Pal was a tall but stooped man. His glasses were smudged, and the eyes behind them, weary. "Yes, ma'am," he said. "How can I help?"

Shannon was immediately deferential. "Sorry to trouble you, doctor," she said. "I . . . I just wanted to ask some questions. First of all, when exactly does Dr. Shahani get into town? And secondly, the pain is unbearable. Can't you give me something stronger?"

The elderly doctor's face was impassive. "You have a broken hip, Miss Carpenter. What you need is surgery to get out of pain. Unfortunately, Dr. Shahani doesn't come back until day after tomorrow."

Shannon winced. "Jesus."

"I'm sorry." Dr. Pal's face softened a little. "Maybe we can come up with a different drug cocktail for the pain. Or, if you're willing, we can schedule surgery with someone else for tomorrow."

Shannon glanced helplessly at Mohan. "What do you think?"

A muscle moved in Mohan's jaw. "Is this other fellow as good?"

Dr. Pal was silent for a moment. "Shahani is our best surgeon. And this is a complicated case because of the old prosthesis."

"Can you check with the pain team, *immediately*?" Mohan said. "To see if they can make her more comfortable? Only then can we make a proper decision, correct?"

Smita looked at Shannon from the corner of her eye, wondering if, despite what Mohan had said, there was something going on between him and her. She had never known Shannon to rely on a man like this. Then again, she'd never known Shannon to be in such pain, either.

Dr. Pal bowed. "I will report back," he said, and left the room.

"Thanks, Mohan," Shannon said. She turned back to face Smita. "Smits," she said, "this is why I asked you to come."

"I'll stay through your surgery and after," Smita said immediately.

"I have tons of vacation time accrued, so it doesn't matter how long you need me."

Shannon shook her head. "No, don't worry about that. I have Mohan here with me." She shut her eyes briefly and then opened them. "Have you been reading my stories about Meena, the woman who is suing her brothers? For burning her husband alive?"

"What? Yeah, sure," Smita said, remembering a few details. She had not paid much attention, her distaste for India triggered by the story.

"Great," Shannon said. "Well, the verdict will be coming soon, and we need someone to cover it. You need to go to Birwad—that's the name of Meena's village."

Smita stared at Shannon. "I don't understand?" she said at last.

"The verdict will be coming," Shannon repeated. "We need the story."

There was a sudden, heavy tension in the room, fueled by the anger sluicing through Smita. She was aware that Mohan and Nandini were both staring at her. Biting down on her lower lip, she tried to recall the details of the phone conversation from the day before. Had Shannon mentioned the reason for summoning her to Mumbai? Come to think of it, she hadn't. *Why didn't Shannon make things clearer?* Smita thought, unable to shake the feeling of being manipulated into coming back to the one city she'd vowed never to see again.

"Why can't a stringer cover the story?" Smita said. "I thought you asked me here to help you." She saw Mohan's head jerk up and noticed the look of understanding that spread across his face.

"I did," Shannon said, puzzled. And then, Smita realized that pain was blocking her friend's perceptions.

"So, here's the deal," Shannon was saying, oblivious to Smita's anger. "I don't know how much you remember of the story. This woman, Meena, was set on fire by her brothers for marrying a Muslim guy. They killed her husband. She almost died, too. Because of the lawyer who took her case pro bono, the police were forced to reopen their investigation." Shannon's eyes kept opening and shutting, as if she was battling both sleep and pain. "In any case, the court is expected to rule soon. And if you know how slowly the courts work in India"—she cast a quick glance at Mohan—"you'll know what a miracle that is. We need to be there when the ruling comes, Smits."

"Of course," Smita said. "But why didn't you get someone from the Delhi bureau to follow up?"

Shannon reached over and pressed the call button. "Sorry. My hip hurts like a son of a bitch. I think I'm due for more meds."

"I'll go get a nurse," Mohan said immediately, but Shannon shook her head. "Nah. We've bugged them enough. Someone will be here right away. They're pretty good."

Shannon turned back to Smita. "James would've normally covered the verdict, but he is in Norway. His wife's about to have a baby. And Rakesh . . . he's taking over the story I'm working on right now. In any case, I'm not sure Meena will even talk to a male reporter, Smits. She's living in an all-Muslim village. It's a pretty conservative area."

"She's right," Mohan said. "I—my parents are from Surat, which is not too far away from Birwad. Just across the Maharashtra-Gujarat border. I know those people. No way would a woman be allowed to talk to a male."

A nurse came into the room, and Shannon asked for her pills. "*Shukriya*," Shannon said, and Smita watched the nurse's startled smile that her American patient had thanked her in Hindi. "No mention, madam," the nurse said.

Shannon moaned softly and squeezed Smita's hand as she waited for a spasm to pass.

"Why don't they have you on a morphine drip?" Smita demanded.

Shannon looked at her wryly. "They don't use it as freely in India the way we do back home. I'm going to write about this issue as soon as I'm better."

"That's crazy."

There was a sudden silence in the room, as if they'd all run out of things to say. Smita turned to Nandini. "Have you been there? To Birwad? How far is it from here?"

"Yes. It's about a five-hour drive from here." Nandini's tone was so sullen that Smita was surprised.

"I see." Smita bit a fingernail, stalling for time, her head reeling. After Shannon's phone call had brought her vacation to an abrupt end, she had made her peace with visiting Mumbai again. Sitting in her hotel room in the Maldives, Smita had reminded herself of their history— she and Shannon had worked together at the *Philadelphia Inquirer*; later, she had gotten her job in New York because of Shannon's advocacy. When Mummy had died eight months before, Shannon, who happened to be in the US at the time, had taken three days off to fly to Ohio to attend the funeral. More than anything else, it was this last act of friendship, this sense of a debt that needed to be repaid, that had made Smita say yes when Shannon asked her to fly to Mumbai. She had believed she was agreeing to spend a few days here to help Shannon get back on her feet. But instead, she found herself dealing with everything that she detested about this country—its treatment of women, its religious strife, its conservatism. But you're the damn gender issues reporter, Smita reminded herself. *It was a no-brainer for Shannon to summon you. Especially since you were a three-hour plane ride away.*

"So, we're talking about what?" Smita said. "Just a reaction piece, right?"

"I'll leave that to you," Shannon replied. "Maybe meet with Meena first and do a short profile on her—you know, what she's thinking, a hopes-and-fears piece. And then do another, a local reaction story once the judge rules. What do you think?" She glanced at Nandini. "Nan is superb, by the way. A total pro. She'll help you in any way she can."

Smita decided to state the obvious. "Well, I don't really need a translator. I mean, my Hindi ain't great, but I think I can manage. They speak Hindi, right?"

"Yeah. And a peculiar dialect of Marathi."

"If I may," Mohan interjected, "the most important thing is, getting there will be a problem. It's very rural. So having someone like Nandini, who knows the way, will help."

Behind him, Nandini scowled. But only Smita noticed.

"There is a train station, but it's not all that close to Birwad," Shannon said. "Even the motel where we normally stay is a good distance from the village. You really do need a car."

Smita nodded. She had no intention of taking a train through India.

The nurse returned with the pills Shannon had requested and bottled water, but Shannon motioned to her to set them on the bedside table. After the woman left, she made a sad face. "Once I take these, I'll be zonked out for hours. I need to give you all the information now."

"Okay," Smita said. Things were spinning out of her control. There was no real possibility of refusing the assignment. What reason could she offer her editor, Cliff, for refusing to cover the story, after she had heedlessly rushed here? Cliff must have given Shannon his go-ahead to contact her. *Hell*, Smita thought, *he probably thought he was doing me a favor, throwing me a great assignment.* But why hadn't he given her a heads-up? Anything that would have spared her the mortification of this misunderstanding.

Shannon gritted her teeth against the pain and began talking faster, even as her hand reached for the water glass and the two white pills. Smita's stomach lurched. She had never broken a bone and was suddenly deeply grateful for that fact.

"If you hand me my phone, I'll give you Anjali's phone number," Shannon was saying. "She's the lawyer who's helping Meena. As far as I know, Meena is still living with her mother-in-law. They live on the outskirts of Birwad. By the way, the brothers are out on bail and walking around free, believe it or not. Talk to them, too. And interview the village chief. He's a piece of work, that guy. He terrorized her even before her marriage." She swallowed the pills. "If you look up some of my past stories, you'll get the name of the brothers' village. Or maybe Nandini remembers. There's also a sister somewhere . . ."

Shannon set the glass down. "Thank you for doing this, Smits. I owe you one."

Smita dismissed the last of her reservations. The truth was, she would have asked for the same favor if the roles were reversed. And Shannon would have helped her without the slightest bit of resentment or complaint. "Don't be silly," she said. "I'll call Anjali today and figure out when to leave. I'd like to be here for the surgery if I could."

"There's no need. Mohan will help . . ."

"That's a good idea." Nandini was nodding vigorously. "We must be here for the operation."

"There's no need," Shannon repeated. "You need to assist Smita."

They talked for another fifteen minutes, and then Shannon shut her eyes. After a few minutes, she gave a loud snort, then began to snore softly.

Smita turned toward Mohan. "How long will she be out?"

He looked at her quizzically. "Out?"

"I . . . sorry. I mean, how long does she sleep after these pills?"

"Oh. I understand. Hopefully, for three or four hours. But often, the pain wakes her up sooner."

"Okay." She looked around the room, wanting to talk to him privately. "Do you think—is there someplace I can get some coffee?"

"Yes, of course," he said immediately. "Shall I go and—?"

"I'll go with you," she said, getting up before he could react. She turned to Nandini. "What shall we bring for you?"

"Nothing, thank you. I am fine."

"Are you sure? You must be so tired."

"I am fine."

"Okay."

"You mustn't be angry at Nandini," Mohan said as soon as they left the room. "She's just very worried about Shannon. Feels responsible."

"Why should she? It was an accident."

He shrugged. "She's a girl from a lower middle-class family. The first in her family to go to college. And she works with this American woman who is good to her and makes her feel valued. And she makes good money working for a Western newspaper. You can see why she feels loyal."

"How long have you known Shannon?"

"About two years."

"You're a good friend," Smita said as they waited for the elevator. "Helping her like this."

"So are you. Interrupting your vacation to come back to your homeland to help her."

"My *homeland*?"

"Yes, of course. You said you were born here, correct?"

"Yeah, but . . . I mean, I was a teen when we left." She shook her head. "I don't know. I don't think of India that way."

"How do you think of it?"

What was with this guy, being so prickly? "I . . . I don't," she said at last. "Think about it that much. I don't mean to be rude."

Mohan nodded. After a moment, he said, "You know, I had this friend in college. He went to London for a month during summer vacation. One month. And when he came back, suddenly he was talking with a British accent, like a *gora*."

The elevator doors opened, and they got in. Smita waited for Mohan to say more, but he had fallen silent. "What's that got to do with me?" she asked at last.

"I hate this inferiority complex so many of our—*my*—people have. Everything about the West is best."

She waited until they were out of the elevator, aware of a young guy riding with them eavesdropping on their conversation. In the lobby, she said, "Listen, I hear you. But I've lived in the US for twenty years. I'm an American citizen."

Mohan stopped walking and looked down at her. After a beat, he shrugged. "Sorry, *yaar*," he said. "I don't know how we got on this stupid subject. *Chalo*, let's get you your coffee. The cafeteria is right this way."

Smita had a feeling that she'd somehow slipped a notch in his esteem. *Fuck him*, she thought. *He's just some kind of a nationalist.*

"I left without breakfast this morning," Mohan said. "Will you take something? Other than coffee?"

"I ate a big meal at the hotel. But you go ahead."

Mohan ordered a *masala dosa*. Smita resisted the urge to order a fresh juice, settling for a coffee. "I used to love sweet lime juice," she said.

"So get one, *yaar*," he said immediately.

"I'm afraid it may upset my tummy."

"Your American tummy." But he said it with a smile in his voice.

His *dosa* arrived, and Mohan tore off a piece of the crepe and held it out to her. "Take it. *Arre*, take it, *yaar*. Nothing is going to happen. And if you do have an upset stomach, look around. You're in a hospital."

Smita rolled her eyes. She chewed on the crepe. Even without the potato filling, the *dosa* was heavenly, better than any she'd tasted in the States. "Sooo good," she said.

His face lit up, and he immediately signaled for the waiter and ordered another. "Go ahead and eat this one. I'll get mine soon."

"Absolutely not. You're the one who's hungry."

"And you're the one who is eyeing this *dosa* like you're a bloody famine victim. Eat. It's obvious that you've missed the taste of home."

The tears that sprang to her eyes took them both by surprise. Embarrassed, she looked away. There was no way to explain that his words echoed what Mummy used to say about missing the sights, smells, and tastes of India.

Mohan sat back and watched her with satisfaction. "See?" he said after a few minutes. "You're still a *desi* at heart."

She stopped chewing. "Why is it so important to you? For me to reclaim my"— she made air quotes—"*homeland*"?

The waiter set Mohan's *dosa* down in front of him. "*Shukriya*," Mohan said before turning his attention back to her. "It's not a question of important or not important, *yaar*. It's just that . . . who could ever leave Mumbai and not miss it?"

"What would I miss? The fact that every time I rode the bus, a stranger felt entitled to touch me? Or that every time I wanted to leave home wearing a short dress, my dad wouldn't let me because of the ruffians on the street? Tell me."

"But that's not fair," Mohan said. "That stuff happens everywhere in the world."

"Sure. Definitely. But I'm trying to make you understand something. That your Mumbai isn't the same as my Mumbai."

Mohan grimaced. "Okay. I get it. My sister has often said the same thing."

"Good." She nodded, finishing the last of her coffee. "How old is your sister?"

"She's twenty-four."

"And she goes to college in Mumbai?"

"Shoba? No, she's married. She's settled in Bangalore. I'm the only one here in Mumbai."

"You are here in the city alone?" she said.

"Yes. Even though I hate being alone."

He looked so sheepish that Smita burst out laughing. Something about him reminded her of her brother, Rohit.

"If you don't mind, I want to order a sandwich for Nandini,"

Mohan said. "You know, she takes two buses to get here. I'm sure she has not eaten today."

Yup. He was very much like Rohit. "That's great," she said. And she didn't even offer to pick up the tab. He was a Mumbai boy, and Mumbai boys didn't allow guests to pick up the check. That much she still knew.

CHAPTER FOUR

—✦—

THEY COULD HEAR loud voices coming from Shannon's room as they approached.

"Oh God, she's awake," Mohan said. "The pain pills didn't work."

"Where the hell have the two of you been?" Shannon snapped as they entered her room, and Smita froze, transfixed by the distress she saw on Shannon's face.

"I'm so sorry," she whispered. "We just got a bite to eat." She took in Nandini's pinched, teary face, and felt sorry for the younger woman.

"Well, I've had it," Shannon said in the same, harsh tone. She turned to Mohan. "Dr. Pal stopped by while you were away. Turns out they can't give me any fucking drugs stronger than what I'm on."

"I'll talk to him—"

"No. It's okay. He's convinced me. I'm going under the knife tomorrow. Pal says this other guy's pretty good. I can't wait another goddamned day."

"Shannon, are you sure?" Mohan's voice was low, his brow furrowed with worry.

"Yeah. I'm sure," Shannon said, dissolving into tears. "I can't take another moment of this pain."

Mohan took in a sharp breath. "Okay," he said. "This is a good idea."

Shannon pulled her hand out from under the sheet and held it out to Mohan. "And you'll be with me? After Smita and Nan leave?"

"Yes, of course."

There was a sound from the corner of the room, and they all startled as Nandini rushed out. Shannon looked at Mohan. "I can't deal with her theatrics," she said. "Go talk some sense into her."

"What's going on?" Smita asked, but Mohan shook his head and left the room.

Smita pulled up a chair next to the bed. She could hear Mohan and Nandini talking in the hallway, the woman's voice high and strident.

"You got Anjali's number. right?" Shannon asked with her eyes closed. "You'll call her soon and find out if she has a date for the verdict?"

"I will. I got it. Now, stop worrying about work."

Shannon smiled. "You're the best. This is why I could trust this story to only you. You'll understand Meena, like none of the other reporters can."

Waiting for Mohan to return, Smita sat watching Shannon as she dozed. After a few minutes, she got up and walked to the window. Outside, the sea crashed against the enormous boulders, spraying spittle into the air. She jumped, realizing Nandini was standing next to her. She hadn't heard her come back into the room. "Oh, hi," Smita said, not bothering to hide her annoyance, dreading the thought of being alone in the car with this strange woman.

"I'm so scared, madam," Nandini said. "My friend's mother had this same surgery. And she died."

Was it fear that was making Nandini act so strange? "She'll be fine," Smita said. "This is a good hospital."

Nandini nodded. "Mohan *bhai* was also saying that to me." She wiped her nose with the back of her hand. "But, madam, Shannon has been so good to me. Better than my own sisters, she has treated me."

Smita had seen this phenomenon all around the world—young women from low-income families, slender as reeds, working insane hours against insane odds to better their lives. And the gratitude they felt toward bosses or benefactors—anyone who tossed a morsel of kindness their way—was so heartfelt, so earnest, that it never failed to break her heart. She pictured the crowded tenement where Nandini lived, the long commute by public transportation, the Herculean efforts to learn English, and at long last, the chance to work for a Western agency or newspaper—the liberation that came from such an opportunity, and the loyalty that this inspired.

"Nandini," she said, "Shannon is otherwise healthy. She will bounce back quickly. And in the meantime"—she took a deep breath—"we will have a good time together, okay?"

"One thing, Smita." The younger woman's eyes swept her body. "You will need some other, more modest clothes, like *shalwar kameez*. It's a conservative area we are going to."

Smita flushed. Did Nandini think she was some kind of a rookie? "Yes, I know," she said. "I will buy some outfits later today. As you know, I was on vacation until yesterday."

"That will be good."

They stood looking out at the sea until a nurse came into the room. She said something to Nandini in rapid-fire Marathi while Smita looked from one to the other. She heard the word "American" a couple of times, the nurse looking visibly upset. Finally, the woman turned to Smita and said, "It is past visiting hours, madam. You must leave."

"*She's* here," Smita said pointedly, nodding toward Nandini.

"Matron has made exceptions for Miss Shannon's caretaker and the tall gentleman. But please, guests are allowed only during visitation hours."

Smita sighed. "Okay." And when the nurse didn't move, she said, "Please give me a few minutes to make some plans."

"Five more minutes."

Smita followed the nurse out into the hallway. Mohan was at the nurse's station, talking to the same young medical resident as before. Mohan spotted her, said something to the young man, and approached her. "You're leaving?" he asked.

"I'm being kicked out."

"They're very strict about visiting hours. But I could try . . ."

"It's okay. It sounds like they've already made an exception in your and Nandini's cases." She heard the bitterness in her voice and knew that Mohan had heard it, too.

"I'm sorry," he said.

She shook her head. "It's fine. The fact is, I still have to prepare for Birwad. I need to contact that lawyer. And also, I was told by Nandini that I must buy more suitable clothes for our trip."

Mohan looked embarrassed. "We are all under pressure," he murmured. He then brightened. "By the way, I just got some good news. They are putting Shannon at the top of the list. Hers will be the first surgery of the day tomorrow."

"Great. What time should I be at the hospital?"

"Let's see. They will take her in by seven. But nothing is going to happen until eight. And it's a long surgery. Even if you came by nine or ten . . ."

"I'll be here at seven."

"There's no need to come that early. You are going to have a long day of travel tomorrow if you leave after the surgery." He smiled. "Nandini has made it clear that she will not leave until she is sure Shannon is going to be okay."

Smita went back into the room. Shannon was sleeping soundly.

Smita gave her a light kiss on the forehead, then stood watching her. Pain had carved new lines into Shannon's face. As she watched, Shannon moaned softly. Smita felt a rush of sympathy. Shannon was usually so gregarious and outgoing that it was easy to forget that she had no family. Once, only once, when they were both drunk after a work party, had Shannon spoken about the childhood spent in foster homes. Smita admired Shannon—here she was, in a country not her own, being looked after by a translator who clearly adored her and a male friend who was ensuring that she was receiving the best of care.

And then there's me, Smita thought. *I dropped everything to rush to her side. Why? For Shannon's sake, for sure, but also to prove that I know how to be a real friend. Well, the joke's on me. Because Shannon doesn't need my friendship or company—she just needs my professional commitment.*

"I'll see you tomorrow," Smita whispered to Nandini, and before the woman could respond, she slipped out of the room.

SMITA CALLED ANJALI'S number as soon as the cab had pulled out of the hospital. It rang a few times before a voice said, "Tell me."

"Oh hi," Smita said, taken aback by the abrupt greeting. "Is this Anjali?"

"Speaking. Who's this?"

Even though Smita knew it would get stiflingly hot in the cab, she motioned to the driver to roll up his window. "My name is Smita. I'm Shannon's colleague. And I'm taking over the Meena Mustafa story for Shannon?"

"Oh yes." Anjali had the clipped accent of upper-class Indians that Smita remembered from her girlhood. "Her assistant said you were flying in from the States."

Smita didn't bother to correct her. "Yeah, I just got in late last night."

"How is Shannon? Did she have her surgery?"

"It's scheduled for tomorrow morning."

"Good, good." There was a hint of impatience in Anjali's voice, the sound of an overworked woman who was routinely pulled in a hundred different directions. Smita knew that tone only too well.

"I was calling about the verdict. Shannon feels that I should leave tomorrow—"

"Don't bother," Anjali said, interrupting her. "We just got word a few minutes ago that there's been a delay. There won't be a ruling tomorrow."

"Oh. Why not?"

Anjali gave a bitter laugh. "*Why not?* Because this is India. Apparently, the judge hasn't finished writing his judgment."

"I see."

"So, will you still be able to come later?" Anjali asked. "Or will the paper not do a follow-up?"

Maybe they'll run a wire story? Smita thought. "Is the Indian media covering the story?" Smita asked. "Maybe we can just—"

"Please." Anjali's tone was dismissive. "Do you think they can be bothered with such a story? After all, these were Hindus killing a Muslim. So who cares, right? It is, how do you say it—dog bites man? No, they're too busy covering movie stars and—*cricket.*"

Smita smiled at the contempt with which Anjali said the last word. "Listen, where are your offices located?" she asked. "I'd love to talk some more with you about why you took this case, and other issues."

"Why? Because no other lawyer would've bothered with it. And we need more women like Meena to speak up for their rights. That's the only way things will change in this godforsaken country."

"Yes, of course. And you are close to Birwad?"

"Not really. Our offices are about an hour's drive from Meena's village and a little more than that from Vithalgaon, where her brothers live. From Mumbai, you will need to drive. You will have a driver, right?"

"Yes."

"Great," Anjali said absently. "Well, do you want me to get in touch with you when we know the date of the verdict?"

A motorcyclist pulled so close to Smita's cab before swerving at the last instant that she had to bite her lip to keep from screaming. The man shook his fist at her driver before shooting ahead.

"Hello?" Anjali said.

"Oh, sorry," Smita replied. "How much in advance will you know?"

Anjali clucked, then added, "Hard to say. At least the day before, hopefully." She paused. "So? Are you hanging around in Mumbai?"

Smita thought for a moment, then came to a decision. "I think we'll take a start the day after tomorrow," she said. "That way, I can stay at the hospital all day tomorrow if I have to."

"But the verdict may not come until the day after . . ."

"That's okay. I'll go meet with Meena. And I'll interview the brothers, too."

"Good idea. But be careful. The older brother especially can be very belligerent. You should see how he behaves in court. But the worst of the lot is Rupal Bhosle. He's the head of their village council. The brothers worship him like he's some kind of god. Too bad I couldn't sue him."

"It's hard to believe that someone could sanction such barbaric . . ."

"Male entitlement, my dear. Bullshit notions of family honor."

Smita heard the anger in Anjali's voice.

The cab driver pressed on his horn, blasting in Smita's ear. She looked around, bewildered. They were sitting in a massive traffic jam. "God," Anjali said. "What's going on?"

Smita leaned forward and tapped the driver on his shoulder. "*Oi, bhai*," she said in her stilted Hindi. "What use blowing the horn? Nobody is moving, *na*?"

The man looked over his shoulder and grinned sheepishly. "Right you are, miss," he said. "What to do? Just a bad habit."

She smiled, disarmed by his sheepishness. "Sorry," she said to Anjali. "We're stuck in traffic."

"Okay, tell you what," Anjali said briskly. "Let's stay in touch the next few days. I'm assuming you're going to stay at the same motel where Shannon stays when she goes to Birwad?"

"Yeah, I guess so."

"And you're traveling with her assistant? What's her name? *Nandita?*"

"Nandini."

"Ah yes, Nandini. She's good. You're in good hands with her."

Smita looked glumly out of the cab window after they'd hung up. She took in the stalks of the ugly new skyscrapers that had sprouted all over the city. She saw the older buildings, all of which needed a fresh coat of paint. And everywhere, there was the bewildering crush of humanity—people pouring onto the roads from the crowded side-walks, darting into traffic, squeezing past the cars and buses and trucks. Unable to bear the heat in the closed vehicle, she rolled down her window and was immediately assailed by the deafening beeps of the vehicles around her. It was like listening to a demented, cacophonous orchestra; she had the strange sensation that the cars were communi-cating to one another, like in some science-fictional, postapocalyptic movie. She fought the urge to plug her fingers into her ears. It was not as if she was a stranger to the third world. But India wasn't a country so much as an unstoppable force of nature. Everything about it bewil-dered her—the *paan*-stained walls in a renowned hospital, the insane traffic, the masses of people everywhere, Mohan's idiotic insistence that she claim India as her homeland. At this moment, India felt inexpress-ibly large—as well as small and provincial enough to choke her. Well, she'd just have to grit it out. You didn't cover the kind of stories and go to the remote parts of the world that she did because you sought comfort. What had Papa said to her during those early, hard months in Ohio? "Being uncomfortable is good, *beta*. It's in discomfort that growth happens."

Papa. She had not told him that she was back in the city that no member of her family had visited since they'd left. As far as her father knew, she was still vacationing in the Maldives. She'd have to call him that night, but she saw no reason to inform him about her change in plans. He'd only fret until she returned home.

Smita turned her head and saw the driver staring at her in the cab's rearview mirror. He looked away as soon as their eyes met, but she felt the heat rise in her cheeks. She glanced down at her T-shirt and noticed that a bit of her cleavage was showing. In Manhattan, the shirt would be so ordinary as to go unnoticed—but in Mumbai, it was enough to attract the attention of men like the taxi driver. There was no question that she would need to buy more modest attire before she left for Meena's village. She leaned forward in her seat, pulling up the neckline of her T-shirt as she spoke to the driver. "Oh, *bhai*," she said. "I need to buy some outfits. Do they still sell clothes at Colaba Causeway?"

"Yes, of course, memsahib," he said. "They say you can buy everything there, from a pin to an elephant."

CHAPTER FIVE

———✦———

SMITA'S HEART BEGAN to flutter, and her hands turned clammy within moments of strolling down the Causeway. Her anxiety wasn't caused by the vendors at the roadside stalls who begged her to examine their leather purses and silver jewelry and wooden statues. It wasn't because she heard her own distant laughter in the laughter coming from the schoolgirls walking ahead of her, saw her former self in the way they half skipped, half walked down the sidewalk.

It wasn't because she passed Metro Shoes and remembered going there with Mummy at the start of each school year. It wasn't because she passed shops selling schoolbags and remembered Papa buying new backpacks for her and Rohit at the start of each school year. It wasn't even because she walked past the Olympia Coffee House and remembered the egg *bhurji* breakfast that Papa used to sometimes treat her to on Saturdays.

Her hands went clammy because she was close to the one street that she'd hoped to avoid forever.

Spencer Road. What does it look like now? she wondered. Would it hold any signs of her family's life there, or had time papered over its absence? Did any of their old neighbors still live there? The ones who would remember that day in 1996? Beatrice Auntie, the kindly Christian woman who had lived across the street from them, was probably long dead. But surely, there were others who remembered her family fondly—who recalled, for instance, how Papa would buy fireworks for all the neighborhood children to celebrate Diwali, the Hindu festival of lights? Some who felt a pinprick of guilt even after all this time? Or had the dark waters of time pooled around that one incident?

Smita stopped walking, coming to such an abrupt stop that the young man behind her almost ran into her. She found a spot under an awning, away from the press of people. Her heart beat so hard, she felt dizzy. It was as if her very body was protesting the incomprehensible thought forming in her mind—she wanted to go see it, her old street.

Don't be ridiculous, she chided herself. *There's nothing there for you to see. Let the past remain the past. You have nothing to say to those people, not anymore.* But a new idea wormed itself into her head: She wanted to visit the old neighborhood not so much for her own sake as for Papa's. At some point, she would have to tell him about her visit to Mumbai. She didn't have to worry about Papa finding out by reading one of her articles in the paper; ever since November 2016, he had stopped watching the news and eventually had let his subscription to her newspaper lapse. "We came to this country believing it was the world's greatest democracy," he'd said when they argued. "And now, look at what damage this man is doing. I mean, banning Muslims from entering the country? Kidnapping children from their parents? Is this the country we came to? I will still vote, *beta*. But I cannot bear to read about what these people are doing. My heart cannot take it."

But Papa would be crushed when he found out that she'd been a ten-minute walk away from their old neighborhood and had not visited. She knew he would be curious about how the area had changed and would pepper her with questions. Buoyed by this thought, Smita began to walk again, ignoring the thudding in her chest. She retraced her steps and cut across one of the by-lanes. Much to her chagrin, she was disoriented within minutes, unable to recognize a single landmark. She stopped and asked for directions to Spencer Road. It turned out she was only two streets away.

When she reached her destination, she stood still, waiting for the pounding in her heart to quieten, her eyes darting nervously as she looked up and down the street. Was it possible that someone would recognize her as the gangly fourteen-year-old girl who had lived there before she left for America? She gazed up at the Harbor Breeze Apartments, the seven-story cream-colored building across the street. Scaffolding covered the front, and she could see that the building was being painted. How shabby and rundown it looked, so different from the posh building she remembered. *Does everything look new and unblemished in our youth?* she wondered. It was only the bougainvillea that draped over the whitewashed outer wall and the single coconut tree that grew in the small front yard that made the place recognizable to her.

Smita didn't dare turn to look at the building behind her, where Beatrice Auntie had lived. She was already nervous; looking at Beatrice's building would make her come undone.

At the sound of a sharp crack, she jumped. It was only the noise of a bat smacking a ball, from the boys playing cricket down the street—but it was enough to make her realize just how jittery and nervous she was.

On the heels of that realization, she felt anger, as sharp and clean as the sound of that bat smacking that ball. What was she doing, skulking around here, cowering on the street? As if *she* had done something wrong, as if *she* had something to hide. Trembling at the thought of running into one of her former neighbors.

Smita remembered with bitterness how traumatic the first few years in Ohio had been for her mother. How terribly long it had taken Mummy to make new friends, to trust anyone outside her immediate family. How she'd rebuffed the friendliness of the other mothers when they tried to include her in their outings and lunches. How she'd sat alone at home during the day while Smita and Rohit were at school and her husband at work, a shadow of the gregarious, warmhearted woman who had once been the beating heart of the social activities of this building.

Through the tangle of memories, Smita thought of Pushpa Patel. Mummy's best friend. Chiku's mother. *Maybe she still lives here?*

Without another thought, Smita stepped off the curb to cross the street. A motorcyclist on the one-way street missed her by inches, but she scarcely registered the words he shouted at her.

In the lobby, she looked up at the large wooden board with the apartment numbers of the building's residents. There was Pushpa Patel's name and apartment number, 3B, as it had always been. She had spent so much of her childhood in that flat. And then, as if tonguing a pain she couldn't ignore, she searched the board again until she found apartment 5C. Their old apartment.

To avoid the battery of questions from the liftman, Smita took the stairs. On the third floor, she recognized the brown, flecked floor tile on which she and Chiku used to play hopscotch. The smell of fried food hovered like an open umbrella over the door to the apartment. The anger that had propelled her in from the street had vanished, and in its place was a heart-pounding nervousness. Hand on the doorbell, she waited for the queasiness in her belly to settle. *You can still leave,* she said to herself, even though she knew she wouldn't. She rang the bell and heard its long ding-dong chime.

A moment passed. *Shit,* Smita thought. *This is a fucking mistake.* But just then the door opened, and there was Pushpa Auntie's rotund face, older but familiar, peering at her. "Yes?" the woman inquired. "Can I help you?"

Smita's mouth went dry. She waited for a flicker of recognition to spark on Pushpa's face, but instead the older woman's brow furrowed in confusion. "Can I help?" she said again.

Too many years had gone by, Smita realized. What a son of a bitch time was, chewing up everything in its path.

The door was closing on her, Mrs. Patel retreating into the apartment. "Pushpa Auntie, it's me," Smita said in a rush. "Smita Agarwal."

But Pushpa Patel looked as confused as before. *How old is she now?* Smita wondered. *A little older than Papa?*

"I'm sorry," Mrs. Patel was saying. "You have the wrong number." As if this encounter were a phone call, instead of a face-to-face visit.

"Pushpa Auntie, it's me," Smita said again. "Your old neighbor from 5C."

CHAPTER SIX

———✕———

SMITA RECOGNIZED THE mahogany trunk in Pushpa's living room. She and Chiku used to hide in it when they played hide-and-seek, while Rohit, two years older, thumped his feet on the marbled floor and pretended to not know where they were hiding. "I remember that trunk," she said. "Chiku and I . . ."

"Thank you," Pushpa said. She sat in an armchair and indicated that Smita should sit across from her. "What will you take?" she asked politely. "Something hot? Something cold?"

"Nothing, thanks," Smita said, not wanting to turn this into a social visit. She looked around the room where she had spent so much time.

"You are still in the States?" Pushpa asked. Her voice was friendly, but her eyes were disinterested. Once upon a time, Pushpa Auntie had been one of Smita's favorite adults. Now, Smita wondered why.

"Yes. I live in New York."

"I see. We have visited. Many times."

Smita nodded. "That's good," she said vaguely. "Did you like it?" She wondered if Pushpa's husband was at home. What was the man's first name? For the life of her, she couldn't remember.

Pushpa made a face. "Some things were good. But there were too many of those darkies, always misbehaving on the streets."

"Excuse me?"

"Those, what you call them? Those blackies."

"The correct term is *African American*." Of course the woman was a racist. Why was Smita surprised?

Pushpa stiffened. She sat back in her chair. "And you? You are married?"

"No," Smita said. "I'm not. What about—?"

"So, you are having no issues?"

Smita stared at her blankly before realizing what the woman was asking. She'd forgotten that Papa's Indian friends often referred to children as "issues." "No," she said.

"I'm sorry," Pushpa said, as if Smita's childless state was something that warranted condolences.

Smita bristled. "How is Chiku?" she asked, wanting to change the subject.

Pushpa's face brightened. "He's fine," she said. "He's a well-known lawyer. He goes by Chetan now, of course. Nobody calls him Chiku anymore. He argues cases before the high court, after all. He and his wife live in Cuffe Parade. They are having three children. All boys, by the grace of God. I got him married as soon as he finished college."

So, she was not just a racist but a sexist to boot. "Rohit is married and has a son, also," Smita said. "You remember my brother, Rohit, right?"

Pushpa made a noncommittal sound as she stared toward the balcony. Both women listened to the cries of the boys playing cricket on the street below. "Ball, ball, ball!" one of them yelled.

"What community—what kind of girl did he marry?" Mrs. Patel asked.

She knows, Smita thought. *She remembers*. Forcing her voice to remain neutral she said, "An American girl, of course. Very beautiful."

"She's a—what do you call them, an African?"

Smita fought down her distaste before she spoke. "Nope. Allison's white." Her sister-in-law was the daughter of first-generation Irish immigrants, with hair as dark as her own. But Smita felt an irrational, childish urge to impress the woman by turning Ali into a WASP. "She's blonde. With blue eyes. Comes from a very wealthy family."

Pushpa looked impressed. "*Wah*," she said.

Smita smiled grimly. "You've heard of Apple computers?"

"Of course," Pushpa said with a laugh. "We are not so backward. Everybody knows the Apple. My Chetan has three Apple phones."

Smita nodded. "My sister-in-law's father is a senior executive at Apple. You should've seen the dowry he gave us, Auntie." Even as the string of lies escaped her lips, she wondered why she was trying to impress this awful woman.

"That's very good," Pushpa said, nodding in a cow-like fashion. Her eyes held Smita's for a moment before she looked away. "And your parents?" she said. "They are well?"

Smita hated herself for the tears that sprang in her eyes. "Mummy died eight months ago," she said.

"My condolences," Pushpa said, as if they were discussing the death of their mailman rather than her former best friend.

Smita felt her anger rise. "Mummy built a good life for herself. But she never stopped missing this city, you know," she said softly. "All her life."

Pushpa looked down at her hands. "Nobody who moves to America misses India," she said.

You bitch, Smita thought. *You fucking bitch*. "That's probably true for people who leave voluntarily," she said. "Not for those who are chased out of their own homes."

Pushpa's head jerked up. "It's best to let bygones be bygones. No use crying over spilled milk."

It was the word "crying" that unleashed something in Smita. It rekindled the memory of those early days in Ohio when she and Rohit would come home from school to find their mother red-eyed and list-less. The two of them overhearing conversations in which Mummy would berate Papa for dragging the family to this cold, wintery *desh*. Papa's voice, low and apologetic at the start of their arguments, then rising and growing more urgent.

"This is your privilege talking, Pushpa Auntie," Smita said sharply. "It's not your life that was upended, right? Until the day she died, my mother wondered why you betrayed us the way you did."

"Don't talk rot," Pushpa said. "You are just like your father. Always blaming others for your problems."

A vein throbbed in Smita's forehead. Nobody had ever spoken about Papa in such a dismissive way. "That's a lie," she said. "My papa . . . He's a thousand times the person that any of you will ever be." As she said the words, she knew why she'd made the trek to this horrible woman's home: to say to her face what Papa was too much of a gen-tleman to ever say.

Pushpa's face darkened. "Have you come back after all this time to create problems?" she hissed. "What is the meaning of all this drama, this *tamasha*? You show up to my door after all these years to insult me? Is this how you Americans treat your elders?"

Smita leaned in. "No," she said slowly, her eyes fixed on the older woman's face. "But is this how you Indians treat your children?"

She heard Pushpa gasp before the older woman stood up. "Get out. Leave. Get out of my house *now*."

Smita stared at Pushpa, aghast at how quickly the conversation had gotten derailed. "Auntie, we got off on the wrong foot," she said.

"Listen, I came here to gain some insight. I would like us to talk . . . Please."

"Jaiprakash!" Pushpa yelled. "Where are you?" And when a dark-skinned elderly man rushed into the living room, she turned to her cook and said, "Show memsahib the door."

The man looked from his employer to the well-dressed younger woman in confusion. Smita put up her hands and rose. "It's okay," she said to him. "I'll go."

SMITA DRAGGED HER feet as she walked back toward the Causeway, angry at herself for this impulsive visit, mortified by how easily Mrs. Patel had turned the tables on her. What had she hoped to gain from this fool's errand anyway? She had hoped to embarrass the woman, to squeeze out an apology that she could carry back to Papa, to remind Mrs. Patel that the past never died. Instead, she had been banished from Mrs. Patel's life for a second time.

Why on earth am I surprised? Smita asked herself as she crossed the street. She had been a journalist for too many years to not know how easily people made excuses for their past misdeeds. Nobody was the villain in his or her own life story. Shame on her for expecting Pushpa Auntie to have lost any sleep over ancient history. Why would she fret over the past when every day a new Mumbai was being built atop the debris of the old city? "Look to the future, child," her father used to say. "This is why our feet point forward, not back."

As soon as she got to the shopping district, Smita stopped at a clothing store to buy appropriate outfits for her trip to Birwad, but the salesman who greeted her in the first store was so oily and effusive, she walked right out. She was spent; she would have to shop the next day, in between breaks from caring for Shannon. *Surely, there will be stores near the hospital?* she thought. Meanwhile, she wanted only to get a bite to eat and then collapse on her bed. But the thought of eating alone in the opulent splendor of the Taj was a lonely one, and so she continued walking, looking for a restaurant that catered to the many Western tourists in the neighborhood. She stopped at the Leopold Cafe and sat at one of the tables overlooking the Causeway.

As she sipped a beer, after ordering a sandwich from the elderly waiter, Smita saw what looked like bullet holes in the Leopold's walls. She blinked, remembering. *Of course.* The restaurant had been one of the targets of the terrorist attacks that had brought this metropolis to its knees for three horrific days in November 2008. What the Leopold had done—refused to paper over its history and instead keep the bullet holes as a permanent marker of those harrowing days—was unusual. Most of the time, the world chose to move on with nary a look back. She saw this in the US after every school shooting: a flurry of news stories, the sanctimonious tweets about thoughts and prayers, the predictable calls for gun control reform and then—silence. Parents and other survivors were left to their private lifelong grief, permanently out of step with a world that had moved on. Bloodstains were scrubbed from school walls before the students returned.

Smita had been visiting her parents and brother in Ohio that November, the four of them glued to CNN as it reported on the young men from Pakistan shooting up the city and setting fire to the Taj. Rohit had looked up from the television set and said, with spite in his voice that made Smita and their parents pay attention: "Serves them right. I hope they burn that whole miserable city down."

"*Beta*," Papa had said reflexively, "to wish ill on millions of innocent people is a sin."

Rohit had shaken his head and left the room.

She'd tried broaching the subject with Rohit later that evening, the two of them perched in front of the TV again after their parents had gone to bed. But he had gestured toward *The Daily Show*. "I'm watching this," he said curtly, and Smita had acquiesced with silence.

The old waiter returned to her table with her sandwich. "First time here?" he asked, nodding toward the wall with the bullet holes.

"Yes. Were you here at the time?"

"Yes, madam. God was with me that day. I'd just gone up to the mezzanine floor. Two of my coworkers were not so lucky. Nor were many of our customers."

She'd heard variations of this recap so many times, ordinary humans trying to solve an enduring mystery: Why had they lived while others had died in the tragedy? No matter what calamity they'd survived—plane crashes or earthquakes or mass shootings—survivors felt compelled to assign some reason, discern some pattern as to why they'd been spared. Smita saw no pattern to such events: she believed that life was a series of random events, a zigzag of coincidences that led to either survival or death.

The waiter draped a dish towel over his right shoulder. "The bastards didn't even come in," he said. "Just stood at the entrance and sprayed bullets as casually as you and I would hand out sweets on Diwali." His eyelids fluttered briefly as he remembered. "There was blood everywhere, people screaming, ducking under tables. And then they threw in a grenade. Imagine that, madam. A grenade into a restaurant. What kind of person does that?"

All kinds of people, Smita wanted to say. *Seemingly ordinary people who rise each morning, eat breakfast, smile at their neighbors, and kiss their children goodbye. People who look and act just like you and me. Until they're gripped by an ideological conviction, or a disruption occurs in their lives that makes them want to rearrange the world or burn everything down.*

The waiter must have seen something on her face—a combination of revulsion and fatalism—because he said, softly: "Same evil happened in your country, isn't it? On 9/11?"

"How'd you know I'm from America?" Smita asked.

He smiled broadly, showing tobacco-stained teeth. "I've worked here for thirty years, madam. Many of our customers are foreigners. *Bas*, you opened your mouth, and I could tell you're America."

"You're America," the waiter said. Not *You're American*. Smita felt that he was right. At that moment, she felt as if she were all of America, as if the red earth of Georgia had hardened her bones and the blue waters of the Pacific flowed in her bloodstream. She was America, all of it—Walt Whitman and Woody Guthrie, the snowcapped Rockies and the Mississippi Delta, Old Faithful in Yellowstone. In that moment, she felt so estranged from the city of her birth that she would have paid a million bucks to be transported back to her silent, monastic apartment in Brooklyn.

"So, what brings you to our Mumbai?" the waiter asked, his chattiness making Smita uneasy. "Holiday or business?"

"Business," she said shortly.

He must have sensed her reluctance and began to move away, his old formality returning. "Enjoy your stay," he said.

She sat at the Leopold even after she'd paid the bill, replaying the conversation with Pushpa Auntie in her head. She was the journalist, and yet it was Pushpa who had seized the narrative. She remembered what Molly, who worked for NBC, had once told her: The most basic rule of broadcast journalism was that you never, ever relinquished the microphone, never handed it over to your subject. Well, old Pushpa Patel—who, as far as she knew, had never held a job, much less interviewed despots and leaders around the world—had successfully wrested the microphone from her. Tomorrow, the woman would gleefully recount the story to all their former neighbors—how this Smita, this mere slip of a girl, had dared to come into her house and insulted her. And how she'd put her in her place.

It was true what they said. You really couldn't go home again. Mumbai had spat her out once, and it had just done so again. How was it that Shannon, who had been based in India for three years, had found people like Mohan and Nandini who clearly cared about her? In Smita's case, there wasn't a soul in this city of twenty million whom she could call. Once she'd escaped India, Smita had lost all connection with her school friends. In recent years, as many of her former classmates had found one another through social media, several had tried contacting her, but she had not replied. How could she have borne their curiosity and their questions? Her parents, too, had not stayed in touch with the handful of relatives they had in Mumbai. No, she may as well have been in Nairobi or Jakarta, for all the difference it made.

She left the restaurant and walked back toward her hotel, the frenzied cries of the vendors reminding her of the squawking of birds at sundown. Sarongs and kurtas. Leather handbags and perfume. They wanted her to buy it all. She ignored their pleas, careful not to make eye contact with any of them.

It was dark by the time she reached the Taj. Despite her fatigue, she briefly considered crossing the street and walking under the arch of the Gateway to the sea at Apollo Bunder, the sea that had been the backdrop to her childhood. Instead, she passed through the metal detectors of the hotel—a legacy of the 2008 attacks, the apologetic young woman receptionist had informed her when she'd checked in—and then took the elevator to her room.

CHAPTER SEVEN

—◆—

IN THE MORNING, Smita got to the hospital with moments to spare. The nurse and ward boy were in Shannon's room, about to transfer her to a gurney to wheel her to surgery. Mohan and Nandini, both of them grim faced, barely glanced at her when she entered the room.

"Smits," Shannon said. "I'm so glad you're here."

The words were a broom, sweeping away the last of her resentment at being summoned to Mumbai. "Me too," she said. "And here's the good news—there won't be a verdict today. So I'll be able to stay with you all day."

She was dimly aware of the fact that Nandini had spun around to stare at her. But the next second the woman continued arguing with the nurse in Marathi, and Smita could only make out a word or two. She heard the words for *bed* and *transfer*, and then heard the nurse say, "*Accha*, fine. We can take her from here only. Okay?"

"Good," Nandini said, with a satisfied smile. She turned to Shannon. "They will transport you to the operation theater on this bed, Shannon. They will not put you on the gurney."

Shannon threw Smita a wry look. *Can you believe this shit?* she appeared to signal.

"Where do we wait? Can we go with her?" Smita asked Mohan.

"What?" He looked at her absently, as if he'd forgotten who she was. "Yes, of course." He turned to the nurse. "*Chalo*, let's go."

Shannon extended her hand to Mohan as the male transporter unlocked the bed. "Thanks a million, love," she said. "I don't know what I would've—"

"No thanks necessary," Mohan said, shaking his head vigorously. "We'll see you soon."

"Inshallah," Shannon replied, and Smita smiled at her effortless use of the word.

Nandini walked beside the bed as they wheeled Shannon to the operating room, Smita and Mohan following. At the large metal door their little caravan came to a halt. "Only patients past this point," the nurse said, looking directly at Nandini, as if bracing herself for an argument. But Nandini nodded wordlessly before taking Shannon's hand in hers. "Good luck," she said.

"Thanks, Nan. Make sure you take an early start tomorrow, okay? You should pick Smita up and—"

"Shannon," Mohan and Nandini said in unison, and Shannon smiled.

"See you all later," she said. "Go get a bite to eat, all of you."

THEY WANDERED BACK to Shannon's room to wait, making desultory conversation along the way. Nandini went immediately to the window and stood there, her back turned to Smita and Mohan. Smita shot him an inquiring glance, but he seemed oblivious to her. The conversation sagged and after ten minutes or so, Mohan leapt to his feet. "I need to go outside for a while, *yaar*," he announced. "Just to get away from this atmosphere."

Smita's stomach sank at the thought of being left alone with Nandini, without Mohan's buffering presence. The young woman turned around, and Smita saw that her eyes were red and puffy. She caught her breath. "Nandini," she said. "Shannon is going to be fine."

"She needs me here," Nandini said fiercely. "Doctor said it will be a long recovery. Shannon said you were born and bred in India. Why you cannot go to Birwad by yourself?"

Even though she understood the reason for Nandini's disdain, Smita was taken aback by her hostility. "I . . . I haven't lived in India in twenty years," she said. "I was a teenager when I left, you see. So I'm not sure if my Hindi is up to the task. And I've never driven in this country."

"Smita," Mohan said, "Nandini doesn't really mean what she said. This is just her worry for her friend speaking. *Hai na*, Nandini *bhen?* You wouldn't really wish for Smita to travel alone, correct?"

The moments ticked by. Finally, Nandini nodded.

"Right," Mohan said briskly, as if he were unaware of the reluctance with which Nandini had answered. "Shannon always tells me what a professional you are. This was just a moment's weakness." He rubbed his hands together. "*Chalo*, good that we have all this cleared up. Now, I can go for a quick walk. Maybe get you something to eat." He looked at Smita. "How about you? Shall I pick up some breakfast for you?"

Smita got to her feet. "Actually, if you don't mind, I'd like to get out for a few minutes, also. Get some fresh air."

Mohan glanced at Nandini. "*Theek hai?*" he asked quietly. "You can always phone us if you need anything."

But Nandini seemed as eager to get rid of Smita as the latter was to go. "Yes, yes, very good," she said, nodding vigorously. "If there is any news, I will call."

"*Arre, yaar*, they haven't even given Shannon anesthesia yet. We will be here for several more hours."

THE SALTY SEA air hit them as soon as they exited the hospital, and Smita inhaled deeply. "It's such a beautiful location for a hospital," she said.

Mohan looked at her curiously. After a moment he said, "Would you like to go look at the water for a few minutes?"

"Can we? That would be lovely. Tomorrow I have to leave town to go cover this story." She heard the whininess in her voice and bit the inside of her cheek in embarrassment.

"Sure," he said, "Follow me."

Mohan took the outer edge of the sidewalk, closer to the traffic, and the absentminded gracefulness of the gesture made Smita smile. Papa used to do this when they lived in Mumbai.

"So, for whatever reason, I take it you don't wish to go to Birwad?" Mohan asked as they walked. His tone was pleasant, conversational.

She hesitated. "Well, I'm not looking forward to spending all this time in a car with Nandini," she said at last. "The woman seems to have taken an intense dislike to me."

"Rubbish," Mohan said promptly. "It's not that at all. You misunderstand. She is just reluctant to leave Shannon, that's all. You see, she obviously doesn't think I'm capable of taking care of her." He smiled. "But may I ask you something?"

"Sure."

"Did you . . . It's just that, you seemed upset when Shannon asked you to cover the story for her. Why did you agree to come if you don't wish to do so?"

Smita sighed. "I thought she wanted me to come help take care of her in the hospital. If I'd known that she was okay, that is, that she had you and Nandini, then I . . ."

"Then what?" Mohan said. "You wouldn't have come?"

Ruminating over Mohan's question, she swerved to avoid the out-stretched arm of the fruit vendor who was holding out a slice of orange for her to sample. "No, I guess I would've come anyway if there was no one else to take over," she finally said. "But I wouldn't have been caught unawares."

He nodded. "You should've seen your expression when Shannon asked you, *yaar*." He made such a grotesque face that Smita laughed.

"Did I really look that shocked?"

"Worse." And again, he pulled a long, doleful face.

"Hey," Smita said, "changing the subject, I need to buy a few outfits for tomorrow. Are there any stores around here where I can buy a few pairs of *shalwar kameez* or something?"

"My friend, you are in Breach Candy. You can buy a new set of grandparents here if you wish." As he spoke, he gestured with his hand to turn right into a park.

Smita's breath caught at the sight of the dark pink bougainvillea bushes. And beyond that, the thin gray lip of the Arabian Sea. Tall coconut trees lined the wide walkway that led toward the stone benches facing the water. "Oh wow," she breathed. "This is stunning."

Mohan looked pleased. "Thank you," he said quietly, as if she had complimented him on his own apartment. "You should come here at sunset. It's heaven on earth."

She thought of all the beautiful, magical places she had visited— Capri, Saint-Tropez, Paros. As beautiful as this park was it could hardly compare with the heart-stopping beauty of the places she'd been. And yet, in the middle of a dirty, crowded metropolis, it was a kind of par-adise. She took in the old couples sitting quietly on the stone benches, watched the affluent residents of the neighborhood walk briskly by, the old gardener watering the pots of flowers that dotted the walkway. But what tore at her heart was the sight of the middle-aged women, fat as dumplings, jogging in their tennis shoes and saris, their bellies jiggling. Something about this sight felt so quintessentially Mumbai.

Or *Bombay*, as her parents insisted on calling their old city. Yeah, this was Papa's Bombay—cosmopolitan, sophisticated, but also resolutely out of step with the rest of the world.

She nodded. "It is," she said.

Mohan turned toward her, surprised, and she realized that he had braced himself for an argument. Had she really made herself so obnoxious the day before that he felt defensive around her? Her feelings for this city were complicated. She was sorry that he had registered only her disapproval.

Mohan pointed to a bench in a shady spot. "Shall we sit for a few moments? The sun is already so hot."

A bird chirped above them, but when Smita looked up, she couldn't spot it. "That sounds so lovely," she murmured.

"It's rare," Mohan said. "The city's mostly overrun by crows. They've chased all the other species out. It's only in this posh part of town that you spot other birds, occasionally. And thankfully in Dadar, we still have parrots."

"Do you own an apartment in Dadar?"

He shook his head. "Actually, I live as a paying guest with a Parsi family. I went to college with their son, but he lives in Bangalore. It works out great—I have my own room, and Zarine Auntie sends a hot lunch tiffin to my office every day."

"Is it because you hate living alone?" Smita said, remembering their conversation from the day before.

Mohan nodded, without a hint of self-abasement. "Yah. Also, rents in this city are absurd. I mean, if it's London or New York, I can understand shelling out so much. But in this bloody city, with its potholes and dirty air? Absurd."

"Oh, so now you're dissing Mumbai?" Smita teased. "I thought you loved this city?"

"I do," he said promptly. "But you don't love something because you're blind to its faults, right? You love it *despite* its flaws."

She nodded. They sat in silence, staring out at the sea. Smita remembered going to the seaside during the monsoon season, how the ocean used to heave and spit, thrilling her with its might and fury.

"What about you? Do you live with your parents?" Mohan asked.

"Are you kidding me?" The words escaped her lips before she could pull them back. She registered the insulted look on Mohan's face. She reminded herself that her not living with her parents probably seemed as odd to him as living with his would have seemed to her. "I don't," she said. "And in any case, my mother is dead. She died eight months ago."

"I'm sorry," he said quietly. "My condolences."

Smita blinked hard, staring straight ahead as she wrestled for control of her emotions.

"I am really sorry," Mohan said after a few minutes. "I cannot imagine what I would do if something happened to my mother."

She nodded, unable to say what she was thinking: What had made Mummy's cancer diagnosis and quick death even more unbearable was knowing that Mummy would die without ever seeing India again. That somehow, the final bereavement had echoed the earlier one, as if Mummy had died not once but twice. The fact that they'd landed on their feet in America didn't diminish the hardship and loneliness of exile: The early promise of Papa's academic career thwarted; the two-year period when Rohit refused to invite his white classmates to their modest apartment after one boy had screwed up his nose and said, "Ew. It smells like curry in here." Smita herself had grown quiet and distant, far removed from the fun-loving, lively girl she'd once been.

"Where do they live?" she asked. "Your folks?"

"In a town called Surat. It's about five hours' drive from here."

"Do you see them often, then?"

He shrugged. "Not so much. They bought another place in Kerala after my papa retired, and they spend a lot of time there. And when I'm working, I put in long hours."

"Can't you go see them now? Since you're off for two weeks?"

Mohan clasped his hands behind his head and stretched back against them. "Well, they're away at the moment. Normally, I would have gone for a few days to check on the house. But now, with Shannon being sick, I don't know."

"Shannon. We should call, no?"

"In a minute." Mohan paused. "I admire Nandini," he said. "From what Shannon says, she's very good at her job. But to be honest, *yaar*, she's gone a bit *pagal* since Shannon's accident."

"*Pagal?*"

"You know? A bit mad." He pointed to his temple and made a circle with his index finger, making the universal gesture.

"She acts as if she hates me," Smita said. It felt good to be able to verbalize this.

"No, don't be silly. I told you. She's, like, mad with worry." He sighed heavily. "It will be better when she gets out of town with you. I'll find it easier to manage in the hospital without all her drama."

"I hate drama, too. That's why I'm dreading traveling with her."

"I understand. But Shannon really respects her." Mohan pulled on his lower lip. "How many days do you think you'll be gone?"

"I'm not sure. I spoke to my editor on my way here this morning. He wants at least a couple of stories." Smita exhaled. "I brought my laptop with me today. I will need to work from the hospital this afternoon. I still have to read Shannon's previous stories, and I probably need to talk to Anjali some more."

Mohan raised his eyebrows. "Nandini will have all that information, *yaar*. Don't worry." He rose from the bench. "Maybe we should head back. But first, we can stop by a few clothing stores."

"Oh, no, that's okay," Smita said hastily. "I can do this later. I didn't mean for you to help with that."

"*Oi*, Smita," Mohan said, "take pity on a poor fellow. Don't make me go back to the hospital just yet. I'm telling you, this surgery is going to take hours."

As they walked toward the exit to the park, Mohan phoned Nandini. "*Sab theek hai?*" he asked her in Hindi. "Fine, fine, good. We will be back in a couple of hours. But call if you need anything before then, *accha?*"

AS IT TURNED out, Smita was grateful for Mohan's company. The salesman at the store sized her up immediately and began to show her the most expensive and garish outfits. Smita protested, but the man ignored her. "Oh, *bhai*," Mohan intervened after a few minutes. "Memsahib is not going to a wedding. She is visiting some very poor people in a village. So show her the simplest cotton outfits you have."

The salesman looked so put off that Smita fought to keep a straight face. "Maybe madam should go to Khadi Bhandar," he muttered, loud enough for them to hear. But he signaled to Smita. "Please to come this way, madam."

In the end, they left the store with four identical *shalwar kameez* outfits, each in a different color. "I wanted to shop at Colaba yesterday but ran into the same problem," Smita said.

Mohan shook his head dismissively. "All these people are *chors*," he said. "Colaba has so many foreigners that it's the worst. They just fleece people."

Smita smiled. "I grew up in Colaba," she said. "It was this way even twenty years ago."

"Oh really? Which street?"

She hated herself for her loose tongue. Across the street, she saw a woman standing behind a wooden cart. "Oh wow," she said. "Fresh roasted corn on the cob with lime. I haven't had that in years." She looked at him. "Can we get some?"

She knew that Mohan had seen through her charade. But after a beat he shrugged and said, "Sure."

The old woman grinned as Smita bit into the corn. Smita caught Mohan's eye. "Sorry. There's so little street food I can safely eat. And I've always loved the spices they rub on the corn."

Mohan reached for his wallet and Smita stopped him. "I'll pay," she said. "I traded money at—"

"Smita," Mohan said. "Please. You are my guest."

"Yes, but—" Smita said. She jumped as the old woman vendor interrupted them. "The man must pay, baby. It is our custom."

"See?" Mohan said, smiling. "Listen to your elders."

As THEY WALKED past the information desk in the hospital lobby, Mohan gave the woman receptionist a curt nod and flashed a slip of paper. "Doctor's pass," he said.

"And for madam, sir?" the receptionist asked. It was the same woman who had made her wait in the lobby the day before.

The change in Mohan was imperceptible, a slight straightening of the shoulders. "It's okay," he said. "She's with me."

"Yes, but sir. Visiting hours . . ."

This time, he stopped and looked closely at the seated woman. "It's okay," he repeated, and the woman nodded. "Come," he said as he took Smita by the elbow and steered her toward the elevators. She knew what she had just witnessed. She stole a glance at Mohan. His entire demeanor was different.

"You know," Smita said as they waited for the elevator, "would you mind if I sat in the cafeteria and worked on my laptop for a couple of hours?"

"Yes, of course," Mohan said immediately. "If there's any news I will phone you or come find you. But it will be many, many hours still."

He walked her to the cafeteria. "Call, *hah*, if you need anything?"

"Mohan. Stop being a mother hen, *yaar*."

He raised his eyebrows at her use of his salutation, then flashed her a quick salute and walked away.

Smita turned on her computer and glanced at her watch. It was late in the US, but Papa was a night owl. She dialed his number.

"Hi, *beta*," her father said. "How's your vacation?"

"It's going great, Papa," she said. How effortlessly the lie had slipped from her lips. "In fact, we're seriously thinking of extending it by another week or so."

"Really?" Despite the slightly crackly connection, she heard the surprise in his voice. "It's that beautiful? I've always heard it was. In fact, your mother had wanted to go there."

"She did?" How come he hadn't mentioned this before?

"Yes. I didn't want to tell you before you left. In case it made you . . . sad. But you should enjoy yourself thoroughly, *beta*. I worry about you, how hard you work."

She waited until the lump in her throat dissipated. "No harder than you do," she said.

"Me? I'm at the fag end of my life, *beta*. No, the future belongs to you and Rohit."

Despite twenty years in America, Papa still used some of his British-Indian expressions. She and her brother had tried telling him not to use the word *fag*, but to no avail. "How is Rohit?" she asked. "And little Alex?"

"Oh, that fat little rascal? Listen to what he said to me yesterday." And Papa was off, telling her a story about his grandson's latest antics. As always, Smita was grateful to Rohit for having procreated and given her parents a grandchild. She had never had a strong maternal urge and shared little of her single friends' angst about the ticking of their biological clocks. Alex was a gift not just to her parents but to her, also.

After she hung up, Smita worked her way through her emails, then left a message for Anjali to call her. She was reading Shannon's features about Meena when the lawyer phoned her back, urging her to leave for Birwad the next day. "From what we're hearing, the verdict could come any day now. And you'd said you wanted to interview Meena and her brothers beforehand?"

"Yes, that's the plan."

"Make sure you talk to Rupal, okay? He's the village head?"

"I was just reading about him," Smita said.

"He's a *pucca* bastard, I tell you. He's the real mastermind behind all this."

"So the brothers . . . ?"

"*Pah*," Anjali said dismissively. "The brothers are just ignorant peasants. But . . . but this man? He's a monster."

Monster. Demon. Satan. In Smita's line of work, people often bandied around such terms to explain away horrendous behavior. Every time there was a mass shooting in America, for instance, there was a rush to label the shooter a crazed monster, rather than place him within the context of a culture that fetishized guns. Every time a cop shot dead a black man, there was an attempt to paint him as a rogue cop. But what about the millions of otherwise normal people who were recruited to massacre strangers during a war? Were they all evil? How alarmingly easy it had been to get millions to participate in genocide during both the Holocaust and Partition. Human beings could apparently be turned into killers as effortlessly as turning a key. All one had to do was use a few buzzwords: *God. Country, Religion. Honor.* No, men like Rupal were not the problem. The problem lay with the culture from which they bubbled up.

"Hello?" Anjali sounded impatient. "Are you still there?"

"Yes. I'm here."

"Okay. So we'll be in touch, then."

"Anjali. Wait."

"Yes?"

"What's she like? Meena?"

There was a long silence. "She's the bravest client I've ever had," Anjali said finally. "But you have to look past her demeanor to see how brave she is."

"Brave how?"

Smita heard the heavy exhale. "Do you have any idea what a risk she's taken, suing her brothers? We had to force the police to reopen the case. She was near death when I first met her. She injured herself trying to rescue her husband. They set him on fire first, and then they actually tried to stop his younger brother from saving *her* life."

"The picture of her in the paper . . ."

"Yes. She's still pretty disfigured."

"And nothing more can be done? To help?"

"To make her look more presentable, you mean? What for?" There was no mistaking the bitterness in Anjali's voice. "You think anyone else is going to marry this poor woman? You think her neighbors will ever speak to her again? You think she will ever be anything more than what she is—a social pariah?"

"Well, then why put her through the trauma of a lawsuit?"

There was a strained silence. When Anjali finally spoke, she enunciated each word slowly and deliberately: "To set a precedent. To issue a warning to the next bastard thinking of burning alive a woman. And hopefully, to lock these monsters up forever. That's all. Not to improve Meena's life. She knew this when she agreed. And that is why she's the bravest woman I know. You understand?"

"I do," Smita said.

After they hung up, Smita closed her eyes, processing everything Anjali had told her. When she looked up, she saw Mohan standing in front of her, frowning as he peered into her face. "Hi," he said quietly.

Fear made her lean forward in her chair. "What's wrong?" she whispered. "Shannon . . . ?"

". . . is out of surgery," he said. "She's in the recovery room. The surgery took less time than they'd thought. It went really well."

"Thank God."

Mohan gave a slight nod. "Well, I just wanted to give you the news," he said. "Carry on with your work. I'll see you later." He turned to leave but stopped, his attention snagged by the picture of Meena on Smita's open laptop. "Is that her? Meena?"

Smita nodded.

He emitted a low whistle. "This poor woman," he said. "Her . . . those scars. Her face looks like a map or something."

That's it exactly, Smita thought. Meena's face was a map created by a brutal, misogynistic cartographer.

Mohan sat down across from her. "Do you ever get used to seeing such misery? I mean, in your line of work you must see this kind of thing often, no?"

She shook her head, unable to answer. Everywhere she went, it seemed, it was open season on women. Rape, female genital mutilation, bride burnings, domestic abuse—everywhere, in every country, women were abused, isolated, silenced, imprisoned, controlled, punished, and killed. Sometimes, it seemed to Smita that the history of the world was written in female blood. And of course, to go into the far-flung parts of the world to tell these stories required a certain amount of dispassion. But getting used to it? That was another thing altogether. No, she wouldn't be worth her salt as a reporter if she ever got used to the injustice inflicted on women like Meena.

"I . . . I don't think so," she said. "But, I'm never in a place long enough to get really involved, you know?"

He frowned. "That's good?"

"It's not a matter of good or bad. It's just the nature of the beast."

"I see." He nodded. "Okay, I should let you work. See you later."

Smita watched as Mohan walked away, took in the loping walk, noticed how he strode with his palms facing backward. She turned back to her laptop and began to read about Meena's sad, ruined life.

CHAPTER EIGHT

———————— ✳ ————————

THREE HOTEL EMPLOYEES had already approached Smita as she stood in the lobby of the Taj with her suitcase, asking if she needed assistance. She reached for her phone to call Nandini.

"Hey." The male voice came from behind her, making Smita jump. She turned around so fast that Mohan took a hasty step backward, raising his hands in an appeasing gesture. "Sorry, sorry," he said. "I didn't mean to startle."

"What are you doing here?" Smita looked around the Taj's lobby. "Where's Nandini? Is Shannon—"

"Shannon's fine," Mohan said hastily. "She has a slight fever, but the doctor said it's not unusual." He hesitated, looking at Smita closely. "But Nandini. Well. She had a meltdown at the hospital this morning. She called me on my mobile, crying. She's refusing to leave Shannon's side."

"What is she, in love with Shannon or something?" The words were out of Smita's mouth before she could take them back.

Mohan looked at her, one eyebrow crooked. "No," he said. "She just . . . cares about Shannon, that's all."

She heard the chastisement in his voice and flushed. But her anger rose again. "I'm sorry. I'm just frustrated, I guess. I mean, she should've backed out yesterday. It's going to be hard to find another translator on such short notice. What if the verdict comes—"

"There's no need for that."

"Yes, there is. I know Hindi, but I'm not fluent and I don't particularly want to drive myself to Birwad," Smita said, her voice rising. Another guest, a woman who was speaking on her phone, brushed up against her, not paying attention, and Smita glared at her. "Excuse me," she hissed, and the woman glanced back, startled.

"Smita," Mohan said, "*I'm* your new driver. And translator."

"What? No way. I'm sorry, but no."

Smita saw the hurt look that rippled across Mohan's face. She opened her mouth to explain, but he raised his left hand to stop her, fishing his phone out of his pocket with his right. He dialed a number. "Here you go," he said. She heard the note of impatience in his voice. "Talk to Shannon." He walked away before she could react.

"Hello? Mohan?" Shannon's voice was weak, groggy.

"It's me," Smita said quietly. "I'm sorry to trouble you."

"Smits. I apologize for all this." Shannon lowered her voice. "Nandini just stepped out to get me some ice water, so I'll talk fast, okay? Can you hear me?"

"Yes," Smita said. Already, it was beginning to feel as if the trip to Birwad with Mohan was yet another thing she had no control over.

Shannon sighed. "Great. Listen, between you and me, I'd rather have Mohan here and Nandini with you. But what can I do? Nan has been hysterical since you left yesterday, and I just don't have the energy to deal with her theatrics. Also, she was up with me almost all night long. To be honest with you, I'd be afraid to let her drive in this state."

"Mohan said you have a fever?"

"I'm fine," Shannon said. "But here's the thing—it's actually better that you travel with a guy on this assignment. This is a very traditional area you're going to, and they'll respect you more if you're with a man."

Smita scoffed, "*You* travel with Nandini."

"That's different. I'm this big, white American broad. Men like Meena's brothers don't even see me as a woman. They're a little afraid of me. You know what I mean?"

"Not really."

"Hang on." Smita could hear Nandini's voice in the background, heard Shannon mutter, "Thank you," and then let out a sharp "Fuck!"

"I'm back," Shannon said. Her voice was hoarse, and Smita surmised that her pain level had shot up again. "Can I ask?" Shannon continued. "What's the big deal about going with Mohan? He knows the area better than . . ."

Even though Mohan had wandered a good distance away, Smita whispered into the phone. "I hardly know him," she said.

"Oh, come off it, Smits," Shannon snapped. "Like you know most of the minders you travel with when you get to a new country?"

"That's true, but . . ."

"Okay then," Shannon said. "I guess we're good?" She sounded as if the matter were settled. "Smits? Are we good?"

"We're good." Even as she said it, Smita marveled at how skillfully Shannon had played her. "Okay, I'll see you soon. You keep getting better."

"Thanks, love. Stay in touch. And remember, I owe you big."

SMITA LOOKED IN the rearview mirror as Mohan pulled out his wallet and handed a few bills to the elderly doorman who had insisted on placing her suitcase in the trunk. She had waved him off when he'd hurried up to them, but Mohan had shot her a disapproving look and asked her to get in the car. As he got in the driver's seat and began to back up the car, she said, "It was just one bag. We could've handled it."

He clucked at her. "*Eh*, what to do? He's almost my father's age and probably needs the tips. I didn't want to insult him."

She nodded, chastised by his generosity. "And you?" she asked. "Have you already packed, or do we need to . . ."

"Yes. My bag is in the trunk, also." He fiddled with the air-conditioning dial. "I'm just glad that girl had the sense to call me before I had left home this morning."

"Me too." She was suddenly grateful for Mohan's lighthearted presence, such a contrast to Nandini's dour demeanor.

Mohan gestured toward the back seat as they pulled out of the hotel driveway. "By the way, we have omelet sandwiches in the cooler, in case you're hungry," he said. "Zarine Auntie is a fabulous cook."

"Your landlady made you sandwiches this morning?" Smita said.

"*Landlady?* She's more like a second mother to me, *yaar*. But it's true. She spoils me rotten."

"Aren't all Indian men spoiled?" Smita said, a smile in her voice. She thought of Papa, who had never cooked a meal for himself until her mother died. *Papa*. How happy he'd been to learn she was extending her vacation by a week, not suspecting a thing.

"Maybe," Mohan replied. He lowered the volume on the radio. "Mostly by our mothers. Not like those poor American children. Forced to leave their homes at eighteen so that their parents can enjoy being—what's that term you Americans use?—*empty nesters*. As if human beings are birds."

"What are you talking about?"

"I've read about it. How you must leave your home the instant you turn eighteen. Whereas here in India, my God. Parents would kill themselves before they would force their child to leave."

"First of all, nobody is *forced* to leave. Most teenagers are dying to strike out on their own. And secondly, didn't *you* leave your parents' home?"

He gave her a quick look. "True, true. But that was for my schooling."

"And now?"

"*Now?*" He sighed. "What to do, *yaar*? Now, I'm in love with this mad city. Once you've had a taste of Mumbai, you can't live anywhere else."

For a moment, Smita hated Mohan for his smugness. "And yet, millions of people do," she murmured.

"Right you are." Mohan swerved to avoid a pothole. "So why did your family leave?"

She was instantly on guard. "My papa got a job in America," she said shortly.

"What does he do?"

She turned her head to see what movie was playing at Regal Cinema as they passed it. "He's a professor. He teaches at a university in Ohio."

"Wow." He opened his mouth to ask another question, but Smita beat him to it.

"You've never thought of settling overseas?" she asked.

"Me? He considered for a moment. "Yah, maybe when I was younger. But life is too hard abroad. Here we have every convenience."

Smita took in the bumper-to-bumper traffic, the blare of the horns, the plumes of smog from the truck in front of them. "Life is too hard *abroad*?" she repeated, her tone incredulous.

"Of course. Here, I have the *dhobi* come to the house on Sunday to pick up my laundry. The cleaner washes my car each morning. For lunch, Zarine Auntie sends a hot tiffin to my workplace. The peons at my office go to the post office or the bank or run any errand I ask them to. When I get home in the evening, the servant has swept and cleaned my room. Tell me, who does all this for you in America?"

"I do. But I like doing it. It makes me feel independent. Competent. See what I mean?"

Mohan nodded. He lowered the window for a moment, letting in a blast of midmorning heat, then rolled it back up. "You must be mad, *yaar*," he said. "What's so bloody great about being 'independent'?"

With his Ray-Bans and in his blue jeans and sneakers, Mohan looked like a modern guy. But really, Smita thought, he was like all the other pampered Indian men she had known in America.

"*Bolo?*" he said, and she realized he was waiting for her reply.

"I . . . I don't even know how to answer that. I mean, being self-sufficient is its own reward. I think it's just one of the most valuable traits a person can . . ."

"Valuable to whom, *yaar*?" he drawled. "Does it help my *dhobi* if I wash my own clothes? How will he feed his children? And what about Shilpi, who cleans my room every day? How does she survive? Besides, you're dependent, too. You're just dependent on machines. Whereas I'm dependent on people who depend on me to pay them. It's better this way, no? Can you imagine what the unemployment rate would be like if Indians became . . . *independent*?"

"Your argument would make more sense if these people were paid a fair wage," Smita said, remembering how upset her former neighbors used to get every time Mummy gave their servants a raise, accusing her of raising the bar for the rest of them.

"I do my best to pay well," Mohan said. "I have had the same people work for me for years. They seem happy."

Mohan fell silent and Smita glanced at him, afraid that she had hurt his feelings. *We all have our cultural blind spots*, she reminded herself. "I guess independence is in the eye of the beholder, right?" she said. "For instance, the freedom I feel in America as a woman? You can't even imagine . . ."

"Agreed," Mohan said at once. "We Indians are in the Dark Ages when it comes to the treatment of women."

"Look at this poor woman we're going to go see. What they did to her, it's barbaric." Smita shuddered.

"Yes. And I hope they give those bastards the death penalty."

"You believe in the death penalty?"

"Of course. What else can you do with such animals?"

"Well. You can lock them up, for one thing. Although . . ."

"And that's better, this locking them up?" Mohan asked.

"Well, you're not taking a human life," Smita said.

"But you're taking away human freedom."

"Obviously. But what do you propose . . . ?"

"Have you ever been locked up, Smita?"

"No," she said carefully.

"I didn't think so."

"Meaning?"

"Meaning . . ." He slowed down as a woman crossed the street in front of them, dragging her three children behind her. "Meaning, when I was seven, I was very sick. For the longest time, the doctor couldn't understand what was wrong with me. But every evening I would get extremely high fevers. I was confined to the house for four months. No school, no playing cricket, no going to movies, nothing. In those days, our family doctor used to make house calls, so I didn't even have to leave the house to go to his clinic." His voice was low, faraway. "I have a small experience of what it's like to be locked up."

"Are you really comparing being sick for a few months to being locked up in prison for life?"

Mohan sighed. "I guess not. Not really. There's a big difference, of course."

They were quiet for a few moments. "Honestly, I can't even remember how we came to this topic," Smita said at last.

"I was saying I hope those brothers are given the death penalty. And you were defending them."

"I did no such thing," Smita protested. "I just don't believe in the death penalty."

"But that's what these *chutiyas* gave to Meena's husband, right? The death penalty?" He said it softly, but she heard the anger in his voice.

Smita was too weary to respond. The debates surrounding abortion, the death penalty, gun control—she knew from her years in Ohio how tightly people clung to their opinions. This is what she liked about journalism—she didn't have to choose sides. All she had to do was present each side of the argument as clearly and fairly as she could. She assumed that she and Mohan were more or less the same age and came from similar class backgrounds. But that's where the similarities ended—he held beliefs that would shock her liberal friends back home. But what did it matter? In about a week or so, with any luck, she'd be flying back home—this trip, this driver, this conversation forgotten.

THE MODEST MOTEL was so off the beaten path that they had to stop twice and ask for directions. As they entered the building, Smita speculated that there were probably no more than nine rooms. Instead of entering through a reception area, they walked up to a small desk. They rang the old-fashioned bell, and after a moment, a middle-aged man appeared from the back room.

"Yes?" he said. "May I help?"

"We'd like to rent two rooms, please?" Smita said.

The man looked from one to the other. "Two rooms?" he repeated. "How many in your party?"

"Just the both of us," Smita replied.

"Then why you are needing two? I can offer one maybe. Someone called earlier today and said a big wedding party may be coming tomorrow."

"Well," Smita said, "we're here today. And we need two rooms."

The man's eyes narrowed. "You are man and wife, correct?" he asked.

Smita felt her cheeks flush with anger. "I don't see how that . . ."

"Because this is a respectable family establishment," the man continued. "We don't need any problems here. If you are married, you can have one room. If you're not, we cannot rent to you. Full stop."

Smita was about to snap back, but Mohan squeezed her arm and stepped in front of her. "*Arre, bhai sahib*," he said, smoothly. "This is my fiancée. I told her that we could stay in one room and save some money. But what to do? She is a girl from a good family. She insists on having her own room. Until the wedding."

Smita rolled her eyes, but the clerk's face had begun to soften. "I understand," he said nodding. "For you, sir, I will make an exception. I applaud your modesty, madam. You may have the rooms. For how many days will you be staying?"

Smita hesitated, but Mohan had begun to reach for his wallet and was pulling out a few hundred-rupee notes. "This is for being so understanding," he said. "We will pay separately for the rooms, of course. But this is just because of the extra trouble. Because we don't know yet how long we'll be staying."

"No problem," the clerk said, sticking the bills in his shirt pocket. "You are visiting for family reasons?"

"Ah, yes and no," Mohan said evasively, his smile filtering any insult.

"I see," the clerk said. He pulled out a pen and pushed a sheet of yellowing paper toward their end of the table. "You please fill out these forms."

Smita reached for the offered pen. The clerk froze. He stared intently at Mohan. "Sir," he said, "only your signature is valid."

There was a short, painful silence. Then, Mohan mustered a strangled laugh. "Oh yes, of course," he said. "Forgive my fiancée. She's a city girl and . . ."

The clerk appraised Smita gravely. "Madam is a foreigner," he said softly. "Not familiar with our customs."

Smita flushed, then walked away as Mohan filled out the form. *A foreigner.* That was exactly what she was. In this moment, she wanted nothing to do with this provincial country in which she found herself trapped.

Even as she fumed at the clerk's casual misogyny, her thoughts turned to Meena. The damage done to Meena was far too grievous for comparison, of course, but it stemmed from a similar mindset, one that saw women as the property of men. She would get out of India in a few days, but someone like Meena probably never would.

A heavy feeling gripped Smita. This was the real India, revealing itself to her in small slights and grave tragedies. She turned her head slightly to give Mohan a sidelong glance, thankful for his presence but also envious of his male privilege. She looked out the window into the parking lot. It was getting late in the day. They would have to wait until the next morning to meet Meena.

"Come," Mohan said quietly. He was at her side, holding a suitcase in each hand. Without thinking, she reached for hers. But he threw her a cautioning look, and she retracted her hand and lowered her eyes, for the benefit of the clerk. She bristled inwardly as she followed Mohan down the long hallway to their side-by-side rooms. He unlocked her door and motioned for her to enter. They looked around the sparse room with whitewashed walls. "It will do?" Mohan asked, and she heard the anxiety in his voice.

"Yes, of course," Smita said. "It's fine." She poked her head into the bathroom and was relieved to see the Western-style toilet. To the right was a shower, with a plastic bucket and mug nearby on the tiled floor. The wall tile looked reasonably clean. "The bathroom is nice," she added.

"Good," Mohan said. He covered his mouth and yawned. "Sorry," he said. "Do you want to go see Meena today? It will be—"

"No. There's no point. We'll go in the morning."

Smita saw the relief on his face.

"Listen, the manager said they have a kitchen and dining room here," Mohan said. "He said they can prepare us any meal we want. Do you know what . . . ?"

"I don't care," Smita said. "You order whatever you want. I'm not even that hungry. All I really want is an ice-cold beer."

Mohan looked pained, and she immediately realized her gaffe. Of course. In a place like this, they probably would frown on a woman drinking alcohol in public. "It's okay," she said hastily. "I don't have to drink."

"No, no," he said, frowning. "Tell you what. Let me go place our dinner order. And then, I'll have him deliver two bottles of beer to my room. You can come drink it there. Or . . . I can just drop off a bottle for you?"

It was Mohan's hesitancy, his thoughtfulness in not foisting his company on her, that helped her decide. "Don't be silly," she said. "I'll come have a beer with you, okay?"

He nodded.

"Hey, Mohan? If they don't allow women to sign here, what did Shannon and Nandini do when they stayed here?"

He shrugged. "Shannon's an American. Different rules, I'm sure. And even then . . . If she'd come with a man, they would've asked for *his* signature."

She shook her head.

"This is not Mumbai, Smita. It's a small, isolated place. You saw. Nothing much around."

"It's like they're living fifty years in the past."

Something flickered in Mohan's eyes. "*Fifty?*" he said. "Wait till we go to Birwad. It's more like two hundred years behind."

BOOK TWO

CHAPTER NINE

———✳———

AT NIGHT, I *see my husband burn.*

In my dreams, I smell the gasoline and see the fire climb like a vine over his body. Over and over again, I watch him turn into smoke before my unfortunate eyes, flames leaping from his hair like from the head of the god Agni.

My husband's name was Abdul. It is a Muslim name meaning "servant." And all his life that's what he did, serve someone. Why did Ammi not name her son after a king? Then, maybe Abdul could have been rich and powerful, like Rupal, the chief of my old village. Rupal is a magic man, strong as a bull, with dark powers. People in my village still remember how Rupal once pulled a live snake out of a woman's mouth and turned it into a bird. With my own eyes, I have seen him walk on hot coals and not burn his feet. No, the burning is reserved for poor people like us.

In the First Information Report, made while Ammi was burying her oldest son and I was still fighting for my life in the hospital, the police wrote

Unknown Persons, *even though everybody knew who killed Abdul. But I demanded that the police register a fresh report and name my brothers as the suspects. In those dark days, Anjali was the only one who insisted that justice must be served.*

Anjali was the one who came to the hospital to give me the news that Abdul was dead. She was the one who ran to get the doctor when I screamed and tried to pull the IV out of my arm. She was the one who raised the money to pay for my three surgeries so that I can now speak and hold a spoon in my melted hand. She was the one who told me she would take my case for free to show the world that I belonged to myself and not to my brothers. And Anjali was the first and last person who said that loving Abdul was not a sin that I should be punished for.

But I will tell you the truth—I was scared. I had never before entered the police chowki. *I had never sat across from the big police inspector–sahib, much less looked at his face. The custom in my village says that inferiors must always sit at a level below their superiors—low-caste people must sit below the high caste, the young must always sit below the old, and women must sit below the men. At home, if my brothers rested on the bed, my younger sister, Radha, and I would squat on the floor. It was always thus. But at the police* chowki, *Anjali insisted that I sit on a chair across from the inspector.*

Everyone was against reopening the case. My mother-in-law asked hadn't I already brought enough misfortune on her head by marrying her son? My Muslim neighbors complained that I was inviting more danger upon our little village. All of them agreed that my Hindu brothers were correct for avenging the dishonor I had brought to my family by marrying Abdul. Even Abdul's old neighbors and friends, those who loved him, felt he had committed an unnatural act, bringing a Hindu bride into his home. In Birwad, we have a saying: "A mongoose cannot lay down next to a snake." Thus it is between the Hindu and the Muslim. Besides, my neighbors said, how could I win against my brothers when nature had made it so that no woman can prevail against the might of a man?

Rupal himself sent word that God had visited him and warned that I would be reincarnated one thousand and one times in lesser forms if I went ahead with the complaint against my brothers. That in my next life, I would come back as a lowly worm to be stepped upon by men. This is the Hindu law of reincarnation and karma, he said. If I stayed on this wicked path, I would endlessly repeat the cycles of life, being born as lower and lower life forms. It was my karmic duty to forgive my brothers and repent for my sins. He warned me to not listen to Anjali. She was a creation of the devil, sent to corrupt me.

When Rupal's messenger told me this, I knew exactly what I must do: Listen to Anjali's advice. Because had I not been stepped upon by men all my life? Had I not already been treated like a worm? Even if God Himself put His foot on my head, how could He crush me lower than I already was?

Also, there was the little seed growing in my belly. What would I say to my child when she asked me what I had done to honor her father and avenge his death? It was for the sake of my little Abru that I kept going with Anjali to the police chowki and asking that they name my brothers as the killers. And Anjali was very shrewd. She took my story to Shannon, the woman with the red hair, who looked like fire. When the police heard that a foreign white woman was asking questions about their bogus investigations, bas, they began to get nervous.

My brothers took my marriage and reduced it to kindling. Rupal tried to scare me by turning me into a worm. Perhaps it was always so: Thousands of years ago, even our Lord Rama tested his beloved wife Sita's virtue with agni pariksha, forcing her to enter a burning pyre. Unlike me, Sita came out of the fire unharmed. But then, I was not the wife of a God, just the wife of a good man.

When I mentioned this to Anjali, she told me to forget these ancient stories. "Listen to me, Meena," she said. "When you look at yourself, what do you see?"

I started to weep. "I see a face that makes babies cry," I said. "I see the hands of a cripple."

"Exactly," Anjali said. "Which is why you have to learn to look inside yourself. It's a new way of looking, to see the true you. The fire took away a lot, but it also left a lot behind. Do you understand?"

I didn't.

So Anjali told me something I didn't know before. She explained to me how steel is made.

Steel, she said, is forged from fire.

CHAPTER TEN

———✳———

MEENA'S GOOD EYE was doe-like and vulnerable, and it took everything in Smita's power to keep her own eyes trained on Meena's disfigured face and not look away. It was as if lava had flowed down the left side of her visage, destroying everything in its path. The lava ran from the middle of Meena's forehead, shutting closed her left eye, and then melting away most of her cheek before stopping just below her lower lip. The surgeons had obviously done the best they could with what remained, but their handiwork was clumsy, as if they had simply given up. As she sat in Meena's humble shack, Smita could sense Meena's mother-in-law's displeasure at having Mohan and her show up without advance notice. The only bright spot in the cramped, dark hut was Meena's daughter, Abru, who sat quietly in the corner of the room and occasionally tottered over to her mother and climbed into her lap. Smita could see Meena's good eye softening each time Abru grabbed a handful of her mother's hair and put it into her mouth.

"How is Shannon?" Meena asked. Her voice was soft, low, and slightly difficult to understand.

"She is okay. She's in less pain now. She sends you her regards."

"I will pray for her." Meena bit her lower lip. "She promised me she would be here," she mumbled. "When the judge gives the ruling."

"I'm sorry." Smita discreetly pulled out her notebook. "So how do you feel?" she asked. "About the verdict?"

The mother-in-law spoke before Meena could. "*Hah*. That foreign reporter promised us five thousand rupees. For telling our story. Now, where's the money?"

Smita kept her focus on Meena, who met her eyes and gave a quick, almost imperceptible shake of her head. Smita turned to face the mother-in-law. "We don't pay for stories, *ji*," she said, thankful that her Hindi was serviceable enough. "You must have misunderstood what my colleague said."

"*Arre, wah*," the older woman said belligerently. "You sit in my house and call me a liar?"

"Ammi," Meena raised her voice a notch. "Stop this talk of money, *na*. It does not suit us."

Smita couldn't entirely understand the string of curses that the older woman let loose, but Ammi's tone made her hair stand on end. "*Besharam*, shameless whore," Ammi said. "First, she murders my poor son and now she disrespects me? Sits like a fat *maharani* all day long, feasting on my bones and then has the gall to talk back? I should've let you die in that hospital instead of fighting to save your life."

The right side of Meena's mouth twisted into a bitter smile. "You didn't even come see me in the hospital, Ammi. Why are you telling these lies?"

The older woman picked up the broom from the corner of the room and struck Meena with it. "Hey!" Smita yelled, jumping to her feet.

"*Bai*," Mohan said. "What are you doing? Stop this at once."

The woman turned to Mohan. Her voice took on a sniveling quality.

"What to do, *seth*?" she said. "With my own eyes I watched my son burn to death. Every day I ask God why He didn't pluck my eyes out first before letting me witness such a heartbreaking sight. Then, my younger son fled the village after saving this ungrateful wretch's life. So that income is also gone. We are poor people, *seth*. I swear on my dead husband's grave, I had a financial arrangement with that American woman . . ."

Smita made a quick calculation. She wanted to talk to Meena outside, away from her mother-in-law. So far, her Hindi was up to the task. If Meena said something she didn't understand, she could always write it down phonetically and check with Mohan later. Better to leave him inside the hut to fend off Ammi. She got to her feet. "Let's get some air," she said to Meena. "Shall we talk outside?"

Meena hesitated, turning instinctively to look at Mohan for permission. He glanced at Smita. "Think you can manage?" he said, and when she nodded, he smiled at Meena. "Go outdoors, sister," he said. "Ammi and I will chat."

The bright clarity of the day belied the dark misery of the straw hut. Meena, carrying her daughter, led Smita to a rope cot. She stood as Smita sat down, then squatted on the ground before her.

"What are you doing?" Smita said. She patted the cot. "Come sit next to me."

"In my old village, we always sat below our superiors, memsahib," Meena said. "It is the custom."

"But you are not in your village, Meena. Muslims don't have these caste divisions, correct?" Smita patted the cot again. "So, come on." She waited as Meena lifted her daughter, looked around furtively, and sat Abru next to Smita before she, too, sat down. The child sucked her thumb, oblivious to her mother's unease.

"How old is your daughter?" Smita asked.

"Fifteen months."

"She's beautiful," Smita said, stroking the child's hair.

Meena beamed. "*Ai*. She is *khubsurat* like her father. Every time I see her face, I remember my Abdul."

"It is not good, what happened to you," Smita murmured, wincing inwardly at the obviousness of her statement but wanting to ease into the interview.

Meena didn't seem to notice. "I told Abdul to forget about me, memsahib. I told him my brothers would never allow our love match. But Abdul believed the world was as pure as his heart. He swore that he would drink poison and kill himself if I didn't marry him." She laughed bleakly. "In the end, I killed him after all."

"You didn't kill him. You were a victim, just like him."

Meena nodded. "That is what Anjali said, exact words. The first time she came to see me in the hospital. I was in such pain—it was like I had no body. Like I was fire itself. I couldn't even remember my own name because of the pain. When they changed my dressing, my skin used to come off with the gauze. And when I would shut my eyes, I kept seeing Abdul's body. It looked like a flowering tree except it was blooming fire."

"So you met Anjali that early on?"

"Yes. Anjali is like my God. She was the one who got me transferred to the big hospital. She raised the money that paid for my operations. And most important, she is the reason the doctors didn't remove my little Abru from my body. I was only a few months with child, memsahib. The doctors decided they must get rid of her, to save my life. Anjali was the only one who asked me what I wanted. And even though I couldn't speak, I said no. That was the greatest gift she gave me. Without my Abru, my Abdul would have left me forever."

Maybe it was from sitting directly under the sun, but Smita felt woozy. She closed her eyes for a moment and Meena noticed immediately. "You will take a glass of water, madam?" She half rose from the cot before Smita could answer, then sat back down. "Or are you not allowed to drink from our cups?"

It took Smita a minute to realize what Meena was asking—whether Smita as a Hindu could, *would*, drink or eat at a Muslim home. Meena had probably guessed at her caste and religion from her name. Good God. It was as if nothing had changed in the years since Smita had left India. What a fossilized country this was, with its caste and class and religious bigotries. Smita took in Meena's disfigured face and knew that her distaste for these customs was itself a sign of privilege. Did she really think India had changed so much just because she herself had managed to escape it?

"I have no problem with it, Meena," she said. "But I'm okay now. Let's not have you go back inside and disturb your mother-in-law."

A look of understanding flashed between the two women.

After a few minutes, Meena asked, "Will you be making the write-up for *your* paper like Shannon did?"

"Yes. Shannon and I write for the same newspaper."

Meena frowned. "But Shannon's paper is in America?"

"It is. I live there, also. I just came to India because . . ."

"They allow Hindustani people to give the write-up in the paper in America?" Meena asked.

"Yes, of course. All kinds of people work there."

"And your village elders never stop you from going to your job?" Meena said.

"Where I live, it's a big city. Like Mumbai. There are no village elders there," Smita said, realizing how little of the world Meena understood.

"*Accha?*" Meena said, wonder in her voice. "Then I pray that God will help you to rise even higher and higher, memsahib."

Smita tapped Meena's bony wrist with her index finger. "Enough about me," she said. "What about you? How are you feeling? Anjali expects the verdict any day now. Are you nervous?"

The young woman stared at the spot where Smita had touched her. "Yes, very much nervous. Even if the judge finds my brothers guilty . . ."

"Yes?" Smita prompted.

Meena raised her head and looked Smita in the eye. "If they are found guilty, there are many who still wish me harm. People in my old village think I have brought shame upon them. Everyone here in Birwad blames me for Abdul's death. My husband and his brother, Kabir, were the backbone of this community. Always joking-laughing with friend and stranger alike. And of course, the Hindu families in the surrounding villages are angry at me for filing the lawsuit against my brothers. I cannot even go to their markets because they are spitting in my face, memsahib."

Surely, Meena meant the last part as a figure of speech? Smita couldn't tell. "Meena," she said gently. "Do you think you could call me by my name instead of memsahib? After all, you called Shannon by hers, correct?"

"That was different," Meena said with a bashful smile. "Shannon was a foreigner."

"Well, if you insist on calling me memsahib, I will have to do the same."

Meena's hand flew to her mouth as she choked back a scandalized laugh. "Memsahib . . . sorry, Smita. Ammi will faint if she hears you call me memsahib."

Even though only one half of her face moved, Meena looked much younger when she laughed.

"So how do you spend your days?" Smita said. "What do you do all day?"

Meena's face went blank. "Nothing. I just cook and clean for my mother-in-law and my little one."

"You don't work at all?"

Meena pointed to her face. "In this condition, Didi?" Smita noticed that Meena had switched to calling her Didi, for "older sister." "Tell me, who will hire me? Also, nobody knows what to think of me. After my marriage, the Hindus treat me like I am a Muslim. But the Muslims in this village still consider me Hindu." She swallowed, then said something in a dialect that Smita didn't understand.

"I'm sorry?" Smita said. "The last thing you said—I couldn't follow?"

Meena brushed away the single tear on her cheek with the back of her hand. "I said, '*I'm the dog who belongs neither in the house nor on the streets*,'" she repeated in Hindi. "You understand?"

"I do."

"You see that hovel down there, Didi?" Meena said. "To your left? That's the only place on this sad earth where I am still at home."

Smita followed the line of Meena's pointing finger, squinting in the sun to see better. All she could see were the blackened remains of a straw hut that stood diagonally across from where they sat, a good distance away from Ammi's shack. Piles of rubbish were strewn around it. It took Smita a moment to realize what it was. "Is that your . . . is that where it . . . happened?" she asked.

Meena nodded. "That was our home. It was even more modest than my mother-in-law's home, Didi, but I tell you the truth—I was never happier than the four months I lived there with Abdul. Every morning he would wake up before me and make me a cup of tea. Cooking beside my husband, walking to the factory together, made me feel like the richest woman in Hindustan."

Smita looked around. "May I ask you something? Why do you and Ammi live on the outskirts, so far from the main village?"

Meena bit down on her lip as her nose turned red. "Abdul bought this land when it came up for sale Didi," she said at last. "His plan was to build his mother a *pucca* house here, out of his factory earnings. As for our little shack? He and Kabir built that in a few days after I ran away from my brothers' house. With both boys and myself all working, we were planning on giving poor Ammi a restful old age."

"Man plans and God laughs." Papa used to say this all the time. Smita wanted to translate this for Meena but she wasn't sure she was up to the task. She was doing well without Mohan's help so far; she didn't want to push her luck. "Your husband sounds like a very good man," she murmured.

Meena didn't answer. After a few minutes she said, "May I ask? What is your earliest memory, Didi?"

Smita knew the answer immediately—it was going with Papa to one of his lectures at Bombay University. Mummy had to take Rohit to the doctor that day, so Papa had taken her to work with him. She had sat quietly in the front row of his classroom, and when they left his college that day, he had bought her a Cadbury fruit-and-nut chocolate bar for being so good.

But she didn't want to get sidetracked. "I'm not sure," she said. "What's yours?"

"It is not a firm memory as such," Meena replied. "It's more a feeling. What I remember most from my childhood is the feeling of loneliness. Even after my sister, Radha, was born, I still felt alone, even though she was my best friend. Evening time, when it was time for Dada to come home from the fields, I would wait outside our hut to greet him. While waiting, I'd look up at the evening sky. I could hear the birds cawing as they made their way home. And it seemed to me that everything—every stalk of wheat, every stone on the ground, every bird in the sky—had its place in this world. Except me. That my true home was inside this loneliness. You understand me?"

"I do."

Meena smiled. "I know you do, Didi," she said. "From the minute you walked into our home, I saw it in your eyes—you have known this curse of loneliness, also."

Smita reddened and looked away.

"I'm telling you this because you asked about my Abdul," Meena continued, her voice a low, steady drone. "He was like a magician. From the time I met him, my lonely disappeared."

"Would he . . . would he have supported you in filing this lawsuit?" Smita asked.

Meena's face crumpled. "He would be so ashamed of me, Didi," she said. "He so badly wanted peace between our two families. After we found out about our baby, he insisted we go to my brothers' house with a big box of *mithai*. He believed they would come around once they understood that he was a good husband." Suddenly, Meena slapped her forehead. "But I should've known better."

"Because?"

"Because my older brother, Govind, would not even let us enter his home. He said I already cut his nose by running away to marry a Muslim. But to carry the Muslim child meant that the stain of dishonor would spread through the generations. He took the box of sweets and threw it on the ground outside his house. He said he would forbid even the stray dogs from eating it."

"Is this why—?"

"It is. That box of *mithai* carried Abdul's death warrant, Didi. We just did not know it then. Who can imagine such darkness? All my life, I gave my heart and soul to my brothers. No matter how sick I was, I used to get up and cook for them. This is how I saw my own mother serve my father, until the day she died. You could say that it was my duty. But I tell you the truth—I didn't do it as obligation. I did it with love. Every extra grain of rice or sugar, every extra piece of meat, went to them. I even took food from my beloved sister and gave it to Arvind and Govind. When Radha complained, I explained to her that they were men and needed their strength. So tell me, how I could guess their hatred for me?"

"Maybe that's why they didn't want you to marry Abdul. They didn't want to lose their servant."

Meena lowered her voice and looked furtively toward Ammi's house. "It wasn't just that. You see, in our village they hate the Muslims. They consider them to be the lowest of the low. Because they are beef-eaters, Didi."

"I understand," Smita said, red-hot anger running through her.

Meena looked startled. "Do you hate the Muslims, also?" she said.

"Me? No. Not at all. Some of my best friends are Muslims." Smita smiled mirthlessly, knowing Meena would not get the joke. "I can't remember. Did you actually convert to Islam after your marriage?"

"I wanted to, out of respect for my husband. Ammi wanted me to, also. But Abdul didn't let me. He said he wanted our family to look like Hindustan itself. Hindu and Muslim living side by side."

Smita stared at the ground. Meena's words had sketched the contours of her desolation and loss, and Smita could at last fully understand the damage Abdul's death had wrought. A young man, most likely illiterate, most certainly poor, had considered his interfaith marriage to be not a source of shame but of pride. He had seen himself and his wife as representatives of a new India, had thought of their unborn child as an ambassador of this new nation. The reason for Abdul's death was simple, really: It was a failure of imagination. Bearing no malice or prejudice himself, he couldn't imagine the contempt and hatred that his brothers-in-law felt for his kind, couldn't have foreseen how they seethed under the scandal and dishonor that Meena had wrought.

She could've told them, Smita thought. She could've warned them. In the end, the old India—severed not only by the political and geographical upheaval of Partition but also by the timeless rivers of hatred that divided its citizens—would triumph. It always did. "Do you think you will win the court case?" she asked, needing to be reassured that she was being unduly cynical. After all, she had lived away for so long. Perhaps, if nothing else, the judiciary had evolved?

Meena looked at her, the good eye unblinking. "I hope so, Didi," she said. "But in the end, it is God's will. What matters to me is that as my little one grows up, she will know that her mother fought for her father's honor. *Bas*, this is all I am living for now—for her. For this reason, I put up with my mother-in-law's taunts, the insults of my new neighbors. I tell you true, Didi. Other than my little Abru, I am having no one in this world. When Abdul was alive, Ammi's house was like a festival. His friends, her neighbors, all used to stop by. Now, no one comes. They fear that our bad luck will haunt their own homes. Even Anjali, even she will soon be gone, after this court case is finished."

Smita's mouth went dry, as if she could taste Meena's despair. "What do you do all day?" she asked. "Where do you go?"

Meena pointed to the charred remains of the hut. "I go there to sleep at night. To be near my Abdul. Crossing from here to my old home—that is the distance I travel."

"You're not afraid to revisit that place?"

"Why I should be afraid? My Abdul is still with me, *na*?" For the first time since she'd met her, Smita sensed Meena's steely defiance.

Smita remembered how she had spent weeks cowering in her Mumbai apartment, refusing to even go to school until Papa had forced her. Remembering, she was ashamed. Ashamed of the sludge-like fear that had settled in her veins; ashamed of having had the privilege of escape. Most of all, she was embarrassed that she had ever considered her early days of adjustment in America to be anything other than what they were—incredibly good fortune. Their wealth and her father's academic credentials had rescued them from India and deposited them into a good life in America. While Meena had been battling for her life and, later, fighting against crippling social ostracizing, Smita had been sitting in cafés in Brooklyn with her friends, sipping her cappuccinos, all of them feeling aggrieved as they talked about acts of microaggression and instances of cultural appropriation, about being ghosted by a boyfriend or being overlooked for a promotion. How trivial those concerns now seemed. How foolish she had been to join that chorus of perceived slights and insults. How American she had become to not see America for what it had been for her family—a harbor, a shelter, a refuge.

"*Kya hai*, Didi?" Meena was looking at her, concerned. "Did I say something wrong?"

Smita snapped out of her reverie, focusing again on the charred hut and, behind it, the overgrown field. She rose to her feet, mopping her brow with her shirt sleeve. "*Nahi*," she said. "I . . . I just need to go indoors for a minute." She saw the aversion on Meena's face at the thought of facing her mother-in-law and added, "But I'll be right back."

Meena smiled, and Smita marveled anew at the transformation.

"*Hah*," Meena said. "You must go check on your husband."

Smita opened her mouth to correct her, then thought better of it. "I'll be right back," she repeated. "I just need to get out of the sun."

What the hell is wrong with you? Smita chastised herself as she walked toward the hovel. She had interviewed refugees, displaced people, and war victims over the years, and despite the grievous injuries and trauma she had witnessed, had always managed to keep her composure. But it was impossible to keep the same emotional distance here. There was a reason she didn't cover stories in India, a reason why she'd asked her editors for that exemption. Her feelings were too biased, too complicated, for her to maintain objectivity. And yet, despite her earlier reservations, she was glad to be here in Birwad and to have met Meena. Already, she was composing the lede to her story in her head. Shannon's stories about Meena had been well written. Her reporting was impersonal and factual, and she had expertly situated Meena's story within the larger story of the treatment of women in India. In fact, Shannon's reporting was like Shannon herself—dispassionate, tough, no-nonsense. But she had not quite brought Meena to life, had not conveyed that combination of vulnerability and courage. Smita knew she could, *would*, be able to do fuller justice to Meena. She understood Meena's plight in her bones, felt that sense of kinship like connective tissue. Her fingers itched at the thought of going back to the motel and getting to work on her laptop.

She bent and entered through the low doorway, then waited for her eyes to adjust to the dark. As soon as they did, she gave a start of surprise—Mohan was sitting cross-legged on a floor mat in front of Meena's erstwhile sulky mother-in-law, who was giggling at whatever he was saying. They both looked up guiltily, conspirators, as she entered. "Will you also take a cup of tea?" the woman asked, and Smita noticed the tea glasses in front of them.

She was about to say no when she thought better of it. "Many thanks," she said. "I would love some." She paused for a beat and added, "And so will Meena."

The old woman scowled. "I cannot waste precious sugar and milk on that cow," she said. "I work like a dog seven days a week in my mistress's home to feed this family. I'm only home today because my mistress is out of town. As it is, she is not paying me while she is gone."

"Then it's okay, *ji*," Smita said as politely as she could. "I don't need any *chai pani*. I am fine."

Ammi looked conflicted, torn between the ancient impulse toward hospitality and her animosity toward her daughter-in-law. Finally, she rose with a grunt and went to relight the stove, grumbling under her breath. As she watched the woman put the pot on the stove, Smita remembered that it was customary for many rural and tribal women to nurse their children well past infancy. "Is Meena still breastfeeding your grandchild?" she asked.

"Sometimes," Ammi replied as she added the tea to the water. "That was all the heifer was good for, but now she claims her milk is drying up. So yet another mouth to feed."

Her journalistic ethics forbade it, but Smita longed to slip a few hundred-rupee bills into this querulous woman's hands. Who, she wondered, would Ammi be if one could remove the financial stressors from her life? Would the better angels of her nature prevail, would she be able to set the grievous loss of her son alongside Meena's loss of her husband, and realize their common pain? Or would she still resent her daughter-in-law for the calamitous event that had been visited upon her household?

As if he'd read her mind, Mohan opened his wallet. Smita pretended not to see as he pulled out several hundred rupees and set the bundle on the floor. "This is for you, Ammi," he said. "To help with the upkeep of your young charges."

Ammi rolled up the money and slipped it into her blouse. "A million thanks, *beta*," she said, placing her hand on Mohan's head. "A thousand blessings to you. When you call me Ammi, it is as if I hear my Abdul and Kabir's voices in my ear."

Cliff or Shannon would have been aghast at this breach of professional ethics. *But Mohan is not here on assignment*, Smita imagined arguing with them, as if they were here in this tiny room. *What am I supposed to do, scold him in the old woman's presence? She'd kick me out of her home and cut off our access to Meena, who is in no position to defy her orders.*

Mohan looked at her, one eyebrow raised inquiringly. Smita gazed at him impassively, neither endorsing nor chastising him for his generosity. "I still need another half hour or so," she whispered as Ammi poured the tea into thick glasses.

"Take as much time as you need," he said. "We are having a good time here."

"Thanks. I really appreciate this."

Smita carried out two glasses of tea. "For me?" Meena said. "She allowed it?"

"For you."

"Thank you, Didi. See? Already, you have brought good fortune into my life."

Smita looked again at the charred shack in the distance, feeling the incongruity of Meena's gratitude for a cup of chai. She thought of the self-help books preaching the importance of gratitude that millions of Americans bought each year. How many of them could muster gratitude for a cup of tea? She thought of the prosperity evangelists who preached about God wanting His flock to be fabulously wealthy. What would that God have to say about women like Meena, who let a cup of tea register as good fortune?

She watched as Meena blew into the glass to cool it and then offered a few sips to Abru. It struck Smita suddenly that she had not heard the little girl speak. "Does she talk?" she said, rubbing the little girl's back as she asked.

Meena looked crestfallen. "Not yet," she said. "Doctor said not to worry. Some children talk late, she said. She is not a mute, Didi. Thanks God." She frowned. "But I am worried. My Abru is fifteen months old. Too old to not talk, no? I think it's because she heard my crying for help during the fire, when she was still in my womb. Or she heard my screams in the hospital when I found out Abdul was dead. And maybe she thinks: *What do I want to say to a world where my own uncles can kill my father and destroy my mother's heart? What good are words in such a world?*"

Smita nodded, even as she wished for a good pediatrician in Mumbai to check out this little girl. "What are your plans for after the verdict comes?" she asked, to change the subject.

"What use making plans? This is my life now. Abdul and I had planned to shift to Mumbai after Abru was born. He used to say that Mumbai was built for people like us, who are unafraid of hard work. We were both *angutha chhap*, Didi. But we dreamed of our Abru becoming a doctor or a lawyer. Abdul said that there was so much money to be made in Mumbai that we could build a brick home for Ammi and Kabir here, and still send Abru to a good school there. But the fire destroyed those dreams."

Smita looked up from her notebook, her eyes moist with understanding. "I'm sorry," she said. She looked away. "What's '*angutha chhap*' mean?"

"Oh. That is what they call people like us, who don't know how to read or write. When we opened our bank account, we must make an ink thumb impression because we cannot sign our names. That is what the words mean—'thumb impression.'"

"You have a bank account?" Smita asked.

Something flashed in Meena's eyes. "*Had*. Ammi made me empty it after I came home from the hospital. Otherwise, she said, she would sell Abru to the Christian nuns after she was born. She said rich women in foreign places pay lots of money for Hindustani babies."

"She said . . . *what*?" Smita fought the urge to spit out her tea.

Meena nodded grimly. Then, her face softened. "What to do, Didi? That poor woman suffered a miserable loss, no? Imagine losing both her sons. All because of me. And in any case, she is the only grandma Abru has. So I let bygones be bygones."

"Does she still threaten to—?"

"No. Not since I gave the money to her. Besides, my Abru takes after her father. Sometimes, when I catch Ammi's eyes resting on my daughter's face, I know she is missing her son. Every day, she is going half mad, trying to decide whether she loves or hates Abru for looking so much like Abdul."

Could an Upper West Side therapist have shown greater psychological insight than Meena had? Could any priest, rabbi, or imam have shown a greater generosity of spirit than she had demonstrated? Smita wanted to set down her pen to take Meena's hands in hers. Instead, she asked, "What exactly happened to Abdul's younger brother? Ammi said . . . ?"

Meena's eye turned cloudy. "He ran away, after he saved my life by taking me to the hospital. Kabir is the reason I am still living." She paused for a long time, then said quietly, "I am tired, Didi. What to do, I am unused to exercising my tongue so much, these days. Also, I must go in and start cooking. I will tell you the rest of my story next time?"

"Of course," Smita said, shutting her notebook.

But the truth was, she was disappointed by this abrupt end to the interview. She had earned the younger woman's trust, but she wanted to know so much more. Would it be better to file a preliminary story immediately and do a follow-up after the actual verdict, as Shannon had suggested? Or should she file a single long narrative piece after the verdict?

Meena rose from the cot, jutting out her hip and resting Abru on it.

"One more thing," Smita said. "You understand that I will also be contacting your brothers, right?"

The younger woman blanched and looked visibly shaken. Smita frowned. Shannon had quoted the brothers in her stories. Then, she remembered. Of course. Meena was illiterate. She had never read any of Shannon's articles about herself.

As if she had sensed the tension in her mother, Abru turned her head to gaze at her. Meena kissed the top of her daughter's head absently. "You do as you wish," she said stiffly. "That is not my concern."

Smita rose from the cot, also.

Meena began to walk toward Ammi's hut, then looked back. "You ask them why they did such evil. Why they stole the only sun in my sky. My brother Govind and I were close as children. He used to call me his *tara*, his little star."

"So this enmity is recent? He turned on you because of your marriage?"

"Even before that. He said Radha and I cut his nose when we took the factory job. All the other men in the village mocked him because we earned more than he did. He kept our full wages, but this made him hate us even more."

"I don't understand—" Smita began, but Meena shook her head and went inside the hut with Abru, leaving Smita to trail in behind them.

Mohan and Ammi were laughing together, their heads almost touching. For some reason, the sight irritated Smita. "Ready?" she said, and from Mohan's expression, she could tell he was startled by the sharpness of her tone.

"Okay, Ammi," Mohan said as he got to his feet. "I will take your leave. But we will meet again, inshallah."

"Inshallah, inshallah. You are welcome anytime, *beta*," the older woman said in a simpering voice that set Smita's teeth on edge.

"Bye, Meena," Smita said quietly. "Be well."

"Bye, Didi. God go with you."

CHAPTER ELEVEN

—✳—

MY SKIN BURNS *again, like it did in the hospital. Since the fire, I feel every-thing on my body's surface. Smita left Ammi's house ten minutes before, but still I felt her sympathy on my skin. How sweetly she caressed my Abru, as if she didn't care that Abru, too, is cursed. Nobody in this small Muslim com-munity of cobblers will send their children to play with my little one. It is as if we have become lepers, and they are worried that their children will catch our disease.*

If Abdul had lived and I had died instead, Abru would have had a bet-ter life. She would have grown up without a mother's love, but Ammi's eyes would have remained soft when they fell on my daughter's face. Abdul would have loved her twice as much, once for her own sake, and once because of his love for me. And she would have still had her uncle, Kabir, to give her rides on his back and to sing Hindi film songs to her at night.

Then, I remember that Abru is still having two uncles. The ones who killed her father.

THEY ARE STILL *walking free, my brothers.*

Even after half of Birwad saw them toss the match and watched as my Abdul was wrapped in flames. Even though they saw Govind yell at my brother-in-law for running toward me with the buckets of water to put out the flames from my body. Even after they heard Arvind and Govind threaten Kabir's life if he helped me anymore.

The police did not come that night. Did Rupal pay them to stay away? In Birwad, we have a saying: "Thieves come when you don't expect them; the police don't come when you expect them." Even if the police had shown up, they would have stood joking and laughing while my family screamed for help. Or maybe they would have burned the other Muslim homes in the main village. Why? Because most of the police are Hindus. Why? Because they are the police and who will stop them?

Kabir had borrowed a truck to drive me to the hospital. He left his own mother with her older son's lifeless body, to save my life. After dropping me off at the hospital, he took off for Mumbai. Ammi received one letter from him before he was lost in the fog of that big city. Months later, when I finally came home from the hospital, my stomach swollen with child, Ammi spat in my face. I let the spit run down the melted half of my face, unable to feel it, unwilling to wipe it away in her presence.

Anjali told me that when the police said that they were unsuccessful in finding Abdul's killers, they were not lying. When they wrote Unknown Persons *on the first report, they were not lying. Because the people they interviewed for Abdul's murder? They were sleeping peacefully in Gorpur, a village three kilometers from Birwad. When the police asked those Gorpurwallas what they were knowing about the burning, they told the truth—they knew nothing. This is how honest our police are in this* desh.

But even after the police reopened the case and talked to the witnesses from Birwad, Ammi still refused to talk to them. They will never charge two Hindu men for the killing of a Muslim boy, she said. But she was wrong. Shannon put her story in the paper, and a few days later, both my brothers were arrested.

They spent fifteen days in the lockup. Then, something strange began to happen. One by one, all our neighbors changed their stories. One remembered staying home the night of the fire because his wife was sick. Another said he took his children to the cinema hall in a nearby village that night. Someone said his TV was playing so loud, he did not hear the rowdy procession of men march through the main village on their way to our home. Just before the police filed the charge sheet with the court, Govind and Arvind applied for the bail. Anjali protested; the charge was murder, she said. How can murderers walk free while a man lies buried in the ground, and a woman is so defaced that babies cry when they see her unfortunate face? But the judge allowed my brothers to post bail. This is our Hindustan, where killers walk free and their victims are prisoners in their home.

SOMEONE ELSE IS in prison, also. My sister. Radha. Her jailer is her husband. Twenty-four years older than she is, with a face like a jackfruit, and one leg shorter than the other. A cripple.

Radha had helped me elope with Abdul. Govind was so furious, he married her off soon after I left home. No man her own age would marry her because of the shame I had brought upon the family. Only a cripple from a distant village, who needed a wife to wait on him like a servant, would agree to such a match.

My crime; Radha's punishment.

CHAPTER TWELVE

MOHAN PEPPERED SMITA with questions as soon as they were back in the car, but she answered in monosyllables as she jotted down last-minute impressions in her notebook. She was beat, emotional, and in no mood for conversation. For the first time, she wished Nandini had accompanied her here instead of Mohan, because as a professional minder, she would have known to leave her alone. Mohan, however, seemed oblivious to her reluctance to chat. After a few more minutes of her noncommittal replies, he finally got the hint. "Is something wrong?" he asked. "Did I offend you in some way?"

"No," she said, looking out the car window at the scenery around them. *I hate this land*, she thought. *Everything about it is cruel and violent.*

"Smita," Mohan said, "what's wrong, *yaar*?"

The fact was, she couldn't explain this dark, nasty feeling that had grabbed hold of her. *The only sun in my sky.* That's how Meena had described what her husband had meant to her. How did one survive such a loss?

"Smita?"

"What?" she snapped. "Can't you see that I want to be left alone?"

Mohan's jaw went slack. "I was just—"

"You were just what?" she demanded, then added before he could respond, "What were you and that old lady laughing and giggling about anyway?"

"That's what you're angry about?" Mohan sounded incredulous. "That I was cheering up an old woman who . . ."

"Damn straight. I'm out there interviewing that poor girl about the brutal murder of her husband, and we come back in to find you two laughing and joking."

"I was trying to distract her," Mohan said loudly. "So that you could talk to Meena and get your story. I thought I was helping you, but instead you are . . . I don't even know what you're saying."

Mohan's anger was so unexpected that Smita felt chastised and immediately regretful of her behavior. "Mohan," she said, "I'm sorry."

"I honestly don't know how to help you," Mohan said. "It's like I have to apologize to you for everything in this country. Everything I see is now filtered through your eyes. And it all looks ugly and backward and—"

"Mohan, no. Please. I . . . I'm just frustrated, you know? But it was wrong of me to take it out on you."

He took his eyes off the road to look at her. "Why do you hate India so much?"

Smita sighed. "I don't," she said at last. "I . . . there are many things I love about the country. And I know that what happened to Meena happens all over the world. Even in America, of course. I know that. I mean, trust me—I cover stories like these all the time."

He nodded, and as suddenly as his temper had flared, the anger left his body. The change was so dramatic that Smita imagined that she'd heard a silent whoosh. "Okay," he said. "Let's drop it."

She looked out the car window as they cut through the main village, shocked by how shabby everything looked. Small houses with corrugated metal roofs squatted next to ones covered merely with blue tarp. Flies hovered above the open drain that ran past some of the houses. They drove past a giant pit filled with refuse. A couple of young boys played desultorily near the pit, even as a strange, moldy smell seeped into the car. Smita thought that these huts looked even more ragged than the slums she'd passed on her way from the airport a few nights before. Then, she remembered: This was a Muslim village, which meant that it was even poorer than a typical one. A few old men, their faces dark against the white of their beards and skullcaps, stared expressionlessly as they drove by. There were no women around.

"Do you want to stop?" Mohan asked. "Talk to anyone?"

Smita considered for a moment, then shook her head no.

"I wanted to ask you," Smita said when they were back on the main road, "do you understand the dialect Ammi speaks?"

He shrugged. "More or less. Some of the people who worked for my family came from villages near Birwad. I think the old security guard at my school was from around here."

"Oh yeah? What school was that?"

"The Anand School for Boys."

"Where's that?"

"*What?*" Mohan said, his voice heavy with irony. "You haven't heard of the world-famous Anand School for Boys?"

"No. Sorry." A beat. "But I'm sure it was great, seeing how it produced a prodigy like you."

"Nicely played." Mohan smiled. "What about you? Where did you do your schooling?"

Smita stiffened, uneasy about sharing any details. But the last thing she wanted to do was offend Mohan again. "I went to Cathedral," she said.

"Ah. Great school. I should've known."

"Meaning?"

"Meaning many of the posh Mumbaikars I work with went to Cathedral."

"We weren't posh."

"No?"

"No," she said. "I told you—my father is a professor." The truth was they could have never afforded their flat in Colaba or any of the other luxuries they enjoyed if it weren't for Papa's inheritance. As much as Papa valued education, he couldn't have sent her and Rohit to Cathedral on his salary.

"What did *your* parents do?" she asked.

"Well, my mother is a housewife."

"And your dad?"

"My papa?" Mohan cleared his throat. For the first time since Smita had met him, he seemed evasive. "Well, my papa was a diamond merchant. You know, Surat is famous for—"

"Are you kidding?"

"No. Why would I?"

"Your dad is a *diamond merchant*?"

"*Ae*, Smita. Relax, *yaar*. He was just a small-time guy."

"I see," Smita said. "You know what they call a small-time diamond merchant, right?" She waited for him to ask and, when he didn't, she said, "A diamond merchant."

"Very funny."

"You know what's *really* funny?"

"What?"

"That you've asked me so many questions about my life and you failed to mention that your father is a diamond merchant."

"Yah, okay, you're right. I should've told you what my father did right at the airport the night I picked you up. Before you mistook me for Shannon's driver."

"Touché," she said with a laugh. But then something went wrong

because she kept laughing, unable to stop. She was aware that she was
being ridiculous, that Mohan was throwing her a worried look. But
something was fueling this hysteria—a combination of fatigue and sadness and anger and . . . the blank looks on the faces of those elderly
Muslim men a few moments before. Ammi's harsh voice as she had
berated Meena. The image of Meena stroking her daughter with her
melted hand. The land outside this car bore so much suffering. *This
land is your land* . . . The words of the Woody Guthrie song she'd
always loved came into her head, but somehow the lyrics seemed
ironic, malicious even. Like it or not, this, too, was her land and she
felt implicated and ensnared in its twisted morality and contradictions.

She pursed her lips, wanting to apologize for her hysterical laughter. But before she could explain, her phone rang. "Excuse me," she
murmured, searching her purse, hoping it wasn't Papa calling. "It's the
lawyer," she whispered to Mohan.

"Hello? Smita? Anjali here." The voice was as brisk as ever.

"Hi. Have they announced the date?"

"The verdict should come day after tomorrow," Anjali said. "That's
what the clerk told my office today. And they will give us enough notice
to get to the courthouse. Are you checked in at the motel?"

"Yes. Since yesterday. But—"

"Good. That's perfect. It's a little over an hour from there to the
courthouse. We will call you as soon as we know what time you should
be there." Anjali cleared her throat. "Have you met Meena yet?"

"We just left her place a short time ago."

"Sad case, *eh*?"

"Yes. Very." Smita made a quick calculation. "Since we have a day in
between, I'll probably go meet with the brothers tomorrow. And then . . ."

"Excellent idea. Okay, well, see you the day after."

"Wait—"

But Anjali had already hung up.

Smita shook her head as she put the phone away. "What's this
woman's problem?" she muttered.

"You can't imagine how busy she must be, *yaar*," Mohan said.

"Do you always do this?"

"Do what?"

"Leap to every stranger's defense?"

He shrugged.

"So, we're going to meet the brothers tomorrow?" Mohan asked after a moment.

"Yes. And the village chief. Anjali thinks he's the one who instigated the brothers." The heaviness was back; she felt its weight. "Mohan," she said, "you have a sister. Is there anything she could do, do you suppose, that would make you disown her? Much less, injure her?"

"What a stupid question, Smita," he said. "You have a brother, no? Would he ever do such a thing?"

A sudden flash of memory. Rohit's distraught face. Rohit protecting her with his body. "My brother would die rather than do what Meena's brothers did," she said.

Mohan nodded. "Exactly."

"You're very much like Rohit, you know. Decent."

He took his eyes off the road briefly, a teasing expression on his face that she was beginning to recognize. "But you are nothing like my sister," he said. He tapped on his brakes as a small animal scuttled in front of their car, then picked up speed again. "My sister is sweet. Simple. Uncomplicated."

She laughed, understanding why Shannon had become close to Mohan. He was good company, and there was a lightness to him that Smita appreciated. Plus, any other guy would have hit on her already, and she was so utterly grateful that Mohan hadn't. Ever since she'd left home at eighteen, Smita had been unapologetically sexual, a reaction to her traditional upbringing. But she had not slept with a man since Mummy had died. Smita took in Mohan's profile and was relieved not to feel the slightest spark of interest.

Life is easier this way, she thought. *Just ask Meena.*

THIRTEEN

———✦———

THE NOISE OF *the sewing machines in the factory where Radha and I worked was so loud that I would get a headache after every shift. As we walked home at the end of each ten-hour day, Radha would carry our tiffin box. But if I made the smallest complaint to Govind, he would pounce on me. "This is what happens when women do the men's job," he'd say. "You have fallen so low, no respectable man will ever marry you. And how will we ever find a match for Arvind after the shame you and Radha have brought on us by working? The whole village is spitting on us because our sisters have turned their own brothers into eunuchs."*

In the beginning, I believed that Govind was right. Our village was hundreds of years old. In all that time, Radha and I were the only two women who had defied its tradition and worked outside our home. Govind complained that even small children laughed behind his back. As for the old men who sat around all day drinking chai and gossiping? They advised him to take the whips used on the farm animals and beat us until we obeyed him. "A woman and an ox must be thrashed often," they said.

Rupal also came over to warn us that sewing men's jeans all day would turn Radha and me into males. I believed him, but Radha shook her head. "Didi, don't listen to that bevakoof," she said. "He's just jealous because we are earning more money than he does doing all his witchery."

But I was not sure. Everybody in the village said that Rupal had magic powers, and a special mobile phone that allowed him to talk straight to God. Whatever God would tell him, he would repeat to us. "What if he's correct?" I asked my sister.

Radha took my hand and held it to my breasts. "Feel those two mangoes," she said. "Do these grow on a man's body?"

The day Abdul started work at the factory, I knew for sure that I was a woman. When he smiled and said, "Namaste. My name is Abdul," and looked at me with eyes the color of light tea, I felt something tremble in my body. He looked at me as if he knew the heart inside my heart, the one not even Radha could see. I felt myself shiver with happiness, but the next minute I cursed my destiny because God was playing a cruel trick on me. From his name and from the white skull cap on his head, I guessed Abdul's religion. A Hindu and Muslim could never be together—everybody knew that timeless truth.

On his first day, I had to show Abdul how we hemmed the shirts. Before I could even finish telling him, he said, "I know. No problem. I am an expert tailor." He took the pile of shirts from me, and I noticed his fingers, long and thin, as if they were designed to play the shennai. Or to touch a woman's body. My cheeks burned, and I pinched myself to keep such evil thoughts out of my mind. Maybe my brothers were correct—by working side by side with strange men, I had become a wicked woman.

I rushed back to my own sewing machine. But after a few minutes, I looked to my left, where Abdul was sitting one row ahead of me. When he turned his head to talk to the man next to him, I took a long drink of his features. His hair was black and shiny as a crow's. His skin was smooth and dark as *a stone. And as he worked, he bent from his neck, so that his back remained straight as a wall. Within half a day, Abdul was already making friends left and right. He was fast at his job—even from one row behind, I could see how expertly he hemmed—but as he worked, he would say funny-funny things that made everybody shake with laughter. Nobody could believe it was his first day. With Abdul's arrival, it felt as if God had dropped a rainbow inside that dark factory. Once, he heard my laughter and turned around to give me a quick wink. No one else saw. A little later, I noticed the foreman walking toward us, and I coughed loudly to warn Abdul. In my heart, I felt the same feeling I had for Radha—protectiveness. I wanted to protect this man I had just met in the same way I wanted to protect my sister. For the first time since we started working, I gave thanks to Radha for forcing me to take this job. It was as if a gust of wind had blown open a window in my heart and a sweet bird had flown in and made a nest. I knew I must shoo it away, but what to do? For the first time in my life, I wanted something to stay.*

RADHA WORKED IN *the ladies' section, making clothes for the ladies of America. It was Radha who had first heard about this factory. She came running home one day, her face shiny with excitement. "Didi, Didi, listen!" she said. "There's a new clothing factory opened in Navnagar. They are paying good-solid wages. I am applying."*

I looked up from where I was sweeping the floor. "Applying for what?" I asked.

She looked at me impatiently. "For a job."

"Little sister," I said, "have you gone mad? You know that this is not the work for womenfolk. In our village, has a woman ever held a job outside her home?"

Radha scowled. "So, we should continue to starve? Govind and I work all day in the fields but without rain, what's the use? And what does that good-for-nothing Arvind do? Lazes around drinking, getting in your way as you sweep and clean."

"Radha," I said, "Govind needs you in the kheti, na? Who will help him if you are gone?"

She did not even let me finish. "That kheti is not big enough to support us all. Govind can manage alone. Or, let Arvind put down his bottle and go help. I am tired of being hungry all the time. I work as hard as our brothers, but they eat first. If we ever buy an egg or goat meat, they get it. Why?"

"Chokri, chup! This is how Ma raised us. In honor of her . . ."

"Ma is dead. She lived in a different time. In Mumbai and Delhi, all the women are working. We are young. Why do we have to sit at home like old women? The factory is paying good money. And the work is easy."

"Our brothers will never allow . . ."

"Who is asking them?" Radha got that angry look on her face, a look I knew from the time she was a baby. "I want to eat an egg every day. Can Govind dig an egg for me from the kheti? If not, who is he to stop me?"

Fear made a knot in my stomach. Govind had a bad temper. Since our father's death, he was the head of our family.

"Let me talk to him," I said. "But if he says no . . ."

Radha shook her head impatiently, as if my words were mosquitoes she had to swat away. "If he says no, I'm still applying. I don't care."

"Little sister," I said, raising my voice, "this is our older brother. His word is law."

"No. Even if Narendra Modi prohibits me, I'm still applying."

IF RADHA COULD have seen all the way to where her stubbornness would take us, maybe she would have buried her desire, and we would have never taken a step out of our village. Because traditions are like eggs—once you break one, it is impossible to put it back inside its shell.

CHAPTER FOURTEEN

——✳——

"I'll say one thing about this motel," Smita said with her mouth full. "They sure have a great kitchen."

Mohan stared at her, an expression on his face she couldn't read.

"What?" she asked.

"Just that—I like seeing you eat. So many women . . . I don't know, *yaar*. They eat like birds or mice in front of men. You don't have such hang-ups."

"In my line of work, when there's food, you eat." Smita checked her watch and then set her fork down. "Having said that, we should probably get going soon, right?"

"Right."

They had pulled out of the motel compound and dodged a sudden flock of chickens crossing the street—the old joke made Smita smile—when she thought of something. "You don't think the front desk guy has been suspicious about the beer bottles you've been bringing to your room the last two nights?" she asked.

Mohan's lips were set in a straight line. "One thing you have to understand about India, Smita," he said, "is that half of these customs exist just to save face. As long as you don't rub it in their faces, nobody cares."

"So, it's a country of hypocrites."

He smiled as if he was wise to her. "No. It's a country that puts a premium on saving face."

"Just like Meena's brothers." Her tone was bitter. "That's what they were doing, right? Saving their family honor."

Mohan nodded but didn't reply. He had come to her room before dinner the evening before with two bottles of beer and a bag of cashews. He had made her splutter with laughter as he told her, in his droll, deadpan fashion, story after story about the pranks he and his friends used to play on their schoolteachers.

Now, he glanced at her. "Everything okay with you?"

"Yes. Why?"

"Only because you haven't argued with me in the last three minutes or so."

"I guess I'm slipping."

"Yah, you're probably pining away for that fat *baniya* who sat at the dinner table next to ours last night. Maybe you liked the way he was licking his fingers?" And he did such an exaggerated pantomime of the man that Smita burst out laughing.

"You know, you have a great laugh," Mohan said.

"Everybody tells me it's too mannish."

He frowned. "Who?"

Truth be told, it was only Bryan who had said that to her once, when they were having problems. But the comment had stuck, the way insults always did. "Everybody," she said vaguely.

Mohan fiddled with the car radio, trying to pick up a station. "Do you have any favorite Hindi film songs? From your childhood?"

"Not really," she said. "Rohit and I were more into rock and roll anyway. But my mom used to listen to *ghazals*."

"Not your papa?"

"Nah. He was more into Western classical."

"What? Almost every member of your family listened to something different?"

"Pretty much." She glanced at him. "How was it in your family?"

"My father is a huge Hindi film fan. So mostly, we grew up on that music. They're pretty traditional people, you know? Teetotalers. Vegetarians. Proud to be Gujarati."

"Did they have an arranged marriage?"

"Yes, of course. In their time, nothing else was possible."

She nodded, suppressing the urge to tell him that her mother had eloped with her father. "So, will they find a bride for you?"

He made a dismissive gesture with his hand. "They've tried. But I told them I wasn't interested."

"Not interested in what? Marriage? Or an arranged marriage?"

"I'm not sure. Probably both at this point. At my age."

"How old are you? Sixty-four?"

"Ha ha." Mohan honked at a car that came too close. "I'm thirty-two," he said. "Getting too old to marry."

"What nonsense," she said. "I'm thirty-four. You're just a spring chicken." She looked at him curiously. "You've never come close? To marrying?"

He was quiet for so long that the silence began to feel uncomfortable. "Hey, I'm sorry," Smita began. "It's none of my business."

"No, it's okay." He paused. "I came close once. But it was many years ago."

"What happened?"

"Nothing. She was with me in college. She wanted to marry while we were students. But I—I wanted to make something of myself before we settled down. In those days, I had an old-fashioned notion that the man had to support the woman. My upbringing, you know? So I hesitated. And she got tired of waiting. She married another classmate."

"I'm sorry."

"Forget it, *yaar*. It was a long time ago." Mohan shook his head. "Besides, she wasn't a Gujarati. So my parents would've probably had a heart attack. It's just as well."

"You wouldn't have defied them?" Smita heard the judgment in her voice and knew that he had heard it, too.

"Yah, probably," he said. "If it had come to that."

They fell into another silence. After a few moments, Mohan said, "What about you?"

"What about me?"

"You never married?"

She shrugged. "No. It never took."

He made a small, enigmatic motion with his head, the meaning of which she didn't get. "Did you ever date a *desi* guy?" he asked after a moment.

"No," she said, suddenly embarrassed. "That is, I went on a few dates that my folks set up. But in my line of work, you know, I don't meet too many Indians."

"Huh. And you don't meet boys outside of your line of work? Like, at parties and all?"

She smiled, acknowledging the dig. But how to explain her nomadic existence to Mohan, rooted, steady Mohan? What would he make of the packed suitcases in her austere Brooklyn apartment? Would he disapprove of the hook-ups she had with the correspondents she met in far-flung places? What would he think of the expensive Sunday brunches she shared with her single friends in New York, during which they lingered over mimosas, complaining incessantly about how all the good guys were married or gay? Would he be bemused or impressed by their chatter, the fact that they talked almost exclusively about indie films and politics and the latest exhibit at the Met? God, how stereo-typical her life in Brooklyn was. How *American*.

She realized that he was waiting for her to answer. "I don't really go to a lot of parties," she said.

"And what about your parents? Were they not pushing you to get married?"

Smita pushed a strand of hair behind her ear. "They would've liked me to, sure. Mummy, especially. Wanting to marry off their children is part of the DNA of Indian parents, right?"

"Why just Indian parents? Don't all parents wish this for their children?"

Don't take the bait, Smita said to herself. "I guess."

After a minute, she said, "Tell me something. Are you sorry you let Nandini talk you into accompanying me? Instead of being with Shannon?"

"Not at all. Shannon sounded so good when I spoke to her yes-terday. They already have her doing physiotherapy. And this is a new experience for me, going on a story with a journalist. Although I'm not sure I should go in with you when you interview those brothers. Because I will want to kill them."

"That's the thing about being a journalist," she said. "You can't let your emotions get in the way. I have to be able to interview them with-out judging them."

"I honestly don't know how you can do that."

But she had done it many times. Smita told him about her first tough assignment, as a young reporter in Philly. How she'd interviewed the two straight men who'd gone into a gay bar, left with a much younger guy, and then brutally beaten him and left him for dead. The boy, from a small town thirty miles from Philly, was nineteen years old and had screwed up his nerve to visit a gay bar for the first time in his young, closeted life.

"Did he die?" Mohan asked as he swerved to avoid a pothole on the road.

"Yes. After a week in the hospital. His pastor-father refused to visit him because that would've meant 'condoning' his sexual orientation."

"I didn't realize America was so backwards, *yaar*. I mean, we see pictures of those gay pride parades and all on TV."

"Well, it's still easier to be gay in the big cities than in small-town America. But things have definitely changed. This is from when I first became a reporter—from before I was an old maid."

"What was the hardest story you've ever covered?"

She sighed, a hundred memories flitting through her head like macabre slides on an old View-Master. War. Genocide. Rape. And that was not counting the everyday outrages like domestic violence, the battles over transgender rights, or the abortion wars. Or stories like Meena's, caused by twisted, patriarchal notions of family honor.

Smita hesitated, not wanting to confess this other thing to Mohan: As horrific as Meena's injuries were, they were not the worst she'd seen. Not even close. And yet, Meena's isolation—her complete dependence on a mother-in-law who hated her and blamed her for her son's death—had triggered a corresponding loneliness in Smita. Perhaps it was as simple as this: She could cover heartbreaking events in Lebanon and South Africa and Nigeria and not feel complicit in those because they had not happened in her own country. But despite her American passport, despite the many miles between her American life and her Indian childhood, there was no denying it—sitting with Meena on that cot, she had felt complicit in what had happened to her. Listening to Meena's slightly slurred speech, Smita had felt a mix of emotions, felt both American *and* Indian, a victim herself, but also someone who had escaped in a way that Meena never would. There was no way, however, to unspool this for Mohan without slitting open the yellowing envelope of her past.

"Smita . . ." Mohan said. "Actually, forget it. You know, we don't have to talk about sad things, *yaar*. Let's change the subject."

She looked at him with gratitude. Every time she'd been with a nonjourno, she'd seen the curiosity in their faces, the voyeuristic curiosity as they probed her for the most sensationalistic aspects of her job. She could see them filing away the anecdotes she shared, adding to their cache of can-you-believe-this-shit stories, fodder for conversation at their next party. None of them had had the grace to restrain their prurient interest, despite her obvious reluctance. "Thanks," she said to Mohan. "But tell me about *your* job. What exactly do you do?"

He spoke in his usual steady way, offering up droll, precise imitations of his colleagues, piquing her interest when he described the artificial intelligence project he was currently working on.

But after a while, she stopped listening. More than anything, she wanted to be engulfed in silence, and India was not a silent place. Smita felt suddenly, acutely homesick for New York. She longed to be flung back into the anonymity of Manhattan, to walk its crowded streets experiencing that thrilling dilution of her individual self. And New York on a crisp fall evening! The weak autumnal sun bouncing off the brownstones, the slow, drunken fall of the orange and gold leaves near the lagoon in Central Park, her face flushed and cold as she walked. She had first seen New York in autumn, when she had started grad school at Columbia, and maybe that was why it was the season she most associated with the city. These days, Smita spent so much time in places where famine or civil war had ravaged the countryside—where floods and hurricanes had uprooted hundred-year-old trees, where loggers or poachers had destroyed old-growth forests—that she felt intense gratitude for the neighborhood parks of Brooklyn and the vastness of Central Park each time she returned home. In the suburban Ohio community where they'd landed after Papa had secured a job at a small liberal arts college, she had felt like an alien, a guest in someone else's country. It wasn't until she arrived in New York that she experienced the sense of homecoming she hadn't known she was missing. The first time she saw the city, it was as if something exploded in her chest—it was that visceral, that immediate a falling in love. New York didn't feel like a city to her; it felt like a country. The nation-state of New York, where the world's restless and ambitious gathered, where the misfits and the misunderstood arrived—and the city didn't so much welcome them as shift just a tiny bit to accommodate them, to test them, to see if they had the right stuff. And if you passed the test, then all of it was there for the taking—the joyful riot of color and smells of Jackson Heights, the eclectic streets of Greenwich Village, the elusive tranquility of Prospect Park, the benches at the Battery, where one could sit undisturbed and stare at the "lady of the harbor." Smita remembered what Shannon had once said: "This city is like some giant social experiment conducted every single day. This place should be a fucking powder keg—but somehow, it's not."

As THEY GOT closer to Vithalgaon, Mohan, too, fell silent. Smita looked out of the window at a grove of trees as Mohan slowed down to let a youth on a wobbly bicycle cross the road. She watched a farmer walking behind two skeletal oxen pulling a primitive-looking plough across a field and felt as if she were watching a scene from two hundred years ago. She noticed the garland of yellow marigolds coiled around the beasts' horns, and for some reason, the tenderness of the gesture broke her heart. This, too, was her country, this inheritance, her birthright. Except that it wasn't. She had been deprived of it, much as Meena had been. Of course there was no comparison between what she had suffered and what was done to Meena—Smita's hand flew involuntarily to her unblemished face. But despite her privilege, her heart ached, and she felt a different kind of homesickness than what she'd felt for New York—the loss of something that had never fully belonged to her.

And yet, none of this—this bifurcated sense of self, this rending—was extraordinary. If her years as a reporter had taught her anything, it was these two things: One, the world was filled with people who were adrift, rudderless, and untethered. And two, the innocent always paid for the sins of the guilty.

A memory floated into her head, distant but breathtakingly sharp. Smita—at age eight or nine?—being pulled into Pushpa Auntie's lap, snuggling into the warmth of the older woman's flabby body, Pushpa's upper arms flapping as she hugged Smita. "See?" Pushpa was saying to her son. "See how she sits in my lap? All cuddly-cuddly. Not like you. Mr. Stuck-up."

"She's a girl," Chiku said contemptuously. "And she's a year younger than me."

What was she remembering? And why was Chiku scowling and rubbing the back of his head?

After lunch at Chiku's flat, the three of them—Rohit, Chiku, and herself—lounged on the sectional. Smita and her brother each read an Enid Blyton novel from their father's prized first-edition collection while Chiku flipped through the pages of *Filmfare*. From where they sat, they could hear Pushpa Auntie yelling at the servant in the kitchen. During one particularly fervent string of insults flung by Pushpa Auntie, Rohit looked up from his book and winked at his sister. Smita winked back. They both loved Pushpa Auntie and knew that the woman's bark was worse than her bite.

"God," Chiku spat out suddenly, "I hate her."

"Who?" they asked in unison.

"*Who?* My mother, who else? She drives me mad."

Rohit and Smita exchanged a shocked look. They couldn't imagine talking about their mummy in such a manner. As if he'd read their mind, Chiku said, "I wish your parents would adopt me."

"But your mummy's nice," Smita said.

Chiku shook his head. "I can't stand her."

Pushpa came into the living room, her cheeks flushed. Smita felt a pang of sympathy. She had always thought of Pushpa Auntie as being as robust and resilient as a battleship. But seeing her through Chiku's hostile eyes, she felt a strange sympathy for her mother's best friend. She wondered if Chiku's mother knew how he felt about her, and her heart ached at the thought. She shut her novel as she got to her feet. "Shall I get you a glass of water, Auntie?" she said. "It's a hot day."

Pushpa Auntie smiled as she settled into a nearby chair. "Thank you, my child," she said as Smita exited the room. Suddenly, she leaned forward and smacked Chiku on the back of his head. "See? See how your friends treat their elders? Unlike you, you worthless *junglee*. When have you ever fetched your poor mother a glass of water? Look at them, reading real books while you read your stupid film magazines."

Chiku rubbed his head as he glared at his mother. He was still glaring at her when Smita returned to the living room, and Pushpa held out her arms and pulled her into her lap.

Even after all these years, Smita could feel Pushpa Auntie's damp skin against her own and smell the woman's signature perfume. How could she reconcile this memory with the cold reception that she had recently received? How could that loving woman, in whose lap she'd felt so warm and safe, betray them the way she had? The two families had been so close, all of them flitting in and out of the two apartments throughout Smita's childhood. Smita tried to imagine her own parents not protecting Chiku if the roles had been reversed, but her imagination failed her. It wasn't as if Papa and Mummy were perfect—they weren't. But that was rule number three she'd learned from her years as a foreign correspondent: In every country, in every crisis, there are a handful of people who will stand against the tide. Her parents belonged to that small minority. Smita's heart tore open with gratitude at this thought, but in the next moment, she remembered that one of those good people was dead. She bit down on her lower lip to keep from crying.

"We're almost there," Mohan said, and Smita nodded mutely, not trusting herself to speak just yet, waiting for the hollow feeling to dissipate before she faced Abdul's killers. Struggling to be "present in the moment," as her yoga teacher in Brooklyn would say.

They followed a dirt road to where a small constellation of hovels stood in a loose, scattershot configuration. Still, it was immediately obvious that Vithalgaon was not as impoverished as Birwad. Chickens, stray dogs, and small children clustered in front of the huts, the dogs howling as they ran up to the car. Two men in *lungis* ambled up to them, staring at Smita. Mohan rolled down his window. "We're looking for the brothers Arvind and Govind!" he called. "Where can we find them?"

One of the men grinned knowingly. "The judge-sahib has ruled?" he asked.

Smita spoke before Mohan could reply. "Can you please direct us to their house?" she asked, her tone icy.

The man leered at her, then walked around the car to her side. "Those two don't live among us little people any longer." He pointed toward the main road. "Go back there and at the first crossing, make a left turn. You will see a small brick house. That's where they live. Thanks to the earnings of their sister. Yes, the same sister that they burned when the money stopped."

"Did you tell this to the police?" Smita said.

The man shook his head. "*Arre*, madam, forget this nonsense about police-folice. Govind is from our caste, no? Why we would get him in trouble with the police?" He scowled. "Even though I don't approve of what he did to that poor girl. Killing that Muslim dog? Fine. But they should not have touched that girl. No, he should have just dragged her back home and kept her locked up to do the cooking-cleaning."

Mohan shot Smita a look and spoke before she could. "Okay, *bhai*, thanks for your help," he said.

"No mention!" the man called. "All this drama will soon blow over. You'll see."

CHAPTER FIFTEEN

———◆———

THE MEN IN *my village were angry when Radha and I kept working at the factory.*

Rupal's voice was the loudest. He warned us, and when we didn't listen, he threatened us. He said he would perform a magic ceremony and make a sea of serpents in front of our home, to prevent us from leaving. Radha laughed and told him she was not afraid. We kept to our routine—leaving the house at dawn and walking the four kilometers each way, six days a week. After we had been working for about three months, we went to leave one morning and almost stepped on the dead goat outside our door. Rupal had skinned the animal and dropped it there for us to see. Radha screamed. For the first time, her courage was shaken. When she finally stopped screaming, she looked at me. "Let's stay home, Didi," she said. "These men will never give up until they destroy us. Their traditions mean more to them than their humanity."

Why didn't I agree with her that day? I had only joined the factory so that Radha would not walk home alone or be harassed by strange men at her job.

But that morning, I felt the iron come into my eyes when I saw that innocent animal lying in the dust, its tongue hanging out, flies already attacking its body. "Wait here," I said to Radha. "We will go to work today for sure. But first, I must take care of something."

I went into the house and found Arvind on his bed, sleeping off his drunkenness from the night before. Govind had already left for the farm. "Ae," I said, shaking him. "Get up, you good-for-nothing." Never before had I spoken to my brother in this manner. But that poor animal who had sacrificed his life for the fake honor of these men put the harshness in my voice. And this also was true: Even as they were telling the world they were against our working, both our brothers were enjoying the fruits of our labor. Every few days, Arvind asked me for money to buy liquor. And just the previous night, Govind had talked to me about getting the government loan to build a house a short distance from the main village. With our salaries, we could repay the loan in a few years, he said.

I had looked at him with surprise. "You tell everyone that your sisters have darkened your face by working outside the home," I said. "The other day when Rupal was visiting, you called me a whore. But you will build a house from our ill-gotten money?"

I saw shame stain his face. "If the soil of this bastard farm yielded more, I wouldn't touch your dirty money," he muttered. "But as it is, I am having little choice." His eyes flashed with anger. "You corrupted our little Radha with your greed. You are a woman who has forgotten her station in life. But since you are defying my authority, I will decide how to spend your money."

My brother had become a stranger. I remembered how he used to carry me on his shoulders when I was a child and tell me that I was taller than he was. How he used to buy me ice candy when he took me to the festival each year. Every Diwali, even as he dressed in tatters, Govind would buy Radha and me a new sari each. But our working at the factory had turned his love into rage, and brought this hard, contemptuous look to his eyes.

Remembering how Govind had looked at me made me shake Arvind harder. "Ai, ai, ai," he complained. "What is it?"

"Get up," I hissed. "Come see your friend Rupal's handiwork, you lazy drunk."

Arvind looked at me. "Have you gone mad, sister?" he said.

"Mad? You care about nothing but the bottle, and you call me 'mad'? Now, hurry up. Some of us are having to work to support this family."

He followed me outside. When he saw the dead goat, he looked like he was going to cry. He has always been a little soft, Arvind. But on that morning, I didn't care. "This is the evil that Rupal did," I said. "Now, you go clean up this mess."

"What? Me? This is not my work. This is . . ."

"We are going to our job, Arvind. The boss yells at us if we are even one minute late. As it is, we are going to have to run the whole way. This poor animal better be gone before we come home. And wash the front of the house with hot water. If I find one drop of blood . . ."

"This is women's work!" Arvind yelled. He spat on the ground. "This is why women are forbidden from having jobs outside the home. Rupal is right. You are acting like a man. I now see the truth of his words."

Radha stood in front of him. She was still shaking, but her face was hot with fury. "Chup re, stupid. Don't show off your ignorance to the whole world. As is it, people make fun of you. Now, do what Meena Didi asked. Otherwise, not one more paisa for your daru. You hear me?"

The look on Arvind's face made the breath catch in my throat. It was pure hatred.

AS CHILDREN, WE were taught to be afraid of tigers and lions. Nobody taught us what I know today—the most dangerous animal in this world is a man with wounded pride.

CHAPTER SIXTEEN

As Smita knocked on the door of the house, she could hear the radio playing within. She waited for a moment, then knocked again, a little louder. She looked over her shoulder as Mohan got out of the car and came around to where she stood. "No answer?" he asked, and she shook her head.

A goat bleated from under the banyan tree to which it was tied. The sun glittered like a medallion in the blue of the sky. Smita wiped the sweat off her brow onto her sleeve. Meena had mentioned that her younger brother was almost always home, her revulsion at his sloth evident on her face. Well, if the fellow was hungover, that would explain why he hadn't come to the door.

She went to knock again, but Mohan gestured for her to step aside. He made a fist and pounded on the sturdy door as Smita gazed up at the house, taking in the brick exterior and tiled roof. So this was the house that Meena had built them out of her earnings. Even though the workmanship was crude and some of the bricks were coming loose, it was a palace compared with Meena's current dwelling.

"*Saala, kon hai?*" They heard the voice from inside, loud and belligerent, before they heard the footsteps. There was the sound of something being knocked over; they heard a man grunting and then swearing under his breath. A minute later, the door flung open. "What?" the man yelled, glaring at Mohan. He was rail thin, with a mop of thick, disheveled hair.

Mohan took a step back. Then, in a haughty, aggressive tone that startled Smita, he said, "How long did we have to knock? And which one of the two are you?"

The belligerence drained out of the other man's face and was replaced by sullenness. "My name is Arvind, *ji*," he muttered. "Are you the police inspector?"

Smita knew in a flash what she had witnessed—the assertion of power by an educated, affluent man against someone of lower status; Mohan telegraphing his dominance simply by striking the right tone and posture. It disheartened her, but she couldn't think about that. Instead, she took a step toward the man. "Hello. My name is Smita. I'm from a newspaper in America," she said, wishing her Hindi was not so stilted. "You've talked to my friend Shannon before. I just wanted to chat a little bit about your sister, Meena, and you know, the court case."

Arvind spat at the mention of his sister. "I know no Meena," he said. "My sister Meena is dead."

Mohan spoke before Smita could. "But she didn't die in the fire," he said softly, his voice coiled with anger. "You know that."

"Not in the fire," Arvind said. He licked his lips nervously but stood his ground. "Before that. When she married that Muslim bastard. The fire was just a warning to the rest of them. In case any of their men were thinking of coming and corrupting our girls."

"Nobody was . . ."

"Mohan," Smita said, gently restraining him with her hand on his arm. She turned to the other man. "May we come in, *ji*? I just have a few questions."

Arvind's face was impassive as he looked at her. "We have already spoken to that foreign lady," he said at last. "What is her name? Sharon something? The one who dresses like a man."

"Ah, yes. Shannon. But she has gotten sick, you see. So she asked me to help her out. She sends her salaams, by the way," she added. "Now, may we enter?"

Arvind's eyes darted about as he considered her request. He craned his neck and looked over her shoulder. "Wait here," he said at last. "I will return in a few minutes." And before they could protest, he was past them, crossing the compound and then running into the fields beyond.

"You think he just took off?" Smita said in disbelief.

"I'm not sure," Mohan said. "But let's wait in the car, okay? It's even hotter here than in Mumbai."

They got back in the car, and he turned on the air-conditioning. "How long do you think we should wait?"

"We have no choice," Smita said miserably. "I can't really write my story without trying to get their comments." She frowned. "It's so weird. In the stories that Shannon did? It's like they brag about what they did in one sentence and then claim they had nothing to do with the murder in the next. And yet, here they are, out on bail. How can that be?"

Mohan shrugged. "India," he said and Smita heard the resignation in his voice.

They waited for about ten minutes, with Smita growing increasingly angry at herself for having let Arvind take off. But what could she have done? Blocked him as he sprinted away? She turned to Mohan to ask him if he was okay with waiting a little longer, when he sat up and pointed toward the field and at the two figures who were hurrying back toward the house. "Is that him?" Mohan asked. "Maybe he went to get his older brother?"

Govind was a bulkier version of Arvind. "*Kya hai?*" he asked. "We have already said all that we are going to."

Smita shot Mohan a silencing look before getting out of the car. "Good afternoon," she said, ignoring Govind's obvious hostility. "I'm so happy your brother fetched you. We just have a few questions and then we'll be gone." Seeing that he was about to refuse, she added, "We want to be fair. Give you a chance to explain things from your point of view."

Govind's eyes narrowed as he took in the incongruity of Smita's affected Hindi and her Indian outfit. He lowered his head to peer at Mohan, who had followed Smita's unspoken request to remain in the car. "You are Hindu?" he asked.

"What?" Smita said, startled. "I mean, yes. But what . . ."

"Good," he nodded once, as if she'd passed some test. "So, you understand our culture. Because that other lady, that foreigner, she didn't understand us. Our values."

Smita quelled the nausea that she felt. "I see," she murmured.

"You are also from the foreign place," Govind continued. "But your modest dress is telling me you are a woman of good morals. That other woman, Shannon. She wore pants. Like a man." He gestured toward the car. "You please ask your husband to join us."

"He's not . . ." Smita thought better of correcting him. "Thanks," she said. "I'll ask him." She walked up to Mohan and murmured, "He thinks we're married."

Mohan gave her a quick nod. He got out of the car and strode toward Govind, his hand outstretched, his manner friendly. "*Kaise ho?*" he said. "Sorry for interrupting your day like this."

Despite the friendliness of Mohan's tone, Smita knew that Govind was aware of the class difference between them. Instead of shaking

Mohan's proffered hand, he folded his own in greeting. Then, he turned to Arvind and smacked him on his head. "Go make our guests some tea. Go." Arvind went into the house, rubbing his head and muttering under his breath.

Govind smiled apologetically. "Since both our women are gone, my brother and I have to do all the cooking-cleaning these days."

"That's okay," Mohan said. "I do everything for myself, also."

"You are big-city folks, sir," Govind said. "Life is different for us. Here it is a matter of dishonor for us to do women's work."

Mohan looked like he was about to argue, so Smita stepped in to preempt him. "What news do you hear about Radha?" she asked as she discreetly pulled out her notebook.

Govind shrugged. "What is there to say? Radha is lucky I was able to find her a husband after the scandal."

"You mean from Meena's marriage?"

His lips curled at the mention of Meena's name. "Yes, of course. But even before that." He chewed on the wad of tobacco in his mouth. "No woman in our village had ever left home to go work for strangers. It is the strictest taboo. It is my misfortune that both my sisters defied not only my authority but also the authority of our village elders."

"Why is it so wrong for women to work?" Smita asked.

Govind looked at her incredulously. "Because it is the law, passed down from our forefathers. God made it so, this division of labor. It is the destiny of women to birth and raise children and keep the house. Men are the breadwinners. Everyone knows this"—Govind threw Smita a contemptuous look—"at least in Vithalgaon."

"I heard you tried to stop them from working at the factory?"

"Memsahib, I did everything in my power. I begged them, pleaded with them, asked them to consider the honor of our forefathers. Our village chief forbade anyone from even speaking to them. We tried everything. But some demon had entered into them. Some people in the village swore they saw a black halo around them when they went to work each morning."

Smita fought to hide her astonishment at Govind's performance. *Talk about playing the victim*, she thought. She considered her next question, but just then Arvind came to the doorway of the house. "What do you wish me to do?" he called. "Bring the tea out?"

Govind hesitated, and Smita saw her chance. "Please, may we enter your home? The sun is really strong today."

"Memsahib, this evil sun is always strong. Working in the fields every day—that is why my skin is tough as leather."

Smita felt suitably chastised. "Indeed," she said.

There was a brief pause, and then Govind appeared to have come to a decision. "Please, memsahib," he said. "Welcome to our home."

They walked into a long, rectangular room with three wooden folding chairs and a small television set. There was no other furniture. Smita caught a glimpse of a mattress on the floor of the next room before Govind directed her attention to one of the wooden chairs. "Please to sit," he said, to Mohan and Smita. And after they did, he sat on his haunches in front of them.

Mohan half rose. "Won't you . . . ?" he said, pointing to the third chair.

Govind smiled bashfully. "It is our custom, *seth*. You are our superior."

Mohan laughed. "*Arre, bhai.* What's all this talk of superior-inferior?"

But Govind remained on the floor. After a moment, he yelled to his brother. "*Ae*, where's the chai, you good-for-nothing?" Arvind appeared with two glasses of tea, handed them silently to the two visitors, and took his place on the floor next to his brother.

Smita took a sip. "It's good tea," she said politely, but Arvind looked back at her blankly. She noticed that he had wetted and slicked back his hair while in the kitchen. She took another sip, set the glass on the floor, and picked up her notebook as matter-of-factly as she could, aware that the brothers were watching her every move. "So," she said, "do you think the judge will rule in your favor?"

Arvind stole a glance at his older brother, waiting for him to speak. The minutes ticked by. In the silence, Smita heard the distant bleating of the goat. "He will definitely vote in our favor," Govind said suddenly. "God is just, and He is on our side. That whore can go to any court in the country, but the truth will prevail."

Beside her, Smita heard Mohan's sharp intake of breath. "The truth?" she asked. "Did you—did you not," she hesitated, wanting to phrase the question as delicately as she could, "did you not try to kill, that is, set Meena's hut on fire?"

Govind's eyes searched the room before resting on Smita's face. "Someone did," he muttered. "Who, we cannot say."

Was the man really lying to her face? But then, why was she surprised? "Meena says it was the two of you. That she saw you with her own eyes."

Govind spat on the floor. "Of course she is saying this. That Muslim beef-eater told her what to say."

"Her husband? How could he? He's dead."

The man's face grew defiant. "Maybe the *kutta* didn't die straight away. How do we know what he said or did?"

Smita felt as if Govind was a large silverfish she was trying to reel in. One false move on her part, and he would slip away. "You're saying you don't know who killed Abdul?" she said at last.

"Memsahib, you are asking the incorrect question." Govind shook his head impatiently. "Who cares *who* burned that dog alive? *Why* did they do it? That is question no one is asking. They did it to protect the honor of all Hindus. To teach those Muslim dogs their proper station in life."

Smita opened her mouth to speak, but Govind raised his hand to cut her off. "It's like this. My brother and I are sitting on the floor before you because this is our rightful place. You understand? We are all having our stations in life. God has made it so. We have allowed these Muslim dogs to live in our Hindustan as our guests. But a dog must know who is its master, correct? Muslims must keep to their own villages and, above all, they must stay away from our women. That is a fact." He lowered his voice. "This is their jihad. You understand? They force our women to bear their children so they can multiply and take over Hindustan."

"But Meena says nobody forced her," Smita said. "She says she loved her husband."

Govind stared at the floor. When he looked up, Smita saw that a muscle in his jaw was convulsing. "How this can be, memsahib?" he said. "What you suggest is against the natural order of things. Can a fish fall in love with a cow? Can a crow fall in love with a tiger?"

Smita gave Mohan a quick glance, but she was unable to read his expression. "So, you have no regrets for what you've—what has happened to Meena?" she asked, hearing the hollowness in her own voice.

Govind smiled faintly. "I have regrets, for sure," he said softly. "I regret that my sister survived. And most of all, I regret that the bastard child she was carrying is still alive. She even brought the infant to court when she appeared before the judge-sahib. Can you imagine? It was as if she wanted to defile the whole court with her excrement."

The blood rushed to Smita's face as she remembered Abru's sweet face. She wanted to stand up and yell obscenities at this vile man, to rain blows on his head. Instead, she looked at a spot on the wall beyond him until she could trust herself to speak. "The child is innocent," she said.

"I made my peace with Meena leaving our home to go live in sin with that man," Govind said. "She humiliated me three times, memsahib. Once when she defied me and took the factory job. The second time when she ran away to Birwad to live with those Muslim *chamars*. The whole village spat at me then, but still I did nothing to avenge the insult. My mistake. But the third disrespect was intolerable. They came to my door with a box of sweets, holding hands, pointing to the evil she was carrying in her belly. The shameless whore and her Muslim pimp came and defiled my doorstep. Holding her head high. As if it wasn't a crime against God, that thing growing in her belly." Govind choked back angry tears. "What was I supposed to do? Tolerate their evil? Allow him to call me his brother-in-law, as if we were equals in the eyes of God?"

"Couldn't you have just asked them to leave?"

"That I did. They ran home with their tails between their legs, like the mongrels they were. But memsahib, when the crops in my field go bad and don't give the good-proper yield, you know what we have to do? We must burn the fields to the ground. Then, the next year, the crops grow back stronger. That is what had to be done—the land had to be cleansed. I just regret that two of the crops are still growing."

There was a sudden, charged silence in the room, as if they all realized that Govind had almost confessed to Abdul's murder. After long minutes, Mohan spoke into the silence. "You say you've seen her in court. So you are aware of the damage the fire has done? Her one eye is melted shut. Half of her face is gone. But it is not enough for you?"

Govind opened his mouth to answer, but Mohan was staring directly at him, holding his gaze, and after a moment, Govind looked away and stared at the floor. "Your ways of life are different than ours, sir," he said at last.

Smita felt Mohan tense and spoke before he could. "What about you, Arvind?" she said quickly. "Do you feel the same way?"

Arvind looked from her to his brother and then back at her. "Whatever my older brother thinks is best," he said.

"But I thought you were close to Meena," Smita said, although in that moment she couldn't recall how she knew this, whether Meena had mentioned the detail to her or she'd read it in one of Shannon's stories.

For a split second Arvind's face softened, but then he shook his head. "It doesn't matter. This my brother's house. He is my elder."

"And yet, this entire house was built from your sisters' earnings, wasn't it?" Mohan said. As the affront registered on Govind's face, Smita wanted to smack Mohan.

"*Arre, wah, seth*," Govind said, his eyes glimmering with malice. "You are a guest in my home, but you are so free with your insults. Yes, you are correct. Our sisters paid for this house out of their ill-gotten wealth."

He turned to Smita, as if he expected a more sympathetic ear. "I had a bride picked out for Arvind. She came from a good family from a nearby village, and they were willing to pay a big dowry. But after word got around about my sisters working at that factory, they called off the wedding."

Arvind was staring straight ahead, his face expressionless.

"Were you upset about this?" Smita asked him.

Arvind laughed dismissively. "They dug their own grave," he said. "From the dowry my bride would've brought, we would have paid Meena and Radha's dowries. That's why only Govind *bhai* was so anxious to get me married off first. Then, he could get rid of our sisters. Two less mouths for us to feed once they became their husband's responsibility. But as it turned out, we didn't have to pay any dowry to that old cripple who married Radha."

Smita had thought that Arvind was the gentler of the two brothers. But she found herself disliking him as much as she did the older one. It was as if Meena's transgressions had destroyed all familial feeling.

"So, tell me something," Mohan said. "Who put up the bail money to get you out of the lockup? Did you have to borrow from the money lender?"

"No, *seth*," Govind said. "We used our own money."

"Your sisters' money? Their savings?"

Govind scowled. "No female has any right to her savings. All their money belonged to me as the head of the household. This is our custom."

"I see." Mohan smiled pleasantly. "Is it also your custom to try and murder your sister because you are angry that she ran away to another man and that her salary had stopped coming to you? Because that's what your neighbors are saying."

"Mohan!" Smita said, knowing he'd gone too far.

But she was too late. Govind was already on his feet, his big, peasant hands clenched in fists. "Please, both of you, leave my house right now. Before something untoward happens."

Mohan rose to his feet, too, and stepped in front of Smita. "You keep your threats for poor women like your sister," he said evenly. "If you so much as look in the direction of my . . . my wife . . . I'll have you hung upside-down and beaten at the police station. You hear me?"

Govind's eyes went flat, opaque. "Yes, sahib," he said dully. "We know the power that you people possess. You can crush ordinary men like me under the soles of your shoes. We know your kind."

"That's right."

"Mohan, stop," Smita said. "This is getting out of hand." She turned toward Govind. "Listen, I'm sorry . . ."

"Don't you apologize," Mohan said. "Don't you dare say 'I'm sorry' to this, this bastard."

"*Arre, bas!*" A shout rang out and they all jumped. It was Arvind, his eyes teary, his chest heaving. "Everybody, stop. And you people . . . Go. Just go."

Smita and Mohan were in the car and pulling away when Govind strode toward them. "Even if they give me the death penalty, it will be worth it." He grinned humorlessly, showing tobacco-stained teeth. "Just to have watched that fucker dance as he burned."

"Are you saying you murdered him?" Smita said.

He spat on the ground. "I am confessing to nothing. Every witness in Birwad has changed their story. Nobody is believing what that whore has to say."

"Let's get out of here," Smita said. "I can't hear another word of this."

THEY DIDN'T SPEAK until the house was a speck from the rearview mirror. Then, a livid Smita turned on Mohan. "What the hell was that about? You actually got in the way of my doing my job. What gave you the right to bulldoze your way into my interview?"

Mohan raised one hand, as if to fend off a blow. "I'm sorry. I lost my temper. Forgive me."

She glared at him and turned away. She looked out of the window even as Mohan spoke. "I don't know how you do this job, *yaar*. I . . . I just wanted to choke him. After seeing how they'd ruined that poor girl."

Nandini wouldn't have interfered like this, Smita thought. *She would've known the importance of dispassion, of allowing sources to reveal themselves in their own time, in their own words.* But Mohan was not a professional. He was merely an acquaintance who had given up his own vacation to help her. He had reacted in the way any sentient human being would. And she needed him for his male presence. It grated on Smita to admit it, but if Govind had not believed that Mohan was her husband, he wouldn't have allowed her to enter his home.

"I want to make one more stop," Smita said. "Let's head back to the main village. I need to talk to that fucking village chief."

CHAPTER SEVENTEEN

———✳———

WHEN RADHA AND I were children, we used to play a game. She would ask, "What is the true color of the world, Didi?"

And I would say, "Green."

"Why green?"

"Because the trees are green. Grass is green. The new buds on the plants are green. Even the parrots are green. Green is the color of the world."

"But, Didi," Radha would argue, "the wheat stalks are brown. My body is brown. The field mice are brown. No, the world is brown."

"What about blue?" I would say. "The sky is blue. And it covers the whole world, like a mother who loves and embraces all her children."

Radha would fall silent, and I would remember that she had known our mother's love for even fewer years than I did. So I would take her in my arms and hold her, to make her know what it feels like to be loved.

Today I know the truth: The true color of the world is black.

Anger is black.

Shame and scandal are black.

Betrayal is black.

Hatred is black.

And a roasted, smoking body is Black, Black, Black.

The world, after witnessing such cruelty, goes black.

The waking up to a changed world is black.

HE COMES TO me at night, when it is only me and Abru, sleeping in our hut. Sometimes, he smells like the last time, smoky, like burnt hair. Like the taste that is forever in my mouth. But most of the time, he smells like he used to—like the river, like the grass, like the smell of our land after the first rain.

Ammi complained loudly when I first began to visit our old hut, but I think she is now happy to have her own house at night. Every time she sees my face, she is reminded of the night when two of the goondas held her back as she screamed and screamed, watching her oldest son ablaze. Of how she cried as she watched me trying to beat the flames off Abdul's body until the heat melted my hands and I passed out from the pain.

It is only when I visit my old hut at night that I feel at peace. Always, I pretend to be asleep when Abdul visits so that he can feel like he is surprising me. I shut my eye and roll over onto my side as I lie on the mud floor. He puts his arms around me from behind, his hips moving against my hips, his knees fitting inside the bend of my knees. We stay like this until he drains all the fear and hatred out of my heart.

Once, a long time ago, when Nishta, my old neighbor in Vithalgaon, had jaundice, Rupal came to her house with a small stone. He rubbed the smooth stone over her body and then asked Nishta's mother to wash her with a wet towel. When the woman wrung the towel outside, yellow water poured out of it. We all saw it. Rupal said it was the jaundice coming out of Nishta's body.

Fear and hatred have turned my heart black. But with his love, Abdul wrings my heart clean every night.

His love.

Abdul's love for me.

AT THE FACTORY, *the boss would give us a fifteen-minute lunch break. There was a large jamun tree in the compound, and Radha and I would sit under its motherly branches and eat our meal. We had never had enough to eat, but now, with both of us working, we stuffed our tiffin box with rice and dal and ate like men. Still, habit made me save a little of my food for Radha each day. Occasionally, two other women, both married, ate with us. But they were from a distant village and mostly kept to themselves. Once, I asked them if the menfolk in their village were also angry at them for working, but they shook their heads no. "See, Didi?" Radha said. "Only Vithalgaon has such backward customs."*

A month after he started at the factory, Abdul began to time his lunch break five minutes after Radha and I would start ours. He'd sit under a nearby tree and unwrap two small bananas and a roti from a big red kerchief. Every day, he ate the same food. It used to hurt my eyes to see him eat the same lunch day after day. I could sense him stealing quick looks at me, but I was careful never to draw Radha's attention to him. Radha had a temper; there was no telling what she would say or do. Even at home, Radha had begun acting like she was the man of the house. Once, I even heard her order Arvind to polish her sandals if he wanted money for his daru. So I made sure to sit in a manner that blocked Radha from seeing Abdul looking at me while he ate. But even without a single word spoken, something began to grow between Abdul and me. When Radha and I would walk home after our shift, he would follow us at a distance. If Radha turned around, Abdul would quickly bend to tie his shoelaces or begin talking to some of the other workers who were also making their way home. About halfway from Vithalgaon, he would turn left and disappear down a side road. That was how I learned the direction to his village.

When the monsoons came, Radha took ill with typhoid fever. I wanted to stay home to take care of her, but she begged me to go to work. She was afraid that the foreman would fire us if we both were no-shows. And we needed my wages to pay for her medicine and the new house.

Because it was raining so hard, the foreman shut all the windows, and even with the ceiling fans running, the tin roof made the room as hot as a furnace. One day, the heat was so terrible I made two mistakes in one morning. I was so upset, I decided to go outdoors for lunch, rain or no rain. Luckily, the sun was out, even though the ground was still wet. But two minutes after I began to eat, Abdul appeared, standing under his own tree. And because there was no one else present on this day, he raised his hand and called out, "Salaam!" I made no reply, shocked at the liberty he had taken with me. If any of the Hindu workers heard his insult to me, they would break his legs. I thought about not finishing my lunch and going back inside, but just then, I heard the song of a koel—and the music the bird made was so beautiful that I decided to turn my back on Abdul and stay where I was.

I was almost finished with lunch when I heard a soft "Excuse me?" Startled, I turned around and there he was, standing next to me, looking as nervous as I felt, his eyes darting this way and that to make sure no one had seen us. "My brother just got back from Ratnagiri," he said in a rush. "And he brought back some mangoes. I thought of you—and your sister." His hand trembled as he held out two beautiful golden mangoes. Of course I could not accept them. If my hand were to accidentally touch the hand of a Muslim, God would surely chop it off before the end of the day.

"Please, ji," he begged. "I carried them all the way here for you."

I looked away, pulling the dupatta that covered my hair even more tightly to hide half of my face. What a risk he had taken. I was a respectable woman. Maybe Abdul had heard the rumors about Radha and me, how nobody in our village would speak to us, how Rupal had convinced them all that we were fallen women. Tears came in my eyes. Like the stink of a rotten fish, the odor of our reputations had followed us here. That could be the only reason why this boy had taken such a liberty with me. "You please go," I said. "Before anybody sees or I tell the boss. The Hindu brothers in here will give you a proper thrashing if you don't leave."

"I'm sorry," he said. "I meant no insult." I heard him begin to walk away across the dusty compound, but I kept my head turned.

I waited until I was sure he had entered the factory, not wanting even his shadow to fall on me. Finally, I turned around. Abdul had left the two mangoes sitting on his red kerchief on the ground. For me. As a gift for me.

I looked around. There was no one else there. My fifteen minutes were already up. I knew I should leave the fruit on the ground. But then I remembered how his hand had trembled as he held them out. Quickly, I picked up the mangoes and shoved them inside my tiffin carrier. I knew that shutting the lid would flatten them, but what to do? Next, I picked up his kerchief, balled it up, and shoved it inside the pocket of my tunic. But just before I did this, I held it up to my nose, even as I prayed to God to forgive me for this blasphemy. I was hoping it would smell like him, but instead, it carried the faint scent of the mangoes.

When I got back inside, Abdul was already at his station. He looked up anxiously to catch my eye, then immediately looked back down. A secret passed between us, like a summer breeze. As I walked past him, I removed the handkerchief from my pocket and dropped it. I was so nervous, I thought I would faint. In my whole life, I had never acted this way with a man. What if someone saw? But we were paid by the number of items we stitched in a day, so everybody's eyes were on the job in front of them. No one saw. After I sat down at my machine, Abdul casually leaned toward the floor and picked up the kerchief, dabbing his neck before putting it in his pocket.

And that was how our love story began.

YEARS AGO, A Christian priest visited our village, telling us tall stories about a man and a woman and an apple and a snake. Radha and I went to the meeting because they were giving free ice cream, but we left early after we realized that the priest was talking rubbish. Why should the woman be punished for eating an apple? Or for taking it back to her husband? This is what women are supposed to do—share their food. "Didi, instead of blaming her, *the husband should have been happy that his wife shared the fruit with him, na?" Radha said.*

I agreed with her.

But after Abdul died for my sins, I understood what the priest was trying to say.

I SHOULD NEVER *have taken a bite of that mango.*

CHAPTER EIGHTEEN

———✳———

RUPAL BHOSLE LIVED in a two-story house at one end of the village. If the house didn't give away his status as the richest man in Vithalgaon, the deference shown to him by his many employees did. A servant had run into the big house to inform Rupal of Smita and Mohan's arrival, and he had come out to meet them in his compound. As they stood chatting, Rupal gave a sudden kick to the young boy who was washing one of his two cars. "*Saala, chutiya*, keep your eyes on your work," Rupal said. The boy bobbed his head and beamed, as if Rupal had paid him a compliment. "Yes, boss. Sorry, boss," he said.

Rupal led them to the back veranda. A large swing hung from the rafters, but he motioned them toward some rattan chairs. The house was surrounded by sugarcane fields, and Smita could see bare-chested men working in the distance. In the fierce heat of the day, their blackened skin made them look like silhouettes against the blue of the sky.

Rupal lowered his lanky frame into a chair across from Smita and blocked her view.

He was a tall man with a lush mustache and a long, dolorous face. His light-brown eyes were framed by thick, dark eyelashes. Smita thought that he would have been handsome except for the twist of his lips that gave him an expression of cruelty. Every few seconds, he glanced at Mohan, who had chosen to wander away and was standing a few feet away.

"Will you take something?" Rupal asked expansively. "Chai, coffee, Coca-Cola?"

"No thanks," Smita said. "We just had tea at Govind's place."

"Ah, Govind. He's a good boy. Good boy." He yawned a prodigious yawn. "So, you say that girl, Shannon, has her wicket down? For how long?"

"Excuse me?"

"*Arre, baba.* For how long will she be out of commission?"

"Oh. I'm not sure." Smita cleared her throat. "In any case . . . As I explained, I'm hoping to write a story about when the verdict comes in. And I thought I should interview you. Because Meena said you . . ."

"Ah, Meena. I tried warning that foolish girl to not step into that den of temptation. But did she listen? No. And so, everything happened just as I had predicted."

"You predicted that she would be burned alive?" Smita tried, but failed, to keep the sarcasm out of her voice.

Rupal looked deeply into her eyes. "I can see backwards and forwards in time, miss," he said. "From the beginning of the world until the end of time. I am having that power."

"And when was that?" said Mohan, walking back toward them. "The beginning of the world?"

Not again, Smita thought, feeling her stomach muscles tense. *Don't fuck this up for me, Mohan.*

But Rupal seemed oblivious to the challenge in Mohan's query. "Easy question, sir," he said. "The universe was created about two hundred years ago. Around the time the demon Ravana and the god-prince Rama were living on Earth."

Mohan's lips twitched. "*Accha?* And you can see all the way back two hundred years? Wow."

"*Hah.*" Rupal nodded, puffing out his chest. "But to predict what end this girl Meena would meet, I didn't even need to go back so far. I just told her brothers the truth—stitching those Western clothes, working beside people from unknown castes and creeds, would corrupt her morals. That is exact-to-exact what happened." Rupal gave a triumphant smile. "And that's why I told them how to end their problem."

"End their problem?"

"Yes. With her falling under the spell of that worshipper of Muhammad." Rupal turned his gaze toward Smita. "What to do, miss? In the old days, we could count on the police to help. A few slaps at the police station, and *bas*, the fellow would have come to his senses. But these days." He sighed dramatically. "These days, even the police and the politicians are too afraid of these terrorists who create trouble wherever they go. They do the same mischief in your country, also, isn't it? With that 9/11 *tamasha*? So it falls upon honest citizens to take matters into their own hands."

"You advised the brothers to . . . ?"

"Of course. As the village head, it is my job to protect the morals of our village, isn't it? And that means, first and foremost, protecting the virtue of our women. I advised Govind to go at night with a can of kerosene and teach that fellow a lesson nobody in his community would ever forget."

Was this detail in the stories Shannon had written about the case? Smita tried to remember. If the man was confessing to her so nonchalantly, surely he had done the same with Shannon? "Did you tell the police this? About your role?"

The man stared at her for a long moment and then let out a loud guffaw. "*Arre*, the area police chief is my cousin-brother, miss. My mother's sister's son. Of course I told him. Gave him the date and time we were planning on doing this. So that they could ignore the phone calls."

Smita went pale. She cast a quick glance at Mohan, who was standing with his hands thrust deep into the pockets of his jeans. "The police knew?" she asked.

"Yes, of course. We are law-abiding citizens. Not like those dogs."

"When? When did you give Govind this advice? After Meena informed him she was pregnant?"

"Yes," Rupal said. "But all of this could've been avoided if he'd listened to me earlier. Govind came to me when he found out that she was whoring herself to that Abdul. At that time, I told him to beat Meena and forbid her from leaving the house. That good-for-nothing Arvind is home all day anyway, *na*? He can watch his sister. I told Govind to take some boys from our village to meet Abdul on his way home from work and give him a good-proper thrashing. Leave him bleeding by the side of the road like the dog that he is. *Bas*, that would've cooled his taste for Hindu flesh. Automatically, he would've gone *thanda*."

"*Thanda?*"

"Cold," Mohan said quietly. "He means, Abdul would've given up."

"Exactly. But that *chutiya* Arvind gets so drunk that the girl manages to run away while he is sleeping. The younger sister swears that Meena insisted that she help her get to Birwad. Next thing we hear, Meena is married. Never in our history has such a thing happened in our village. Still, Govind decided to do nothing to avenge this insult, the bloody eunuch."

Rupal removed a *paan* leaf from a tin can, placed some tobacco and *supari* inside it, folded it into a triangle, and inserted it into his cheek. Remembering his manners, he offered a leaf to Mohan, who declined. "What else you want to know?" he asked, chewing on the betel leaf, his mouth turning scarlet.

"I'm confused," Smita said, even while she marveled at the man's audacity, the nonchalant manner in which he was incriminating himself. "You said the burning was your idea?"

"*Hah*. After they came to Govind's house when Meena was with child, he came to see me again. The poor boy was almost mad with shame and worry. Thank God that by then he had managed to get the younger sister married off to that cripple from out of town. Radha was lucky. No boy from our village would've married her, despite her beauty. But Govind must also think about making the marriage for his younger brother, no? Tell me, which decent family will allow their daughter to marry a boy who is having a Muslim niece or nephew? So I says to him, the only way to restore his family name is to burn it all down."

"I see," Smita said.

But she didn't. In Mumbai, there were shopping malls and fancy French and sushi restaurants springing up everywhere. The Indian economy was growing at twice the American rate. The entire affect was that of a city and a country on the rise. Coming to Vithalgaon was like going back in time, to life from two centuries ago, a place where the rivers of communal hatred and religious enmity still flowed unabated. What struck her most about Rupal was his matter-of-factness. Not only was he implicating Govind, he was also describing an upside-down world where wrong was right and men like him were unaware of the brazenness of their claims and how convoluted their thinking was. She had seen it in other places, of course, this righteousness that people felt about their beliefs. However, she had usually witnessed this cognitive distortion on a larger scale, sweeping over places like Syria or Sudan. Almost always, behind the religious or ideological rhetoric, lay a strategy for economic gain—land grabs, claims to water and other natural resources. In her reporting, she had typically followed the money. But this manufactured enmity with Abdul seemed to have no financial basis.

A thought struck her, and she sat up, remembering what Mohan had accused Govind of earlier that day. The money. Of course. "Was Govind upset about the lack of income, after Meena left?"

Rupal frowned and looked away. When he turned to Smita again, there was a different expression in his eyes. "She had saved some household money before she decided to run away. That's the one decent thing she did—she left that for her brothers. She took nothing with her. Govind paid the government loan from that money for many months." Rupal leaned forward and peered at Smita. "God is great," he said. "I made sure they went to Birwad on the last day of the month, when Meena and Abdul got paid and cashed their salary before coming home. Before they lit the match, the men went inside their home and removed the cash. That's the money the brothers used. To pay for their bail."

The ball of grief that had remained coiled inside Smita since she'd met Meena the day before burst open. "They used Meena and Abdul's money? So that they can walk around free? Govind told me they paid for the bond out of *his* earnings."

Rupal's eyes flashed with anger. "How is it *her* money? Every *paisa* she earned belonged to Govind. If she had not married that swine, it would be his."

"Didn't half of it belong to Abdul?"

Rupal shrugged. "That is of no consequence."

Smita felt Mohan stir behind her. "Tell me something," she said to Rupal. "Were you surprised when you heard about the lawsuit?"

Rupal gave the *paan* a vigorous chew and then spat out a scarlet streak on the ground in front of him. Smita instinctively moved her feet away from the spot. "It's that lady lawyer who instigated Meena," he said. "Coming here, poking her nose in our business." He paused. "But we will take care of the situation when the time comes."

Smita felt a chill run down her spine. "Meaning?"

"Meaning I am a man with many powers. Sitting in my home, I can unleash a plague upon New Delhi. I can make a plane fall out of the sky. I can send a hundred snakes into that lawyer's office. You mark my words, if something happens to those two brothers . . ."

"Is that so?" Mohan said suddenly. "*Wah, ustad.* You are more powerful than Prime Minister Modi. *Wah.* Okay, tell me, what is the name of the village where Meena's sister now lives?"

"How am I to know? This is not my business."

"Oh. Okay, what's her phone number?"

"I don't know. How would I know if she even has a phone?"

"*Arre,* you are so powerful, *bhai.* You cannot look into her house and see if she has a phone? Do some of your *jadoo* right now, no?"

Rupal chewed on the *paan,* then tucked it into his left cheek, making it bulge. "Mister is mocking my powers," he said finally.

"He doesn't mean it," Smita said hastily. "He is joking around. Sorry."

But Rupal was not appeased. "Joking-fooling about such matters is not good. Everybody in this village defers to me. People come from other villages to ask my advice when they are sick or need their marriage horoscope read. Ask anyone."

"I believe you," Smita said. She waited a beat. "So what do you predict? About the judge's ruling?"

Rupal shot her a look she couldn't decipher. Then, he shrugged volubly. "Who knows? Either they will remain free, or they will get the death penalty and become martyrs. Either way, they have restored their family name." He looked at his watch. "Now, if you can excuse me, it is time for my panchayat meeting. The village council meets every week at this hour. Many important cases we are having to decide this week."

"May I attend? I'd like to see what . . ."

"How can this be? Only men are allowed at our meetings. Even if a dispute involves a wife or a sister, the woman has to stand outside the house and call out her complaint."

Rupal gave Mohan a pitying look. "You take care of your missus, city *babu*. You have learned a few of our customs today. Maybe they will help you."

Rupal rose from his chair and then waited until Smita did so, also. "Good day," he said touching his forehead with his right hand. "I will walk you to your car."

"That's okay. I think I will walk around the village a little bit. I'd like to . . ."

Rupal smiled politely. "Miss," he said deliberately. "It is not advisable for a woman to walk around my village with her head uncovered. We understand your customs are different. But you must respect ours."

Smita opened her mouth to argue, but Rupal cut her off. "No one in the whole village will talk to you without my permission. Which I will not give."

"Why not?" Smita asked, but he merely gazed at her impassively.

Smita shut her notebook and the three of them walked toward the front door. There, she stopped, struck by a thought. "One more thing. When we visited the brothers, they were still living in their house. How are they managing the bank payments now? You said . . ."

"We take care of our own, little miss," he said. "I am giving them a loan, of course."

"You are loaning them money to pay off their bank loan?" Mohan said, not bothering to hide his incredulity.

"That's so."

"At what interest rate?"

Smita could tell that Rupal was uncomfortable, but he held Mohan's gaze. "Under these sad circumstances, I have given the boys a discount. They pay me thirty percent, only."

Smita gasped. *That's highway robbery*, she wanted to say. Instead, she said, "They can afford to pay you and still eat?"

"How is this my business? If they cannot pay, they will lose the house. It is that simple. As it is, I allow Govind to hire out his drunkard brother to me three days a week, to pay down the debt."

"What does Arvind do for you?"

"What does he do? Whatever big-small jobs I am needing him to do. Three days a week, his scrawny neck is in my hands."

Rupal raised his index finger to cut Smita off before she could speak.

"One final thing, miss. What I said about giving advice to Govind about the fire? I was only joking with you. Please don't put such a silly notice into your newspaper."

"Nobody jokes about such a serious thing to a newspaper reporter," Smita said.

"We are just ignorant farmers, miss," Rupal said. "What do we know about the rules of talking to a reporter? Besides, no one will believe such a story. I will deny it all."

Before Smita could react, Rupal gestured toward their car. "Be careful on these roads," he said. "They are hard to travel once it gets dark. All the ghosts and spirits come out at night."

CHAPTER NINETEEN

———

SMITA AND MOHAN were quiet as they drove back toward the motel. Smita felt numb, exhausted, spent. She sifted through the interview in her mind, trying to locate the exact moment when it had gone off the rails. But the fact was, Rupal had controlled the conversation from the very start, and he had decided when to end it. Not to mention the fact that he had virtually thrown them out of the village. *How dare he?* And what was wrong with her that she'd let him? She was not on the top of her game, and to do Meena's story justice, she needed to be.

Mohan groaned.

"What is it?" she asked.

He turned to her, his eyes red. "What is this country?" he cried. "How can we be this backwards? Did you hear what that bastard said? He ordered the burning? And he's sitting there like a king, unharmed? How can this be so in this day and age?"

Smita nodded in sympathy. But some small part of her was gratified to hear Mohan's distress, to see that this trip had pierced through his privilege. She remembered how reflexively defensive and proud of India he'd been when they'd first met. She didn't wish this loss of innocence on him. But she was glad that they were on the same page.

Maybe even the son of a diamond merchant can be made to face the truth, she thought grimly.

SMITA FILLED THE bucket in her bathroom with hot water, then used the plastic mug to pour water over her body. She thought with longing about her hotel room at the Taj, with its powerful shower and marbled bathroom, then felt guilty about such a bourgeois desire. But who was she kidding? Soon, she would be back in her luxurious condo in Brooklyn, with its granite countertops and the rain shower in the bathroom. Papa had forced Rohit and Smita to take their share of their mother's inheritance soon after Mummy had died. They had declined, but Papa had been insistent. Rohit had bought a car and put away the rest in Alex's college fund; Smita had had her bathroom and kitchen remodeled.

What would little Abru's inheritance be? The gravesite of a father she would never know, but whose specter would haunt her entire life. The ashes of her mother's dreams, which she would taste in her own mouth. Her grandmother's grief, which could manifest itself only as anger, in a harsh word or a quick slap whenever the little girl did something that reminded Ammi of her dead son. Abru's life would be marked by hunger—an emotional hunger never sated, its roots in a time before her birth. And the physical hunger, the emptiness in her stomach that would feel as real to her as a shoe or a stone. Poor Abdul had thought that his daughter would be the heir to a new, modern India. Instead, she had become a symbol of the old, timeless India, a country scarred by ignorance, illiteracy, and superstition, governed by men who dropped the poison pellets of communal hatred onto a people who mistook revenge for honor, and blood lust for tradition.

Smita made a sound, sorrow bubbling up from her lips. The bathroom went blurry, and she dropped the mug into the bucket, the water splashing onto her feet. She rested her forehead against the bathroom wall and sobbed. She cried for so long that after a while, her outrage at Meena's fate tipped over into the deep sorrow for the confused, fearful twelve-year-old child Smita herself had once been, the resurrection of a sorrow that she had spent years beating back.

She felt lighter when she emerged from the shower, as if her tears had washed away some of the pain she had been carrying around. She dressed and, with a quick glance in the mirror, left her room. She walked swiftly down the hallway and knocked on Mohan's door before she could change her mind.

"Hi," she said, when he answered. "Can I come in?"

"Yes, of course," he said, letting her in and closing the door behind them.

CHAPTER TWENTY

———◼———

TWO DAYS AFTER *Abdul gifted me the mangoes, I packed a ladoo for him. I didn't place it in our tiffin box. Instead, I wrapped it in newspaper and carried it separately. At lunchtime, I put the sweet in my pocket and walked to my usual spot under the tree. Radha was still sick, so I ate alone. I sat with my back to Abdul, but still my neck got hot as I felt his eyes on me. After I finished my lunch, I walked to where Abdul was sitting. He rose to his feet immediately. I placed the wrapped ladoo on the ground near his tree. "For your kindness," I said to the tree trunk, my back to him. "The mangoes were very sweet."*

He replied, but the blood was rushing to my head and it drowned out his words. I walked quickly back into the factory. The old woman sitting at the machine next to me saw the sweat on my face. "Ae, chokri," she said to me. "Are you taking sick?"

She did not know how correct she was. I was sick, but this was a sickness of the heart.

Every day after I gifted him the ladoo, *Abdul and I began to find a way to talk without words. Sometimes, he would sing a love song while working that I knew was meant for my ears. Sometimes, I dropped a chocolate on the ground between our two trees on our way back from lunch. When Abdul returned to his seat, he would open the wrapper and pop the candy into his mouth, his eyes briefly meeting mine. And every evening, he would walk home behind me, remembering to stay a good distance away.*

Then, one day as I finished using the outdoor latrine, he was waiting for me. He pretended to tie his shoelaces as I passed by. "I am working overtime next Sunday," he whispered. "Maybe you can apply, too?"

I applied for the overtime shift the same day.

ONLY A FEW *of us were working that Sunday, so the foreman shuttered half the room and made us crowd together in the other half. As we looked for a seat, Abdul took the spot at the machine next to mine. Nobody noticed but me.*

At first, we were so excited to sit next to each other that we stole glances every few minutes. But then the work picked up, and we had to concentrate on our consignment. Sweat ran down our faces, but we couldn't stop to wipe it off. For six hours I worked, my body stiff with heat and fear. My heart was singing like a transistor radio, and I was afraid that everyone there would hear it play Abdul's name. But when I looked up, no one was watching. Everyone was busy meeting their quota.

I left work that evening with a small group of women, but one by one, they got off the main road and went toward their home village. When it was only me, I stopped and looked over my shoulder. Abdul was alone, also. He hurried to catch up with me, but walked on the other side of the narrow road, close to the ditch. From there, he called out, "Your name is Meena! I know."

My heart was fluttering. I pulled my dupatta closer to my face.

"My name is Abdul. You must be remembering?"

I didn't reply.

"I am from Birwad. My father is dead. I live with my ammi and my younger brother."

A man came toward us on his bicycle, and Abdul stopped talking. After he had passed, Abdul said, "Please don't take this the wrong way. I want to tell you, you are very beautiful."

I turned my head away.

"I don't mean any insult. I have great respect for you. I see how kind you are, how you help other people at work. Please. I am not like other men."

I said nothing.

"Who is in your family? Other than your sister? Radha, isn't it?"

I kept quiet. Then, like the rains during the monsoon, the angry words poured out of my mouth. "I have two brothers. Who will give me a thrashing if they find out I am talking to a Muslim man."

He kept quiet for so long, I thought that maybe he had disappeared into the fields on either side of us. I turned my head slightly to take a look. He was still walking, with his head bowed. Then, he looked up and our eyes met. His eyes burned hot, like the earth beneath our feet. "What difference does that make?" he demanded. "We are both Hindustani, no? The same Mother India has given birth to all of us, isn't it?"

His voice was not angry. Rather, it was sad, like the music from a flute playing alone at night. But in that one minute, my whole life changed. His words cut open a belief I had held my whole life, but when I looked inside, there was nothing there. "This is not what I think," I said. "It is what my brothers believe."

A man and a little boy came toward us from the opposite direction, and we stopped talking again. "Salaam, how are you?" Abdul said to them as they passed, and the father nodded. I knew we were getting nearer to the side road that led to his village, and I slowed down. When the man and child were a good distance away, Abdul said, "Look to your right. There is a little road there and it leads to the river. If you wish, we can go there for a few minutes and talk in peace. No one will see us there."

My heart was tight with fear. What had I done, to let this man think that

I was the kind of woman who would go to the river with a stranger? I prayed for the earth to swallow me whole then and there.

"Meena ji," Abdul said, "please don't take offense. I know your good character. I am only asking this because I wish to share what is in my heart."

I walked faster, wanting to get away.

"Please. Even if you refuse my request, please don't be angry at me. I mean no disrespect. I would sooner disrespect my ammi than to disrespect you. Please believe me."

I held my silence and kept walking. I walked past the little road where he had asked me to turn right. Soon, I thought, he would give up and I would make my way home alone.

Home. I saw the four of us at dinner later that night: Radha, angry because she had been stuck at home all day. Arvind, drunk as always. Govind, complaining nonstop about this and that. I saw us in that sad house, eating food that Radha and I provided, having to endure Govind's insults and abuse. Govind, who would never forgive Radha and me for defying his orders. I felt the full weight of his darkness.

I stopped. I turned around and walked back until I reached the small side road that led to the river. Abdul made a small, joyful noise, but I ignored him.

And then, without looking at him, I turned onto that dusty road and walked into my rise and fall.

CHAPTER TWENTY-ONE

———✳———

MOHAN HAD SUGGESTED that they drive to the seaside. Walking bare-foot in the sand, the wind steady in her face, Smita felt free, as though she had more in common with the birds on this beach than with the woman who had sobbed in her bathroom a couple of hours earlier. "Thank you for this," she said.

"Of course," Mohan said.

"How come it's so quiet here?" Smita asked, looking around the beach. "I thought it would be teeming with people, like every other place in India."

"Oh, they will come when it gets dark," Mohan said. "All the couples wanting to do hanky-panky."

She laughed, watching Mohan's face, translucent in the orange light. His shirtsleeves were rolled up to his elbows, and his feet were as brown as the sand. "Can we sit for a moment?" she said.

"Sure." They climbed up away from the water and sat on their haunches, staring at the sun setting into the sea, listening to the mesmerizing sound of the waves washing away the memories of the day.

Smita gave a start of surprise as pellets hit her back. She spun around. Three young urchins were perched behind a boulder, giggling and snickering as they threw small stones at her. "Kissy-kissy," one said, contorting his face, wiggling his hips and pursing his lips. He lifted his arms in an exaggerated pantomime of an embrace. His performance was so hyperbolic that despite her annoyance, Smita laughed. But this only emboldened the youngest child, who stooped to pick up another stone. Mohan rose to his feet and raised his hand in a mock threat. "*Saala* idiot!" he roared. "You want me to call the police?"

The boys scattered almost immediately, but their laughter signaled how lightly they took Mohan's threat. When they were a safe distance away, they looked back and made a kissing sound. But when Mohan took a step toward them, they fled.

He turned to her. "Sorry," he said. "They meant no harm."

"Mohan," Smita said, "you don't have to apologize for everything that happens in India, you know?"

He stood uncertainly for a moment, then sat back down. They continued looking at the slow descent of the sun into the water, turning the waves orange and gold. There were more people at the beach, couples and children appearing, the women in their saris squealing as the water tickled their bare feet.

"It never gets old," Smita said. "No matter how many times one sees a sunset, it's always as beautiful as the first time. Why do you suppose that is?"

Mohan began to give her a laborious, detailed explanation about human evolutionary genetics and other subjects she barely understood. She turned her head to hide her smile. He really was a science nerd.

Her stomach growled without warning, and he stopped midsentence. "Sorry," she said, making a rueful face. "Go on."

"No, it's okay. I forgot that we didn't have lunch today. We should head back."

"That sounds good, actually," she said. "I want to get to bed early tonight so I can be ready tomorrow morning when Anjali calls to tell us what time to be in court."

Mohan held out his hand to help Smita up. His skin felt warm and slightly damp. They made their way to the car and just before getting in, Smita looked back at the sea one last time. And as she did so, she had a strange thought—*I will never see this beach again.*

THREE FAMILIES HAD arrived earlier in the day, so the dining room at the motel was noisier than the previous two nights. Which was why Smita didn't know that Anjali had called until she reached for her phone after dinner. "Oh shit," she said. "I have a missed call from Anjali." She gestured toward Mohan's glass. "You stay and finish your beer."

Smita stepped outside to phone Anjali. "You got my message?" Anjali said in greeting.

"What? No. I haven't listened to my messages yet."

"Well, there won't be a verdict this week. You may as well go back to Mumbai for a long weekend."

"You've got to be kidding," Smita said, her irritation rising. "I thought you said . . ."

"I said I'd let you know when we knew something." Anjali's tone was sharp. "I can't be responsible for the entire criminal justice system in this country."

"But what happened?"

"Who the hell knows? They just announced that the judge is going to be out of town until next week."

Smita pulled at her hair in frustration. She had spent a small fortune to get an expedited visa, left Shannon at the hospital in Mumbai, and there was yet another setback. She'd be stuck in India for at least another week. How long did Cliff expect her to stay? Surely, one of the Delhi-based correspondents was free to take over? At the same time, her heart sank at the thought of someone else writing this story. Not after what she'd sacrificed to get to India. Not after the connection she'd established with Meena.

"Hello? Can you hear me?"

"I'm sorry." Smita forced herself to focus. "Can you repeat that?"

"I said I will phone as soon as I know something next week."

Smita hung up and stood peering into the darkness, taking in the half moon and the silhouettes of the trees. It was a still, humid night, and the heat made her blouse stick to her back. She pulled it away from her skin, airing her body. Okay, she thought, trying to regroup, they would drive back to the Taj the next morning, and she would spend some time with Shannon, now that her surgery was behind her. Maybe she could catch a ferry from the Gateway and go to the Elephanta Caves for a few hours on Saturday morning. She hadn't been there since she was nine years old.

She turned and walked back into the dining room. Mohan was reading on his phone, but he looked up as she approached. "What time tomorrow?" he asked as Smita sat down.

"There's no verdict yet. The judge is apparently out of town. So no decision until next week."

"What?"

"Anjali advises we return to Mumbai and await her phone call."

Mohan was shaking his head before she was even finished. "That makes no sense. How can we be sure that we will reach the courthouse in time? It's at least a five- to six-hour drive. What if they call us that same morning?"

"I don't know," she said, irritably. "I can't think anymore. I—I don't want to be here for three days if there's no need. I mean, this place ain't exactly the French Rivera. I'd rather go back to Mumbai."

Mohan swore softly under his breath.

"What?"

"Nothing." He was silent for a minute. "It's just that I told Zarine Auntie I won't be back for a few days."

"So? You changed your mind. What's the big deal?"

"She has an old college friend visiting. The woman is staying in my room."

Smita sighed in exasperation. One more complication. This week had been nothing but a series of complications.

Mohan appeared to be oblivious to her annoyance. "Also, I was hoping we could check on my parents' house in Surat while we were here, *yaar*. After you were done with your interviews, of course. We are close enough."

"I thought they were in Hyderabad," she snapped.

"Kerala," he corrected absently. "And I said I wanted to visit the *house*, not them."

She scowled and he noticed. "What is it?" he asked.

She opened her mouth to tell him, but what could she say? Mohan had given up his vacation to accompany her to this godforsaken place. He had been generous and kind to her all week. He had every right in the world to want to go check on his family home without her being upset at him. "Nothing," she said. She bit the inside of her cheek as she thought. The prospect of sinking into her soft, luxurious bed at the Taj after a nice hot shower seemed dimmer with each passing moment. But Mohan was right. Driving back from Mumbai in time for the verdict was much too dicey.

"So how would this work? You'll go to Surat while I'm here?" *Stuck here without a car*, she thought miserably.

"No, don't be silly, *yaar*," Mohan said. "You're more than welcome to go with me."

"No thank you," she said.

Mohan rolled his eyes. "Oh, come on, Smita. You know I'm not going to leave you here alone for three days. Okay, forget it. I don't have to go to Surat. Just let me know what you want to do."

"I don't want you to change your plans because of me."

"Smita—honestly, it doesn't matter." He got up, ignoring her look of surprise. "I'm going to the loo. Can you do two things while I'm gone?"

"What?"

"Order me a chocolate ice cream when the waiter comes. And two, make up your bloody mind about what we are doing."

When he returned, she said, "How far from Surat to the courthouse?"

"Maybe an hour or an hour and a half, tops. Depends on traffic."

"Well, that decides it. We'll go to Surat. I'll go with you. It's the only sensible thing to do."

CHAPTER TWENTY-TWO

———◆———

THERE WAS A big tree near the river where Abdul told me to go. Two large branches extended over the water, and Abdul sat on one branch while I sat on the other. Nobody else was around. At first, I kept looking over my shoulder, afraid of someone approaching, but Abdul's manner was so respectful, I began to relax. He asked me question upon question: Who all lived in our house? What did Arvind and Govind do? How old was Radha? What did I like to do for fun? Then, he told me about himself: How his father died in a truck accident when he was five. How he learned to do the tailoring work to support his ammi and younger brother. The way he talked about them, the softness that came into his eyes, told me that he was a man of good character.

After a few minutes, he slapped his forehead and said, "In all this excitement, I nearly forgot." He jumped off the tree branch and removed a small Cadbury chocolate bar from his pocket. "This is for you," he said. "Sorry, it is all melting." He sat back down on the branch after handing it to me.

I felt shy again when I took the chocolate from him. I thought maybe I should take it home for my Radha, but he looked so eager for me to eat it that I opened the silver wrapper. "Will you take some?" I said, offering it to him.

"Ladies first," he said. "I will take a piece only after you eat."

No man in my life had ever asked me to eat first. My mother served my father before any of us. We always served our brothers first. Maybe in these Muslim families, they did things upside-down? I took a bite of the chocolate. "Now you?" I said, and he smiled and asked me to break off a small piece for him. I was grateful for this courtesy. Abdul was a good man, but I was not ready to risk the wrath of God by having a Muslim take a bite of my chocolate.

We sat on the low branches, swinging our legs as if we were children again. I thought that perhaps I had never felt so happy in my life. Abdul was telling me about his younger brother when I heard myself say, "Why did you ask me to come here?"

"Because I am thirsty to talk to you. All day at work, I watch you, and I see how you take over the job of the old lady sitting next to you when she falls behind on her quota. I see how you give extra food to your sister. I know your good heart."

My face burned with shame at the thought of him having watched me so closely. Suddenly, I was afraid. I must leave at once, I thought. Before someone comes and catches us. Before he makes another indecent remark.

"Meena," Abdul said, "I have no bad intentions toward you. Please do not misunderstand me."

"You just insulted me by speaking so familiarly, but . . ."

"Insulted you? If loving you is an insult, then I insult my ammi. Then I insult my God."

"Ae, Bhagwan. What blasphemy is this?"

"Meena," he said, "don't you understand? I love you as much as I love my ammi. The way I love Allah."

"Then you must find a woman who, like you, also worships Allah."

He gave me such a long, sad look, it ruined my heart. "I wish. I wish I could find her. But it is too late. Because from the first minute I saw you, my heart was in your hands."

"How can it be so?" My voice was thin, angry. "How can a Muslim love a Hindu?"

He covered his face in his hands, as if he could not bear to look at me. They were the same color as Govind's. I thought: Are Abdul's hands Muslim? Are his fingernails Muslim? Is his skin? What made him a Muslim? What made me a Hindu? Just the family I was born into?

I wanted to share my thoughts with Abdul, but I could not find the words. I cursed my lack of schooling. I could not make the pretty words the way he could.

Abdul looked up and stared at the river. "I am a Hindustani first," he said quietly. "First, I worship my desh. Next, I worship my religion. I am not looking for a Hindu or Muslim or Christian girl. I just want a fellow Hindustani."

"You don't even know me," I said. "Bas, a few minutes of watching me work each day, and you think you understand me."

"I know your heart, Meena." His eyes shone like the pebbles in the river. "I know your good heart. My intentions are honorable. I want to bring the marriage proposal for you to your brothers."

In our caste, it is common for the bride and groom to meet for the first time on their wedding day. A matchmaker or a relative brings the match. Horoscopes are drawn. Inquiries about the family are made. The dowry amount is settled. Most importantly, the groom and bride are from the same caste. Only then are the wedding plans drawn. Abdul was talking as if he didn't know about any of these timeless traditions. Maybe in his religion the rules were different?

"My older brother would never allow such a match," I said. "Not only are you not from our caste, you are a Muslim. You don't know Govind. He will be insulted. When he gets angry, he acts like a wild water buffalo."

Then, Abdul said something that showed me that he was either a saint or a mad man. "What business is it of his, who you marry? I'm wanting to marry you, not him. So it's up to you to reject or accept me."

"You are pagal!" I yelled, jumping off the tree branch. "A total loss. I am a girl from a decent family. My brother is like my father to me. How can I marry without his permission?"

Abdul looked at me with his sad, hurt eyes. His sadness cut me so deeply, I wanted to cut him back. "Everyone knows you Muslims are not children of God. But my religion teaches me to respect our elders," I said, walking away.

He slid off the branch and began to follow me, but I yelled, "Don't take another step toward me! Do you understand what will happen to you if I tell anyone how you insulted me?"

He stopped. "I meant no harm. Please hear me out."

But I didn't. I ran down the road and back to the main path. I ran almost the whole way until I reached our house.

It was only when I went to sleep that I allowed myself to remember Abdul's hands. And once again, I tried to solve the puzzle—what exactly made him a Muslim? I imagined myself examining a long row of hands. How would I know which ones were Muslim?

And even if I did, would I pick the Hindu hands?

CHAPTER TWENTY-THREE

———■———

IN THE MORNING, Smita got to the dining room first. She waited, rebuffing the waiter's repeated attempts to get her to place her order. She was debating whether she should call Mohan when she saw him hurrying in. He was carrying his car keys. "What's up?" she said. "You went out this morning?"

"Yah." Mohan's face was sweaty. "I went to the market to pick up a few things."

After breakfast, Smita fetched her suitcase and met Mohan in the parking lot.

Mohan popped open the car trunk. There were three large cloth sacks, containing sugar, dal, and rice. "Are we taking food to Surat?" she asked. "So much for just a few days?"

"No," he said. "These are for Meena and Ammi."

"Mohan," she began, "you know I can't do this. I looked away the other day when you gave Ammi cash. But as a journalist, I can't pay for stories. As sorry as I feel for them, it's unethical for me to take them gifts."

"So, don't do it, *yaar*," he said softly. "You're not the one doing anything, right? But *I'm* not a journalist. I'm just a . . . concerned citizen."

They continued staring at each other, and then Smita looked away. "Okay," she said. She walked toward the door on the passenger side.

"Really?" Mohan said. "You're giving in that easily?"

"Yup," she said as she slid into the car. "I know when I've lost an argument."

"HELP ME CARRY the sacks in?" Mohan asked when they got to Meena's house.

"I can't. It's unprofessional. I can't have them think that these are gifts from me."

Mohan took a swig from his now-warm can of Coke. "Do you know how insulted they will be if they feel your displeasure?"

"You see how complicated this is getting? This is why I didn't think buying them food was a good idea."

As Mohan carried the groceries into Ammi's house, Smita walked toward the clearing between the two huts, her eyes drawn to the burnt hovel. It looked blighted, a black heap that stood like an insult against an innocent blue sky. Given the ferocity of the fire, it was surprising that there was anything left of the structure.

Meena emerged from the hovel. She stood at the entrance, her left hand on her hip, her right hand shading her eyes from the sun as she peered at Smita. Behind the hut, the tall wild grasses moved lightly in the breeze, a contrast to Meena's stillness. The next minute, Meena's face flooded with recognition, and she broke out in a startled smile. Even from this distance, Smita could see the awful, irregular geometry of Meena's face as past and present, normalcy and deformity, beauty and monstrosity, collided.

"Hello," Smita said. "I hope we are not intruding."

Meena took Smita's hand in both of hers and held it. "Didi," she said. "I'm so happy to see you. What brings you back so soon?"

Meena's scarred hands felt rough against her own. "I wanted to talk to you a little bit more," Smita said. "And Mohan wanted to drop off a few things for Ammi. For you and Abru, too." She looked around. "Where is your little one?"

Meena pointed toward the other hut. "With her grandmother."

"I see," Smita said, unsure of whether to enter Ammi's hut or wait for Mohan to emerge. As she hesitated, Abru came out. She was holding Mohan's index finger with her right hand and sucking her left thumb as she tottered beside him. Mohan took short steps as he tried to match his strides to the little girl's.

Meena inhaled sharply. "*Ae*, Bhagwan," she murmured. "She thinks he is her father. He is the first man who has entered our home since she was born."

Mohan got down on his haunches to talk to Abru. He whispered something to her, and Abru stared back with her big dark eyes. After a moment, Mohan rose, as if to walk away, but Abru reached out for him with her hand and gave a wordless cry.

"Look at her," Meena said, her tone incredulous. "Just like—" She fell silent. Mohan had picked up Abru and was approaching them. He was making funny snorting noises as he rubbed his nose against her belly. The girl giggled helplessly.

A lump formed in Smita's throat. Abru looked like a child transformed, with no indication of the sad, forlorn girl who had clung to her mother a few days before. Smita had been so busy with her interview that she had paid the most cursory attention to Abru. How little attention the child had required to come to life. Smita filled with regret at having protested Mohan's generosity. What harm would it do for her to look the other way while Mohan dropped off a few groceries? The professional codes of American journalism had no bearing on the lives of people like Meena. Why had it not occurred to her to alleviate Meena's suffering in the most basic of ways—with food that would outlast their visit; or by playing with a child who was so clearly starved for attention? She admired Mohan for how quickly and correctly he had read the situation.

Mohan stood before her, still holding Abru. "You want to hold her?"

Smita had no choice but to take the little girl in her arms. How light the child felt, her bones as hollow as a bird's. She imagined Abru was light even by Indian standards. Could this be the reason why the girl wasn't speaking yet, due to malnourishment? Smita remembered how her mother used to send milk and eggs home each day with the sweeper who cleaned their Mumbai apartment, so that the woman could feed her children a protein-rich diet. How Papa used to buy ice cream for the street urchins whenever they went to Chowpatty Beach, instead of giving them money. "How much does she weigh?" she asked and then regretted the question as she watched shame infuse the younger woman's face.

"I'm not sure," Meena murmured. "Anjali took Abru to the doctor a few months ago. She gave us a list of powders to help her gain weight. But . . ." Her voice trailed off, but Smita found it easy to fill in the blanks. No money for the supplements and no ability to earn any.

Smita cleared her throat. "Will you return to the factory someday?" she asked as gently as she could. "After, you know, Abru is a little older?"

"There is no factory. The owners closed it after the union strike." Meena's voice was bitter. "They say that the building is just sitting empty. We heard that they moved the whole business to another *desh*, where they pay people less money than us."

Smita nodded. It was an old story—capital chasing labor to an even poorer country. Most likely, they had left India to move to Cambodia or Vietnam. Or maybe they had relocated to a more impoverished part of India. "Do you remember who gave you this news?" she said. "Was it Anjali?"

For the first time since she'd met Meena, the woman looked cagey.

"It was a message. From my sister. She got away from her husband's house to use a telephone after she heard about my lawsuit. She found the number for Anjali's office and left a long message for me."

"You've been in touch with her?" Smita asked sharply.

"No, no, no, Didi. How could I? Radha didn't leave a number. *Bas*, there was just that one phone call."

Smita nodded, then ducked to prevent Abru from tugging at her hair. The child lurched silently toward Mohan. "I think she wants you," Smita called, and Mohan hurried back to them, taking Abru from her arms. The girl grabbed Mohan's sunglasses and twirled them in her hand.

Smita turned laughingly toward Meena but was horrified to see that the younger woman was crying. "Forgive me, Didi." Meena brushed away her tears. "What to do? These tears are traitors. They fall in times of sorrow and of happiness. Today, they come from happiness. Your husband has drawn laughter from my daughter's lips. May God bless both of you with many children of your own."

"What else did your sister say?" Smita asked.

"Mostly she was calling to let me know she was sorry."

"Sorry?"

"For dragging me to the factory job against my wishes. Because I only went to protect her."

"Because that's where you met Abdul?"

"Yes. At first, we managed to hide it from Radha. But once she found out, she begged me to stop my romance." Meena looked into the distance. "Then, it was my turn to be defiant."

"Did she . . . was she the one who told your brothers?"

Meena shook her head. "She would never betray me. My Radha." Suddenly, she slapped herself on the cheek. "No, I was stupid enough to tell my brothers myself. Because once love blossomed between Abdul and me, we did not want to hide it, Didi. We were so proud of our love.

That is how unworldly we were. Abdul begged me to inform them myself, before the news reached them."

"Do you mind if we sit?" Smita gestured toward the rope cot outside Ammi's hut. "And I will take some notes?" Mohan, she saw, had gone back inside Ammi's hovel.

The two women sat side by side. "So many times I wonder, did I make a mistake telling Govind about Abdul?" Meena said.

"Why did you? Since he hated Muslims so much?"

Meena's eye was cloudy as she stared ahead. "Because love had softened my heart, Didi. Abdul's kind nature made me kind. I was happy, so I wanted to share my happy with others. At night, I would look at Govind's tired face, and my heart would ache at how miserable he looked. I would remember how much he had loved me when we were young. It was as if my love for Abdul made me see other people's pain. But it also made me blind to the evil in the world. Do you understand my meaning?"

"I'm not sure," Smita said.

"Radha begged me not to tell. But I said, 'Little sister, Abdul and I wish to marry. How long can I keep this secret? Better he hears it from my lips than from someone else.'"

"So what happened?"

"Govind went to Rupal for advice. And Rupal called a village council meeting." Meena spoke in a monotone, her face immobile. "He had already punished Radha and me by forbidding all our neighbors from talking to us. Think of that, Didi. Friends we had grown up with, grandmothers who had known us from the moment of our birth, people we had celebrated and mourned with—none of them speaking to us. With a snap of his fingers, Rupal had turned us into ghosts."

"Everybody listened to the council?" Smita asked. "No one defied it?"

Meena looked shocked. "How can they do this? Anyone breaking his order would be punished themselves. Even if we went to the market, the shopkeepers wouldn't talk to us. *Bas*, we had to put the money down on the counter. They took whatever amount they wished. No bargaining, nothing. Oh, and we could not touch the fruits or vegetables. We must take whatever they gave us."

A long-forgotten memory sliced through Smita, its edges sharp. Her thirteenth birthday. Mummy and she coming home carrying a cake from the Taj and noticing Pushpa Patel coming from the opposite direction. Pushpa crossed the street to avoid talking to them. She forced herself to focus on Meena instead. "What did the council decide? About you and Abdul, I mean."

Meena stared at the ground for a long time. "They decided to test me," she said at last. "To examine if . . . if Abdul had defiled me." She swallowed. "Rupal wanted to do . . . a private test. An inspection. To. . . find out."

"Meena, if this is too hard . . ."

"No. It's okay, Didi. You put this in your newspaper. So that the world will know what is this Hindustan." She made an effort to look Smita in the eye. "I refused. I told Govind that if he allowed such shamelessness in his own home, I would walk into the river and drown myself."

"Did Rupal let up after that?"

"They had to come up with another test to check my purity. They ordered me to walk over hot coals. If my feet got burned, it meant I was not . . . a virgin."

Smita's mouth went dry. She longed for the water bottle she had left in Mohan's car. But there was no way to interrupt this interview to walk back to the vehicle. And unless she wanted to be laid up with dysentery for days, it was unthinkable to ask Meena for a drink of the dirty, unfiltered water in her home. She wished Mohan were around, but he was inside Ammi's house. She could hear the older woman's soft laughter in response something he was saying. "That's absurd," Smita said. "I mean, how could you possibly?"

"Rupal is a magic man, Didi. He had done this many times, no problem. But me?"

"So you refused?"

Meena began to cry. "They tied me. Tied me with a rope, like these Muslims tie a goat before they butcher it for Eid. They dragged me all the way to the village square, down the same road you just drove on. My own blood did this, Didi. And they forced me to walk on those white-hot coals. I took four steps only, and my feet smoked and crackled, just like those coals."

Smita felt sick to her stomach.

"I fainted, and they pulled me out of the pit," Meena said, in a low monotone. "Rupal had made his point. He made them believe that I was a soiled woman."

"And, and, your feet?"

In reply, Meena lifted one leg and crossed her ankle over her knee. She pulled back her foot so that Smita could see. Even though Meena's foot was dusty, Smita could see the raised burn marks. "Meena," she said. "I just can't . . . Oh God. I'm so sorry."

"It's nothing," Meena said. "These scars are nothing. It is these scars that gave me the four months of happiness with my Abdul."

"What do you mean?"

"They are what gave me the courage to run away."

Before Smita could respond, Mohan and Ammi came out of the house. Abru was holding Mohan's hand. "What's up?" Smita said, annoyed at the intrusion.

"Maybe it's time for us to take our leave," Mohan said in a tone that signaled to Smita that the interruption was not his idea. "We still have a long drive."

Smita gave Meena an apologetic look. "I'm sorry," she said.

"Yes, yes, you two go, *beta*," Ammi said, addressing Mohan. "This one here has nothing better to do than lie around in leisure, unlike us working folks. Ya Allah, if someone had told me that I have to work at my age, while this lazy cow lounges around at home, I would've asked Him to strike me down and bury my bones. What has the world come to?"

Smita caught Mohan's eye, imploring him to intervene. But he simply gazed back at her and she turned toward the old woman. "I'm sure it's difficult for Meena to work given her . . ."—she struggled to find the Hindi word for *disability*—"condition. But, Ammi, taking care of a child is also full-time work, no?"

She saw Mohan shake his head in warning.

The old woman's voice grew high-pitched and aggrieved. "Out of respect for you, I will keep my mouth shut, madam," she said. "Because we are beholden to you, I will not tell you what a snake I have let into my household." Ammi slammed her open palm against her forehead. "I must have some awful debts to repay. That's why I am the only unfortunate in this whole community to be saddled with a Hindu daughter-in-law. Whose lowlife brothers are the reason my son is dead. How much I begged my Abdul to not allow this travesty into our peaceful home. But no . . ."

As Ammi keened and beat her breast, Smita suspected that the theatrics were for their benefit and was reluctant to console her. Mohan, too, stood rooted in place, as if he was trying to figure out what to say or do, while Meena sat on the rope cot, staring down at her feet.

There was a sound, soft at first and then louder. Smita looked at Mohan, puzzled, then looked down. Abru, who was still holding Mohan's hand, was making a funny noise, moving her tongue rapidly against her upper lip, and it took Smita a moment to realize that she was imitating Ammi's keening. She fought to keep down her startled laughter but burst out laughing anyway. Ammi ceased her commotion abruptly. In that sudden silence, they all listened to the child and the half octave of sounds she was making. As it dawned on Ammi that she was being mocked, she rushed toward the girl, who turned and hid behind Mohan's legs. "*Oi*, Ammi," Mohan said in his most appeasing tone. "Let it go, *yaar*. The poor child is just having some fun."

Even though Mohan's tone was light, Ammi immediately lowered her hand. *India*, Smita thought, even as she was grateful to Mohan for his intervention. A country where a man of Mohan's stature could prompt immediate deference from a woman twice his age. She hated thinking of what Ammi might say or do to Abru once they left.

There was no way to resume her conversation with Meena. "I'll see you next week, okay?" she said gently. "After the verdict comes? We'll need to talk then."

Meena's face was unreadable. "As you wish."

"Listen," Smita said quietly, "this is going to be behind you, soon. Once your brothers are sentenced, you'll be able to . . . to make a fresh start."

Meena looked at her with a strange smile on her face. "What good will that do, Didi? Will it bring my Abdul back? Will it give me the use of my left hand? Or give me back my looks?"

"But you filed . . ."

Meena shook her head. "I told you. I pursued this case for her sake." She pointed to Abru.

Smita felt Mohan's presence by her side. "*Chalo, ji*," he said to Meena. "We will take your leave. But our prayers are with you."

Meena rose immediately from the cot. She covered her head with her sari, then bowed her head and folded her hands. "God's blessings to you, *seth*," she said. "May He bless you with ten sons."

Mohan laughed. "*Arre*, Meena *ji*, be careful with your prayers. I will have to work ten jobs to feed ten sons."

Meena kept her gaze toward the ground, but Smita could see her smile.

"*As-salamu alaikum*, Ammi," Smita said, as they walked past the old woman.

Ammi looked startled. "*Wa alaikum assalaam, beti*," the old woman replied. "Be well."

"HATS OFF TO you, *yaar*," Mohan said after they got in the car. "Where did you learn that Muslim greeting? I loved how casually you said it, too. Like it rolled off your tongue."

Smita shrugged. "Don't forget, I lived in this country for fourteen years."

"I know. But that was a long time ago, *dost*."

"True," she said.

"Hey. How come your family left India when you were a teenager?"

"I told you," she said. "My father got a job in America."

"It's an odd age to move, right?"

She shrugged. "I was happy to go."

"Why?"

"What do you mean, *why*? Who doesn't want to move to America?"

"I don't. I don't have the slightest desire."

Smita eyed him cautiously. "Okay."

Mohan looked as if he was about to say more but let the subject drop. "So, what did Meena say today?" he asked.

She told him about the coal pit. She described the raised, cordlike marks on Meena's feet.

And was gratified to see Mohan's hand tremble on the steering wheel when she was finished.

CHAPTER TWENTY-FOUR

———※———

AMMI IS IN *a good mood. It makes me sad to see what a sack of sugar and a bag of rice can do for her. To remember that if Abdul had lived, Ammi would not be working at her age. The plan had been for Abdul and me to send money home from Mumbai to Birwad each month so that Kabir could leave his mechanic's job and become a farmer. Then, after a few years, they would have shifted to Mumbai, also.*

I look out at the fields behind my house, overgrown with grasses taller than a man. Kabir would have enjoyed cutting down those grasses and taming that land. Now, it is simply a field of buried dreams. Sometimes, I play hide-and-seek with Abru in the grass and speak to the ghosts of the two brothers. Other than this, the short distance between Ammi's house and mine has become my country, my cage.

But today, talking to Smita has made a restless wind inside of me. Today, I want it to carry me away like a seed and plant me in new soil. What had Smita said? That after the judgment, I could make a fresh start. But even if

I were the kind of woman who could abandon Ammi, where would I go? Is there a place where my face will not cause babies to burst into tears? What foolish employer would hire a woman such as me? No, there is nowhere for me to live other than in the place where my life ended.

"So much food," Ammi says. "God bless that boy. Maybe I will invite Fouzia for dinner tonight."

My heart twists at those words. Fouzia is Ammi's childhood friend. During the first four months of my marriage, before the calamity came, when our house shook with laughter and Ammi's eyes landed like butterflies on her sons' faces, Fouzia used to come over each afternoon to take tea with Ammi. Fouzia was like a second mother to Abdul and Kabir, but her real son has prohibited her from visiting us, afraid that our bad luck will spread to his home. Mohan babu's gift has made Ammi briefly forget how all of Birwad has shunned us. Fouzia will not step into our misfortune.

Then, her face gets dark with anger as she remembers how alone she is, stuck with a daughter-in-law she hates and a granddaughter whose resemblance to her son is a thorn in her eyes. But she recovers. "More food for us," she says. "That Fouzia eats like an elephant. Always did." She begins to plan dinner, rubs her belly as if the meal is already in her. Abru looks at her carefully, ready to run away from her if scolded, ready to run into her arms if called. Now, Ammi is promising Abru some kheer, and from this I know that Mohan babu must have also given her some money. How else would she be able to afford the milk for such a treat?

Perhaps Ammi will take Abru with her to the marketplace, and I will have the peace to do the only thing that brings me peace—dream of my Abdul. It is only in my dreams that I can still see his face properly. He is beginning to fade from me, like the moon rising higher in the sky. I am ashamed of myself for such faithlessness. What kind of wife forgets her husband?

I HAD WANTED to tell Smita about how my burnt feet led me to Abdul.

If Rupal had not forced me to walk on those hot coals, if my own blood had not roped and dragged me into the village square, maybe I would have listened to Govind's warnings about marrying outside our faith. Maybe my fear of God would have overshadowed my love for Abdul. Because a woman can live in one of two houses—fear or love. It is impossible to live in both at the same time.

But even as my brothers tied and dragged me like a dumb beast, I knew I was not an animal. As the smoke rose from my hissing feet and just before I fainted, I said to myself: I am a woman who has walked on fiery coals and lived.

For the next two weeks, I remained at home with Radha and Arvind. Govind left strict instructions with Arvind to make sure I didn't leave the house. Every day Radha put ointment and cool rags on my feet. My whole body burned with fever. Rupal came one afternoon to check on me, but Radha chased him out of the house with a broom. I smiled when she told me. Little Typhoon, I used to call her when she was little.

Radha helped me run away.

When the fever finally left my body and I began to speak again, I told her the truth: If Govind forced me to marry some someone else, I would take rat poison and kill myself. Radha cried the first time I spoke of this. "Why, Didi?" she yelled. "Why do you want to marry that Muslim fellow? He will take four wives and have twelve children. Why do you choose such a life?"

"Abdul? Take four wives?" I laughed. "He's not like that, Radha. He wants us to be a modern couple. Like, like . . . Shah Rukh Khan and Gauri."

Radha blinked. Shah Rukh Khan was Radha's favorite actor. She was mad about him. "But, Didi," she said at last, "that's different. They are living in Mumbai. We are stuck here in this tiny village. Govind dada will never allow this marriage."

Love against fear.

In the end, Radha's love for me proved stronger than her fear. She did what I asked: We took some of the money Govind gave us for household expenses and bought Arvind a bottle of daru. For his birthday, Radha said. "Save this for dinnertime," she told him. Of course he drank the full bottle before it was noon. When he was passed out, lying with his mouth open, she helped fit me into the slippers she had made, with layers of leaves and cotton wool at the bottom. The cotton stuck to the ointment on my cracked feet, but I did not complain. Like thieves, we crept out. I took one last look at the house I had helped build with my sweat. But there was no time to linger.

Even in the special slippers, walking on the ground was like walking on the coals. I was sweating so badly as we walked that I was sure the fever was coming back. Instead of the shortcut through the village, we took the main road. Some people we passed stopped and stared; others spat on the ground and turned their backs to us. But because of Rupal's command, nobody talked to us or asked where we were going. Maybe they were hoping we were leaving the village forever.

A truck slowed down, and a strange man asked if we wanted a lift, but we looked straight ahead and kept walking, too scared to reply. Walking. Walking. I felt every step I took, cried out with every stone my foot touched. I felt the fire of the earth under my feet. I didn't care. Soon, I could not feel anything but my heart. It banged thum-thum-thum like a tabla; and after a while, it was the only thing I heard. The birds in the trees fell silent. The cars going by disappeared. Even Radha's voice drifted away. All I was hearing was my heart song. It was singing Abdul's name. It was reminding me that with every step I took, I was closer to turning my heart over to his care.

I WALKED FOR a long time on feet that were burnt black. Just when they were so numb that I wondered if I should crawl on my knees, we reached Birwad.

When we got there, Radha refused to enter. "This is where we part, Didi," she said through her tears.

Even for me, Radha would not enter a Muslim village. That was when my heart stopped singing. What had I imagined? That after marriage, Radha would visit me and my husband. That Abdul and I would return to seek Govind's forgiveness and that slowly, Govind would come to see Abdul's honorable character and give us his blessings. I saw us all sitting together, my old family and my new, in the home that I had built. I imagined Abdul teasing and joking with my sister who was now his sister. Not this. Never this. Not

that my Radha, my sister who I had raised like my child, would already be
turning into stone, a polite stranger. Love and fear. At this moment, they
were holding hands and becoming one.

"Sister," I said, "you will not come in with me?"

She shook her head. "No, Didi." Her eyes shone with tears. "It is hard
enough living in our village," she said. "But if they find out I entered this
place." She shuddered. "Govind will cut my throat."

Now, only now, did I understand what she had risked. What danger I had
put her in. I stared at her in silence. Then, I folded my hands as if I was in the
temple and she was a deity. "In a million lifetimes," I said, "I cannot repay
my debt."

She pulled down my folded hands and fell into my arms. "Didi," she
sobbed. "Didi, you take care of yourself. God be with you." And then, just
when I was thinking this was good, we could stay like this this forever, she
pulled out of my arms and ran down the road from which we had come.

I watched her for as long as I could. "Radha!" I called, wanting to see her
delicate face one more time, but she did not turn around. I watched until she
became a dot, smaller than the stones at my feet. I watched until she disappeared into my past and became a sacred memory.

I turned around to face whatever awaited me, even while thinking that I
had made a terrible mistake, that if my feet were not so damaged, maybe I
could walk back to my village.

There was a commotion in the distance. I looked up to see Abdul running
toward me, calling my name, running zigzag, his arms opened wide, like the
protective wings of a giant bird. A big smile on his face that called me home.

CHAPTER TWENTY-FIVE

———————

Smita stared at the tall iron gates of Mohan's family home. She had not expected the house behind the gates to be this stunning, couldn't have imagined the lovely stucco walls, the red tiled roof, or the lush front yard with the flowering bushes. This looked like a house in Beverly Hills, rather than in small-town India.

"Namaste, *seth*," the old watchman said as he hurried toward the car. "To what do we owe this honor?" He peered in, his gray eyes appraising Smita.

"*Ho*, Ramdas," Mohan said. "What news? How have you been?"

The old man grinned as he straightened. "*Theek hu, seth*," he said. "Thanks to God."

Mohan nodded. "And the wife and children?"

"Everybody is well, by the grace of God." Ramdas bent and looked into the car again. "And who is this young memsahib?"

"Ah, this . . ." Even without looking at him, Smita knew Mohan was flushing. "This is my friend. Smita is her name. She has some work nearby. And so I offered her our home. Just for a few days. Until Monday or so."

Ramdas folded his hands. "Namaste, memsahib," he said with supreme dignity. "Welcome."

IN THE ENORMOUS living room, Smita took in the beautiful Indian artwork on the walls, the expensive furniture, the marble floor. So this was what a diamond merchant's home looked like. As she stood examining one of the paintings, she could hear Ramdas and Mohan chatting in the kitchen. The *chowkidar* appeared before her. "You'll take something, memsahib? Coca-Cola? Tea? Lime water?"

Smita didn't want to offend him by asking whether they boiled their drinking water. As if he'd read her mind, Ramdas smiled. "Or *pani*? Filtered water, we are having," he said.

She nodded. "Thank you. But I can help myself."

"You take rest, memsahib. I will bring." Ramdas looked around. "Has young sahib shown you the guest bedroom?"

"Not yet."

Ramdas picked up her suitcase. "I will show," he said in a proprietary tone that told Smita he had worked for Mohan's family for a long time. "This way."

Her room opened up to a small garden. A single handloom print hung on the wall behind the bed.

Ramdas pulled out a small stool and stood on it to turn on the air conditioner. "Room is a little hot," he said. "When they are away, I keep everything shut off. No point in wasting money."

"You stay here by yourself? When they are gone?"

"Yes, memsahib. The cook travels with them. But I stay here to watch the house. Too many ruffians around these days. Not good to leave a house unoccupied for too long."

She heard the protectiveness in his voice. "And your own family?" she asked. "Do they—"

"They are back in the village. Wife and two children. Big *seth* built a house for them many years ago. They are comfortable there."

"How often do you get to see them?"

"When big *seth* and his wife are away, I come and go as I like." Ramdas suddenly looked sheepish. "I was telling Mohan *seth*, just now only—I was planning on leaving for my home village today or tomorrow. My younger brother's boy is getting married. Naturally, as the elder, my presence is required. But if you wish for me to remain to serve you, I will cancel."

It took her a minute to realize that Ramdas was asking for her permission. "Oh," she said, "that's between you and Mohan. But we will manage fine, I'm sure."

Ramdas appeared relieved. But the next moment, his face fell. "But what about your meals?" he said, as if a new obstacle had presented itself.

"I'm sure we'll be okay. Mohan must know of some nearby restaurants."

He bowed his head. "If you are sure. But . . . let me fetch you the glass of water, memsahib."

SMITA HAD INTENDED to take a short nap, but when she awoke, the clock said 5:00 p.m. She got up and, in her bare feet, went to look for Mohan. She found him on the living room sofa, snoring softly, the magazine on his chest rising and falling with each breath. She stood watching him for a moment, then turned away. But her knee knocked against the crystal fruit bowl on the table nearby, and the sound woke him. He sat up almost immediately, running his hand through his hair.

"I guess we both zonked out," she said.

"*We?*" He cocked his right eyebrow. "I already dropped Ramdas off at the train station and stopped to buy a few provisions. I must've dozed off for less than ten minutes."

"Sorry, *yaar*," she said, adopting his favorite slang.

"Be careful," Mohan said. "Or else you'll turn into a *pucca* Indian." He stifled a yawn. "Listen, I thought we would eat at home tonight," he said. "We can make pasta if you want."

Pasta? After the spicy Indian dinners they'd been eating all this time, Smita felt as if she'd give her right arm for pasta.

CHAPTER TWENTY-SIX

———

THE SUNDAY I *found out that I was pregnant, Abdul had gone to the factory to work an extra shift. Soon after he left that morning I vomited, just as I had the previous night. I blamed it on the food I'd eaten the night before. I went to my cot to lie down and didn't wake up until Ammi came in. "Kya huya?" she said. "It's eleven in the morning, and you are still sleeping?"*

I forced myself to rise. "Sorry, Ammi," I said. "I'll make your breakfast."

"Shoo—" She waved me away. "Forget breakfast now. I had a chapati with ghee at my house."

Sick as I was, I took pride in Ammi's words. With the wages Abdul and I were earning, we were giving Ammi a good life. Now, she could afford to spread ghee on her chapati.

"Sorry, Ammi," I said again.

But my mother-in-law was staring at me with her eyes narrowed. "What is the matter with you? You look unwell."

"God only knows. I threw up after dinner last night. And this morning I did so again."

"Are you with child?"

As soon as Ammi said the words, I knew it was so. I remembered now that I had not been visited by my menses the month before.

"It's not that, Ammi," I lied. "I think I ate something rotten last night."

She nodded before telling me the reason she had come. She needed to borrow some sugar and rice to make kheer for her friend, Fouzia. "Take what you wish, Ammi," I said. "Our house is your house."

"But of course it is," she replied. "After all, this is my son's house, no?"

I had wished that Abdul's mother would be like a mother to me, that she would grow to love me the way Abdul loved both of us. My own mother had died when I was six, and she left in me a hunger as big as the sky. But as I watched Ammi go through my jars of sugar and rice, without even putting the lids back on properly, I knew that my mother-in-law would never make me her own.

As soon as Ammi left, though, I was filled with a joy more powerful than I had ever known. A baby. Our own baby. I looked around in wonder at our small, humble hut. I stared at my thin, brown body. I thought of Abdul's hands on my body, his lips on my lips. Out of our love, we had stitched together our baby. It was the oldest story in the world; it was the newest. Every single thing that I had lost in my own life, every motherless moment, I would make up for with my own child. I was laughing-crying at the miracle of this, at this second chance to take this crooked world in my hands and set it correct. "Ae, Bhagwan, Bhagwan, Bhagwan, I thank you for Your gift," I prayed. And then, feeling guilty, I chanted, "Ya Allah the Beneficent, thank you."

Another wave of nausea came over me, but I laughed. This was the first sacrifice for my child that I would make, in a long line of sacrifices. What was a little vomiting? What was the pain of childbirth, compared with the miracle of a new life? In the face of God's will, what was the wrath of my brothers, or the judgment of my former neighbors? Because this was God's

will. If He did not will it so, this would have never happened—and so soon
after our wedding. Because God lived in His heavenly castle, and not on
Earth, He looked for different ways to speak to us: through our dreams, in
the pictures made by clouds, by this announcement of new life. This little one
was God's messenger sent to us, proof that Abdul was right: We were the new
India. This little one would thread Abdul and me together forever: Hindu
and Muslim, man and woman, husband and wife. Forever.

I stood up; I paced; I sat down. The tiny hovel was choking me, my happiness leaping over its straw walls. My Abdul had built this home for us, and
for that reason, I loved it. But today it felt small, too small, to hold all my
joy, my hopes, my overflowing love. What should I do? Abdul was the first
person I had to tell, which was why I did not confirm Ammi's suspicion. I
wished Radha was here with me. But Radha had disappeared, as if Govind
had shoved her into a gunnysack and thrown her into the river. One month
after I ran away, he got her married to some old cripple. Abdul heard the
news from someone at the factory, but the man did not know the name of
her husband or that of the village where Radha now lived. My sister, my first
love, had disappeared from my life wholly.

Because I couldn't think of Radha, I forced myself to think of this new joy.
But how to pass the hours until Abdul came home, when each minute was a
pinprick, when I was aware of every heartbeat? How it beat, my heart. My
heart, and now, my baby's heart. And that thought calmed me down. I was
not wasting my time as I awaited Abdul's return. Rather, even as I lit the
stove to make myself tea, my body was doing its job—feeding my baby, building its bones. Even as I waited, I was not waiting at all. With every passing
minute, I was growing my baby. Our baby.

When Abdul came home that evening, I could tell that he was hungry and
tired. I looked at his face, so serious and beautiful, and I thought, Please
God, let my son look just like his father. In that moment, I was sure I was
carrying a boy.

He caught me looking at him and smiled. "You miss me?"

"Me? No, not at all," I said, smiling back at him.

He grabbed me by my waist. "Then why you're looking at me as if I'm a box of chocolate?"

I shook myself loose. "Eat your dinner," I said. "Mr. Chocolate."

As always, Abdul waited until I ate the first mouthful. Even then, this ritual felt fresh and new to me. Before our wedding, Abdul made me promise: Everything we did, we did equal. He wanted a wife, he said, not a maid. He only made one request—that I would take care of Ammi, just as he did. "Did Ammi eat?" he asked.

"I dropped off her dinner. Same as usual." I said. Every Sunday, Abdul and I ate alone in our house. The rest of the week, we cooked in Ammi's hut and took our meals with her and Kabir.

"I will stop by and see her after we are done here."

I took his hand. "Not tonight. I have some news."

"What?"

"You eat while the food is hot-pot. I will tell you afterwards."

He frowned. "Is it your brothers? Are they harassing you?"

"No, no." Then, I saw the worry in his eyes and felt sorry for him. "It's not that. It's good news."

"Good news? Arre, Meena, didn't anyone teach you? Bad news can wait. But good news you must share immediately. Tell me."

I placed one finger on my lips. "Shoo. I will tell after you finish eating."

A strange look came over Abdul's face. He stared at me while chewing his food. He swallowed. "Meena," he said, his voice sounding as if the food was stuck in his throat, "tell me now. Are you carrying our baby?"

I screamed and made a fist to hit him. "You spoiled my surprise!" I said. "How did you know?"

But Abdul was unable to speak. He sat looking at me, and then he began to cry. Suddenly, I was terrified. "Are you not happy?" I asked.

He got up and washed his hands. Then, he came up to me, took my face in his hands, and kissed my lips, my eyes, my nose, my forehead. "My wife," he whispered, "what a foolish question. Today is the happiest day in my life."

He sat next to me, rocking me like a baby, and I thought, Whatever Abdul does to me, he's doing to our baby. If he kisses me, he is kissing our son. If he rocks me, he is rocking our baby. *The thought made me shiver.* "Shall we go give Ammi the news?" I asked.

Abdul looked deep into my eyes. "Later," he said. "Tomorrow. Tonight, I want to be alone with my wife. And my daughter."

"Daughter?" I said. "I pray that it is a boy."

"It can be a boy or a girl—it makes no difference to me. I love the baby already because my wife made it for me."

"You helped," I said.

Abdul's eyes were bright. "Let me help some more," he said, and untied my sari.

CHAPTER TWENTY-SEVEN

SMITA LOOKED UP from the newspaper and wondered where the past two days had gone. It was a mellow Sunday morning, and she and Mohan were sitting on the patio, sipping tea and reading different sections of the *Times of India*.

What was Meena doing at this moment? Smita wondered. Was Ammi berating her for this reason or that, or had the groceries brought by Mohan cut some of the tension between them? How on earth did Meena spend her days? Was there even a radio in that dismal shack? Smita gazed at the lush garden around her—the fruit trees, the flowering bushes—and thought of Meena's barren patch of earth.

Mohan looked up from the newspaper and stretched lazily. He caught Smita's eye and smiled. She smiled back. *This is nice*, she thought. *I could get used to this.*

She sat up taller, bewildered by that complacent sentiment. She supposed it was a measure of how close a friendship she and Mohan had formed in the cauldron of a hectic, emotional week that such a thought had crossed her mind. They had already promised to stay in touch, but Smita knew how impossible that would prove to be. They would exchange emails for a few weeks; he would write a wry reminiscence that would make her feel briefly nostalgic. And then she'd shut her laptop and resume whatever task she was doing in New York.

If the verdict came the next day, as she hoped, they'd return to Mumbai by midweek, after she'd completed a few more interviews. Once back at the Taj, she would finish writing her story while Mohan spent time with Shannon at the rehab center. Smita had already resolved that she wouldn't fly home without trying to contact Chiku Patel. They had once been close friends; surely, he would not greet her with the hostility that his mother had. Maybe he could add some fresh perspective. Of course Chiku would defend his mother. But still . . . All she wanted was a plausible explanation for that day in 1996. Chiku had been thirteen at the time—old enough to remember.

Smita then remembered that she hadn't phoned Papa in several days. Ever since Mummy's death, she had done her best to call him regularly from wherever she was traveling. She glanced at her watch—it was nighttime in the US, the perfect time to reach him.

"More tea?" Mohan said, reaching for the pot.

Smita hesitated. She wanted to go inside the house and use her cell phone while Mohan was still in the garden. But it was so lovely right there. "Sure," she said. "Just a little bit more. But I need to make a quick call to my father before he goes to bed."

"Of course," Mohan said. "You can use the phone in the living room."

"That's okay," she said. "I can call on my cell."

"Whatever you wish." He stretched languidly. "What do you feel like doing today?"

The truth was, she was content to laze around and not leave the tranquility of the house. "Do you have stuff you need to do? Errands? Friends to see?" she asked.

"*Nahi, yaar.*" He smiled sleepily. "I just want to make sure you . . ."

"I'm happy to just hang out."

He laughed. "What an old couple we are."

She registered that Mohan had referred to them as a couple, but knew he meant nothing by it.

"What is it?" Mohan said after a moment. "You look upset?"

"You called me *old*," she said. "What girl wouldn't be upset about that?"

He laughed. "You're the last person who would care about something like that."

She got to her feet, pleased that he knew her well enough to understand that about her. "Well," she said, "I'll go call my father. See you soon."

"HI, PAPA," SMITA said. "It's me."

"*Arre, beta*, how are you? Why no phone call in several days? I have been going mad with worry."

Smita's heart sank. Despite Papa's reassurances that he was coping better with his grief, he had clearly slipped some. She had hoped that he had turned a corner. "I'm so sorry," she said.

"Ah, forget it. But tell me. Are you enjoying yourself? How is your holiday going?"

"Oh, it's just fantastic."

"And the weather in the Maldives?"

She would soon have to tell Papa the truth. The less she lied, the better off she'd be. And yet, hearing the eagerness in his voice, she heard herself say, "I tell you, Papa, it is just so wonderful. Blue skies, clear water, white sand. It's heaven on earth. It's like a perfect day today. I'm having a great time."

"*Accha?*" She could hear the lightness in her father's voice and was gratified.

But the next moment, Papa's worry resurfaced. "Listen, *beta*. You stay away from those cafés where the Western tourists hang out, okay? Those are the places that the terrorists target, you know?"

Smita's mind flashed to her visit to the Leopold Cafe. Was that really just around ten days ago? "Oh, Papa," she said, laughing. "The Maldives are pretty safe. Don't worry. I'm fine. In any case, we are hardly leaving the resort."

Papa told her about Alex's latest escapades and then about the dinner party he'd attended earlier in the evening. Even though he kept up a lively conversation, Smita's heart ached at the loneliness she heard in his voice. *He misses Mummy*, she thought. She knew how hard it was for him to attend parties by himself. She would go visit him soon after she got back.

"*Chalo*," her father said after a while. "This phone call must be costing you a great deal."

"It's not. Don't worry."

"Well, *beta*, to be honest, I'm pretty tired. That party was difficult for me, you know?"

"I know you miss her, Papa," Smita said. "I do, too."

Papa sighed. "What to do, Smita? She had everything but the gift of years. Nothing we can do. What cannot be cured must be endured."

They were quiet for a moment.

"Well, good night, my darling," he finally said. "*Khuda hafiz*."

"*Khuda hafiz*, Papa. You take care," she replied as she hung up.

SMITA LINGERED IN the bedroom for a moment. Should she call Rohit to ask him to check on Papa? *Not tonight*, she thought, turning to leave the room. Mohan was standing in the hallway, holding the newspaper in his hand. From the expression on his face, Smita knew that he had overheard at least part of her conversation.

Smita shifted from one foot to the other. "What're you doing here?" she said at last.

"I came in to make us more tea."

"Oh." There was a silence, painfully awkward, and Smita felt herself flush.

"How is your father?" Mohan said.

"Fine," she said cautiously. "Sounds like you heard part of my conversation."

"Yup. I heard. Something about you still being in the Maldives? Instead of in India?"

"Yeah, well, I didn't want to worry him."

"Why would he worry about you being in India?" And before she could think of an answer, Mohan added slowly, "Also, you said '*Khuda hafiz*' before hanging up."

"So what?"

"So . . . It's a Muslim greeting, right?"

The suspicion in his voice ignited her anger. "I don't appreciate you snooping on my conversation with my dad."

"Snooping? I was simply crossing the hallway to go toward the kitchen when . . ."

"Then you should've kept moving along."

Mohan's face turned red. "Excuse me? You're going to tell me how to behave in my own house? What I should do and not do?"

"I'll leave," Smita said immediately. "Just call me a taxi, and I'll leave. I don't have to take this."

Mohan stared at her, as if he was seeing her for the first time. "Smita, what is going on?" he said, bewildered. "What just happened? Why does your father think you're in the Maldives? Why are you lying to him? And to me?"

She shook her head, stiffening, unable to respond. Could she trust Mohan? Could she count on him to understand? And then she thought: *When has he been anything but kind and trustworthy?*

Still, she hesitated, her heart racing. She wiped her clammy hands on her pants, trying to slow down her thoughts.

"Smita?" Mohan said.

Then, relief nipped on the heels of her apprehension. Relief at the thought of untying the secret that had stayed knotted for over twenty years. She had carried the burden of a double life for as long as she could. Here, at last, was the thing she'd welcomed and dreaded—the end of the road.

"Okay," she said. "I'll tell you." She moved toward the living room couch.

Mohan followed her slowly and sat across from her. Smita's heart hurt at the wariness she saw on his face. "Who are you?" he said. "Why did you lie . . . ?"

She held up her hand to stop him. "I'm trying to tell you. I'm going to tell you."

She took a deep breath. "My birth name is Zeenat Rizvi. I was born a Muslim."

BOOK THREE

CHAPTER TWENTY-EIGHT

———— ✦ ————

SMITA AGARWAL WAS born at age twelve.

Before that, she was Zeenat Rizvi.

ZEENAT'S FAMILY LIVED in a large, airy flat in Colaba. Her parents had met in 1977 when Asif had gone to visit his college friend at his home in Hyderabad. Zenobia was the friend's first cousin, a gregarious girl who had immediately captured Asif's slightly melancholy heart. Upon his return to Mumbai, called Bombay back then, he wrote Zenobia passionate love letters. After a year of letters, Zenobia, knowing that her parents were determined to marry her off to a distant relative, left for Mumbai and eloped with Asif. A small scandal ensued until it was determined that the couple would live with Asif's parents while he finished his PhD.

If Asif's father thought it was strange that his son intended to be a scholar of Hindu history and religion, he never said. Perhaps he held out the hope that his only child would eventually come to his senses and

join him in the family construction business. Perhaps in the Bombay of
the 1970s it was still possible for a father to not worry too much about
such cultural hybridity. In any case, good fortune continued to favor
Asif. Zenobia proved to be loving and kind, and within a year of marriage had become an integral part of the Rizvi clan. Both his parents
doted on her. One of the happiest gifts of Asif's life was listening to his
wife and mother chatting away as they cooked in the kitchen while he
wrote his dissertation.

The apartment in Colaba, perhaps the most cosmopolitan neighborhood in the city, was a graduation gift from his father. Asif and
Zenobia, who were more than content to continue living with Asif's
parents, protested such extravagance, but the old man insisted. "It's
your money in the end, *na*, son?" he'd argued. "Who else am I going to
leave it to, the sweeper's son? At least I'll have the satisfaction of seeing
you enjoy part of your inheritance while I'm alive, isn't it?"

The Rizvis's first child, Sameer, was born after they had shifted
to the Colaba apartment. After Sameer's birth, Zenobia continued
to spend part of each day at her in-laws'. She'd bathe and dress her
son and leave for her in-laws' home by midmorning. "A child needs
his grandparents," she'd say, a wistfulness in her voice that only Asif
heard. Zenobia's parents had come around to the marriage, had even
visited them once in their new apartment, but still, the humiliation of
her elopement lingered.

Asif was hired as a professor at Bombay University soon after he
graduated. Some of his former professors had expressed unease at the
thought of a Muslim professor of Hinduism, but Asif had so distinguished himself as a doctoral student, that there was no real argument
against the hire. Also, Asif was no bearded, praying-five-times-a-day
mullah type. He was a modern, secular man and could hold his liquor.
He spoke disparagingly of Pakistan as a failed state and believed that
Kashmir belonged to India. It was easy to forget his provenance.

By the time Zeenat was born, two years after Sameer, her father had made a name for himself as a scholar. She grew up in a happy, close-knit family, distinguishing herself at school with her strong writing skills (a fact of which Asif was inordinately proud), popular with the neighborhood kids, protected from schoolyard bullies by Sameer, and secure in her parents' love. On weekdays, she'd come home from school to the small snack her mother had prepared for her, finish her homework, and then go to play with the other neighborhood children until she was called up for dinner. In the summer, there were trips to Goa and Ooty and Dharamsala.

When Zeenat was eight, her grandmother was killed when a tree limb fell on her during the monsoons. Asif's father was so brokenhearted that he sold his business, took to reading the Qur'an daily, and went to the *masjid* every evening. Asif and Zenobia tried getting him to move in with them, believing that their children might mend his broken heart, but he declined, politely at first, and then with increasing vehemence. "My place is here," he insisted, "in this house where I lived with my beloved."

A year later, he passed. The doctor wrote *Natural Causes* on the death certificate, but Asif knew the truth: his father had died of a broken heart.

Asif missed his parents terribly, when, six months later, his second book was published. In the past few years, his research had focused on Shivaji, the seventeenth-century Maratha warrior-king, who had fought so valiantly against the Mughals. Asif's book, *The Myth of Shivaji*, posited that the king's contemporary cultlike status among Hindus paralleled the rise of anti-Islamic sentiment in India. The book was published in 1994, the year after the Bombay riots, during which Hindus and Muslims had slaughtered one another following the demolition of the historic Babri Masjid by Hindus. Its publication proved to be timely. Asif Rizvi's star was ascendant; a leftist magazine in India ran an excerpt from the book. A few months later, a small college in Ohio invited him to its conference on the global rise of religious fundamentalism.

Still, other than a few of his colleagues, no one in their circle paid
much attention to what the professor-sahib wrote. Their upper-middle-
class Hindu neighbors remained friendly with the Rizvis, the only
Muslim family in the building. The men watched with approval as Asif
downed pegs of Scotch with the best of them. Zenobia played bridge
with the women in the building every Saturday and chaired their kitty
parties. Her best friend, Pushpa Patel, who lived two floors below, was
vice chair.

Bombay was convulsed by another riot in 1996, and this time,
the flames spread to their affluent neighborhood. Asif and Zenobia
watched in disbelief as Muslim-owned cars and shops were vandalized
and burned by mobs wielding kerosene cans. Still, they kept quiet and
laid low, putting their faith in their Hindu friends and the imperme-
ability conferred by their wealth. "*Arre*," Asif would say, "I know every
bloody person up and down this lane. Nobody is going to hurt us."

But one night, the family came home from a play and found a copy
of a column that Asif had written for the *Indian Express* pinned to
their front door, a large red *X* running through it. The column, already
a year old, had mocked the improbable claims made by Shivaji's most
devout and fundamentalist followers. *You Islamic bastard*, a note read.
Next time you won't be so lucky. We are coming for you.

Asif's face turned pale. "Take the children and go inside," he whispered to his wife. "And pack a suitcase. I'll be right back."

"Where are you going?" Zenobia asked, but he was already taking
the elevator back down.

He came home a half hour later, heavy-footed and shell-shocked. He
made sure the children were in their rooms before motioning his wife
to sit beside him on their bed. "I went to see Dilip," he said. "Since he's
president of the building association and all. I told him about the threat
and suggested that we hire more security for the building immediately."

"And?"

Asif paused. "He phoned the other co-op members to come over.

They came. And they said they didn't want any problems with the thugs. They all blamed me for bringing trouble to their doorstep. And they said that . . . that the best thing would be for us to shift."

"Shift? Shift where?"

Asif nodded absently and stared at the floor. When he looked up again, his eyes were cloudy. "That's what I asked. They said we should move out until things cool down." Then, at last, the tears came to his eyes. "Not one of them said they'd come to our aid, Zenobia. Not one."

"Asif, they all have their families to think of. These are hard times."

His anger had finally found its target. "Don't. Don't take their side. These people, these bloody people. How many times have they come to our parties? They have eaten our food, drunk my liquor. And this is who they are? In our time of need?"

They talked late into the evening. They considered moving in with a distant cousin, but when they called, the petrified woman said that Muslims were being beaten on the streets in her neighborhood. In other homes, the phone rang and rang, and they surmised that the occupants had fled.

Finally, at 11:00 p.m., Zenobia said, "Beatrice Auntie."

Beatrice Gonzales was an elderly Anglo-Indian woman who lived in the building across the street. She had been the librarian at the children's school, was already ancient when Sameer had started there, and had retired the year Zeenat entered third grade. Every week, Zenobia dropped off a couple of meals for the elderly spinster, who was getting more and more infirm.

Despite the lateness of the hour, Zenobia called. Beatrice's voice was drowsy when she answered, but as soon as she understood the reason for the call, she was wide-awake. "Come over," she said immediately. "Bring the children and come over now. Asif, too, obviously."

"Pack some clothes for a few days," Asif told his wife. "Until this blows over." He pulled on his goatee. "I don't want any of our neighbors to know where we're going. I will call Jafar *bhai* and tell him to bring his taxi around in a half hour. We should tell our neighbors we're leaving town."

"You want a taxi to go across the street?"

"That's the whole point. We will have Jafar go out to the main road. Then we can drive around her building and go in from the back entrance. Understand?" He stopped, struck by another thought. "Call your friend Pushpa and tell her we're bringing all your jewelry to her for safekeeping."

"Is that a good idea? I can go to the bank tomorrow and put it in the security box."

"Zenobia, it's better if we don't leave Miss Gonzales's house for a few days. Pushpa has that big safe, remember? You only told me when Gaurav bought it for her. She can keep our belongings in there."

Pushpa nodded gravely as she accepted the heavy cloth bag of gold necklaces and diamond bracelets. "Be safe!" she cried as she hugged Zenobia. "Phone me, and I will tell you when it's safe to come home."

"Where to, Asif sahib?" Jafar said when they were in the cab. "Churchgate or Victoria Terminus?"

"Drive," Asif said. He pulled out a hundred-rupee note. "This is for your trouble, *bhai*. Just take us around to the next street and then pull up to the back entrance of Royal Apartments. We had to make a show of leaving, you see?"

Jafar, a fellow Muslim, understood immediately. "Excellent idea, *seth*."

He helped them rush into the building and carried their suitcases up the two floors to Beatrice's apartment.

The old lady opened the door at the first knock. After his wife and kids had entered, Asif faced Jafar. "You know you can't . . ."

"Sahib, you gave me the down payment to purchase my first taxi. My family eats because of your largesse. I am forever in your debt. You don't have to . . ."

Asif smiled, a cold smile that didn't reach his eyes. "Unusual to find a man who remembers his debts, in this city of ours," he said.

Sadness suffused Jafar's face. "These are hard times for us, sahib," he said. "But they will end."

"Inshallah."

"Inshallah. Stay safe, sahib. And remember, if you need anything, I am your servant."

"You take care, Jafar *bhai*. You and your family, also."

THE FIRST FOUR days in Beatrice's apartment went smoothly. Zenobia cooked all their meals, and Beatrice declared she was already gaining weight. Asif read the newspaper and listened incessantly to the news on TV. Sameer played his Walkman and read his Tintin comics, while Zeenat was immersed in her Nancy Drew novels and *Mad* magazines. Despite their haste, Zenobia had remembered to pack everything the children needed. In the evenings, Asif and Sameer played game after game of Scrabble on Beatrice's old board.

The trouble came on the fifth day.

"LISTEN," MOHAN SAID. "You don't have to do this. You don't have to tell me. I can see how hard this is."

But once Smita had started, she didn't wish to stop. Part of the reason was relief at no longer having to hide the truth. And part of it was revenge. Mohan had looked at her with suspicion. She wanted him to come face-to-face with his own privilege.

"It's okay," she said. "I want to." She paused. "But I want you to know—I've only told this story to one other person. My best friend back home. No one else. You're only the second person. Ever."

He bowed his head. "Thank you. But you don't . . ."

"I want to," she repeated.

THE TROUBLE CAME on the fifth day.

A Sunday.

Over Zenobia's vociferous objections, Asif insisted that they attend the luncheon where he was getting a literary award.

"Have you gone mad, Asif?" Zenobia said. "Do you know how dangerous it is?"

"*Fffft*. The streets are already quiet. We will go and come, just like that. Three hours, tops."

"And what about all our neighbors who think we've gone out of town? You made me lie to them for what reason?"

"I have it worked out." Asif gave his wife a beseeching look. "But, darling, I want you to come with me. In fact, I won't go without you."

Jafar was once again employed to smuggle them out of their hideaway and drive them to Flora Fountain. Zenobia protested that she didn't have anything to wear, but she'd had the foresight to pack one good silk sari, and Beatrice loaned her a gold chain and pendant.

"Mummy," Zeenat said, "you look beautiful."

Zenobia pulled her daughter toward her. "You be good. Papa and I will be back in no time, *accha*? Don't give Beatrice Auntie any trouble."

Zeenat rolled her eyes. "Bring me a chicken roll from Paradise on your way home."

Zenobia looked distressed. "I wish I could, darling. But we just want to go long enough for Papa to give his speech and pick up his award."

"Fine."

"As soon as this nightmare ends, we'll go there for lunch, okay, my baby?"

"Mummy, it's fine. Go."

THE CHILDREN ATE lunch with Beatrice before the old woman went to take her siesta. Unlike their own apartment, Beatrice's flat didn't have air-conditioning and even though they wore T-shirts and shorts, Sameer and Zeenat were hot and miserable as they sat in the living room. "I'm bored," Sameer said, stretching his arms over his head.

Zeenat looked up from her book. "I have an idea. Let's call Chiku," she said. "Maybe he can come over."

Sameer hesitated. "Papa said no one should know where we are."

"So? Chiku's not going to tell anyone."

She could see that Sameer was tempted. "You know we can trust him," she said. And before Sameer could react, she picked up Beatrice's phone and dialed Chiku's number.

"Hello, Pushpa Auntie," she said when Mrs. Patel answered. "It's Zeenat. Is Chiku there?"

"Hello, *beta*," Mrs. Patel said. "What news of all of you? How is your mother? Let me speak to her."

"She and Papa are out." Zeenat coiled the phone cord around her finger. "Can Chiku come over to play?"

"Play? But, darling, aren't you out of town?"

"We're just across the street, Auntie," Zeenat laughed. "At Miss Beatrice's house. Chiku can be here in two minutes. Papa didn't want all the neighbors to know."

There was a long silence. When Pushpa Patel spoke, her voice had ice chips in it. "I see. Well, Chiku cannot come. He is busy. With his *friends*."

"Is he coming?" Sameer asked, after Zeenat hung up. He noticed the stunned look on his sister's face. "What is it?"

Zeenat cocked her head. "I don't know. Pushpa Auntie sounded angry. But I don't know why."

"I told you. You shouldn't have called."

"I'm sorry. Don't tell Papa, okay?"

"Listen, don't worry about Pushpa Auntie. She was probably fighting with her servant again." Sameer smiled at his sister. "Come on. Forget about Chiku. Want to play Scrabble?"

They were in the midst of a game, Sameer beating her as usual, when the doorbell rang. "Yay! They're home!" Zeenat exclaimed.

"So soon?" Sameer said. He went to the door and opened it.

But instead of Asif and Zenobia, there were five men, each one carrying a long iron rod. Sameer froze for a moment, then tried slamming the door, but they pushed him aside and entered the living room. The men looked around, eyes narrowing as they saw Zeenat. One of them approached her, even as she tried to pull her T-shirt as far down over her shorts as she could in a vain gesture of modesty. He laughed at the futility of her effort.

"Muslim bitch," the man said. He ran his index finger against Zeenat's barely developed breasts.

"Hey!" Sameer yelled. His eyes bulged with rage. "Don't you dare. I forbid you to . . ."

One of the other men pushed him so hard that Sameer stumbled a few steps before righting himself. "You forbid us? Muslim scum."

Sameer met Zeenat's eyes. "There's a mistake," he said. You have the wrong house. We're not Muslim. We're . . . Catholic. Our auntie lives here."

The first man laughed. "Is that so? And who is your auntie, *chutiya*?"

"It's our Beatrice Auntie. We're just visiting . . ."

The man slapped Sameer across the face so hard that he fell back into the couch, whimpering. Zeenat screamed. Before Sameer could catch his breath, another man yanked him off the couch. "Go," he said. "Go get the old lady." He pushed Sameer, who, after casting a helpless glance at Zeenat, went into Beatrice's bedroom.

"*Ae, chokri*. Tell me. Are you a Christian, too?"

Zeenat opened her mouth to speak, but no sound emerged. The man slammed his hand on the Scrabble board, upsetting the tiles. "I asked you a question."

"Yes," she said. "We all are."

"Your mummy and daddy, too?"

"Yes."

"And where are they?"

"They are out."

"Out, *eh*? Gone to eat beef somewhere, *eh*?" The man spat on the floor. "Muslim vermin."

"My parents are not vermin," Zeenat said angrily. "They are . . ."

"Kill the pigs, kill the pigs!" someone chanted. Zeenat could feel the men around her stiffen, and she rushed into the center, where Sameer stood. Her brother's eyes widened with fear when he saw her. "Get out of here, you idiot!" he yelled. "Run."

But there was nowhere to run. Boss was standing next to them. He held up his hand and the crowd hushed. "This sisterfucker says he's a Christian," he said with a laugh, and the crowd roared with laughter. Then, Boss grew serious—and the crowd grew serious, too. "You see how they mock us?" he said. "Even their children are raised to mock and lie to us. You know why? Because they think we Hindus are ignorant fools." The crowd stirred. Zeenat could see the hardness enter the men's eyes, their faces tight with grievance. She looked down the street, hoping that one of their neighbors would see them and phone the police.

"Look at these two spawns of the devil!" Boss yelled. "Look at their Western clothes and expensive tennis shoes, while our children go hungry. This is how they've humiliated us, from the time of the Mughals, who ruled and demeaned us. But do you know who fought against the Mughals?" Boss scanned the crowd. "Do you?" The men were silent. "It was Shivaji." The men cheered at the familiar name, but Boss raised his hand and they fell silent. "Shivaji, our Hindu king. And the father of these two bastards writes fake books and newspaper articles where he desecrates our leader."

The crowd was restless. Sameer took two steps toward his sister, positioning his body to protect her.

"Today, we are going to teach that professor a lesson he will never forget," Boss continued. "Let him write his future books in his children's blood."

Zeenat froze. And Sameer, sensing her terror, yelled. "Just let my sister go! You can do what you want . . ."

"*Chup.*" Boss slapped the boy across the face.

Holding his cheek, whimpering a little, Sameer said, "Please. I told you. We are Christians."

The man grabbed her by the nape and pulled her to her feet. His face was inches away from hers, his breath hot and fetid. "Pimps and whores. All of you. Polluting our country with your presence."

"Right you are, Boss," one of the other men said.

There was a commotion in the next room, and they all stood still. Zeenat's heart leapt with hope when she saw Beatrice Auntie enter the room. "What is the meaning of this?" Beatrice thundered. But as Zeenat took in the sight of the elderly woman in her floral dress and Bata flip-flops, her heart sank. Beatrice Auntie was old and frail. She would be no help at all.

"Who are you?" Beatrice said. "How dare you? I will phone the police if you don't . . ."

The men looked at one another and burst into laughter. When they could finally speak, the man called Boss said, "Go back into your room, Auntie. Our quarrel is not with you. It's with these butchers here."

"These are children!" Beatrice cried. "What religion says to injure children?"

Boss turned toward Sameer. "*Chal, chutiya,*" he said. "Come with us."

Both Zeenat and Beatrice spoke at the same time:

"Where do you think you are going with him?"

"Don't you dare touch my brother."

Boss motioned to one of the men. "You stay with this old fool." He pushed Sameer in front of him. "I told you to move, motherfucker. Now, move."

They led Sameer out of the apartment. With one final look at Beatrice, Zeenat ran out of the apartment after them, dodging the man watching over Beatrice as he tried to stop her.

On the street, a mob had gathered. The children would have recognized many of the men who hung around the neighborhood, but they were too petrified to focus. The mob was chanting, braying for blood. Boss threw Sameer into the center of the crowd.

"*Arre, chutiya*, if you are Christian, prove it. Drop your pants."

The emboldened men laughed; someone clapped his hands, and the chant began: "Dropyourpants, dropyourpants, pulldownhispants, pulldownhispants."

Zeenat stared at them, confused. She had no idea what they meant. Sameer was obviously pretending that they were not Muslim, but why did they want him to undress?

Boss grinned. He approached Sameer from behind and placed him in a chokehold.

"Help!" Zeenat screamed, looking skyward, praying for some *farishta*, or angel, to come to their rescue. And for a moment, it looked as if her prayers were to be answered because several of their neighbors were standing on their balconies, straining to see what was happening below. Her eyes moved to the familiar, third-floor balcony. How many times had she stood in the street and yelled for Chiku to come down to play? And there he was, Chiku, standing next to his mother. Did they not understand what was happening? Or had they already called for the police? "Chiku!" Zeenat yelled as loudly as she could. "Help us." A pair of hands reached for her just then, but not before she saw Mrs. Patel pulling her son back into the apartment.

But there was no time to think because . . . a hand was reaching for her from behind and pushing itself down the front of her shorts and . . . Zeenat felt as if she would pass out from shame and humiliation. Then, a sharp pain as the hand found its target. Her face drenched in sweat, she tried to jackknife around but was held in place as the man's hand roamed inside her shorts.

She cried out in pain and terror, then looked over to see Sameer on the ground with his shorts and underwear pulled down to his ankles. A smaller crowd had gathered around the boy, jeering. "Christian, *eh*?" Boss said. "Then why the fuck are you circumcised, *chutiya*?"

There was a scuffle at the outer edge of the crowd; heads turned and suddenly, there was Zeenat's father, panting, sweating, pale. His eyes were wild as he took in the sight of his children. The hand digging into Zeenat froze, then extracted itself. Asif rushed to his daughter and pulled her toward him. "What is happening?" he yelled. "Your grievance is with me, not with my children." He spoke directly to Sameer. "Get up. Get up, son. Straighten yourself," as if it had been Sameer's idea to lie in the middle of the street with his pants down. And miraculously, the crowd took a step back and allowed the boy to rise. Still, Zeenat knew better than to think that the danger had passed. She worried that they would injure Papa. She glanced up in desperation at their apartment building again, but the neighbors who remained on their balconies stood immobile.

Papa turned toward Boss. "Aren't you the mechanic at Contractor Auto Repair? Your employer, Pervez Contractor, is a good friend of mine."

For the first time, Boss looked apprehensive. But he stood his ground. "So? My religion is more valuable to me than any job."

Zeenat could see her father fighting to control his fear. "And your religion encourages you to mistreat children?" he said.

Boss was instantly furious and raised a threatening hand. "*Saala*, I will chop off your tongue if you insult my religion."

"I have made it my life's work to study Hinduism," Asif said, raising his voice so that the crowd could hear. "I know more about your religion than you will in five lifetimes. Tell me, can you quote the immortal words of the Ramayana? Or the Mahabharata? I can."

A murmur went through the crowd, and Zeenat could sense a shift in its mood. Her heart surged with love and admiration for her father.

Asif must have sensed the same small victory because he pulled both children toward him, a protective hand on each of them. "Now, come on, let's stop all this madness and everybody go home," he said dismissively.

It was a mistake. The mob would disperse on its terms, not on terms set by the Muslim professor, no matter how learned he was. In fact, his very erudition was a poke in their eyes, even if they had momentarily cowered under it. Boss smacked Asif across the mouth. "Nobody leaves until I say so," he said. "You understand, motherfucker?"

Asif nodded.

"Your boy says he is a Christian," Boss said.

Asif stayed silent.

"Maybe you butchers should convert. Then, instead of the Catholic missionaries trying to convert us Hindus, they can focus on you heathens."

"I am a believer in all religions," Asif said. "All roads lead to one God."

"*Chup re,*" Boss said, striking Asif on the back. "You talk too much, professor." He was quiet for a moment, and they all watched to see what he would do next. "Shivaji was a great warrior," he said out of the blue. "Say it. *Say it.*"

"Shivaji was a great warrior," Asif repeated dully. Then, as if he couldn't help himself, he added, "But I never claimed otherwise. You misunderstand what . . ."

"Papa!" Sameer yelled. "Shut up. Just shut up."

Boss tossed back his head and laughed. "*Wah,*" he said. "The son is smarter than the father." He jabbed his index finger into Asif's face. "Yes. You shut up."

Asif fell quiet.

Boss paced for a minute, lost in thought. "Where's your wife?" he said suddenly.

The breath caught in Asif's chest.

"I asked—where is your wife?"

He swallowed. "She's upstairs. With the old lady. I beg you . . ."

Boss chewed on his tongue, thinking. "We have kerosene here," he said conversationally, almost pleasantly. "We could set all four of you on fire. But first—see these rods? First, we'd beat your children to a pulp. In front of you. Then, we would go fetch your wife. While you are still alive. And then . . ."

Asif howled and fell to his knees. The sound was so sudden that even Boss took a step backward. Zeenat stared at her father, transfixed. Out of the corner of her eye, she saw Sameer's face harden with contempt before he looked away.

"*Bhai,*" Asif said. "I beg you. Take whatever you want from us, but please leave my wife and children alone. We have lived in peace with all of you all these years. Ask any of our neighbors. They will all vouch for us."

"Ask your neighbors?" Boss laughed. "*Saala,* who do you think told us where you rats were hiding? You lied to them, too, *eh*? But your daughter couldn't keep her mouth shut."

Asif looked stricken. "I beg you," he said. "Spare my family."

Boss addressed the crowd. "You see? These fuckers are tough as soldiers when they're left unchallenged. But when we fight back, we see their true, cowardly selves." He turned to one of his henchmen. "What should we do with this pile of refuse?"

The man shrugged. "Kill them?"

Boss appeared dissatisfied with this answer. He pulled on the hair on his chin and then turned his face upward, as if he had been struck by a bolt of inspiration. "Convert!" he proclaimed. "Convert to Hinduism, and you can live. Renounce your Allah publicly. In front of your children."

Asif had never been a particularly religious man. But his face twisted at what Boss was asking of him. He looked up at the man towering over him. "Please," he said, but just then a flash caught his eye and he saw a blade as it gleamed in the sun. It was being held to his son's throat. He knew that one false move by the panicked boy would result in tragedy. "Whatever you wish!" he yelled. "Thy will be done," he cried, and then collapsed in sobs as he saw the blade being removed from Sameer's throat.

"Swear it," Boss said. "Swear on your father's head that you and your family will convert. That is the only way you walk out of here alive."

"I swear. I swear in Allah's name. I swear on my father's head."

A huge smile flashed on Boss's face. "Well done," he said. "You have chosen wisely." He turned to the crowd. "*Arre*, one of you good-for-nothings help this poor gentleman to his feet, *na*," he said humorously. And when Asif stood weakly, Boss enveloped him in a bear hug. "*Hindu-Hindu bhai-bhai*," he said. "Now, come. Today is a day of celebration. Tomorrow, I will return with the priest." He snapped his fingers. "*Ae*, Prakash. Go quickly and bring madam downstairs. Tell her, her Hindu bridegroom awaits her."

"She won't come," Asif said miserably. "Let me go get her."

"Okay," Boss said magnanimously. "We'll keep the children here. And one more thing. Don't bother calling the police, *accha*? Nobody is going to come."

AND SO, IT was done.

Zenobia accompanied Asif back down to the street and was informed about her husband's vow. Not a single neighbor came out to see the Rizvis being escorted back into their apartment. That night, Boss had two of his men stay in their apartment to keep an eye on them. He also made sure that their house phone was "confiscated for one day only, okay?" (They never saw that phone again.) Boss, whose real name was Sushil, returned the next day with a Hindu priest. Several of their neighbors were invited to witness the rites of conversion.

"Listen," Sushil said, just before the ceremony started. "I myself will bestow upon you your new Hindu names."

Henceforth, he proclaimed, Asif Rizvi would be known as Rakesh Agarwal. Zenobia would be renamed Madhu, after Sushil's own sister. They could choose the children's names themselves, he declared benevolently. He would give them a few minutes to decide.

The priest lit a fire in the small urn that was placed in the center of the book-lined living room. He chanted the Sanskrit hymns. Zenobia wept throughout the entire ceremony, but Asif stared resolutely ahead.

Sushil thumped Asif on the back when it was over and shook his hand heartily. "You have assured me a place in heaven, sir," he said, as if the conversion had been Asif's idea.

After their stone-faced neighbors had departed, Sushil produced a box of sweets. "Come on," he said, winking at Asif. "Let's go around the building, distributing the sweets. Now, the building is pure, one hundred percent Hindu."

Seeing Zenobia's head jerk back in revulsion, Asif cast a warning glance at her. "Let's go," he said to his wife.

The three of them left together, leaving the children behind with the old priest, who sat cross-legged on the floor, chewing his tobacco as placidly as a cow chewing cud. Zeenat looked over at Sameer, who had barely said a word since the events of the day before. "How are you?" she said.

"Fine," he said.

"But are you—"

"I told you. I'm fine. Leave me alone."

Zeenat nodded, her twelve-year-old face flooding with comprehension. She would always mark this moment as her initiation into adulthood—the knowledge that only anger could cover up her brother's humiliation and shame. At that moment, with terror and guilt coursing through her, she was in no position to reflect on her own trauma.

Later, when her parents returned to the apartment—the box of sweets empty, their eyes vacant—they looked ten years older. After Sushil left, her mother said, "They all looked at us as if we were strangers. Pushpa said"—and then she began to cry—"Pushpa actually said that it was our fault. For putting them in danger."

"Don't ever mention that woman's name to me again," Asif said bitterly. "That woman, whom you considered your closest friend. She's the one who told them where we were hiding."

"Pushpa?" Zenobia cried. "That's not possible. How would she even know? Did someone see us?"

Asif looked at Zeenat in silence. She stared back, her nose turning red.

"We were bored," Sameer said. His tone was hostile. "It's not Zeenat's fault. You shouldn't have gone out."

Zenobia dropped to the sofa, smacking her forehead as she did. "Ya Allah. I never knew my children could be so stupid."

"Darling," Asif said, "don't blame them. Sameer is right. I let my vanity get the better of me, to go chasing after a stupid prize. We never should've left them alone at home."

Zenobia rose to her feet. "I agree. It *is* your fault." She was almost out of the room before she turned to look back on the three of them. For a moment, Zenobia's face softened. Then, the bitterness came back. "Don't call me *Zenobia* again," she said to her husband. "You may as well start calling me by the new name that animal gave me. *Madhu.*"

ASIF WAS, BY nature, a happy, optimistic man. For several weeks, he kept assuring his family that things would eventually go back to normal. Zenobia scoffed at his reassurances. The children, too, had learned firsthand the limits of their father's ability to protect them. Sameer, especially, was furious at his father: for his chosen profession, for his foolhardy area of scholarship, for leaving them at home alone—and most of all, for the abject way in which he had fallen to his knees and begged for mercy. For weeks, the boy was rigid with mortification at the thought of his friends and neighbors looking down from their balconies and seeing him with his pants down, his dick hanging small and pathetic for all to see—and at the realization that they had seen his father prostrate himself before a common lout, the kind of man who normally wouldn't have dared look someone like Asif in the face. Out of all of them, Sameer embraced his new identity most fervently. The shedding of his Muslim name, his Muslim past, seemed to come as a relief, as if his small, humiliated body was a pebble he wanted to lose in the roaring waters of their new identities.

But even after the riots ended, things didn't blow over. Sushil took a proprietary interest in them, acting like a scientist who had discovered and named a new planet. He insisted on accompanying them when they went to formally register their new names. He drove them to a temple for the first time, making sure they had front-row seats during the *pooja* ceremony. He took to stopping by their apartment whenever he wanted, referring to their mother as *bhabhi*, or sister-in-law. Zenobia's hair began to fall out. She began to grind her teeth at night.

All invitations to the bridge tournaments and the kitty parties stopped. One afternoon, she knocked on Pushpa's door and gave full rein to her rage at Pushpa's betrayal.

"You put my children at risk, Pushpa. For what? We were like sisters."

"You lied to me. You told me you were going far away."

"I didn't. I just said we were going away temporarily. And even if you were angry at me, why would you take that out on my children?"

"Don't blame me. Blame that stupid husband of yours, for not knowing his place."

Zenobia was about to turn away when she remembered something. "In any case," she said, "I have come to take my jewelry back."

Pushpa stared at her coldly. "You will have to wait until my husband comes home. He has the key to the safe. I will send your bag up with my servant. Now, if you will excuse me."

Zenobia stood outside the woman's apartment, blinking in disbelief over the fact that Pushpa had shut the door on her. She heard the doors to the elevator open. Three of her former bridge partners walked out, along with a new woman she didn't recognize. "Hello, Zenobia," one of them said stiffly.

She took in their flawless hair and crisp linen clothes and suddenly was aware of her own damp armpits and stained dress. "I'm no longer Zenobia, remember?" she spat out. "Now I am Madhu. We were forced to convert against our will. While all of you watched."

"Oh, stop being so dramatic," one of them said before being shushed by another.

Zenobia's eyes were wild. "*Dramatic?* My daughter was molested in the middle of the street. My son was . . ."

"Yes, it's very unfortunate," said Priya, a slender, fair-skinned woman who had two children of her own. "But I don't know what you were thinking. Pushpa says she pleaded with you to get out of town for a few weeks. But you didn't listen. And honestly, if your husband wants to jeopardize his own family with his stupid newspaper articles, that's one thing. But he put all of us in harm's way. Those *goondas* would've come for our children next for associating with you people. And still you stand here and blame us."

Asif came home that evening to find Zenobia in bed. She hadn't made dinner, and the children had not eaten. When he woke her up, she said only one thing: "Get me out of here. Get me out of this cursed building, as soon as possible."

Pushpa's servant rang their doorbell at 9:00 p.m. Asif came back into the bedroom, looking puzzled as he held out a cloth sack. "I may be wrong," he said, "but it doesn't feel like they've returned all your jewelry? It feels so light."

His wife looked at him with dull eyes. "What does it matter?" she said. "And how are we going to prove anything anyway? We are luckier than most. At least she sent some stuff back."

Asif nodded. But at that moment, he resolved to move the family as soon as he found someone to buy their apartment.

He spent the next six months looking for a buyer. The first, a wealthy Muslim merchant who wanted to move into a "cosmopolitan" locality, was summarily dismissed by the building's co-op board. "Forget it, *yaar*," Dilip, the head of the building association, told Asif. "We are now an all-Hindu building. Let this man go live with his own kind."

Three other buyers were rejected by the board before Dilip made his intentions clear. It turned out that his brother was looking to relocate to Mumbai. He of course wished to live near his family. Would Asif reduce his asking price and sell to his brother? It would be a win-win-win for all of them.

"How is it a win for me?" Asif asked.

Dilip smiled. "*Arre, yaar*, you want to sell eventually, right? How you will do that if I don't approve the sale? You see? Win-win-win."

Asif went home, called his broker, and told him he had changed his mind. He wasn't selling just yet. Because he had come to a decision. There was no point in simply moving to a different neighborhood. He no longer wished to live in this godforsaken country.

Sushil had given them a new identity. Asif had been forced to shed the name bestowed upon him by his father and instead take a name chosen for him by an illiterate street thug. Everything about them was new. What was that term Christians in America used? *Born again.* They had been born again.

They would start afresh in a new country, among new people. He would move heaven and earth to get an appointment at a university in America.

CHAPTER TWENTY-NINE

━━━

THEY SAT IN silence in Mohan's living room, Smita sobbing quietly, Mohan riveted in place. Finally, after the longest time, Smita spoke. "I'm sorry. You see, I couldn't . . ."

"Don't," Mohan said, his voice hoarse. He crossed the room, sat next to her, and took her hand in his. Everything that the gesture telegraphed—sympathy, solidarity, caring—made Smita come undone, and she began to cry harder.

"One impulsive phone call," Smita said. "With one phone call to Chiku, I upended all our lives. It was my fault, you see? Everything that followed was my fault."

"Smita, no, no, no," Mohan said. "How can you believe this? You were a child."

Smita barely heard him. "We had never thought of ourselves as anything but Indian," she said. "We were not a religious family, and Mumbai was the only home we knew . . ."

"Yes, of course."

"But, Mohan. This incident changed more than just our lives. It changed how we saw ourselves. We were suddenly made to feel like strangers in the only home we'd ever known. In some ways, we felt more welcomed in Ohio than we did in my old neighborhood, after Sushil entered our lives."

Mohan put his arm around Smita's shoulders in a comforting gesture. "I'm sorry. I'm so sorry."

Smita opened her mouth to say more when her phone rang. It was Anjali calling. On a Sunday morning.

Reluctantly, she pulled away from Mohan and reached for her phone. She took a moment to compose herself before she answered, aware that Mohan was watching her.

"Hi, Anjali," Smita said, brushing the tears from her eyes. "How are you?"

"Fine. I have news. We have a firm date. It's on Wednesday. Okay?"

A few days before, Smita would have been dismayed by the delay. Now, she didn't mind so much.

"Of course we won't know the exact time until that morning," Anjali said. "It's at least a five-hour drive from Mumbai. So maybe you should stay at the motel the night before."

"Actually, I'm in Surat. So it won't take as long—"

"*Surat?* What's in Surat?"

"I—I'm just visiting a friend."

"Oh, I see. Well, it will be a shorter drive. I don't know how many hours of notice we'll get."

"That's what I was worried about."

"Okay. Good. Give my salaams to Shannon when you talk with her."

"I will." Smita hesitated. "Anjali?"

"Yes?"

"What—what happens after the verdict?"

"What do you mean? Hopefully, they'll be locked up for years."

"Yes, I know. But I mean, what happens to Meena?"

There was a lengthy silence, and Smita's heart sank. "I don't know," Anjali said at last. "I guess she'll continue living with her mother-in-law." Smita was silent.

Anjali sighed. "Look, I know you want a different answer. But I'm a straight shooter. Okay? This isn't America, unfortunately. This is India."

"But you will . . . Will you stay in touch with her?"

There was another strained silence. When Anjali spoke, she sounded distracted. "Can we talk in person on Wednesday? I have so much paperwork to do today."

Smita felt immediately chastised. "Yeah, of course."

"Sorry, not to be rude, but . . ."

"No. I understand. I do."

Smita hung up and looked down at her chewed-up fingernails. When the hell had she started chewing her nails? India was a fucking wrecking ball, affecting her nervous system, her psyche.

"I could hear what she was saying," Mohan said. "She sounds like a cold fish."

She smiled at his attempt at sympathy. "I don't think she is. Can you imagine how hard it must be, doing the kind of work she does day in and day out?"

"I can't. But honestly, I also cannot imagine doing the work you do."

"I love my job," she said. "It's a privilege, telling people's stories."

Mohan swiveled on the couch so that he faced her. "But what about *you*? Who do you have to tell your story to? Who takes care of you?"

Mummy used to express a similar sentiment. She'd visit Smita in her austere apartment in New York, take in the black-and-white photographs on the gray walls, the sparsely furnished living room—and a look of worry would cross her face. "Let's go buy some real furniture, *beta*," she would say. "A nice, bright couch, maybe? All you have is this cold, hard furniture." It took Smita a few years to figure out that Mummy wasn't really critiquing her taste in decorating. She was concerned about her daughter's solitary, nomadic existence. The minimalist apartment was simply a metaphor for a minimalist life, one shorn of any long-term obligations or relationships.

"I look after myself," she said. She was aiming for nonchalance, but the words fell flat.

"You don't have to be brave with me, Smita," Mohan said. "What you've endured is shocking. That man destroyed your whole life, *yaar*."

Smita shook her head. "No, Mohan. He didn't destroy my life. I didn't let him. Because if I had, he would've won."

"You're right," he said immediately. "You're absolutely right."

"You know," Mohan said after a while, "until I met you, until I met Meena, I really believed India was the greatest country in the world. I mean, I knew there were problems, of course. But after hearing *your* story? I . . . I just . . . I feel like I've been asleep my whole life. The fact that nobody came to your rescue? I just can't believe it."

"I remember this one woman who lived in the neighborhood," Smita said. "I went to school with her daughter, but we weren't friends. One time she ran into me and Mummy, about a year later. And she apologized to us for what had happened. She was only a distant acquaintance, but she had tears in her eyes. 'It's not right what happened to you,' she said. 'I am so ashamed. We should have spoken up.' It meant so much to us, Mohan, the fact that she acknowledged it. Mummy remembered her kindness for years."

"Well, I'm ashamed, too. Ashamed of my country."

She knew that Mohan was trying to express his solidarity, that his words were meant to console. But they made her feel awful. "You don't have to dislike India for my sake, Mohan," she said. "Really. I mean, *I* don't. Not anymore."

"How can you possibly say that? After what you've shared with me?"

Smita was flooded by memories: The horns of the bull plowing a field, decorated with marigolds. The strange democracy of children and dogs and chickens and goats coexisting in the villages they had passed. The line of women walking down the side of the road with clay pots on their heads, carrying water back to their villages. The older women at the park in Breach Candy jogging in their saris and tennis shoes. The waiter at the Taj who had given her a single white rose. Nandini's fierce, protective love for Shannon. Meena's rootlike hand stroking Abru's back. Ramdas's pride in a home that didn't belong to him. Each one of those tender things was India, too.

And this man sitting next to her, his eyes wet, torn between his need to console and his desire to be forgiven. How to make him understand that the very casualness of him, his unthinking acts of kindness and generosity—allowing the doorman at the Taj to carry her suitcase to the car, hoisting large bags of rice and dal into Ammi's shack, his playful manner with Abru and Meena, his impressions of his coworkers that kept her entertained, all of it, all of *him*, had become India, too? That having spoken out loud the secret that had dirtied her for two decades—and seeing his fine, clean anger and outrage—had set free some part of her that had remained calcified for much too long?

"I don't know," she said. "I can't say. But it's true."

"And you're glad you told me? Even though I badgered the truth out of you?"

"I am."

AFTER SOME TIME, Smita rose from the couch, walked toward the kitchen and then looked back. "Can I ask you for a favor?"

"I will."

"You will what?"

"I'll keep helping Meena and her daughter. In fact, I'll send them a monthly check. And I'll stop by every time I come to Surat. I promise. Although, I cannot imagine going there without you, *yaar*."

She made a rueful face. "I know. But we will remain friends."

He nodded, but she knew what he was too polite to say: He was more likely to keep his promise than she was to keep hers.

CHAPTER THIRTY

———— ✳ ————

ANJALI SENT HER assistant to drive me to the courthouse. I wanted to take Abru with me but Anjali had said absolutely not—we may have to sit for many hours before our case number would be called. The assistant said to leave Abru with Ammi, who grumbled about taking her granddaughter to her job with her. Her mistress does not like little children.

I HAVE NOT seen my brothers since I saw them in court the last time.
   I am very scared.
   I am praying Smita and Mohan babu will be there.
   I am hoping God will be there.
   I am not sure if I should pray to the Muslim God or the Hindu one.
   If Abdul were alive, he would say there is only one God—and that I must pray to the God called Justice.
   But I am going to court because Abdul is dead.

Maybe, when people die, they become a speck in the eye of God?

Maybe it is Abdul to whom I must pray.

Maybe he can do in death what he couldn't do in life: save me from the devils I must face in court.

CHAPTER THIRTY-ONE

———✳———

"MOHAN. SLOW DOWN, please. You're going to get us killed."

He glanced at her, irritated. "You only said we can't be late."

"I know. But I also . . . Jesus." She flinched as another car brushed past them, blaring its horn as it did.

He raised an eyebrow. "Jesus?"

"It's an expression."

"I know." He flicked a piece of lint off his cheek. "So . . . Speaking of Jesus, did you ever see Beatrice again?"

"Of course. Although the poor woman was so wracked with guilt, she could barely look us in the eye for several months."

"Yah. It's always like this. The innocent ones feel guilt. Whereas the true bastards, like these two brothers we're about to see, walk around like they own the world."

Smita gave him a sidelong look, debating whether to ask the question that had been bugging her. "And you, you . . ."

"What?"

"Nothing."

"*Smita*. Come on. What is it?"

"It's just that, I was wondering. Does it change anything for you? Knowing, you know, that I was born a Muslim?"

Several seconds passed before Mohan spoke. "I guess it does. To tell you the truth it makes me ashamed to be a Hindu. And it makes me wish I'd known you back then so I could've protected you."

Others had expressed their solidarity with the Rizvi family. Poor Beatrice Gonzales had apologized profusely for being unable to protect Sameer and Zeenat. The chair of Asif's department had thundered his disapproval when he'd heard about Asif's decision to convert. A neighbor's servant had muttered an apology the next time he had run into Mummy. But nobody had wanted to renounce their religion because of what had happened. Nobody had wished they could have scaled the time-space continuum for them. And there was no hint of pity in what Mohan had said. There was just sympathy, a clean sympathy that burned as pure as alcohol.

"Thank you, Mohan."

After a few minutes Mohan asked, "Your father didn't think of shifting immediately? You lived in that neighborhood for another two years?"

THEY DID.

Asif, the only child of an only child, had a handful of distant relatives in Bombay. When word of the conversion got to them, they cut off all ties. And of course, there was no way now to move into an all-Muslim neighborhood, even if they'd wanted to. In any case, Asif, cosmopolitan and agnostic, had no desire to live in a homogenous place, not after living in the most bohemian part of the city. Where would he go? Forced out of one religion and into another, to whom would they turn? Who were their people? For the first time in his life,

Asif Rizvi, aka Rakesh Agarwal, secular humanist, faced an identity crisis.

He had been to America before, had guest-lectured at a few universities in the Midwest. Like academics everywhere, his American colleagues had complained about the lack of respect for the humanities, the heavy teaching loads. Asif had nodded sympathetically, but he'd thought: *You don't know how good you have it.* Because he had lectured to attentive, polite students, strolled around beautiful redbrick campuses, visited the airy, book-filled homes of his American counterparts. Most of all, he had thrilled to the notion of academic freedom, that a professor could be in charge of his or her classroom, with no interference from the university administration, much less from ignorant government bureaucrats.

Now, faced with a hostile wife, a sullen son, and a traumatized daughter who refused to leave the house except to go to school, Asif wrote letters to every American contact that he had, explaining his situation. A few wrote back immediately, sympathetic to his plight, informing him of openings at other universities, promising to follow up on any leads on his behalf. This fraternity of academics became Asif's lifeline during that dark time, helping him remember who he was and the importance of his work. In a few years, a new millennium would dawn; despite his own personal misery, Asif was hopeful that the new century would usher in an age in which the world would finally transcend the tired tropes of caste and creed and national boundaries. Look at what had happened in Europe, with the formation of the European Union and the melting away of national borders. Surely, that was the way of the future. The more oppressive the realities of his home life became, the more Asif longed for the life of the mind. His true compatriots were not ignorant ruffians like Sushil, crippled by not knowing what they didn't know. They were people like Sam Pearl, professor of religion at the small liberal arts university in Ohio that Asif had visited a few years before and with whom he had since coauthored a paper.

After hearing of Asif's plight, Sam went to speak with his dean—and a year into Asif's search, he was offered a visiting professorship. Asif's contract would start in fall 1998.

Asif saw the offer as a lifeline that could pull his family out of India. He accepted immediately, then approached his real estate broker. Find me a new buyer, he said. I will lower the price. Next, he invited Sushil to dinner. Nowhere too fancy, like the Taj or Oberoi, which would have made the young man envious and resentful. He took him to Khyber, a good restaurant and better than anything Sushil could afford on his mechanic's salary. Asif ordered a beer for each of them and then a lavish meal. As soon as the waiter left with their order, he took out a large envelope and pushed it across the table. "What is this?" Sushil asked.

"It's twenty-five thousand rupees." He heard Sushil's intake of breath. "And it's only a partial payment."

"For what?

"For your help. In convincing one of my neighbors."

Sushil waited.

"I am going to confide in you." Asif forced himself to look directly into Sushil's face. "Because I believe you are a man of honor."

Sushil's eye twitched. Still, he waited.

"I am leaving India. I am taking my family and going." He raised his hand to stop Sushil from interrupting. "Wait. My wife has a brother in America," he lied. "We are moving there."

"But—"

"But I need your help. Dilip Pandit, you know him? Yes, well, he's the head of our building association. He's blocking me from selling my apartment at a fair price." Asif leaned forward. "I want you to go see him. Persuade him. I know how persuasive you can be." He smiled a no-hard-feelings smile. "And after the sale, there will be another twenty-five thousand waiting for you. As a thank-you gift."

Sushil stared at him for so long that Asif suddenly worried that he had made a huge mistake. He could imagine Zenobia's wrath when she found out. "Two hundred thousand," Sushil said at last. "That's what it will cost you."

"*Arre*, Sushil, be reasonable . . ."

"Reasonable? Okay, two hundred and fifty thousand."

Asif knew he had lost. Swallowing his distaste for the man sitting across from him, he forced a grin upon his face. "*Baba*, you are a tough negotiator." He offered his hand. "Okay, you win."

But Sushil didn't take the offered hand. "There's one more thing."

Asif closed his eyes briefly before opening them. "Tell me."

"You must promise that you will not convert back after you leave India. That you will live your life as a Hindu."

With his intellectual curiosity piqued, Asif examined the man sitting before him. "Why does this matter so much to you?" he asked.

Sushil looked offended. "Because it's my dharma. My faith."

"I see," Asif said, nodding. Even though he didn't quite see. Still, he had no choice other than to say, "*Accha*. We have a deal."

"I don't want a deal. I want your word."

What a strange and complicated creature Man was. Here was a man who had just extorted a larger bribe from him. And yet, here he sat, completely sincere in his efforts to gain four converts to his religion.

Distrust was gathering on Sushil's face. "So? Do you promise or not?"

"I promise."

But Sushil shook his head. "Swear on your children's heads. Swear."

Under the table, Asif's hand curled into a fist. But he kept his face blank. "I swear."

LATER, AFTER THEY'D sold the apartment and most of their possessions, after they'd left Mumbai at night and arrived in America during the day, after he'd settled his family in America and started his job, Asif had thought about converting back to Islam. And found that he couldn't. First of all, his passport bore his new name, as did his visa and immigration papers. Secondly, between new modes of teaching, enrolling his children in new schools, getting used to doing housework that had previously been done by servants, he had his hands full. And truth to tell, given his area of scholarship, it was better to publish under a Hindu name.

But the most important reason for not changing his name a second time was the promise he had made in that restaurant that day. The best way to honor the religion of his forefathers was to keep his word, even to a man who had extracted it under duress.

"*WAH.*" MOHAN EXHALED. "Your father is a remarkable man. Imagine honoring a promise made to a thug."

Smita remembered how angry she and her brother had been at their father for uprooting the family and moving them to America. And how, as they adjusted to their new life, that anger had softened into gratitude. "He is," she said simply. "The most remarkable man I know. Present company excluded."

Mohan did a double take. "Wow, *yaar*," he said. "That is high praise."

"I mean it." She felt sad as she said those words. Mohan and Papa would never meet.

"Will you come to America someday?" she said. "To see me?"

"Definitely," he said at once. "Inshallah."

"God willing," she translated. "My papa says 'inshallah' all the time."

They fell silent. After they'd driven a few more kilometers, Mohan reached for a Kishore Kumar CD and played it. He sang along under his breath.

"*Zindagi ek safar hai suhana / Yahan kal kya ho kisne jaana?*"

"It's a pretty song," Smita said.

"You don't know it?"

"I don't think so."

"It was a very popular Hindi film song. The lyrics say, 'Life is a beautiful journey / Who knows what will happen tomorrow?'"

They played the song on repeat as they drove toward the courthouse, knowing that they were coming to the end of their journey together.

CHAPTER THIRTY-TWO

———✳———

THE GOTHIC EXTERIOR of the courthouse had lulled Smita into antic-
ipating an equally gorgeous interior. But the crowds that packed the
long hallway that led to the individual rooms made it impossible to
linger as they inched their way to courtroom 6B. "This is more like a
train station at rush hour," she said. "I don't know how we'll ever find
Anjali."

When they passed a storage room, Smita gasped. Stacks of yellowing documents tied in string were piled from floor to ceiling. Small frag-
ments of paper lay ground up into the floor. "Don't they computerize
their records?" she asked. But instead of answering, Mohan grabbed
her hand and pulled her along, positioning his body so that no male
hand brushed against hers.

They entered the large, cavernous courtroom. It appeared as if every
chair was occupied, and people were constantly rushing in and out.

Had they arrived too late? Anjali had said that it was possible that their verdict would be announced first, given the severity of the charges. Smita looked to the front of the room and was relieved to see that the judge had not yet arrived. But how would she find Anjali in this commotion?

She was about to dial Anjali's number when Smita heard her name being called. She spun around to see Meena hurrying toward her. The girl threw herself into Smita's arms. "Oh, Didi," she said. "I am so happy you are here. I am so nervous."

Smita returned Meena's hug, then pulled away from her. Her heart sank. Meena looked as if she could barely stand up on her own. Perspiration coated her face, and her eye was wide with terror. "It's okay," Smita whispered, looking for Mohan, needing his help, and irritated to find him gone.

"Where did you go?" she hissed at him as he hurried up to her.

Mohan gestured to the woman standing next to him. "This is Anjali," he said.

Anjali Banerjee was in her early forties, with short curly hair. She wore a small, worried frown that Smita imagined was etched in place. She gave Smita a quick smile; her handshake was as firm and brisk as her phone conversations had been. "Sorry, sorry, sorry," she said. "I was just looking at the docket. They've postponed the judge's appearance by half an hour or so." She spotted the cowering Meena. "Hi, Meena, how are you?"

Without waiting for an answer, Anjali began to walk away, leaving the others to exchange puzzled looks before following her. Mohan caught up with her, the two of them walking ahead while Meena linked her fingers with Smita's as they hurried behind. Smita didn't mind. She was way past the point of trying to remain dispassionate about Meena's fate.

They were almost at the door when she felt Meena's hand go limp. Smita tensed as Govind sauntered up to them. Arvind was nowhere to be seen. "Whore," Govind said to his sister without preamble. "Cocksucker. We will show you."

Meena made a piteous noise.

"The judge is in our pocket," someone said from behind them, startling Smita. It was Rupal. "We are going to win. Mark my words."

"Anjali. Mohan!" Smita called, but the noise in the corridor overpowered her voice. "Mohan!" she called again, and he turned around, a puzzled look on his face. She saw him take in the scene as he hurried back, Anjali at his heels.

"Don't you dare talk to my client," Anjali barked as soon as she reached them. "I will let the judge know and you'll be . . . "

To Smita's mortification, Rupal chuckled. "Come," he said to Govind. "Let's leave these big-city folk alone. God has already ruled in your favor."

ANJALI LED THEM to a semiprivate room off the hallway, where the four of them huddled together. She appeared to notice Meena's terror for the first time. "What did that bastard say to you?"

But Meena was past the point of speech. She looked at Anjali mutely, tears spilling from her eye.

"The brother insulted her," Smita said. "And the other one said something to the effect of, 'The judge is in our pocket.'"

She smiled, expecting Anjali to laugh at the absurdity of Rupal's statement.

Anjali frowned. "That's not good news."

"What do you mean?"

"It means that they've bribed the judge. Obviously."

Her tone was so matter-of-fact, so detached, that Smita felt her temper rise. "*Obviously?*"

"Excuse me," Mohan said. "I'm not a lawyer, but . . . a question. If it's so obvious that they've bribed the judge, what's to stop you from doing the same thing?"

There was a long, painful silence. Then, Anjali's nose turned a rusty red. "I won't do that," she said, in a low voice. "That's not what we do." She flashed a quick look at Meena. "We had explained this to her. Before we took the case. In our organization, we are trying to change the system. If we . . . If we play dirty like the other side does, then there's no social change happening, correct? We're perpetuating the same system."

Smita had a hollow feeling in her chest. She wished Meena were not present so she could speak candidly to Anjali. "So, what is she?" she said. "The sacrificial lamb?"

Anjali flushed. "We never hid the risks from her," she replied. "Everything was explained." She shook her head impatiently. "Look, this was never a clean case anyway. Every single eyewitness turned hostile. Why do you think those goons are walking free? Do you know how unusual it is to get bail in a murder trial?"

"Then why proceed?"

"Because we need to inform the public about how corrupt our police and court systems are."

Smita felt a vein pulsate in her temple. "So, you're not a lawyer," she said. "You're a political activist."

Anjali's eyes flashed with anger. "You should come work with us for a few months. Before passing judgment."

"Didi, Anjali, what's going on?" Meena cried. "I'm not following."

They all turned to look at her, their faces sober. "Come, Meena *bhen*," Mohan said. "I will sit with you until the judge calls your case. And don't worry about your brothers. I'm here, *na*?"

"Look," Anjali said, when it was just the two of them. "Would it help if I told you that I didn't know they had bribed the judge until now? I honestly didn't think they had the money."

Smita shook her head. "I shouldn't have said what I said to you. I can't even fathom doing what you do for a living."

Anjali's eyes welled with tears. "You can't imagine," she said.

"Sometimes, I hate my job so much, I just want to quit. Move to America and practice corporate law maybe. But then, I come across a case like Meena's. And I take it, in the hopes that someone like her can win."

She checked her watch. "We need to head back. Just in case this bird called justice flies off the endangered list and shows its face in court."

EVERYTHING SOUNDED SO far away, muffled, as if Smita were deep inside a tunnel and the voices were traveling toward her from a great distance. She heard the roaring in her ears, which drowned out the other human voices.

The roaring had begun the instant she had heard the two words: "Not guilty."

The judge was mouthing other words, his nondescript, bespectacled face impassive as he spoke, but his words were disjointed, out of order. From a distance, Smita heard screams, then yells of jubilation, but she didn't have the energy to turn her head. She was still trying to make sense of the two words—*Not guilty*—was struggling to cut them up and rearrange them so that they somehow formed the word: *Justice*.

Justice.

How fine a word.

How rare.

And then, at long last, the judge stopped speaking, and Smita emerged from the darkness of the tunnel and into the glare of reality. Here was Meena, crumpled over. Here was Anjali, her face a patch-work of anger and disgust and disappointment. Here was Mohan, his mouth agape, as if he, too, were trying to right the world on its axis.

The shouting came from behind them. It came from Meena's broth-ers, and several other men who had accompanied them. They were chanting something. Recognizing the chant before Smita did, Anjali swore softly. Then Smita heard it—*"Jai Hind, Jai Hind."* *Long live India*. In the mouths of these animals, a patriotic cheer had suddenly

become a communal taunt. "Your Honor!" Anjali yelled. "This is inex-
cusable. The defendants must . . ."

"What defendants?" Rupal shouted. "These are free men, falsely
accused by these whores."

"Order, order!" the judge thundered. He turned to the constable
standing to his right. "Clear these people out. Okay, next. Case number
21630."

And just like that, it was done. They walked out of the courthouse,
Meena leaning so hard against Smita that Smita thought she might lose
her balance.

A cavern opened up in Smita's heart as they emerged into the day-
light. She turned helplessly to Anjali. One look at the lawyer's crushed
face made her regret her earlier outburst. She realized what it had taken
to even bring charges against the brothers. "What happens next?" she
whispered.

"What happens? Anjali said. "Nothing. We lost." Her face fell.
"This judge is actually one of the better ones. Not nearly as dishonest
as the others. I thought we had a slim chance."

"He's honest?"

"I didn't say that." Anjali bit her fingernail. "Maybe you're right.
Maybe I shouldn't have taken this case. I thought the glare of publicity
in a foreign newspaper would make a difference. I was wrong." She
opened her mouth to say more but was drowned out by the drumming. They all turned to see a small group of dancing, celebratory men
looking for all the world like participants in a wedding procession.
They watched incredulously as Govind and Arvind were hoisted up
by the men, as if they were heroes, or athletes who had won a cham-
pionship. Rupal was distributing sweets to people walking past them.
Smita realized that they had expected no other outcome other than
victory. Otherwise, why would they come prepared with drums and
sweets?

"Shameless bastards," Anjali muttered, casting a worried glance at

Meena, who appeared to be folding into herself, trying to make herself as small and invisible as possible. But Govind noticed her from his perch. "*Ae*, whore!" he called out. "You really thought you would win against your own brothers?"

Anjali strode toward the group, but her assistant blocked her way. "Madam, don't," she said. "You know they are just trying to provoke us."

"Come, Meena," Anjali said, taking the younger woman by her elbow. "You don't need to listen to this garbage anymore."

"It's okay," Meena said in a flat, dull voice that made Smita's hair stand on end. "There is nothing anyone can do now."

"That's nonsense," Anjali said, but the uncertainty in her voice did not reassure any of them.

"How is she getting home?" Mohan asked, ever practical.

"We'll drop her," Anjali said. "But first we need to take her to our office. There are a lot of loose ends to tie up."

"And you?" Mohan said to Smita. "What would you like to do?"

She thought quickly. There was no way to interview Meena while she was in this catatonic state. Also, she needed to file a brief story about the verdict. The longer piece could run later, after she'd interviewed Meena again. Turning to Meena, she asked, "Can we stop by your house tonight? I would like to talk a little more. And to see Abru and Ammi, of course."

"Ammi," Meena repeated, and Smita heard the dread in her voice. Was there anything she or Mohan could do to persuade Ammi to be gentle with her daughter-in-law for the next few days?

"Didi," Meena said, "can't you come home with me now?"

"But you're not going directly home, Meena," Smita said. She turned to Anjali. "How long will she be at the office?"

"Let's see. By the time we get to my office from here, do all the paperwork, and then drop her home, I'd say five or six hours. You're welcome to follow us to our offices if you like."

Smita felt the beginning of a bad headache. It would be easier to file her story from Mohan's house. She longed for some ibuprofen, a few uninterrupted hours of work, and a shower before she met up with Meena again.

"How about we stop by later tonight?" she said. "Say around six?"

"*Theek hai*," Meena said. She turned away listlessly. "Whatever you wish."

CHAPTER THIRTY-THREE

———

Smita broke down as soon as Mohan pulled away from the courthouse. "I don't understand, I don't understand, I don't understand," she cried.

"What's there to understand?" Mohan's voice was infused with anger. "It's simple—they offered the judge a bribe and he took it."

"But why didn't Anjali anticipate this? Why didn't she—?"

"Don't blame her. She probably juggles fifty cases at a time. Once in a while, she wins. Most of the time, she loses. It's like gambling. The house always wins."

But that was exactly it. The judicial system wasn't supposed to be rigged like a casino, with the decks stacked against the plaintiffs.

Smita caught herself. *What's the matter with you?* she lashed out at herself. *You act as if you have never covered a wrong verdict before. Hell, how many times have the cops gotten off after shooting an unarmed black man in America?*

"I've been thinking," Mohan said. "Maybe I can ask my father to employ Meena. Allow her to do a few odd jobs and in exchange, give her a roof above her head. We would send Abru to school."

"Do you think he'll agree?" Smita said hopefully.

"They already have a full-time cook who lives with them. And Ramdas does the cleaning. It will be a little awkward. The cook is very territorial. But something can be worked out."

"Oh, Mohan. That would be ideal."

"It won't be that easy," he said. "All this is assuming Meena will agree to move."

"What do you mean? Why shouldn't she? You've seen for yourself how isolated she is."

"*Ammi*. You forget about Ammi. Do you think Meena will abandon her so easily?"

"Abandon her? Mohan, Ammi hates her. You know she blames her for what happened."

"Exactly. And Meena blames herself. In fact, she agrees with Ammi that she's the reason why Abdul is dead. So she may feel obliged to stay. And in any case, my parents are not going to be back for a few months."

The hope that had flared, died out. It would have been so wonderful to have carried this lifeline to Meena this evening. Smita knew that Mohan's parents would have treated Meena well. But she had the sinking feeling that Mohan's assessment of Meena's character, of her fealty to the mother-in-law, was accurate.

Smita remembered how furious Mummy had been when she'd learned that Asif had bribed Sushil to help sell their apartment. Zenobia had accused him of collaborating with their persecutor, the man who had terrorized their children. "Where is your *izzat*, Asif? Or should I say, *Rakesh*?" she had taunted her husband. "First, you sold out your religion. Now, even your honor?"

Smita and Rohit had sided with their mother at the time. But after all these years, Smita felt a profound sense of gratitude. Papa had done whatever he needed to do to pull his family to safety. In the depths of his despair, he had refused to play dead. And the rewards for that one compromise had been plentiful: The university had created a tenure-track position for him at the end of his visiting professorship. Mummy eventually began to volunteer at the local library and built a new life; Rohit was happy in his marriage and business. Smita felt a sudden urge to call Papa and thank him for what he'd sacrificed. In fact, she'd do it in person when she visited him, take him to his favorite diner in Columbus and tell him the story of her unexpected visit to India. Papa would forgive her for lying to him, his love for her unwavering, unconditional.

"I'll talk to her," Smita said.

"Talk to who?" Mohan replied.

"To Meena. Tonight. I'll . . . share some of my story with her. If need be. I'll try and stress the importance of getting away from that wretched place. If not for her sake, for the sake of her child."

Mohan was silent.

"What?" she said. "You don't think I should?"

"I don't know. I'm not sure." He paused. "I . . . I just think that enough damage has been done to this young girl by us. By people like us. I mean, Anjali helped save her life when she was in the hospital. That's good. Very creditable. But then, she decided to use her for her cause. To fight a battle that she knew Meena couldn't win."

"I know. But what I'm . . ."

"How do you know?" Mohan demanded. "How do you know that asking her to leave Birwad is the right thing to do?"

"How can you ask that?" Smita didn't keep the incredulity out of her voice. "I mean, after everything I shared with you about my own family's experience?"

"How do you know there will be the same happy ending for her?" Mohan said. "And even in your case, Smita, how do you know that you wouldn't have been happy here? Eventually? Listen. I'm not trying to insult you or your family. I'm just saying, I've seen the expression on your face when you look around the countryside when I'm driving."

"How do I look?" she asked.

"Hungry. As if something that was yours was stolen from you. And that you wish to get it back."

"Oh, come off it, Mohan," she said. "I think that's wishful thinking on your part."

He frowned. "How is it wishful thinking?"

She couldn't say what she believed—that despite everything, Mohan wanted her to love India as he did. Still, he wasn't wrong. She was bristling precisely because his observations cut too close to the bone. Her feelings about India had certainly gotten more complicated, and somehow Mohan had gotten entangled in that internal debate. His blunt assessment made her feel vulnerable, his words stripping away the armor she needed to get through the rest of her time in India.

And then she thought, *Why do I need an armor? What exactly am I holding on to?* For years she'd clung to a dream, imagined a tableau of recriminations and remorse from her former neighbors: Pushpa Auntie realizing the error of her ways; Dilip's widow confessing that her husband had always regretted his treatment of Papa; Chiku telling her how ashamed he was of his mother's perfidy. But in a flash of insight, Smita saw that these images were cartoons, the revenge fantasies of a twelve-year-old girl that were frozen in time. No wonder reality had not obliged and played along.

Smita glanced at Mohan, took in the tightness around his mouth. The last thing she wanted to do, on this devastating day, was get into a meaningless argument with him. "You may well be right," she said. "I feel like I don't know anything anymore."

"Me neither."

They both exhaled, the tension in the car abating.

BOOK FOUR

———

CHAPTER THIRTY-FOUR

THE COLD THAT entered my body after the judge-sahib gave his ruling is still present. Ammi's ugly words, hot with contempt, didn't chase it away. Abru's warm hands, slipped into mine as soon as I got home, did not melt it away. I'm lying with my daughter in our hut, waiting for Abdul, but he is a no-show tonight. I wonder if, like Ammi, he is angry with me. The thought cuts my heart. Does Abdul believe I let him down in court many months ago when I told the judge my story?

The last time she interviewed me, Smita asked what future I saw for myself after my brothers went to jail. At that time, all I could see was a long, empty road ahead. I pictured myself doing the same thing day after day—cooking, cleaning, worrying about when my Abru would begin to talk and how I would pay for her schooling. I saw myself take one sodden breath after another, for my daughter's sake.

But now I know that the jackals who killed Abdul can come again at any time. With no fear of the court, they could come for me, for Ammi, and even *for my little one. And I would be unable to do the only job I was put on Earth to do—protect my child.*

When I left Anjali's office today, I took her hand in mine and thanked her for everything she had done. Her nose turned red when I said this. "Kiss Abru for me," she said.

"You come and kiss her yourself."

"I will. Next time I'm in the area, I'll stop by."

The way she said it, her eyes not meeting mine, I knew I would never see her again. "You have been a farishta *in my life," I said. "I will never forget you."*

Anjali began to cry. "I just wish we had won. I did my best. But I failed you, Meena. I'm so sorry."

Ammi is calling me. I know she wants me to start dinner, as if today is an ordinary day, instead of the day when the last bird of hope died. I know that no matter how tasty the food is, she will complain tonight—too much salt or too little; rice too soft or too hard. It will be her way to punish me for losing in court. Because even though Ammi refused to talk to the police, she wanted us to win. To avenge her son's useless death.

I pick up my daughter and walk to my mother-in-law's house.

ABRU HEARS IT *first, looking up from her plate. I see her curious face and then I hear it, too. It sounds like thunder, coming from far away. As we listen the sound rolls nearer, and now I know what it is—it is the beating of drums. "Kya hai?" Ammi says, cupping her hand behind her ear. "Someone's wedding procession so late in the evening?"*

But I know what it is.

This is no wedding celebration.

This is a funeral procession.

I GRAB ABRU'S *dirty hand. "Get up," I say, pulling her to her feet. "Come on, get up." I listen again. The drumming is closer. They are marching through the village. I turn Abru's head toward me. "Listen," I say. "The bogeyman is coming. Run into the field behind our house and hide in the grass. Don't come out until Ammi or I call for you." She looks back at me, dumb as a cow, sucking her thumb, and I smack her hand. "Go. Run!"*

"Hai Allah, hai Allah," Ammi says, finally understanding what's going on. I turn to her. "Ammi!" I yell. "You go with Abru. Hide in the field with her, I beg you."

Ammi picks up Abru and runs. Halfway to the field, she turns around. "You come, too."

I shake my head. "Go. Now!" I say. If no one is home when they arrive, they will burn the field down, looking for us. I turn to look at the road. That's when I see the tips of the torches, carried by the men coming my way.

I turn quickly to look back at Ammi. Carrying Abru is slowing her down. She will need a few extra minutes to find a good hiding place deep in the grass. Help me save our daughter, Abdul, I pray. Then, I bend down and pick up as many stones as I can hold in my hand.

I straighten up. My fear is gone. Even as the torches move closer, one thought keeps hammering in my head: I must keep my daughter alive.

Stones in hand, I greet the men who have come to kill me.

CHAPTER THIRTY-FIVE

TRY AS SHE might, Smita couldn't keep down the queasy feeling. She debated whether to ask Mohan to slow down as he took the curves in the road, but they were already late heading into Birwad. She had fallen asleep after filing her story and woken up two hours later with her heart thudding, certain that Meena was in trouble. Mohan had not been able to convince her that she was wrong.

"Smita. Calm down, *yaar*," Mohan said, even though she had not said a word. "You're worrying for no reason."

"I'd promised Meena we'd be there by six. And I just have this awful feeling."

"Listen, if you're this concerned for her welfare, we can try convincing Ammi and Meena to leave their village. I'll do my best to help situate them in Surat."

She shifted in her seat. "I hope to God Anjali made plans to ensure Meena's safety."

"Exactly," Mohan said. "See? Don't you think Anjali knows the situation better than you? Do you think she would've put Meena in harm's way? After she saved her life?"

Smita nodded, wanting to believe him. But there was that fluttering feeling in her stomach. The headlights of the car lit the road ahead of them, dark fields on either side.

THEY ENTERED BIRWAD fifteen minutes later. The first thing they noticed was the eerie silence and lack of activity. It was as if the whole village had decided to go to bed by seven o'clock. The only sound was the distant howling of a few dogs. Smita could feel her hair stand on end. "Something is wrong," she said, rolling down the window. "This place is dead."

As soon as she said the word *dead*, she knew. And at that exact moment, she heard the sound from down the road, coming toward them like rolling thunder. "Mohan!" she cried. "It's coming from the direction of Meena's house. Something is going on there."

The car screeched to a halt. "We need to call the police," Mohan said. "There's no way we can go in there if you're right."

He reached for his phone, but Smita yelled, "Are you kidding me? I need to get to her. Drive, Mohan. *Drive.*"

"You're not thinking straight. If it's a mob, what can . . ."

"Mohan, for fuck's sake. They will not dare harm us. They know I'm an American. *Drive.*"

He swore under his breath but gunned the car through the village and toward Meena's home. As they got closer, the roar grew louder, as if they were driving into a storm. Then, they saw the source of the sound—a mob of angry, raging men, the fire from their torches lighting up the night. They had formed a circle in the clearing between the two hovels. As Smita looked on in horror, she could see that many of the men were pelting stones at the center of the circle. Mohan came to an abrupt halt at the perimeter of the crowd. Smita leapt out of the car and plowed her way through, feeling the heat from the torches as she made her way to its dark, throbbing heart. Mohan followed behind her. She smelled the distinct scent of masculine sweat, the scent of danger, but she felt reckless, unafraid for her own safety.

She came to the opening and halted. For a moment, in the flickering light of the torches the men carried, she thought she saw a large, bloodied creature they had killed for sport. And yet, she knew at once that it was Meena. *Meena.* Images flashed before Smita's eyes—Govind sauntering up to them just before the verdict and insulting his sister; the aggressive, celebratory drumming outside the courthouse, each beat a threat; Meena asking her to accompany her to her house immediately rather than waiting until the evening. Surely, the girl had had some kind of premonition. And Smita had refused, why? Because she had wanted to file her story? Her fucking story?

Smita lifted her head to the dark sky and screamed, a long, endless scream that unfurled like a black scarf. Dimly, she saw a man stop midkick and recognized Govind, who was staring at her in incomprehension. In the poor light of the evening, Govind looked monstrous, but instead of making her fearful, the image enraged Smita. She hurled herself at him, beating him wildly with both hands, striking his face and chest. Smita felt something rough under her fingernails and realized that she was clawing at his face. And Govind, who had been stunned into immobility by her sudden assault, finally grabbed her wrist and twisted it away from his face. Just then there was a shout, and Mohan threw himself between them. "*Khabardaar,*" he warned. "You lay a hand on her and I swear, I will bring the wrath of God down on you, you motherfucker."

Behind them, the mob stirred; a few men inched forward. Smita drew closer to Mohan. "Remember one thing, *chutiyas*!" Mohan shouted, spinning around so that they could all hear him. "This woman? She's an American. You hurt one hair on her head, and even your corrupt police and courts won't be able to protect you. I tell you, they will send in the American army to hunt down each one of you."

"We are having no quarrel with her, *seth*!" someone yelled. "We are only here to take care of the whore." He pointed toward the ground where Meena lay.

"Get away from her. You've killed her. Now, leave her corpse alone!" Smita screamed. And when she saw that they weren't about to give an inch, she moved toward Meena's mangled body and dropped to the ground. She crouched, one arm over Meena's lifeless body, to protect it from being further assailed by their kicks and beatings. The nauseating smell of fresh blood and ripped flesh filled her nostrils.

"Didi." The voice was so faint, Smita didn't know if she was imagining it. But then she heard Meena's raspy breathing. "You're alive," Smita whispered, aware that Govind and Mohan faced off less than three feet away.

Meena's mouth moved, but no sound emerged. Smita leaned in. "Abru," Meena gasped. "With Ammi. Hiding."

"You please leave, sahib!" Govind yelled. "We are not wanting trouble with you. But please do not interfere in our domestic affairs."

Smita was aware of the terrible risk Mohan was taking. The only thing protecting him was his status as a wealthy outsider. But that protection would not last much longer; the mob had had a taste of blood, and it would turn on her and Mohan next. And yet, she couldn't think about that.

Smita bent closer to Meena. Her good eye closed, then opened again, but there was little life in it. "Didi," she whispered. Smita put her ear against the girl's mouth to hear as best as she could over the yells of the crowd. Meena's tongue was lolling in her mouth as she spoke, making it harder to follow her words. "In the field . . . Hiding." Her right hand fluttered in the dust, and Smita realized she wanted her to hold it. She held it. "You take. To Am'rica. Promise. My Abru."

"I promise," Smita whispered, just as a pair of hands grabbed her from her armpits and yanked her away. In that moment, a foot struck Meena in the jaw. Smita saw the girl's head jerk so hard that a spray of blood flew out of her nostrils. She screamed and tried to get out of the man's grip as she was being dragged away, but Meena's lifeless face, her eye rolled back in her head, signaled to Smita that the kick was the fatal blow. They had killed her. *They had killed her.*

"You fucking bastards!" Mohan yelled, and she saw that they had gripped him, and at long last—when there was nothing she could do to protect Meena—she was afraid. "Mohan!" she screamed, and he turned his head to look at her, the expression on his face inscrutable.

She began to struggle harder as she realized she was being pulled toward Ammi's hut. Surely, they would set it on fire with her and Mohan inside. But a man emerged from the hut and said, "Miss, it is better for you if you don't fight. We wish you no harm." She recognized the voice. It was Rupal's.

The hands gripping her slackened, and Smita pulled away to face Rupal. "You call yourself a man of God?" she shouted. "You allowed an innocent woman to be murdered? In cold blood?"

Rupal put his finger to his lips, signaling her to be quiet. He gestured to Smita's captor to lead her into the hut. A single lantern lit the room. As Smita looked around, she gasped. Either Ammi had put up a mighty struggle, or they had ransacked the hovel. Then, she saw that the provisions Mohan had purchased for Ammi were gone, and she knew that the men had taken away everything of value.

Rupal followed her with his eyes. "We helped ourselves to a few items," he said pleasantly. "Seeing that the old lady has absconded with her bastard grandchild."

Smita flinched at the insult. "The child is innocent," she said. "Of course, so was her mother."

Rupal's eyes were hard. They flickered slightly as Mohan was pushed inside as well. "That child is living proof of our disgrace, miss,"

Rupal said. "To be honest, it's more important for us to find her than it was to kill the whore. And we will. After all, how far can an old grandmother and a young child go?"

Smita's heart flooded with fear. They would hurt Abru, the silent, wounded toddler with the sweet face and birdlike manner. These monsters would hurt a child. Meena's final words came to her. Abru was hiding somewhere, not too far from the hut. How long before these bastards hunted her down?

She forced herself to laugh, hoping that Rupal wouldn't hear her insincerity. "Good luck finding them," she said, keeping her eyes on Rupal but speaking loudly enough for Mohan to hear. "Anjali knew you goons would be up to no good. She insisted that Ammi and the child stay in town with her. You will never see them again."

She heard Rupal's sharp intake of breath, saw the disappointment on his face. But the man was nothing if not cunning. "Then why did the whore return?" he said.

Smita's mind froze.

"We warned her." Mohan spoke into the silence. "We begged her to stay with that lawyer. We even invited her to go with us to Mumbai. But Meena was crazy. She insisted on returning to the land where her husband died."

Rupal looked from one to the other. "Wait here," he said. He strode out of the hut.

Smita turned immediately to Mohan. "Call the police," she hissed. "Now."

"It's a risk. They're all standing right outside," he muttered. "They'll hear me."

She bit her lower lip. All she could think of was the men searching in the tall grasses for Abru. How long had she and Ammi been hiding? How long could they continue to do so? "Call," she said.

He nodded and fished out his phone from his pocket. He dialed the number to the station, muffling the ring the best he could. The phone rang and rang. "Where are they?" he asked desperately. "Why aren't they answering?"

And suddenly, she knew. "Hang up," she said. "Hang up."

"What the hell?" He ended the call.

"They've been paid off. They won't answer. Otherwise, don't you think someone from the village would've let them know? And they would've been here by now?"

Mohan swore under his breath.

Smita moved closer to him. "The child is alive. She's hiding with Ammi in the field behind Meena's house."

"How would you—"

"She told me. Just before she died. We have to keep them from searching the field. I don't know how, but that's what we have to do."

Mohan stared at her for a long moment. In the light of the lantern she could see his face, bleary with fatigue and stress. He went to the entrance of the hut. "Rupal!" he yelled. "Govind, come quickly."

"What is it?" A man they'd never seen before sauntered up to the hovel. "They are busy."

"*Busy?*" Mohan thundered. "*Arre, saala*, they are going to be busy in jail for the next fifty years if they don't show up here in one minute. Tell them the police are on their way."

The man laughed and spat on the ground. "Police knows not to . . ."

"Not the police from your little tadpole pond. This is the big shark that's coming here. They will be here in less than a half hour, *chutiya*."

The man turned and left.

"What are you doing?" Smita hissed. "You will get both of us killed."

"Trust me," Mohan said.

She was about to chastise him when Govind entered the hut. The front of his tunic was spattered with blood. Smita stared at it, her stomach heaving.

"You're lucky to be living," Govind said insolently. "My men could . . ."

"Your men can do nothing," Mohan said haughtily. "You are out of time. I just called the big inspector-sahib at his home. He is a friend of my father's, but still he was not happy to be disturbed at home at this hour. And you know what he said, fucker? He said he was going to come to see for himself the bastard who would kill his own sister. They will be here soon. And I am going to sit right here and watch the *tamasha*."

"You shouldn't have done this, *seth*," Govind said. "Big mistake."

Mohan opened his mouth to reply when the room lit up from the bright light outside. For an insane second, Smita thought someone had set off a bomb. Then, as she realized what was happening, she made to dash out of Ammi's hovel. But Govind blocked her way. "Let it go, memsahib," he said. His voice was flat. "This is the funeral she deserves."

They watched the flames shoot skyward from Meena's hut. After a moment, Smita bent over, moved to the right of the hut, and threw up. The wind carried a foul odor toward them, making her retch even more.

When she straightened up, she turned to Govind. "May worms come out of your eyes every time you sleep," she said. "May you never know a moment's rest ever again for killing your sister."

"What sister?" Govind pointed to the blaze. "You see that? That stupid girl was so upset with the judge's verdict, she set herself on fire."

He turned to Mohan. "Come here, *seth*," he said. He pointed to where a small group of men were working, each of them bent at the waist. "You see what they're doing? They are washing and sweeping the area. When they are done, there will not be a drop of blood on the ground. *Bas*, we came like the wind, and we will disappear quiet as ghosts."

"You came through the village with your drums and torches, no?" Mohan said. "You don't think the people there saw you?"

Govind spat. "You think those Muslim eunuchs will open their mouths? Why should they interfere? If that old woman and the child are truly gone, we have no need to enter Birwad again. As you can see, the saga with Meena is—finished. We have restored the good name of our ancestors."

Smita looked around. "Where is your brother?" she asked.

"That useless drunk? He didn't wish to come." He looked at Mohan. "*Chalo, seth.* Time for you to clear out of here."

"We will wait," Mohan said evenly, "for the big inspector to arrive. You are the one who should disappear."

"Why did you create trouble for us, *seth*? Our customs and traditions exist for a reason. Why must you dishonor them?"

Mohan's face darkened. "Listen," he said. "I will make a deal with you. I will wait here for the inspector. And when he arrives, I will tell him I was mistaken. That the girl set herself on fire. But you need to be gone, along with all your friends."

"Why will he believe you?"

Mohan tilted his head back slightly, an imperious gesture Smita had never seen him make before. "It's not a question of him believing me. He is a friend of my father's. We move in the same circles. Whatever I wish him to do, he will do."

Govind's mouth twisted in bitterness. "The ways of the rich and powerful."

"Exactly. Bribing the police or bribing the judge. What's the difference?"

Govind looked indecisively at both of them. "Why I must trust you?" he said at last.

"Why? Because you have no choice. Because a man like me can crush a hundred men like you. You said so yourself. And because, now that that poor girl is dead, I have already lost interest in your sad life."

Govind flinched. Still, he stood his ground. Smita watched him, her heart in her mouth. The moments ticked by. Smita could see Mohan working himself up into a fury. She couldn't tell how much of it was performance.

"I will go," Govind said at long last, "but on one condition." He glanced at Smita. "Your missus insulted me in front of my community. She must apologize."

"*Saala*, just get out of here before the police come," Mohan said. "Your honor won't be worth five *paisa* in prison."

"You don't understand, *seth*. I will never be able to raise my head and look at my neighbors if your wife doesn't apologize publicly. I would rather grow old in jail than tolerate such an insult."

"*Apologize?* To a thug like you? She will do so over my dead body."

Smita looked in horror from one man to the other, all the while thinking of Abru: *What if the child wandered out of the field? What if Ammi was not with her? How long did they have?*

She stepped forward and looked Govind in the eye. "I'm sorry," she said. "I apologize."

"Smita, don't," Mohan said, but she dismissed him with a wave of her hand.

Govind threw Mohan a gloating look. Then, his face hardened. "Not here. In front of all the men. Outside."

Beside her, Mohan made a guttural sound. Smita ignored him. She walked out of the hut to where a cluster of men stood, Govind at her side.

"*Arre*, listen, all!" Govind called. "Memsahib, who has come all the way from Am'rica, has something to say to us."

The men walked closer to where Smita stood, looking at her curiously. She could feel the heat from Mohan's body behind her. She closed her eyes for an instant, thinking of what Papa must have faced when he'd agreed to convert, his responsibility to his family blinding him to all else. This is what it meant to care so much about another human being that you were willing to sacrifice everything, even pride and self-respect. Let Govind and his ilk cling to their misguided notions of honor. She was her father's daughter. He had taught her well.

"I'm sorry," she said loudly enough for all of them to hear. "I apologize for attacking you. I was wrong. I ask for your forgiveness."

She had a feeling that Govind was not fooled by her performance. But it didn't matter. She had allowed him to save face. He smiled magnanimously. "You are forgiven," he said.

The mob began to hoot and holler, mocking her words. But Govind shushed them. "*Chalo*, hurry. Police will be here soon. Gather your things and let's go."

Smita could sense Mohan's anger as the two of them stood watching the men destroy the last bits of evidence. "Forgive me," she whispered to him. "I had no choice."

Mohan didn't reply, and she knew he was not appeased. She understood. But unlike him, she knew about limited choices.

The minutes ticked by. Several of the men began to extinguish their torches.

Rupal sauntered up to them. "Get out of here, motherfucker," Mohan said. "Otherwise, you will be the first to hang when the police arrive."

"I was only coming to say . . ."

"*Chup*. Not a word from you. And listen." Mohan took a deep breath. "My men will be keeping an eye on you. You harass one more woman in your village, you make one more woman walk on coals or pull any of your stunts, and every government official in the state will be after your hide. You understand me?"

Rupal looked at him sullenly. "You misunderstand . . ."

"I told you. One more word, and I'll make sure you hang." Smita could see the sweat on Mohan's face. "Now, go. All of you!"

The men extinguished the last of their torches and took a different road back to Vithalgaon to avoid marching through Birwad. After they were gone, a sudden silence descended on Ammi's hovel. Mohan retrieved the lantern, and they walked to Meena's hovel and stood, watching it burn.

"She asked me to come back here with her," Smita said. "But I was too stupid to agree. As long as I live, I'll never forgive myself. I could've saved her."

"That's doubtful." Mohan's voice was hollow. "Or say that you'd saved her today. But what about tomorrow? A week from now? No, not even God could've saved that poor girl."

"She's in there. My God, Meena is in there. I can't believe they killed her."

"Smita. I have no idea how long this ruse is going to work. Those men may come back. I don't even know how we are going to find that child in the dark. Let's move."

"Meena said they were hiding in the field behind her hut."

"Are you sure that she recognized you, much less spoke to you? I mean, she was . . ."

"She did."

They got in the car and turned it around so that the headlights shone onto the dark, overgrown field. They exited the vehicle and stood gingerly at the edge of the tall grasses. Smita glanced at Mohan, reluctant to confess to her fear of rodents and snakes. Screwing up her nerve, she took one step forward, as if dipping her toes into chilly waters.

"Ammi," she whispered. "Abru. Are you here?"

There was no response.

"Ammi!" she called, a little louder. "It's Smita. From the newspaper. Are you safe?"

Mohan plunged into the grass. "Abru!" he called, his voice urgent.

Smita felt a sob growing in her throat. Where was the child? Was it possible that she had misheard Meena's garbled speech? She turned around to say something to Mohan and froze. He was singing. *Singing.*

"*Ae dil hai mushakil jeena yahan / Zara hat ke, zara bach ke / Ye hai Bombay meri jaan,*" Mohan sang in a low voice.

"What the fuck are you doing?"

"Shhh. I sang this song to Abru the other day. She loved it. This way, she'll know it's me." He began again.

Something rustled, and then a tiny animal flung itself at Mohan.

Smita screamed, then covered her mouth with her hand. A startled laugh escaped her lips. Of course. It was little Abru, hugging Mohan's legs. They had found her.

"*Oi*, little one," Mohan said, bending down to pick up the girl. "Where's Ammi?"

The child pointed vaguely behind her. "Ammi!" Mohan called again, a little loudly. "Where are you? We need to get out of here."

They heard a groan, and then Ammi lifted herself from the ground and tottered toward them. "Ya Allah," she said, when she reached them. "Is it really you? Are those mad dogs gone?"

Ammi looked toward the smoldering hut. "They burned it," she said to no one in particular. "A second time." She took Smita's hands in hers. "I heard her. I heard her screams. They tortured her like an animal in the slaughterhouse." She glanced at her granddaughter. "I covered the child's mouth before I remembered she doesn't speak. So I covered my own mouth. But what I should've done is covered my ears. So that I didn't hear what I heard."

Smita fought against the nausea gathering in her again. "Get in the car," she said to Ammi. "We have to leave here."

In the car, Smita took Abru from Mohan and held her in her lap. No matter what happened from this point on, even if those bastards were waiting for them down the road, she would never let them have Abru. She had failed Meena; she would not fail her daughter.

Mohan locked the car doors as they pulled away. They drove down the country road with the headlights turned low, one excruciating kilometer after another. When they had gone past the crossroads where Govind and his crew could have waited for them, Smita exhaled. They were gone. She could scarcely believe that they'd managed to make it out of there alive with Ammi and Abru. Once she knew they were safe, Smita began to shake uncontrollably, the horror of the evening catching up with her. She tried to control herself, but from Abru's expression, she knew that the child was feeling her anxiety. She forced herself to smile at the girl in what she hoped was a reassuring manner.

"Do you think we should go register a complaint at the local police station?" Smita asked. "While there still might be some evidence?"

"No way I'm taking that chance," Mohan said. "The police will more than likely turn the child over to the brothers."

Ammi spoke from the back seat. "Where are you taking me, *seth*?" she asked, in her nasally voice.

"Where would you like me to take you? I'm assuming no one in the village will give you shelter?"

Ammi snorted. "Those cowards? No. In this age, who will stick their neck out to help an old woman?" Suddenly, she struck herself forcefully on her forehead. "Why did my Abdul go and marry that heifer? Ruined my life. Look at me now, driven out of my own home and community."

"Please," Smita said sharply. "Your daughter-in-law has just been killed." She glanced quickly at the child, wondering how much she understood. "Show some decency."

Ammi fell into a stunned silence. Then, the wailing began. "Better if those animals had killed me, also!" Ammi cried. "What am I going to do now with this child? With this burden around my neck, I'll have to spend my days begging for a living. As it is, that Meena was eating me out of house and home."

Involuntarily, Smita kissed the top of Abru's head. The girl continued looking at her silently. "No need for you to concern yourself about the child," she heard herself say. "We will take care of her."

The wailing stopped. *It's like she's the toddler*, Smita thought, at last acknowledging her dislike for the woman. But Ammi did have a point. Where would she go?

"You will come with us to my family home in Surat tonight, Ammi," Mohan said. "Tomorrow, we can decide what you will do."

"Allah has brought you into my life, *beta*," Ammi said. "May He bless you and your children's children." The old woman sobbed in gratitude. "Perhaps you can drive me tomorrow morning to my employer's home? If I don't have to worry about the child, they may give me a live-in position."

"Let's see," Mohan said, and Smita was thankful that he was not encouraging Ammi. Meena's body was likely still smoldering in the straw hut. It felt indecent to make plans about any of their futures so soon. Even as she was dying, Meena had saved the lives of her daughter and mother-in-law. But no use telling this to Ammi. Smita lowered her window a little as she struggled to keep her nausea at bay. The night air blew in, warm and innocuous, and the sweet, cloying perfume of *harsingar*, night jasmine, filled the car. It made Smita furious, that fragrance, how it masked the sinister enmities that defiled this land.

Ammi was saying something about Abru, and Smita forced herself to listen. It was clear that the old woman had no interest in keeping the child. Smita was relieved. If they could settle Ammi somewhere, she might be able to keep her promise to Meena. *Meena*. Smita saw again the young woman's writhing, tortured body. Would she ever be able to forget that image? She shook her head, trying to concentrate on the child in her arms, pulling her in even closer. There was no possibility of taking Abru with her to America, as Meena had asked. But once they got back to Mumbai, she would do her best to place Abru in a home. Mohan would help. Surely, Anjali would help, also. Maybe Shannon would have some contacts. Between all of them, they would work something out.

Abru had fallen asleep. She smelled of grass and the earth, a rich, loamy smell.

But the small gesture of pulling the child closer had awakened the girl, and she looked deeply into Smita's face. Her eyes grew wide with confusion. For a few seconds, they stared at each other solemnly.

And then the child who never said a word—who, according to her mother, even cried silently—was suddenly wailing at the top of her lungs and spoke.

After a moment or two, Smita could distinguish the repeated word: *Mamaaaaaaamamaaaaaaaamamaaaaaammamamamamamamamama*.

Abru was crying for her mother. But she was staring into Smita's face.

CHAPTER THIRTY-SIX

———✦———

EVEN THOUGH IT was late when they reached Mohan's home in Surat, Smita phoned Anjali as soon as they got there to share the news of Meena's murder. Anjali was distraught, inconsolable, her usual cool cracking like a thin sheet of ice. "Why didn't I anticipate this?" she said. "*Why didn't I?*" she kept repeating. "I should have arranged protection for her. Oh God, oh God, oh God. I can't believe this. How did I let this happen?"

There is enough guilt to go around, Smita thought when she finally hung up.

She next called Cliff in New York. "She's dead?" Cliff said. "And you witnessed it? Oh my God. This is one helluva story, Smita."

There was a time when she would have shared Cliff's enthusiasm. Now, his reaction felt voyeuristic, macabre. A woman was dead. A child was orphaned.

"How quickly can you file?" he asked.

"I don't know," she said. "Not tonight. This isn't a breaking news story. Let's not treat it as one."

"*It's not?*" Cliff sounded shocked. "Smita? Are you kidding me?"

Smita gritted her teeth in frustration. "I would like to hold the story until we figure out what we're doing with the child," she said.

"Hold it? Hell no. I want to run it as soon as you can file it."

"What if the brothers find out that she's with us? What if they claim family rights?"

"How are they going to do that?" She could hear the bafflement in Cliff's voice. "Didn't you say they're almost illiterate? They probably don't even know where America is on the map. And who the hell is going to give them custody?"

Smita fell quiet, wondering if the horror of what she had witnessed was clouding her professional judgment. Cliff sounded so damn sure. "I envision this as a long narrative piece," she finally said. "I need a few days to work on it, to get quotes from people on the record. I mean, Meena is not famous. Her death is not breaking news. No one else is covering this story. I'd prefer to situate her story within a larger context."

She pictured Cliff chewing on his pen as he considered the shape of the piece. "You gonna write it as a first-person account?" he asked.

"Cliff. It's been a very long day. I—there's a lot going on here. I won't know until I start writing it. You're going to have to trust my judgment on this."

Cliff exhaled. "All right, kiddo. Let's talk again tomorrow."

Smita grimaced. *Kiddo?* Cliff was just two years older than she was. "And hey, Smita? Good work."

Yeah, Smita thought, as she hung up. *Good work that your source is dead. It makes for a better story.* She shook her head, knowing she was being unfair to Cliff and that she was being cynical about a profession she loved. Meena was dead. Nothing could change that fact. Smita's failure to reach Meena in time would haunt her the rest of her life.

She went out into the living room, walking quietly so as to not disturb Ammi and Abru, who slept together on a pallet on the kitchen floor. (Smita had looked askance when Mohan had suggested this arrangement during the ride home, until he had reminded her that Ammi—who had slept on a mud floor her entire life—would find the softness of a bed intolerable.) The house was dark and quiet, and Smita felt ghostlike as she went looking for Mohan. She had not changed out of her clothes since arriving, and they smelled of smoke and gasoline. She shivered at the thought of Meena's incendiary death. Still, she didn't want to go back into her room to change. The numb, hollow spot in her chest felt as if it was growing.

Mohan wasn't in the living room. Surely, he couldn't have gone to bed, leaving her alone to deal with the horror of what they'd been through? Smita's throat ached. *Vodka*, she thought. *I need a shot of vodka*. In her travels, it was her drink of choice—after a long day, the foreign correspondents would gather in a hotel bar, ordering shots. Or, if she was on assignment alone, she'd return to her room and raid the minibar as soon as she walked in. She needed a stiff drink to forget what her eyes had seen: Meena's brutalized, bloodied body. Her hand seeking Smita's. The foot smashing Meena's jaw. The hut exploding in flames. Abru's face as she screamed for her mother—the first spoken words out of the child's mouth an elongated river of longing, an endless cry of grief and loss.

What good did Anjali's involvement do Meena? Smita wondered. In fact, had the court trial hastened Meena's death? Anjali's justification for taking on the legal case was similar to what Smita had herself often said—that she had become a journalist to be a voice for voiceless women like Meena. But as Cliff had reminded her, it was a fine line they walked between journalism and voyeurism. *Poverty porn.* Is that what she did, ultimately, in her travels to the far-flung places of the world—sell poverty porn to her white middle-class readers back home? So that they could feel better about their own "civilized" lives and country, even as they tsk-tsked while reading about oppressed women like Meena? Smita herself had repeated the platitudes about the humanizing effects of literature and narrative journalism, how each medium cultivated empathy in readers. But toward what end? The world remained as sad and brutal a place as ever. Was it simply vanity that made her believe that her work made a difference?

A choking sound escaped her lips, then another. Out of the corner of her eye, she saw a stirring in the darkness and realized that Mohan was in his room and that he'd heard her.

He was sitting at the edge of the bed, holding his head in his hands. Smita watched him, knowing that he was broken, that *she* had broken him. Now that they were home, safe from danger, he was also replaying the images of the evening. Mohan looked up, and from the light cast by the outdoor patio lights, Smita could see his face, dirty, teary, worn-out. There was no trace of the irreverent, playful man who had breezily offered to give up his vacation to drive her into hell. *We will never be the same*, Smita thought. Mohan extended his right arm toward her. Smita moved across the room, sat next to him on the bed, and put her arm around Mohan. It was the mirror image of how he had consoled her a few days earlier, and Smita was glad to be of use. They sat this way for a long time, in the still, in the dark. At some point, Smita felt the salt on her face, but didn't know whether they were her tears or Mohan's. One of them must have swiveled to bridge the space between them, one of them must have initiated the kiss that the other received thankfully— but Smita didn't know who had led the way. Grief was the great leveler. The dark stripped them of language and inhibitions and doubt. They clung to each other in this fashion, each pulling the other in.

They stopped; Mohan drew back. Was it remorse Smita was reading on his face? He ran his fingers through his hair. She could feel him receding.

"Mohan," she said, the single word a cup, holding her terror, her loneliness, her guilt, her confusion.

Mohan cradled her face, his own close to hers. His eyes searched hers, reading her, and then he traced her mouth with his index finger. "*Jaan*," he whispered, and bowed his head and blotted away the world until she didn't know where he began and she ended, where any of them did: Meena and Abdul, Mohan and her, India and America, past and future, life and death. She was no longer sure if she was the consoled or the consoler, the healed or the healer. And the last conscious thought she had was that it didn't matter—the only thing that mattered was that neither one of them would be alone for the night.

THE NEXT DAY came hot and still, with a cloudless blue sky.

Inside the house, Smita felt the irregularity of the weather patterns— she was warmed every time Mohan's eyes fell on her as they made Ammi and Abru breakfast and felt the chill each time he left the room and was out of her sight. Light and shadow. Heat and cold.

What she had wanted to do was to stay in bed with Mohan all day and refuse to face the intrusions the new day would bring. She wanted him to block away the knowledge that Meena was dead, wanted Mohan's kisses on her eyes to keep them from seeing the horrors that lay behind their lids, wanted his mouth on her mouth to keep her from screaming.

But Mohan had woken up at six this morning with someone else's name on his lips:

Abru's.

ANJALI CALLED AT eight. Smita heard the exhaustion in her voice and knew that she hadn't slept. She wanted to offer her sympathies but couldn't bring herself to console Anjali. In a few days she might, but right then, she couldn't escape the thought that Anjali had fucked up. If she and Mohan had not arrived when they did, Ammi and Abru would have been killed, also. The thought of the child being harmed landed like bloody lashes on Smita's skin.

At Anjali's behest, Smita and Mohan went to the police station nearest to Birwad later that morning, leaving Abru at home with Ammi. The inspector who took their complaint looked so disinterested as he picked at his teeth and kept his eyes glued to Smita's chest, it took all her willpower to not ask him how much he'd been paid off by Rupal. The only time the man showed the slightest passion was when Smita mentioned that she was writing a story for an American newspaper. Then, he met her eyes and accused her of maligning India's reputation abroad.

Her anger fueled by the police inspector's disinterest, Smita longed to start work on her article. Maybe she could persuade an Indian newspaper to pick up the story? She had spoken to Shannon on her way to the police station, even though she'd hated giving her the news about Meena while she was in rehab. Shannon had promised to follow up on the story when she returned to work.

"Do you want to go back to Birwad?" Mohan asked as they left the police station. "To, you know, see about giving Meena a proper funeral?"

Smita considered his suggestion. "I want to get back to Abru," she said. "And I need to begin work on my story." She hesitated. "I know that sounds awful. I don't mean to be callous. But honestly, under the circumstances, I think Meena would want us to focus on her daughter, not on her remains."

Mohan nodded as he put the car in reverse. "You don't sound callous. Besides, didn't you tell me that Meena said the four months she shared with her husband were the happiest days of her life?"

"Yes?"

"Then we will leave her where she was at her happiest."

They had not yet discussed what had happened between them the night before. Smita didn't regret it, just the circumstances that had led to such intimacy—and the fact that there had been no opportunity to distinguish love from need, pleasure from grief, desire from solace.

Would any warm body have done last night? she asked herself, but she knew the answer immediately. It was only Mohan who could have consoled her; it was only Mohan that she wanted to console. Their lovemaking had been solemn, tinged with desperation, but also extremely sensual. She had slept deeply for a few hours—and when she'd startled awake, hearing Meena's voice in her ear, Mohan was right there, his arm around her, holding her in place, keeping her from splitting in two. All morning, she hadn't wanted to be away from him for even a moment—and it was taking all her control to not stroke his cheek as he drove or take his hand in her lap. He was allowing her to take the lead, to decide whether their night together was an aberration, something they would never mention—or something of consequence. Of course it was this decency, the very Mohanness of it all, that made her want him even more. But it was also a measure of the warmth she felt toward him that made Smita decide she couldn't risk hurting him. She would help him settle Ammi and Abru; she would file her story; and then, she would leave. She had to get out of India before either of them got too entangled. Their lovemaking may have been born of circumstance, but one thing she was sure of—one of them would get hurt if they continued, and that person would be Mohan. Smita was willing to risk heartbreak. Their intimacy the night before had opened up a hunger in her that felt as big and complicated as India itself. That hunger made her want to pull Mohan into the deepest part of her and hold him there; it also made her want to push him away. It was what had made her so good at her job, this ability to walk away without a look back, to not get pinned down to places or people. But with Mohan, walking away would not be so easy. It was best if she left him the hell alone.

"Everything okay?" Mohan said quietly, looking straight ahead, and Smita knew that he was aware of her agitation.

"No," she said, pretending to misunderstand his question. "Meena is still dead."

THEY WENT OUT that evening to purchase a large bottle of Grey Goose and drank it from cups in Mohan's bedroom after Ammi and Abru had fallen asleep. "I feel like I sleepwalked through this day," Smita said, feeling a little light-headed.

Mohan nodded. "Yes."

"And we didn't accomplish anything at the police station."

"I know."

"Is it okay to sleep with you tonight?" Smita said. She tensed, waiting to regret her words, thinking she would be angry at herself for how blithely she had cast away her earlier resolution.

But Mohan was already pulling her toward him. "It's the only thing that's gotten me through this day."

ALL THROUGH THE next day, Smita worked on her article while Mohan made phone calls. First, he phoned a lawyer friend in Surat to find out what papers they needed for Ammi to give up her rights to Abru. The woman promised to courier the appropriate documents immediately. Next, he called Ammi's employer to gauge her interest in hiring Ammi as a live-in maid. The woman said she needed to check with her husband. While Mohan awaited her reply, he phoned several of his relatives to ask if they were looking for an elderly servant.

Ultimately, he determined that Ammi was best off with her current *bai*. It turned out the employer lived so far away from Vithalgaon, poor Ammi took two buses to and from her job each day—which meant there was no threat to her safety. Ammi herself was pleased with this solution. With the matter decided, she seemed anxious to start her new life. Smita and Mohan went to the market in the evening and bought Ammi a small suitcase, six saris, and some toiletries. That night, Ammi signed the custody papers and gave her granddaughter a perfunctory hug, as if the parting was to last a few hours instead of a lifetime.

ABRU WAS TOTTERING around the back garden, gleefully pulling at the leaves and flowers. Smita watched her from the patio as she sipped her morning tea and waited for Mohan to return. He had woken up early to drive Ammi to her new home, putting Abru next to Smita in bed before leaving. Smita had not seen them off, having said her goodbyes to Ammi the night before.

Abru looked up sharply at the sky, and Smita's hair stood on end. Had the child felt her dead mother's presence? It was so hard to know what Abru understood and what she remembered. But then, Abru went back to pulling on the petals of a white flower, and Smita relaxed. After a few minutes, Abru came up to her. Smita could see that she was tired. Since crying for her mother during the ride back to Surat two nights before, Abru had lapsed into silence again. But Smita marveled at how much she was able to communicate without words.

She picked up the girl. "Do you want something to eat?" she asked, and Abru shook her head no. "Okay," she said, carrying her back to the bed. They lay on their sides, staring into each other's eyes, a trickle of affection stirring in Smita's breast. She stroked the child's hair. Within minutes, Abru's eyelids fluttered, and she drifted off to sleep.

Smita fell asleep, too. She woke up when she heard Mohan's car and then hurried to the door. Mohan walked in, looking exhausted. "How'd it go?" she asked.

He lifted an index finger, signaling her to hold her questions for a minute, and went into the kitchen to get a tall glass of ice water. Carrying the glass into the living room, he sat next to her. "It's bloody hot outside," he said. He looked around. "Where's Abru?"

"Napping." Smita said, then frowned. "Is this normal? She sleeps a lot."

"I think so. She's so little. Just a baby."

"And so terribly undernourished."

"That will change—now that we have her. Don't worry. She will be fine."

"Don't you think it was odd," Smita asked, "how Ammi just gave her a quick hug goodbye last night? As if she has no feelings for her own grandchild."

Mohan was silent for several minutes. "We talked on the way to her *bai*'s house," he said. "She asked me to adopt Abru."

"Ha," Smita said. "That's rich."

"I'm thinking about it."

"*What?*" Smita said, startled.

He shrugged. "Why not? I'm not going to place her in a children's home. Do you have any idea what orphanages are like here? What happens to the children?"

"But how? You have a job and—"

"Most people with children work for a living, Smita."

She heard the reprimand in his voice, and it made her bristle. "You know, Meena asked me to take care of her. *Me.*"

"Well, Meena assumed we were married. But okay. If you want Abru, you take her. She'll be safe with you."

Mohan's tone was reasonable, placid, but Smita detected a hint of impatience in his voice. She looked down at her hands, her nose turning red. "Are you mad at me?" she asked at last.

"No, of course not. Why would I be?" Mohan rubbed his cheek. He had not shaved this morning, Smita noticed. "I'm just exhausted, *yaar*," he said. "Things are moving too damn fast. And now there's a child to think about."

"So why did you say what you did? About me taking her?"

Mohan's eyes flashed. "Because, Smita, I'm trying to do what's best for the child. And you made it sound like it was a bloody custody battle."

"I'm sorry. I'm just surprised, is all. I mean, you don't even have your own apartment. How can you manage a child?"

"What does one have to do with the other? Zarine Auntie can watch her while I'm at work. I mean, where there's a will, there's a way."

How effortlessly, Smita thought, *Mohan has carved me out of his life with Abru.*

"Smita," Mohan said, looking exasperated. "What is it? Why are you crying?"

"I don't know. I just feel sad. And confused. Meena put her in my charge. With her final breath. I feel as if I'm failing her."

They stared helplessly at each other.

"The papers," Smita said after a few minutes. "The ones that Ammi signed. Who did she name as the guardian?"

"She didn't. She left it blank." Mohan exhaled. "But, Smita. This is going to be a bastard of a process. First of all, we have to make sure there are no other claims on Abru. We'll have to track down Meena's sister and make sure—"

"She's most likely in no position to take in a child," Smita interrupted.

"Right. But the courts may insist we find her. As for the brothers—" Mohan stopped briefly. "Look. If you really want to take her to America, I'll help you. I would be delighted. I just won't put her in an orphanage."

"But that's just it, Mohan. There's no way I can. I travel most weeks out of the year. My lifestyle just wouldn't allow me to be a single parent."

He grinned mirthlessly.

"What's so funny?"

"Nothing. Just that, when did it become a *lifestyle* instead of simply *life*? It sounds like a fashion parade or something."

"Yeah, well. That's Brooklyn for you," Smita said vaguely. "But really, I also can't stay in India long enough to get through the red tape."

"You could leave her with me," Mohan said. "I can do all the paperwork for you. That's what all the rich Americans do, right?"

"And you would do this? You wouldn't get too attached to her?"

"I'm already attached to her." Mohan's tone was rueful. "But I would do this. For you. If you needed a child that badly."

Smita was suddenly irritated. This sounded too much like their arguments about India being her homeland. Motherhood was another box that Mohan was placing her in. "I don't need *a* child. This is not about me. I just feel a sense of responsibility for *this* particular child."

"That's a bad reason to wish to become a mother, Smita. Because you feel responsible."

"Dear God, Mohan. Who said anything about becoming a mother? I just said—"

"So how are you going to adopt Abru? As your sister?"

"Okay. Touché. But if *you* were to keep her, what would you be? Her father?"

Mohan cocked his head, puzzled. "Yes, of course."

"I see," she said. "And that . . . that doesn't scare you?"

His eyes widened slightly, as if he finally understood what she was asking—as if he had figured out what made her tick. "Yah. It scares me. All the important things in life are supposed to scare you. My first day in graduate school, I was scared. Same thing the day I started at my job at Tata. Hell, the first time I met you, I was scared."

"You were scared of me?" She laughed. "Why?"

"Because I knew within minutes that I wanted to spend more time with you. And I didn't know how or why."

Mohan was looking at her with such vulnerability, Smita's breath caught. Unable to bear the beating of her own heart, she looked away. "Well," she said, "I'm sure you would've run for the hills if you could've seen into the future."

"Not really," he said. "I'm not saying any of this has been easy. And I would've given my right arm to have been able to save poor Meena. But I don't regret a moment."

"Thank you," she said, burrowing her face into Mohan's chest. They sat like this, Mohan murmuring something against Smita's ear.

"What did you say?" she said, raising her head.

"I said, would it be so bad to stay?" Mohan repeated.

"Stay *where*?"

His eyes flickered with impatience. "You know where. Stay in Mumbai. With me."

"Oh, Mohan," Smita said regretfully. "You know that's impossible."

His grip around her tightened. "It's impossible?" he asked. "It's more impossible than it was for your papa to move his whole family to America?"

"Oh, but that's not fair. That's not the same thing."

"What's the difference?"

"The difference is, we did it out of desperation. We didn't really have a choice."

"I see. So desperation is a better reason to move to a country than love?"

She stared at him openmouthed. *Love?* Had he just used the L-word? "Mohan, we barely know each other," she began. She stopped. Was this some bizarre test? A prank? "Are you . . . are you just positing some theoretical . . ."

"No. I'm really suggesting it."

"That I give up everything in the US, give up my whole life there, to be here with you?"

He smiled. "You don't have to make it sound so terrible, *yaar*."

It had been a mistake, she realized, sleeping with him. This was precisely the kind of entanglement and heartache she had wished to avoid. "Mohan. Sweetie. Come on. You must know how preposterous this sounds."

"Does it?" He played with her hair absentmindedly. "Okay, I'll tell you what. Take a leave of absence. And then, if you are not happy here—if you miss America too much—I will follow you there."

Move to America? Mohan was suggesting it as if he were proposing buying a new tie. This was a side of him she didn't know. Did he have a clue how complicated such a move would be? Smita thought of her friends back home. What would they say? Would they be aghast at his presumptuousness?

"I thought you loved your job," she said.

"I do."

"Then why would you give it up?"

"Because I love you more."

"Come on, Mohan. You have no idea what a bitch I am." She forced a laugh, trying desperately to lighten the mood. But despite herself, Smita was moved. "Because I love you more"—would any of her previous boyfriends have been willing to give up their careers for her? Of course not. A month before, she would have been contemptuous of any man who said such a thing—would have considered him needy and pathetic. Now, she was touched. Somehow, India had worked its spell on her, had made her vulnerable to such sentimentality. When she returned to New York, she wouldn't be the same person she'd been when she'd left.

She studied Mohan's face, suddenly so dear to her. "In any case, where would I stay?" she said. "I can't afford to stay at the Taj indefinitely."

"You could stay in my room."

"At Zarine Auntie's apartment? She wouldn't care?"

"I don't think so," Mohan said. "And if she minds, I can always buy a small flat."

"For six months or so?" Smita said incredulously. "Until we decide what happens with Abru?"

"Those are all just details, *yaar*."

There she was, sitting in a posh bungalow, beside a man who was spreading out a banquet of options for her. Smita thought suddenly of Meena's life, its parsimoniousness, the lack of choice. What had she ever done to deserve such good fortune?

"Don't," Mohan said. "It will only make you sad."

"What are you, a mind reader?"

"Yes," he said. "But that's only because you have the most delightfully transparent face."

Smita shook her head, bemused. "We have both lost our fucking minds. You realize how crazy this whole conversation sounds, right? We barely know each other."

"How long did your papa and mummy know each other before they eloped?"

"That was different. They wrote letters back and forth for a long time."

"So, I will write you a letter. Every day."

"Very funny. They also didn't have visas and passports and shit to deal with."

"So? They had other difficulties, *na*?"

Smita closed her eyes, beginning to get irritated by his persistence. "Mohan, please let's drop the subject. I care about you, but this is making me uncomfortable."

He was immediately contrite. "I'm sorry. You have to remember, this is what I do for a living—solve problems. And somehow, I can always figure out the solution. So it's easy for me to think that life is just another puzzle to solve."

She kissed him on the cheek. "It's okay," she said. "Let's just enjoy the time we have together."

He smiled, then cocked his head, listening. "Abru," he said, and Smita heard the long wail coming from the other side of the house. Together, they ran into the bedroom. Abru was lying on the tiled floor beside the bed. She was holding her head. "Oh shit!" Smita cried as she lowered herself next to the wailing child. "Sweetie, what happened? How did you fall?"

Abru was inconsolable as Smita gently pulled her hand away from the child's head, feeling the small bump forming on the side. "Can you get me some ice?" she called to Mohan, who was already running toward the kitchen.

Smita cradled Abru in her arms as she held the wrapped ice cubes to her head. After a while, as the ice water trickled onto her face, the toddler stuck out her tongue and began to lick her lips. Mohan laughed. "She seems to be enjoying this," he said.

"Can you take her from me?" Smita whispered. "My arm is beginning to cramp."

He lifted Abru and placed her on the bed. The screaming began again. "*Ho ho ho*," Mohan chided. "Nothing wrong with your vocal cords. It's okay, little one. We are right here."

Abru inserted her thumb in her mouth and looked at Mohan with her big dark eyes. Then, she tugged at his sleeve to get him to lie down with her.

"Okay, okay. I'm here with you," he crooned to her.

Smita stood watching as Mohan lay down next to the girl. *They would love Mohan*, she thought wistfully. Papa would enjoy discussing technological issues with him. Rohit would appreciate his sense of humor. As for Mummy, she would have taken him on her morning walks and showed him off to all her friends.

Smita waited until Abru dosed off, then got into the left side of the bed, so that Abru was sandwiched between them. After a few minutes, she reached for Mohan over the child's body, and the three of them slept that way, Smita and Mohan holding hands.

CHAPTER THIRTY-SEVEN

———✴———

IT HAD BEEN almost a week since they'd returned to Mumbai, and their days were mostly devoted to Abru.

But the nights belonged to Mohan and Smita.

Now that her story had been published, she was free to spend time with Mohan and Abru. Every evening, Mohan—who had spoken to his boss about his new circumstances and extended his leave—took Abru back to his landlady's apartment and then returned to the Taj.

Smita watched him as he slept next to her, snoring softly. *If only we'd met while living in the same city*, she thought, *and dated like a normal couple*. Out of the blue, she heard Meena's dying rasp in her ear.

She must have twitched, because Mohan's eyes flew open. They darted around the room as he tried to get his bearings, and in the second before his eyes focused on her, Smita had a revelation: *Here lies a man with his own sacred inner life, his own inviolate soul*. She was filled with an intense desire to study Mohan, like learning a foreign language that would open up new vistas.

"What is it?" he said. "Why are you looking at me like that?"

She nuzzled his cheek. "Nothing. Go back to sleep."

But they were both wide awake. After a few minutes, Smita leaned against the headboard and reached for her laptop. It had been three days since her story had run, but the reader comments were still pouring in. She propped up the computer against her body, even though she was a little conflicted about sharing the comments with Mohan. Most of them struck the right notes of indignation and compassion, but there were the usual number of hateful posts, with several people referring to India as a misogynistic, shithole country, as if stories like Meena's never happened in the West. A month before, such comments would have made Mohan's hackles rise. But he, too, had changed. Cliff had told her how his phone was blowing up with calls from readers wanting to know if there was a GoFundMe account for Abru, and even though Mohan had immediately refused the help, he was touched by the solicitousness of her American readers.

"Any more developments?" Mohan asked after she shut her laptop.

"Anjali called earlier. I forgot to tell you. Her group is demanding the police investigate Meena's murder. My first-person story helped, she said."

Mohan nodded. "I'll probably have to go back at some time to give a statement."

"Will I need to come, also?"

"*Jaan*, things move slowly in India." He smiled grimly. "You'll be long gone by then."

"I hate feeling like I'm leaving you holding the bag. I mean, it's bad enough that you're moving ahead with Abru. But now, to also have to testify against Govind . . ."

Mohan shrugged. "I'll manage."

"You really want me to come for lunch tomorrow?" Smita asked after a few minutes. "To Zarine Auntie's house?"

"Smita, why do we have to go over every damn conversation? She wants to meet you. You accepted. I thought the matter was decided."

"Please don't be angry at me, Mohan. I can't bear the thought of you being mad at me."

"I'm not angry. I'm sorry . . . It's just that everything happened so fast. And I keep thinking of that poor girl."

"Me too," she whispered. "I can't get her out of my head. I wake up thinking about her. How she reached for my hand just before she . . ."

"Don't. Force yourself to think of something else. That's what I'm trying to do."

They fell silent, co-conspirators, witnesses. Smita shifted in his arms and looked up, memorizing his face.

"*Ae*," he said. "Stop looking at me like that. I am here. We still have a few days together. And even after that . . . It's not like you're going to the damn moon, *yaar*. I'll come see you in America."

CHAPTER THIRTY-EIGHT

———

THE NEXT MORNING, they went to see Shannon at the rehab unit. Nandini had not yet arrived. "She's coming late today," Shannon said. "It's her younger brother's birthday, so there's some ceremony at home or something."

"Do you want me to stay?" Smita said. "I'm supposed to go to Mohan's for lunch today, to meet his landlady. But I can cancel?"

"Ah yes." Shannon smiled. "The infamous Zarine Auntie."

"You've met her?

Shannon shook her head. "No. I've just heard him talk about her. He thinks the world of her."

She broke off as Mohan entered the room. "Mohan, love," Shannon said. "Will you do me a favor?"

"Of course."

"Do you think you could go buy me a fresh coconut from the

vendor outside the hospital? Nandini brings me one daily. She claims the coconut water helps promote healing after surgery."

"She's right," Mohan said. "I'll be back in a jiffy."

Shannon used her walker to scoot closer to Smita as soon as Mohan was out of the room. She sat on the edge of her bed. "How are you doing?" she asked. "You've been through some crazy shit."

Smita exhaled. "I'm still in shock. I still can't believe Meena is dead. I keep seeing her body, hearing her gasping for breath."

"I can imagine," Shannon said. "It's a terrible profession we've chosen in some ways."

"In some ways," Smita said. "But I can't think of doing anything else for a living."

"Me neither. Listen, I hope you don't mind my asking. What's going on between you and Mohan?"

"Nothing, really. I mean, I—I care about Mohan. But it's not, you know, serious."

"But Mohan's pretty serious about you, Smits," Shannon said. "He's going to be devastated."

"He told you this?"

"No. Not at all. Both of you have been unforgivably secretive since you've returned from Surat. But I see how he looks at you. And you're going to leave Abru with him?"

Smita heard the disapproval in Shannon's voice. She frowned. "You know, when you called me in the Maldives, I thought you were asking me to come here to help you. After your fall."

"Smits, I'm sorry. I didn't realize that. But what's—"

"Wait. Let me finish." She took a deep breath. "I had vowed never to step foot into India again. Because of something that happened in my childhood. But I came, Shannon. I came because it was you. And then, everything kind of fell apart. I had no intention of hooking up with Mohan. Okay?"

"Smita. Please. I wasn't trying to—"

She brushed aside Shannon's apology. "What am I supposed to do?" she said. "Upend my whole life for the sake of a guy I just met? Mohan actually asked me to stay on for half a year. As if it's that easy. What about my job? You know how hard both of us worked to get to where we are."

"Okay, relax." Shannon patted the edge of her bed. "Come sit next to me."

"I'm okay."

"Smits, don't be an ass. Come here. I'm sorry," Shannon said, pulling Smita toward her. "Listen, I shouldn't have said anything. It's just that—I've known you for a long time. Far longer than I've known Mohan, obviously. And you two look so suited for each other. I've never seen you the way you are around him."

"How's that?"

"I don't know how to describe it. You look—I dunno. Happy, for sure. But it's more than that. You look . . . contented."

"Oh, bullshit." Smita said lightly. "You're not used to seeing me with a brown dude, is all."

Shannon mustered a perfunctory smile. "You know me better than that, Smits." She paused. "Fuck. I'm going to miss you."

"I'm gonna miss you, too. But I'll see you in New York soon?"

"Not for a while. Cliff offered to fly me home and have someone take my place for a few months. But I refused. I like it here. Besides, Nan would be distraught if I took off."

"No kidding. I think she's, like, in love with you or something."

"Are the two of you making fun of Nandini?" Mohan said. He was smiling as he walked toward the bedside table, carrying a large coconut, its hacked top hanging as if from a hinge. He held it against a glass and flipped it, so that the coconut water drained into the glass.

"Here you are, my dear," he said to Shannon.

"Thanks, Mohan. You're the best."

"So, what trouble are you planning?" he asked.

Mohan's playful tone reminded Smita of how he had acted around her when they'd met, before Meena had died—before they'd assumed responsibility for Abru. And before they'd made the mistake of sleeping with each other.

"Nothing," she replied. "We're just talking shop."

"'Talking shop,'" Mohan repeated. "I tell you, no one can beat you Americans when it comes to strange expressions."

Shannon let out a yawn. "Okay, you two. You need to get going, right? I'm tired. And ready for my nap."

Mohan glanced at the clock. "Be serious, *yaar*, Shannon," he said. "It's not even noon. How could you possibly be sleepy again?"

Smita gave Shannon a hug. "See you tomorrow?"

"That'll be nice."

"Ready?" Smita said, turning to Mohan.

"In a minute." He bent to fluff Shannon's pillow. Shannon threw Smita a bemused look. "He'll make some lucky woman a good wife someday," she said.

"Very funny. Okay, ciao. I have to get this one here to Zarine Auntie's for lunch."

"COME IN, COME in, come in," Zarine Sethna said. "Please, welcome, welcome."

"Thank you," Smita said, suddenly shy. She stepped into a well-appointed room, filled with Chinese vases and antique furniture, and smiled at Mohan's landlady. "Thank you for inviting me to lunch."

"Definitely, definitely." Zarine was a tall light-skinned woman with curly gray hair. She pushed her rimless glasses back up on her nose. "Mohan has told us so much about you."

"Thank you." Smita looked around. "Where's Abru?"

"Taking her afternoon nap," Zarine replied. She smiled. "You are worried about her? You want to see her?"

Smita nodded.

"Go take her to see the child," Zarine said to Mohan. "Then we can eat."

"It's very nice of you to take all this trouble . . ."

"*Arre, wah*," Zarine interrupted. "No trouble. Mohan is like my son."

They went into Zarine's bedroom. "She already looks plumper," Smita whispered. "Or is it my imagination?"

"She ate three ice-cream cones yesterday, remember? You've been spoiling her." He pretended to frown. "Once you leave, *bas*. I am putting her on a diet."

Smita laughed, but her heart hurt at the thought of Mohan having Abru all to himself. "And Zarine Auntie is okay with the arrangement? She'll watch her while you're at work?" She hesitated. "If you are paying her to take care of Abru, I can send a monthly contribution?"

"Yah, right. So that Zarine Auntie and Jamshed can kill both of us. For insulting them like that."

"Jamshed?"

"Her husband. I told you about him, remember? They are both in love with this child."

"But you will be her primary guardian? You won't let them . . ."

He touched her wrist. "Smita. Stop fretting. I told you—" He broke off as Zarine entered the room.

"Please. Come to the table," Zarine said. "What will you drink? Something hot or cold?"

"A soft drink, please," Smita said.

Mohan placed his hands on the older woman's shoulders. "Come on, Zarine Auntie," he said. "You've been cooking since morning. Smita and I can do everything else. I mean, at your age, you should not tire yourself."

Zarine grinned. "See how he teases me?" she said to Smita, who

had noticed that Mohan's accent sounded thicker, more Indian, when
he spoke to Zarine. There was also no mistaking his affection for her.
Was he like this around his own mother? The thought of never finding
out saddened her.

SMITA SAT SIPPING her raspberry soda while Zarine and Mohan
brought the dishes to the dining table. "Auntie," Smita gasped. "So
much food?"

"Eat, eat, *deekra*," Zarine Auntie said, spooning some *sali boti* onto
Smita's plate.

"Oof, Auntie," Smita groaned. "Stop."

"Smita," Mohan said with his mouth full, "eat up, *yaar*. You will
never get food like this in America."

She nodded and did as she was told. A peaceful silence fell at the
table, interrupted by Smita's occasional murmurs of appreciation.
"I remember this drink from my childhood," Smita said as she took
another sip of raspberry soda. "My father had a lot of Parsi friends.
Any time we visited, they served us Duke's raspberry."

Zarine snapped her fingers. "Go to the fridge and get your friend
another bottle," she told Mohan, who rose immediately, a broad smile
on his face.

The older woman followed him with her eyes until he was out of
the dining room. "So how long have you known my Mohan?"

"Ah, er, not really that long," Smita stammered. "That is . . ."

Zarine shook her head dismissively. "Doesn't matter, doesn't matter," she said. "When two people love one another, time doesn't matter."

Smita kept her gaze on her plate. She jumped as she felt Zarine's
hand cup her face. "So beautiful," the woman murmured. "No wonder
my Mohan is *lattoo-fattoo* over you."

"*Laddoo-faddoo?*"

Zarine laughed. "Not '*laddoo*'—*lattoo*. It means, how do you say?
'Head over heels.'"

Smita smiled back. Then, she yelped. Zarine had pinched her forearm.

"Don't you dare hurt this poor boy," Zarine said. Her eyes were blazing. "All these years I'm knowing him, and this is the first time he's brought a girl home."

"Auntie," Smita said. "You . . . you know that I live in the US, right?" She waited until Zarine nodded. "So, you know that I'm scheduled to go home in three days?"

Zarine looked stricken. "*Three days?* What about Mohan? And the child?"

"I—I wanted to place Abru in an orphanage. But Mohan said no. He said he . . ."

"*Chokri*"—Zarine rose to her feet—"have some sense. Do you know what would happen to a girl in an orphanage? Of course Mohan said no. I thought you were more intelligent than that."

She will blame me for hurting Mohan, Smita thought with dismay. She looked toward the kitchen. She could hear Mohan dispensing ice cubes into a glass. The food sat heavily in her stomach. Was this lunch an ambush? And if so, had Mohan been part of it?

But the puzzled expression on Mohan's face as he came back in assuaged her suspicion. "*Su che?*" he asked Zarine in Gujarati. "What happened?"

"Nothing, nothing," Zarine said as she sat back in her chair. Then she added, with effort, "Eat some more, *deekra*."

Smita shook her head. "No thank you," she said.

There was a strained silence. "I will make some Parsi-style tea," Zarine said. You will take? And we have *lagan nu* custard for dessert."

"*Arre*, Zarine Auntie, give this poor girl a break, *yaar*," Mohan said. "Let's wait ten, fifteen minutes before we begin to eat again, okay?"

Zarine's face softened. "You know what they say about us Parsis," she said. "While we are eating breakfast, we are already planning the lunch menu."

They laughed, and the chill in the room dissipated. "I will go warm the custard in the oven," Zarine said. "Do you want to show Smita your room? I will call when it's ready."

They were both shy as they entered Mohan's bedroom. Smita took in the bare walls, the neatly made double bed, the single chair with a pair of jeans draped on it. Mohan's room looked as spare and impersonal as her own condo. Somehow, despite his friendly nature and the fact that he lived with other people, his was as monastic an existence as her own. The thought made her emotional, a fact that he noticed immediately. "What is it?" he said.

"Nothing. I'm just happy to see your room. To know where you live."

He got the embittered look that she'd begun to dread, the look that came over his face each time he was reminded of her imminent departure—and she braced herself for a caustic remark. But he said nothing, and she walked toward his dresser and picked up a framed photo. "Your parents?" she asked.

"Yes."

"You look a lot like your father."

"That's what everybody says."

She set the picture back down, absentmindedly flicking off the lint from the frame as she did so. He noticed. "It's so dusty here," he said. "You clean, and a half hour later, *bas*, it's dirty again."

"And yet, it's your beloved city," she teased.

But Mohan's face remained unsmiling. "It is. Of course it is." He gazed at her for another moment. "Come. We should keep Zarine Auntie company."

"Can I help you?" Smita asked in the kitchen.

"You want to make the tea?" Zarine said.

Smita hesitated. "Do you . . . I just use tea bags?"

"Tea bags? Nonsense. We use real tea leaves. And mint leaves. And lemongrass." She turned to Mohan. "Take this American girl and go sit in the living room. I will bring us a nice hot-pot cup of tea."

As Smita and Mohan entered the living room, they walked past the old teakwood armoire. Half of the cupboard was faced with a full-length mirror, and Smita glanced at it. But instead of seeing her reflection, she saw an older couple. They were rushing around a kitchen, assembling a school lunch. Smita recognized the couple immediately—it was Mohan and her, ten years older. The temporal distortion made her woozy, and she stumbled.

"Smita? What's the matter?" Mohan asked, steadying her.

She turned to him, disoriented, confused. "The bathroom?" she said. "I feel a little faint."

Smita held on to the sink as she stared at herself in the bathroom mirror. *Relax*, she told herself. *You're under a lot of pressure. So you had a weird . . .* But what exactly was it? A hallucination? A premonition? A feeling of déjà vu?

Then, she knew: It was wishful thinking, a moment's indulgence, a case of the If Onlys. A phantom image created by intense longing. All she had to do was wait it out, and the moment would pass. In fact, it had already passed. She knew from experience that no matter how much she loved a place or a person, she just had to wait for the fever to break. It always did. During her first year in the States, she had refused to eat any of Mummy's Indian dishes, had been adamant about learning to love mac and cheese and hamburgers and pizza. It was her way of forgetting India. Yes, she determined, she would simply wait out her love for Mohan, allow it to subside into affection.

Smita splashed cold water on her face, dried herself, and stepped out of the bathroom. Mohan was perched on the edge of his bed, but he rose immediately. "Are you sick?" he asked. "Do you need to lie down?"

"I'm okay." She forced a smile. "I'm much better."

They walked back into the dining room. "Come, *beta*," Zarine said, patting the chair beside her. "Nothing like a good cup of tea to chase away all ailments."

"Is it time to wake up Abru?" Smita asked as she sat down. The thought of leaving Zarine's flat without seeing the child awake was too depressing.

"Sure," Mohan said. "I'll go get her."

"I'm sorry," Zarine said as soon as Mohan was out of the room. "I forgot my manners. What to do? I love that boy so much. I cannot bear to see him hurt."

"It's okay, Auntie," Smita said. "It means a lot to me that he has someone like you who cares for him."

Zarine shook her head in wonder. "*Accha?*" she murmured. "You love him that much?"

Smita flushed. "I do."

"I see." Zarine peered at Smita from the top of her glasses. "So, take him back with you. Who does the poor boy have in Mumbai except for my husband and myself? Two oldies? All he does is work, work, work. He may as well live in America."

"Auntie. You don't understand. It's not that easy."

"I see. It's not that easy." Zarine blinked furiously. "Tell me something. Is it easier to break this poor boy's heart? To leave him stuck with the child all alone?"

Zarine was making her head spin, adding to the disorienting quality of the day. Besides, how was this any of her business? There was a noise in the hallway, and then Abru came running into the room, her hands raised. Before Smita could get up, the child flung herself at her and tried to climb into her lap. A startled laugh escaped Smita's lips as she lifted Abru and hugged her. Was there anything more flattering than being the object of a child's affection?

"Do you want some custard?" she said to the girl, who stared back at her.

"*Wah*," Zarine said. "Look at her. She thinks you're her mother."

There was a painful silence in the room. "Okay, Zarine Auntie," Mohan said. "Enough drama. Please."

"I'm sorry," Zarine said.

Smita busied herself feeding bites of dessert to Abru. "This custard is superb," she said. The dessert reminded Smita of the cardamom *kulfi* her mother used to make. What would Mummy say if she could see her now? Would she be proud of her for fighting her fears and coming to India? Smita had a feeling that she would.

"Thank you," Zarine said. "It is my mother's recipe. Her brother was a wedding caterer."

"Hmmm. I remember going to a Parsi wedding when I was a child," Smita said. "The food was out of this world."

"What was the name of the couple?" Zarine asked.

Smita laughed. "Auntie. I have no idea. I was a kid."

"Yes, yes, of course." Zarine had the grace to look abashed. "When did you leave India?"

"In 1998. I was fourteen."

"I see. We had a chance to go. When we were first married." She looked at Mohan. "Your Jamshed Uncle had a job offer. But we didn't take it."

"I didn't know this," Mohan said.

"It was donkey's years ago. Ancient history." Zarine leaned over to wipe Abru's mouth with her napkin.

"Do you regret not going?" Smita asked.

"*Regret?* No. I was so busy taking care of my old parents and my son—who had time for regret-fegret?" Zarine smiled. "Besides, home is where the heart is. As long as I'm with my Jamshed, even hell would feel like paradise."

"Jaasd," Abru said suddenly.

"Oh my God," Zarine squealed. "She's talking. She just said my Jamshed's name, I swear."

Mohan took Abru from Smita's lap after they were finished with lunch. "Do you want to go for a walk?" he asked. "I can show you around Dadar Parsi Colony and the Five Gardens before we head back?"

"I'd like that." Smita turned to Zarine. "It was so nice to have met you," she said. "Thank you for your hospitality."

Zarine grinned. "So formal," she said to Mohan, as if Smita were not present. She pulled the younger woman into her arms. "Safe journey to you. God bless."

"God bless," Smita repeated.

CHAPTER THIRTY-NINE

————✳————

On the way to the airport, Mohan played a Hemant Kumar CD. Smita listened as Mohan sang along to a particularly haunting song by the velvet-voiced singer: "*Tum pukar lo / Tumhara intezaar hai.*"

"That's so lovely," she said.

"I love this song."

"I can see why. What do the lyrics mean? What's '*pukar lo*'?"

"He's saying, 'Call out to me—I am waiting for you.'"

Smita took his hand and held it in her lap, trying not to cry. She wanted to reassure him and repeat what she'd said the day before—that she'd try and visit any time an assignment brought her to Asia. But the time for promises was behind them.

After a few seconds, she cracked the window slightly, and India rode in on the night air and entered the car, a third passenger who, she suddenly realized, had been present from the moment she'd met Mohan.

THE POLICE OFFICER stood under the large signs that read: *Ticketed Passengers Only*. But Mohan slipped into the airport terminal with Smita, wheeling her bag. "I still cannot believe you don't check in a suitcase," he said. "Don't you know that traveling abroad with bags as big as dining tables is part of our national heritage?"

"Years of practice traveling light," Smita said. She looked around nervously. "Security is going to catch you. If not now, then on your way out."

Mohan clucked dismissively. "Don't worry about me," he said.

They moved away from the main doors. She took in his tousled hair, the shirt that clung to his body due to the humidity. "Thank you for everything, Mohan," she said. "I don't know what I would've done without you."

He stared at her wordlessly, his Adam's apple bobbing. "So?" he said at last. "I guess this is it."

The other passengers rushed past the two of them as they stood gazing at each other. The last time she'd left Mumbai, twenty years before—with Sushil accompanying her family to the airport—Smita couldn't wait to get away. This time, she held herself still, as if her body were a clay pot filled to the brim with grief. One false move, and all her emotions would spill over.

Mohan looked at his watch. "You should go," he said. "There's usually a long line at security and immigration."

She took his hand in hers. "You'll write? You'll keep me informed about how things proceed with Abru's paperwork?"

"Yup."

"And . . . and you promise not to be too sad? For my sake?"

"I'll be fine," Mohan said, and smiled that new, cynical smile. "Once I'm back at work, I won't even have a chance to miss you."

"Good," Smita said, pretending to believe him. "Good."

She kissed his cheek. "Bye, my Mohan. I'll miss you."

He touched the spot where she'd kissed him. "Bye. Be safe. Phone me when you're at the gate. I'll be waiting in here or outside. Just in case your flight is delayed."

"Mohan, it's getting late. It's going to take you forever to get back home. You should leave now. Please."

He frowned. "Don't be silly, *yaar*. I'll wait until your flight takes off."

"But that makes no sense . . ."

"Smita." He put his finger to her lips. "It's an Indian tradition. Now, go."

"Bye. Love you."

"Bye."

SMITA PHONED MOHAN as soon as she was settled in the lounge. The phone rang and rang, but Mohan didn't pick up. Had he changed his mind and left? She hung up, resolving to try again after she went to the restroom. She still had plenty of time before her flight. But just as she was about to place the phone in her handbag, it rang. "Sorry, *yaar*," Mohan said. "They kicked me out. I'm standing outside with what seems like half of Mumbai. And it's so bloody noisy, I couldn't hear the phone."

She hated the thought of Mohan standing in the thick crowd behind the barricades. "My flight doesn't take off for another two hours. What's the use of you waiting? Everything went smoothly."

"Smita, in my family, we always wait until someone's plane takes off. What if there's a delay or something?"

She rolled her eyes. "Okay. I can tell I'm not going to win this one."

They talked for another ten minutes, and then Smita said, "Hey, I want to go use the restroom. I'll call you from the plane before takeoff, okay?"

"Okay," he said. "Love you."

"Love you, too."

SMITA FOUND A seat across from a family of four when she returned
to the lounge. She smiled at the harried-looking mother, who seemed
responsible for the two young children, a boy and a girl, while her husband walked around the room, stretching and yawning languidly. The
woman smiled back at her self-consciously. "My first time to Am'rica,"
she said in heavily accented English.

"Beautiful children," Smita said. "How old are they?"

"He is five. She is two."

Smita nodded, then shut her eyes, the events of the day finally catching up with her. Earlier, she and Mohan had taken Abru to Hanging
Gardens, where the girl had been transfixed by the roadside antics of a
dancing bear. Then, they'd returned to Zarine's apartment to drop off
the child. The older woman had made her disappointment and disapproval crystal clear, barely speaking to Smita. "Bon voyage," she'd said
stiffly when Smita and Mohan were leaving for the airport.

Smita decided to get a cup of coffee. She turned to the woman
across from her and motioned to her suitcase. "Can you watch this
for me?" she said. "I'm just going to go get something to drink." Even
as she asked, she was aware of how she'd never make this request of a
stranger in post-9/11 America. She had a hunch that Indians had not
yet embraced the culture of distrust and fear that had permeated every
aspect of civil life in America.

The woman nodded. "Of course."

When she returned, the woman's daughter had knocked over Smita's
suitcase and was sitting on top of it. "Sorry, sorry," the woman said.
"These children . . ."

Smita smiled. "It's perfectly fine." *If you knew everywhere this
suitcase has been,* she thought, *you'd know that this is the least of its
maltreatment.*

Smita sat down, sipping her Nescafé. She'd had a cup at lunch, Mohan sitting across from her—the two of them barely speaking. She had sensed him pulling away from her, transferring his affection to Abru. Even though she was hurt, she had envied Mohan his ability to love so effortlessly. Mohan, Abdul, Meena. They belonged to a different tribe, men and women who were willing to risk everything for love. Perhaps she would have joined their ranks, too, if Sushil had not scarred her at age twelve. Sushil's menacing face, possessive and haranguing, rose in front of her, and she closed her eyes to escape the image.

Something hot and wet touched her thigh, and she yelped in pain. Smita saw the coffee stain spread on her pants and looked up to see the little girl giggling and running away. She pulled the linen away from her skin as the mother rose and grabbed her daughter. Heads turned as the child screamed bloody murder, a sound that immediately transported Smita back to that awful night when they had fled Birwad and Abru had screamed. Smita forced herself to focus on the present. The child before her was in full meltdown, and the father, who was at the far end of the lounge, was hurrying back angrily.

Frightened by the look on his face, Smita rose and blocked his path. "Please," she said to him. "It's nothing. Just a little coffee. A little accident, is all."

The man gave her a puzzled look before turning to his wife for an explanation. The woman, still holding the screaming child, spoke to him urgently in a language Smita didn't understand.

"Sorry, *ji*," the man said to Smita.

"It's fine. It's perfectly fine," she said, and then smiled broadly to accentuate her words. She decided against heading into the restroom to wash out the coffee stain, not wanting to do anything to add to the parents' embarrassment.

The man nodded and sat down across from Smita. He turned to his daughter, who was still fighting her mother. "Meena," he said, "stop this nonsense immediately."

Smita's breath caught. "Her name is Meena?" she asked.

"*Hah, ji.*"

It's a common name, Smita told herself. *It's like meeting someone named Mary in Ohio, for crying out loud. Probably half the women at this airport have that name.* But then she looked down at the coffee stain on her pants. She had been burned. A girl named Meena had knocked hot coffee on her pants and burned her.

Smita stood up abruptly. Then, she slowly sat back down. *This is ridiculous*, she thought. *You're acting like one of those superstitious idiots that Papa loves to mock. The ones who see an image of Christ in a grilled cheese sandwich. You call this little spill a burn? After what you've seen? Shame on you for dishonoring Meena's suffering. Now, get a grip. Pull the paperback out of your suitcase and distract yourself. All you have to do is sit still until you're on that plane. Because—and you know this because you've done it a hundred times before—the cool, disinfected atmosphere of a plane is designed to make you forget whatever hot, humid, smelly city you are escaping from. It is designed to anesthetize you against remembering home.*

Home? Had she just thought of Mumbai as home? The city that she had resented and feared for most of her life? A city filled with evil men like Sushil. *But then*, she argued with herself, *hadn't the same city also coughed up a Mohan? Hell, hadn't it birthed and shaped the bones of a good and honorable man like Papa?* How could she have let a man like Sushil blind her to this essential truth?

Out of the blue, Smita heard the laughter: Rohit and herself. Chiku and Anand, the boy who had lived one building over. And Anand's little sister. What was her name? *Tinka*, that was it. Other children from the neighborhood, too, Christians and Parsis and Hindus, all gathered in the compound of the Harbor Breeze apartments, their heads tilted upward as they watched the rockets and comets explode in the night sky. As always, Papa had spent hundreds of rupees to treat the local kids to the fireworks display during the Hindu festival of Diwali. That was India, too—that nonchalance, that secularism, nobody blinking twice at that easy melding of different traditions and faiths.

The memories came faster, like coins falling into a slot machine: Mumbai flooding during the monsoons and strangers helping one another—men giving away their umbrellas to women, commuters rescuing those stranded in buses and trains, housewives serving hot tea and chapatis to the homeless families huddled on their street, teenagers wading through waist-deep waters to run errands for their elderly neighbors. Even as a child, Smita used to thrill to the camaraderie that infected the whole metropolis then.

Mohan would be one of those people, she thought, and she felt a sudden yearning to see that side of him, to discover Mohan not in the charged, explosive, compressed amount of time that they'd shared, but in ordinary ways: What were his favorite movies? Was he handy? What were his favorite foods? What size shoes did he wear? Mohan, as the ordinary hero of his everyday life. Mohan, who was waiting outside and would wait until even the contrails of her plane had dissipated. Smita knew—there was no way to love Mohan and not love India; there was no way to love India and not love Mohan. Because he was the best of what it had to offer. It was almost as though, by introducing Mohan to her, the country was trying to make up for what it had once taken away.

Smita caught herself. *Enough of this sentimental claptrap*, she thought. *You are not one of those women who give up their jobs and identities to be with a man. This is the dangerous part of India—feudal, traditional, patriarchal India—that is messing with your head. You have worked too hard to get to where you are to risk losing it for someone you barely know.*

But surely, she argued with herself, life was more than this relentless getting ahead? Surely, there was more to life than self-actualization and ambition and success? What was wrong with linking one's happiness to that of another human being? Why should fifty years of peak capitalism eradicate something that the Eastern philosophers had taught for thousands of years—that life is about interconnectedness, interdependence, and yes, even sacrifice? Smita remembered how she used to try to boost Mummy's spirits during the radiation sessions by telling her stories about her travels and adventures. Mummy, of course, was always proud of her achievements. But once in a while, she'd get a sad, embarrassed look on her face, as if she saw through the bravado to the loneliness at Smita's core.

Maybe there were other options. Her first-person account about Meena's death had generated a lot of buzz and earned her tremendous goodwill within the newsroom. Shannon was still incapacitated. She could ask Cliff to let her use India as her base for a few months while Shannon recovered. This would give her a chance to get to know Mohan better, and she could spend more time with little Abru. Because the fact remained that Meena had bequeathed Abru to her. Even Mohan knew this. She had allowed herself to believe Mohan's beautiful lie about Meena intending him to be an equal partner.

Could this be a way to give the twelve-year-old who had cowered in her apartment in Colaba for three months after the assault a second chance to walk the public streets of Mumbai with her head held high? A chance to realize that the shame she had embraced didn't belong to her? A chance to remember all that she had loved about India, unsullied by what had followed?

She and Mohan could pour into Abru, a child born out of Meena and Abdul's improbable love, everything that was good and courageous about themselves.

The four of them could raise this child together.

Smita could try to set aside her own insecurities, her wariness of the old India—and instead believe in Abdul's brave, idealistic dream of the new India.

Yes, that would be a way to honor the memory of that fine man

Abdul. That would be a good way to avenge Meena's melted face, her one good eye, the bloody pulp of her body.

Smita's heart beat faster as she realized something: If Abdul and Meena could have foreseen the opportunities she and Mohan could provide for Abru, they would have sacrificed their very lives for their daughter. They would have embraced every moment of misery and suffering for the sake of that happy ending.

She imagined retracing her steps and walking out of the airport to where Mohan stood. She allowed herself to picture the delight spreading on his face as she hurried toward him. But then she thought of all the complications that would ensue, and her heart sank at the bureaucracy and the paperwork and the other hurdles involved: Cliff might refuse her request to be stationed in India; Mohan might prove to be disappointing; Papa might not support her temporary move to India. Humans were not migratory birds, able to fly from one country to another, she reminded herself. Homo sapiens had feet, not wings. Above all, there was the irrefutable fact that she barely knew Mohan, outside of the cauldron they'd found themselves in for the past month.

Oh, Mummy, she thought with a groan. *Help me. Tell me what to do.*

She turned her eyes upward, to the ceiling, as if she half expected to see her mother float down toward her, like some descending angel. Her eyes fell on a wooden sign that hung on the wall above the sliding doors of the lounge. YOU ARE HERE, the sign read.

Smita blinked. *You Are Here.* Here, in Mumbai, with only the length of the airport separating her from the man she loved. And half a city away from Abru, a child she could grow to love as dearly as her own.

Abru. If she abandoned Abru, wouldn't she be proving Sushil right? The man had considered her family subhuman because of its faith, and there she was, acting as if she weren't human. Because what sentient being could abandon an orphaned child as blithely as she had? She remembered the contempt she'd seen in Zarine Auntie's eyes and realized that it wasn't just because she was breaking Mohan's heart. It was because a person who could abandon a child without so much as a backward glance was in fact beneath contempt.

She thought of Mohan, standing at his lonely post outside the airport until her plane took off. Waiting, along with thousands of others, all of them choosing to do the hard, inconvenient thing. Why? Because that's what you did for your loved ones. She used to think it quaint that her parents drove to the Columbus airport to pick up their visitors, even though the guests could have taken a taxi. But Mohan was cut from the same cloth as Mummy and Papa. She remembered him heaving the bags of rice and sugar and dal into Ammi's hut. At every step, Mohan had done the difficult thing, and had done so matter-of-factly, as if there were no other choice. Maybe, in the end, that's all that love was—doing the hard thing. Not roses and valentines and walks on the beach, but simply being present, day after ordinary day. The extraordinary romanticism of ordinary life.

But what if, in the end, she and Mohan couldn't make it work? What if her greatest fear came true—that Mohan would prove to be disappointing? The men she'd dated had been smart, talented, hard charging, and high achieving. But after a while, they had become ordinary, too. Their feet stunk when they removed their boots or shoes at the end of the day; they had bad breath in the morning. They told the same damn jokes and stories over and over again. Spinach got stuck between their teeth. They had issues with their fathers. And her unfortunate tendency to focus on the small, irritating things, rather than keeping her eyes on the big picture, eventually made her lose interest.

Smita had never forgotten something Bryan had once said when things were still sweet between them. She'd been at his apartment in Brooklyn, complaining about his couch being covered with cat hair. Bryan had taken her face in his hands and said, "You know what your problem is, Smita? You focus on the cat hair. Try focusing on the cat."

Perhaps that's what love was—an embrace of the commonplace? Perhaps that's where wisdom lay—in recognizing the grandeur of everyday domestic life? If so, she had a lot of learning to do.

Smita dialed Mohan's number again. *Say something*, she thought, *say something, Mohan, that will help me decide one way or the other*. He answered on the fifth ring, sounding breathless, as if he'd been sprinting. "Are you boarding?" he asked.

"What? No. No, I just . . . I just wanted to hear your voice again."

"Oh, okay." He was silent for a moment. Then, he said, "Hold on a second. It's so crowded and noisy here, I can barely hear myself."

She waited until Mohan came back on the line, but it was obvious that he was distracted by the jostling of the crowd around him. They had a desultory exchange, and then Mohan said, "I'm sorry. I can't hear a word. Can you call back in a few minutes?"

She hung up. The whole conversation had been so disjointed, and she was no closer to making a decision than before. And then she thought: *First Mummy and now Mohan*. Since when had she started relying on others to help her decide what to do? At this rate, she figured she may as well draw straws or flip a coin. *Surely*, she thought, *Mohan deserves better than someone this unsteady in her love for him*.

Smita thought back to something that Rohit had said when he'd quit his job to start his own business: "Look, I know it's a risk. But at some point, you have to jump. I'll either land on my feet or I'll land on my face. But either way, I'll own the fall. You see what I'm saying?"

Rohit's words had inspired her to go skydiving the summer after, despite her fear of heights. She had landed on her feet.

Smita paced up and down the lounge, trying to control her agitation. She returned to her seat and sat down. The other passengers looked at her curiously. A moment later, she rose again. The woman across from her smiled. "Bathroom?" she said. "I will watch your luggage."

"It's okay," Smita said. "I—I am leaving."

The woman looked at her, confused. "Leaving, madam?" she said. "The plane will be departing soonly."

"I know. But I will not be on it." Smita turned around, then looked back. "Give Meena a kiss from me."

A long line had formed at the counter where the gate agent stood. Since Smita had not checked a suitcase, she could simply walk away. But in a country already on edge after several terrorist attacks, Smita knew the consternation and delays her unexplained absence would cause. She pushed her way to the head of the queue, ignoring the howls of protest behind her.

The gate agent glared at her. "Madam, please go back and wait your turn," she said.

"I'm leaving," Smita replied, and she felt an immediate lightness of spirit. "My name is Smita Agarwal. I don't have a checked bag, so there shouldn't be a problem."

"You're leaving for what? The flight is on time."

"I'm not boarding the flight. I'm—I'm going back."

The agent blinked at her in incomprehension. "Going back where?"

"Home. I'm going home."

SMITA TRIED DIALING Mohan's number again as she hurried across the terminal, but for some unfathomable reason, Mohan's line was busy. Smita bit down on her lip in frustration. She'd promised to phone Mohan from the plane—why on earth was he on another call? Then, she realized that they wouldn't be boarding her flight for another half hour. If she knew Mohan, he was probably talking to Zarine, checking up on Abru. The child had intuitively known that something was amiss when Smita had kissed her goodbye earlier that day and had started wailing inconsolably. Zarine had glared at Smita, picked up Abru, and taken her to the balcony to calm her down. Smita, overcome with guilt, had barely been able to make eye contact with Mohan as they'd walked to his car.

She dialed again. This time it rang but, when Mohan answered, there was so much static that she hung up. When she redialed, the call went directly into voice mail.

Smita was almost to the exit door. Another minute, and she would be outside. She debated whether to continue trying Mohan's phone from the air-conditioned refuge of the terminal or step into the sultry, humid night. But even as she asked herself the question, she knew that her excitement was too great. She walked outdoors and was immediately hit by the familiar blare of traffic horns, the acrid smell of diesel fumes, and the chatter of people waiting for their loved ones. She panicked, wondering how she would possibly find Mohan. A man broke through from the crowd and approached her. "Taxi, madam? I fetch a taxi? Where you going?" he asked. "Good rate I'm giving."

She tried shaking him off, knowing that any eye contact would only encourage him. But the man was persistent, following her as she walked along the sidewalk, peering into the crowd. In desperation, she dialed Mohan's number again, and this time he answered.

"Mohan!" she yelled. "Where are you?"

"Still here, just like I said . . ."

"I know. But *where* are you? I'm outside looking for you."

There was a sudden silence. "You're here? You . . . you didn't go?"

She smiled at the wonder she heard in his voice. "*Jaan*," she said. "I'm here. Where are you?"

"I . . . I . . . Tell me where you are, and I'll find you," Mohan said. "Which way did you exit?"

After she told him, Mohan said, "Okay. Stay where you are. I'll be there in two minutes. I'm walking there now. Don't move."

"Okay, but . . ."

"Smita, stay put. I will spot you in a minute. Just wait there."

She scanned the crowd for him, but she saw only a wall of unfamiliar faces, all of them straining against the barrier, searching for their own families. Her eyes swept from left to right, then back to the left—and there was Mohan, almost directly in front of her, standing still. They were probably twenty feet away from each other, separated by the metal barricades. But the look on Mohan's face was a homecoming. "Smita!" Mohan called, raising his right hand in greeting and holding it high. There was an expression on his face that she'd never seen before.

Smita ran.

She rolled her suitcase alongside herself and ran.

She didn't stop running until she reached the spot where her future stood, waiting for her to catch up with it.

CHAPTER FORTY

———⋆———

ABRU.

It means Honor.

I NAMED HER this in memory of her father, a man who made this word bloom with every word he spoke and every deed he did.

I named her this to erase how my brothers had twisted this fine word and made it ugly with their bloodlust.

I named her this to tell the world that you can burn a man alive but still not put out the nobility in his heart.

I named her this to make sure that my daughter would keep Abdul's flame alive within herself. Even when I couldn't offer her anything more than my breast milk, I could offer her this name. To remind her of whom she belonged to and from where she came. To strengthen her and tie her to her history.

FOR THESE REASONS, *I gave my daughter this name.*

My daughter, whose face I kept under my eyelids as the kicks and rods destroyed my remaining body.

My daughter, whose life I saved with my dying breath.

My daughter, whose face was the last face I saw in my mind before my end.

My daughter, who will remain, as proof that Abdul and I met, lived, and loved.

My daughter, who may yet live to see the new Hindustan that Abdul believed in and dreamed of.

My daughter, whose name was my last breath.

My daughter.

My breath.

ABRU.

ACKNOWLEDGMENTS

THIS NOVEL WAS inspired by the news articles about India written by Ellen Barry for the *New York Times*. The characters and events in the book are fictional, but I have borrowed a few ideas about the treatment of women in rural India from her articles.

I am enormously grateful to Peter S. Goodman, global economics correspondent for the *New York Times*, for his timely and generous help in answering my questions about the life of foreign correspondents. Thank you to attorney Ramesh Vaidyanathan in Mumbai for explaining the workings of the Indian court system. I couldn't have written this book without their help.

I am thankful to my sisterhood of fellow women writers for their support, friendship, and inspiration: Thank you, Caroline Leavitt, Hillary Jordan, Lisa Ko, Tayari Jones, Katherine Boo, Laura Moriarty, Mary Grimm, Tricia Springstubb, Regina Brett, Barbara Shapiro, Deanna Fei, Meg Waite Clayton, and Celeste Ng, for being the brilliant, unstoppable forces of nature that you are.

To my literary brothers Jim Sheeler, Ben Fountain, Wiley Cash, Dave Lucas, David Giffels, Philip Metres, Michael Salinger, Salman Rushdie, and Luis Alberto Urrea, thank you for your friendship and inspiration.

Cheers to my fellow Pen Gals—Sarah Willis, Loung Ung, Sara Holbrook, Karen Sandstrom, and Paula McLain—for margaritas and giggles and fierce love. Kris Ohlson, we still miss you.

My colleagues at Case Western Reserve University inspire me

daily to do better. Special thanks to Athena Vrettos, Chris Flint, Kim Emmons, Georgia Cowart, and Cyrus Taylor.

Kathy Pories, this novel is greatly improved thanks to your skillful edits and insightful suggestions. Thank you, Dan Greenberg, for helping this novel find its way to Kathy.

Thanks to my friends Judy Griffin, Anne Reid, Barb Hipsman, Bob Springer, Bob Howard, Hutokshi and Perveen Rustomfram, Feroza Freeland, Sharon and Rumy Talati, Dav and Sayuri Pilkey, Kershasp Pundole, Rhonda Kautz, Diana Bilimoria, Kim Conidi, Paula Woods, Regina Webb, Ilona Urban, Marcia Myers, Jenny Wilson, Merilee Nelson, Diane Moran, Kathy Feltey, Marsha Keith, Suzanne Holt, Mary Hagan, Denise Reynolds, Cathy Mockus, Sandra West, Tatyana Rehn, Claudio Milstein, Amy Keating, Wendy Langenderfer, Terri Notte, Brenda Buchanan, Subodh and Meena Chandra, Kathe Goshe, Kate Mathews, Jackie Cerruti Cassara, Gina DiGiovine Goodwin, and so many others. My life would be greatly diminished if you weren't touring the planet at the same time that I am.

Jim Sheeler, you may be gone, but you will live forever in the hearts of those of us who loved you. Thank you, Annick Sauvageot and James Sheeler, for sharing Jimmy with us.

Lasting thanks to my family, Homai and Noshir Umrigar and Gulshan and Rointon Andhyarujina.

Eust Kavouras, H/S forever.

HONOR

Reclaiming Honor
An Essay by Thrity Umrigar

Questions for Discussion

RECLAIMING HONOR
An Essay by Thrity Umrigar

IN 1993, my middle-aged father stood on our balcony and watched helplessly as the apartment building across the street burned. It had been set on fire by a mob of angry Hindus who had heard that a Muslim family lived on the ground floor.

By this time, I was living in faraway America, safe from the paroxysm of insanity and violence that gripped Bombay—the erstwhile most tolerant and cosmopolitan of Indian cities—during that terrible period. But I can still hear the bewilderment in my father's voice as he later recounted the incident during our weekly phone chat. I immediately worried about my family's well-being, but he brushed aside my fretting. We were Parsis, a small, prosperous, and educated religious minority in India; the joke was that there were so few of us, nobody saw us as any kind of threat.

What I learned much later was that the Muslim family who lived next door to us had brought all their jewelry to Dad for safekeeping before they fled the neighborhood for a few weeks. There were many sad stories of families returning home after the riots ended and finding that those whom they'd trusted with their assets had swindled them. My dad, on the other hand, had made our neighbors put their jewelry in his locker themselves and then given them the key to it. "When you return," he said, "please come and use the key to remove your belongings."

The whole experience stayed with me, even though I heard and read about it secondhand, even though I was no longer in the city of my birth. But I certainly wasn't thinking of it as literary material, just a personal story that made me worry about my father even as it made me more proud of him.

Then, a few years ago, I came across a series of stories written by Ellen Barry in the *New York Times* about the oppressive conditions of women in parts of rural India. Barry's description of the punishment meted out to those who strayed from tradition made my hair stand up. Things we take for granted, such as women working outside the home, were considered transgressions punishable in ways that recalled the Dark Ages. Naturally, Barry's stories also described the corrupt police and politicians who allowed such barbarity to flourish.

The world that Barry described was alien to me. I was a city kid, raised in a tolerant, Westernized, middle-class family that took for granted that women had to be educated and independent. But even so, I had spent the first twenty-one years of my life in India. How had my privilege blinded me to such injustice? I was aware of urban poverty, of course, and had written about homelessness and the struggles of the working poor, but I was as stunned by the medieval punishments Barry described (making women walk on coals?) as I was by the patriarchal mindset. But at the same time, I was impressed by the determination displayed by the women of the village who rebelled against the old ways.

It was that respect for women who persisted against insurmountable odds, who questioned traditions that had prevailed for thousands of years, that gave birth to Meena, one of the two protagonists of *Honor*. She came to me, urgent with the need to tell her own story. She shares that story with Smita, a young Indian American journalist haunted by a family secret, tormented by her own love-hate relationship with India. Smita is everything Meena is not—emotionally closed off, terrified of intimacy, afraid of love. In a traditional "privileged savior" novel, the modern, worldly Smita would lead the impoverished, illiterate Meena to enlightenment and safety. But what if Meena were the teacher in *Honor*?

THE WORD HONOR has been abused and shorn of its meaning in traditional, male-dominated societies, where it is simply a cover for the domination of women by their fathers, brothers, and sons. The sexual politics of the so-called honor killings are impossible to avoid. Women are raped, killed, and sacrificed to preserve male pride and reputations.

In this novel, I wanted to reclaim the word and give it back to the people to whom it belongs—people like Meena, a Hindu woman, and her Muslim husband, Abdul, who allow their love to blind them to the bigotries and religious fervor that surround them, who transcend their own upbringing to imagine a new and better world. It seems to me that every time we read a story about an honor killing, it's always told from the point of view of the killers. But my interests lay in the victims. I wanted to tell the story of their everyday lives: how they met, how they fell in love, how they lived. There is something incredibly tender and beautiful about people who have never known a day's freedom deciding to love whomever their heart chooses.

By telling Smita's and Meena's love stories—one taboo, the other not; one constrained by societal prohibitions, the other by her own inhibitions—I wanted to examine notions of privilege and inequity, and the simple luck of the draw that separates a Meena from a Smita. But there's also another love story at the heart of *Honor*, one that describes Smita's love-hate relationship with India itself. The novel poses the question of whether it is possible to love a country when you're ashamed of its politics and practices. What form and shape does that love take? Millions of us all around the world are currently grappling with that question. It is my hope that readers will see themselves in the internal and external struggles of the novel's two female characters, and in their search for home.

QUESTIONS FOR DISCUSSION

1. Smita tells Mohan that her India is not his India. What does she mean?

2. How is Meena's India different from Smita's? What explains the differences?

3. Meena relates her story to us directly, in the first person. Why do you think the author chose this point of view?

4. Meena's brothers think they are doing the moral thing, the right thing, by punishing their sister and her husband. Honor killings are a fact of life in many parts of the world. What do you think it will take to change this cultural practice?

5. What do you think of a system where the village council and the head of that council have so much power? What are the consequences of those positions being held by men?

6. Why didn't Smita's father change their name back to their family name after settling in America? Do you understand why he didn't?

7. Smita and Meena both fall in love. How do their cultures inform their relationships: the level of intimacy, communication, decision-making

for each woman? If you are in a committed relationship, how do you think it would have been affected if it had begun in a different culture?

8. As strange as the customs and traditions described in this book may seem to an American reader, did you recognize any common touch-points across the two cultures? What aspects of the novel reminded you of life in America?

9. Trace Mohan's evolution in the course of his travels with Smita.

10. What do you think of Smita's decision at the conclusion of the novel? What do you foresee for Smita and Mohan?

11. There are many different levels of privilege described in this book. What are some of them and how do they affect the characters' behavior?

12. There is a moment when Smita remembers the marigolds tied around the oxen's horns, and it makes her feel tender toward India. Why?

13. The notion of objectivity is the foundational belief in mainstream American journalism. What happens when journalists cover places and people whose culture is completely different from theirs? Should they strive to be objective or should they identify a moral ground from which to report a story? If so, how do they determine what that moral ground should be? Or are we imposing our morality on others?

14. What do you think of the final chapter? What function does it serve?

15. What are the various meanings of the book's title?

© Laura Watilo Blake

THRITY UMRIGAR is the bestselling author of nine novels, including *The Space Between Us*, which was a finalist for the PEN/ Beyond Margins Award, as well as a memoir and three picture books. Her books have been translated into several languages and published in more than fifteen countries. She is the winner of a Lambda Literary Award and a Seth Rosenberg Award and is Distinguished Professor of English at Case Western Reserve University. A recipient of the Nieman Fellowship to Harvard, she is a prizewinning former journalist who has contributed to the *Boston Globe*, the *Washington Post*, the *New York Times*, and *Huffington Post*.